Castles and Catwalks

Castles and Catwalks

Sex as segue to the sinister

Merlin T. Williams

Copyright © 2022 by Merlin T. Williams.

Library of Congress Control Number: 2022910213
ISBN: Hardcover   978-1-6698-2786-3
                Softcover   978-1-6698-2785-6
                eBook   978-1-6698-2784-9

All rights reserved. No part of this book may be reproduced or transmitted in any form or by any means, electronic or mechanical, including photocopying, recording, or by any information storage and retrieval system, without permission in writing from the copyright owner.

This is a work of fiction. Names, characters, places and incidents either are the product of the author's imagination or are used fictitiously, and any resemblance to any actual persons, living or dead, events, or locales is entirely coincidental.

Scripture quotations marked NKJV are taken from the New King James Version. Copyright © 1982 by Thomas Nelson, Inc. Used by permission. All rights reserved.

Any people depicted in stock imagery provided by Getty Images are models, and such images are being used for illustrative purposes only.
Certain stock imagery © Getty Images.

Print information available on the last page.

Rev. date: 06/01/2022

To order additional copies of this book, contact:
Xlibris
844-714-8691
www.Xlibris.com
Orders@Xlibris.com

843080

Dedication

To John DeNora, a teacher who orchestrated an 'off-the-grid', high school curriculum, which included avant-garde, study hall, music. When most people waltzed through life in three quarter time, he introduced his students to the music of Brubeck, Davis, Coltrane and Evans. Discordant except in the hands of the gifted, 5/4 time became the marching beat for the select few seeking participation, by proxy at least, in President Kennedy's New Frontier.

To a man as well, who lived life style choices never hinted at by parents, by pulpit pundits, nor by principals in wing-toe shoes. His was the voice, the steady, baritone drizzle of 'off-the-cuff' social commentary in a post McCarthy, buttoned-down era.

White, Anglo Saxon dominance in the country would disappear in our life time, John had said so. Having Black friends was hip. John lived the thought. An automobile was built for performance only if it had a standard, four-on-the-floor, transmission. John's Triumph TR3, was just such a machine. And more, fascist police brutality was not relegated to the third world. John, with a Cheshire cat grin, had opined so!

John DeNora, through his broad strokes of scathing social synopses, his bond with unbound music and the frequent musings he chose to share with his students, was a gifting Magi in an otherwise starless, night sky.

Chapter 1

"OK Mister Michael, Sir. Here's the deal! Here is my proposal for your consideration. Today I will not lift a finger to clean your bloody room. It will remain as it is and today there will be no twisted towel that looks vaguely like a throttled swan either. You will get new towels, soap and shampoo. That is all!

And, in return, yes, in return…, you will get twenty minutes of me. Do you like that proposal? And, oh yes, when you have finished, no, only when we have finished…, then you must agree to fill in the hotel card on the desk stating your degree, your sterling degree, of satisfaction with the room service you have received to date. Are we in accord Mister Michael, Sir? Let's shake on it then, shall we!"

Taking her cue from the wide grin on my face and my fingers that lingered along hers, Elithia made short work of removing the beige bottom half of her hotel uniform. She stood before me, like a sturdy senior high school rugby player, half in and half out of school colors. She placed her hands on her hips and peered back toward the room door which had been left ajar.

Her cart, with its wheels braced, had been placed across the door way. It became the large, "Do Not Disturb" sign. It would prompt passing guests to exhibit a greater interest in pinching some of the body preparations in plastic tubes than in peering into the room to glimpse the mundane spectacle of a woman wrestling with the bed sheets.

This was not a spontaneous, serendipitous event. It had been in the making for some time. Ever since I first took up residence at The Coral Reefs at Grace Bay.

From the outset, Elithia and I had engaged in banter which was always of short duration and, almost always, long on sexual innuendo.

"Another day in paradise filled with the radiant colors of the rainbow. Right Elithia." That had been one of my recent, banal remarks delivered to her as I strode toward the door to allow her to do her job without interruption.

"You are right, but only for those who have the eyes to see. For most gentlemen who come to the Turks and Caicos, it has been my experience that the only color they show any interest in seeing is black. And I am not referring to the midnight sky either! I am sure that you have heard the expression, Once you go black, you never go back."

Without thinking I responded.

"Yes, but the committee that makes up those profound catch-phrases also added an after-thought.

Once you go white and take flight, it is sheer delight. Racial equality at work…, maybe."

We had grinned at each other knowing that the heat had just been turned up below the cauldron in which both of us were willing, unbound captives. I knew then that the feast of physical fulfillment would be plated and served up soon. Very soon!

Satisfied with her door barricade, Elithia looked at her watch and quickly squirmed out of her panties. She half squatted and ran both of her hands through her pubic hair. She smelled her fingers tentatively and with two great strides rushed forward and pushed me backward over the arm of the sofa.

"Now you just stay there. Stay there…, just like that. Don't move. Here, I'll get you a cushion for your head. You do want a ring side seat for the main event, don't you?"

"Yes but one of the combatants, the one who is still wearing shorts and boxer trunks seems to be out for the count before the match even begins."

I burst out laughing at the sight of my body arched over the arm rest. It was caught by the far mirrored wall. I felt like a patient pyramid positioned on a proctology table. Only wrong side up.

My legs dangled down toward the floor and my head and upper torso were arched, bow-like, back and below my mid-section.

"Well let's rectify that inequality right now shall we."

With that Elithia deftly undid the front of my short pants and, just as expertly, removed both them and my Jockey underwear in one fluid motion.

"Now Mister Man, now Mister Michael, nothing is left to your imagination and…, and now nothing is left to mine either. Ohh, yes, this will be fun."

Elithia leaned forward, looked into my eyes and gently started to massage my nostrils with the tips if her unseen fingers.

"Well my blue eyed man of the morning, what color are you thinking of now?"

"What is the color of desire? I don't think one pigment would suffice. An impressionistic explosion in oils on a large canvas might come close."

"Who talks like that? No one else I know. That is for certain. I think that I want to wrap you up in a laundry bag and take you home. But enough of this. Kiss me Michael. Quickly now, just kiss me hard!"

Kissing someone on the lips, on the lips for the first time, someone for whom there was considerable attraction, and no small amount of budding affection, was delicious.

Michael, your mouth makes words and your tongue suggests love making that is not at all American. Where exactly do you come from anyway?

"My passport was issued by the island nation known as Pleasure. It's not to be found in any world atlas I have ever seen, but the place is very real…, at least as far as I am concerned."

"Yes, well be that as it may, you are here, right now, with me. And nothing else matters, does it!"

With her fingers lingering long around my nostrils, she tongued her way down to my stomach, blew lightly on, what in silhouette would have appeared as a bump on an otherwise smooth, supine body, and, like a ravenous fish, struck the bait and engulfed it completely.

"I like to swallow my man right away, Michael. I like to feel him grow in my mouth. I have liked it ever since I was fourteen. I liked it even before I started to have real sex."

Elithia was one of those women who was, it seemed, 'born ready' for admission to the carnival that was the carnal.

Her comments, delivered between oral thrusts with one hand acting as a tourniquet around the base of my penis, was quickly followed by the result she sought. Elithia mounted me as she squatted and balanced herself on the sofa arm rest that was to serve as our fornication fulcrum.

"White, flight, delight, white, flight, delight," she whispered into my face as she gyrated and rapidly thrust up and down on her latest creation.

Mere moments passed when, just as abruptly as she had inserted me, she disengaged herself and, looking toward the door, dismounted from her perch. Popping the cork in a wine bottle would have been an appropriate analogy. Tightness of fit, cork to glass and cock to next up from ass, produced an audible "popping" noise that signaled our separation.

Elithia quickly turned around and remounted the arm of the sofa.

"I'll keep watch on the front door and you Michael, ha-ha, and you can keep a sharp eye out for intruders at my back door, the one that is winking at you, ha-ha!"

'Shake that booty girl, shake that bodacious booty', could have been the title of a video taken of our love making. In fact, that expression captured all Caribbean women of African descent when they danced at festivals, when they partied with friends and when they were in full, pre-orgasmic flight.

Their mid-sections seemed to take on lives of their own. It was as though their ball and socket hip joints magically morphed into elastic, universal connections, ones that defied the biological limitation experienced by other, less capable, mortals.

I could manage no more than to just hold on to the mechanical bull which Elithia had become. But just as I was losing my grip, she stopped.

I immediately thought that she had caught a glimpse of her manager walking by the door. But I was wrong.

Gyrations were replaced by heavy breathing and long, slow, deep thrusts.

"Poles in holes, poles in holes. It's my favorite game Michael. Poles in holes, yes, poles in holes."

The machine above me, the one which had no "on/off" switch, now afforded me the opportunity to prove that I was the keeper, the one in charge of the back door. With my moistened thumb, I plunged past compliant cheeks and beyond anal sphincter. My meat thermometer was immediately given more than a merely fond embrace.

She groaned and squeezed my legs, just below the knees and fought to muffle the guttural sound that did not want to be contained. She rocked back and forth on me until the spasms that convulsed her body subsided.

Less than ten strokes were needed, aided by her flattened palm that glided over the head of my penis, to make me come. Like a basking shark with mouth agape, she gathered in my involuntary spill, held it in her mouth for a few moments, mischievously winked at me, and then spit everything in her mouth in the direction of my stomach.

"Now, that's my version, no actually that's our version of an impressionistic explosion in oils done on a not so large canvass. Do you like it Michael? Remember, I had limited time to create it and I had only one tube of paint to play with.

Anyway, I call it, "White on White by Black". Do you like it, Michael?"

Elithia did not wait for a response. She did not have to. Her summation was court room counsel perfect.

"Alas, playmate of mine, fun time is over for today. Quickly now, you clean yourself up with a used towel and…, and…, don't forget the guest satisfaction card. Bye-bye for now my lovely, blue-eyed man."

The promised new terrycloth and tubes were tossed on the floor and Elithia, throwing a kiss in my direction, quietly shut the door.

* * *

The Turks and Caicos Islands were a disappointment to me. Lying east, south-east of the Bahamas and due north of Haiti and the Dominican Republic, the British protectorate was only a ninety minute flight from Miami. But the place seemed to be at the opposite end of the earth. If rococo and raunchiness made for not so strange bedfellows in Miami then, in the Turks and Caicos, quiet and comatose could have been viewed as synonymous terms.

Forty islands in all, give or take those that drowned daily at high tide, and none was more than fifty feet above sea level. Only twenty percent of those rocky dots were large enough to support human habitation. Permanently dry land and potable water being the determining factors.

The Turks and Caicos Islands, despite the trumpeting of travel brochures, were nothing more than a series of small, limestone rocks jutting out of the depths of the Atlantic Ocean, rocks that were surrounded by beautiful but treacherous coral reefs. Great for divers but dreary for the island denizens, the so called, 'belongers', who preferred to remain ashore.

Flora and fauna did abound and given the symbiotic relationship between the eaters of the plants and their resulting role as agents of seed dispersal, the islands did sustain a distinct lushness. However, in the absence of greater bio-diversity, many of the plants and animals indigenous to the splendidly isolated island chain were short listed as endangered species.

Every living thing, even the lizards, seemed to be on a scale that was Lilliputian. All of the creatures that creped, hopped, or crawled on two or four legs, had demonstrated the capacity to adapt, not unlike their human counterparts, to sparseness. Prickly cacti and dense mangrove thickets dominated the sun baked landscape.

With a meager, permanent population of less than fourteen thousand, the place was akin to residing in a glass house. The native population had bathed and been baptized in the same gene pool for generations. As a consequence, it seemed, everyone was related by blood to everyone else, and of course, everyone knew the business of everybody else.

Personal and family secrets, like nude sun bathing and pornography, were not permitted on the Turks and Caicos Islands.

This weather beaten habitat for humanity did, at least, enjoy a very low level of street crime. Residents thought nothing of leaving their doors unlocked at night.

And to chain a valuable item, such as a bicycle, to something sturdy was a foreign concept practiced only by tourists.

The notable exceptions to this cloak of civility were those, native or otherwise, who swam in the treacherous, rough waters of smuggling and international finance.

I had developed a fondness for the Mahi-Mahi Bar. It was located at the western end of my hotel away from the loud Miami guests who wore 'obnoxious' like the reigning designer label of choice.

But when the ocean decided to wear a civilized face and the wall of sliding glass panels were pushed back into their enclosures, the panoramic view, the unblemished expanse, the olfactory seduction which was of the sea and its creatures was…, was worthy of the toast it always received from my first scotch of the day.

Designed to resemble an old fishing wharf, the bar was festooned with all manner of nautical paraphernalia. Ripped fishing nets hung from the walls. Large wooden net floats, all of which had seen better days, dangled in red and white perfusion.

And salvaged ships' wheels, most with broken or missing spokes, the last vestige of derelict vessels that, in their day, had provided a livelihood for many of the male inhabitants of the islands, ringed the walls like clocks that could no longer tell the time.

On the wall behind the bar a huge, stuffed Mahi-Mahi, a dolphin-like fish, peered down indifferently at the machinations of the transient men and women at play.

Kitschy, I thought, but the breathing of the ocean brought in by the prevailing breeze more than compensated for the tourist-trap, banality that verged on the vulgar.

The bar stools and chairs placed around the thirty or so tables, all comfortably complimented with cushions, invited patrons to linger longer at their version of the mating game.

Few hotel guests ever visited the bar during day light hours. A suntan was a must have acquisition for most. Meager huts with thatched roofs ringed the beach. These oases that dispensed alcohol made baking, while being basted in booze, effortless.

I was aware of only one other person who frequented the bar at midday on a regular basis. Caucasian, he was a man for whom forty, as a reason for a candled cake, had long passed into distorted memory. Outfitted in shorts that were stained with sea salt, a pair of equally encrusted canvas running shoes, a loose fitting shirt and a wide brimmed, brown hat, he followed a practiced routine that was almost religious in its adherence to ritual.

He would carefully place his long, fly fishing rod in the corner behind the bar, set his creel down beside it, remove his hat and place it on top of the wicker box. After running his fingers through his salt and pepper hair, he would glance around the room, then, and only then, sit down at the bar and chug-a-lug half of the Budweiser beer that was waiting for him.

He would slowly sip the remainder of it, then abruptly stand up, collect his gear and be gone within thirty minutes of his arrival. He neither talked to nor made eye contact with anyone other than the barman on duty.

Curiosity got the better of me. As the next scotch was ordered, I slid a sawbuck across the table in the direction of the palm tree shirted man who had responded to my nod.

"I find it strange that the gentleman who just left with his fishing gear always arrives at the same time every day but he never seems to have caught anything…"

"Oh, that's Mister Jonathon. He is a regular in here at this time of year. He is a professor somewhere in America, Baltimore or maybe it's Boston. I'm not sure. Anyway, he is on something that he calls a sab…, sabbatical and when he visits Provo, all he does each and every morning is fish.

He just loves to fish. Makes his own lures too, down at his house, in the back corner of the hotel property. It's really just an old storage shack but he likes to call it his Caribbean castle. Ha, ha, his Caribbean castle…, get it! Ha ha.

You noticed, of course you noticed, that he never seems to have any luck. Actually, he catches a lot of fish. Every day, well, almost every day anyway. And you will never guess why he always comes in here empty handed. Well, believe it or not, it's because he files the barbs off all of his baits. He calls it 'catch and release', I think. Yes, that's it, 'catch and release'.

Yes, I must say that Mr. Jonathon enjoys his own, peculiar ways…, but he is always generous…, and, and, courteous to me and the other barmen. Yes, he is very much a gentleman. Of that there is no doubt."

Ten bucks well spent I thought. Gossip made perfect through practice was not necessarily a bad thing.

But why catch and release when the ocean shallows were teaming with fish that would treat anyone's palate. Why yank some creature around by the mouth, for minutes on end, only to look at it up close for a few seconds and then let it go.

That was adolescent behavior. It was what a fourteen year old boy would do. He would delight himself, on afternoons alone in his room, by flipping through the pages of a glossy, men's magazine mesmerized by the visual magic of reclining young women. Engage, enjoy, but never to the point of orgasm or ejaculation for that matter. That kind of evidence would 'stain' his secret. Bull fighting with no final blood by the sword. No death by design in the afternoon.

Mister Jonathon would have to be met and, unlike his penchant for play with no point, I would fashion a series of verbal baits, like some of his 'Royal Coachmen', that would be to his liking. I would lure and land him with taut conversation and then consume the story he would divulge with great relish. Banish my boredom, for a short time at least and…, and, maybe even get lucky, get served up a fish story of sufficient weight to tip the scales of my considerable incredulity.

Sipping slowly at the surface of the Chivas Regal, pausing long to allow the ice cubes to work and rework their magic, I wondered about the floating mass that some glacier up North had calved that was this Mr. Jonathon.

An informed guess could have been made as to the hazard quotient of the real beast, the glistening white mountain of frozen, fresh water that floated, mostly submerged, in the sea. One seventh of its mass was all that was visible above the surface. Mr. Jonathon fit the definition of an iceberg. Only he floated in an ocean of predictable, distinctly adolescent, self-gratifying, certainty.

Confident in my wild guess, about the man who occupied the Caribbean castle at the back of the hotel property, my gut told me that this self-anointed king would however, prove to be not quite as clean as his floating counterpart.

Life's complications clung to a man like barnacles to a boat bottom. That was inescapable. And unlike my sea borne, moving metaphor, his striations and the detritus that had undoubtedly collected around him would render his claimed academic posting somewhere along the Atlantic seaboard of the US, dubious at best. And therefore his supposed sabbatical would be reduced to the sham it probably was when viewed through the lens of persuaded disclosure. But if not sabbatical, what then?

This Turks and Caicos version of the spent fisherman, Santiago, from 'The Old Man and the Sea', this misanthrope, Mr. 'J', presented even less to the world around him than did any iceberg. An iceberg glistened in its grandeur while the secretive Mr. Jonathon barely broke the surface of the water filled world in which he floated. He seemed to be content to tread water more than taste it.

Sure, both were inert and innocuous when viewed from afar. But the danger posed by both of them could be real, very real, and proximity to them was the determining factor of lethality. Better to be cautious when approaching the man. Better to observe him from afar a little while longer. He wasn't going anywhere anyway. Nor was I, it seemed!

Chapter 2

Mr. Jonathon, Mr. Jonathon! Was he merely an animated oddity that fit in well with the other tourist trappings in the Maki-Maki bar, or was he a floating channel marker whose warning bell, if left unheeded, could spell disaster! Maybe both, maybe neither! Who knew!

I was bored being stuck in Provo. Hence, perhaps, my fascination with the non-descript man. But I could smell the nefarious in him though. He had a story to tell and I wanted to be his rapt audience. Another wedding guest maybe, in the Rhyme of the Ancient Mariner!

I felt confident that I could handle whatever my digging would dredge up from his murky depths.

Lost in the tawny liquid in front of me, my peripheral vision caught the movement of someone who had just entered the bar. I looked up to see who had interrupted my contented contemplation of the uncharted island, Mr. Jonathon, the man who continued to loom large in front of me.

He, along with the iceberg, suddenly sank beneath the waves of conscious thought.

Striding into the bar from the hotel lobby was a woman. Dressed in a grey, pin striped, well-tailored business suit, she appeared to be in her early thirties.

Instantly, I was transported back to the early 1960's. I was Dick Clark and the Maki-Maki bar became the set for American Bandstand. And the diminutive Connie Francis, or her double, one generation removed, had just made her entrance.

I was ready to mouth the words to her bubble gum song, "Lipstick On Your Collar", which I knew she had come to sing, or at least lip-synch, for the live audience of maybe thirty preppy, white kids. Everyone knew that her presence in front of the cameras was to promote record sales via the magic of black and white television exposure. But nobody cared. Connie was the female teen idol of the day.

Always the lady, graceful, good looking, and gracious to all, she owned the stage in a natural, unassuming way. And she always delivered on the expectation of performance. Even my mother liked her.

"Try to find a girl like her, dear. She looks like she would really enjoy camping. Young ladies like that who are full of adventure, are the most fun to be with, you know."

My mother saw 'no-nonsense', practical girls as perfect marriage material. Ones whose concept of a temporary erection went no further than the image of a rude dwelling composed of canvas, metal poles, ropes and pegs.

But given the fact that Connie was the main squeeze of Bobby Darin, an innovative male singer poised to take over from Frank Sinatra as the country's main heart throb, she obviously knew how to do more than just pump the plunger on a Coleman lamp to keep the mantle glowing brightly at night!

Connie leaned over the bar toward the barman. She looked like she was telling him her whole life story. The barman glanced at me half way through her monologue, grinned his recognition as to what it was that she had finally decided upon and nodded his recognition of the subsequent course of action my Marcel Marceau mime implied.

The sugar, lime juice, dry gin, and soda water were poured over ice in a tall glass and stirred. A large slice of lime and a cherry added the finishing touch. The concoction was placed on the cork coaster which was in front of the woman.

Without tasting her toast to the Turks and the tropics, she gulped down the first half of the drink like she was trying to douse a fire somewhere down below deck. Only when the fizzy tartness had reached her stomach did she turn to acknowledge the fellow patron who had paid for her Pepto-Bismol with a punch.

"That's in recognition of the most beautiful woman in here," I said with a grin.

"But I'm the only woman in here."

"Hence the superlative perhaps. Cheers!"

The Connie who was dressed for the court room, slid from her perch and, with her Tom Collins in hand, strode over, with a bemused grin, to my table.

This gin maiden was a single woman. I could tell by the way she made her clothes do the fitting for her. The fastidious attention to detail required to mold pumps, purse and even pedicure into a unified whole was more photo shoot preparedness than pavement practiced common sense. To compensate for a short stature she wore heels that were too high. She wobbled when she walked. Her severe color co-ordination spoke of unlimited self-indulgence in high end shops. Too much time and too much money spent on too few people.

There appeared to be no one in her life to whom she could pose the question, the defining question, 'How do I look, dear?'

She did not anger the Chinese gods with perfection. She merely bored them to death with the banality of always looking her uncorroborated best.

"OK cowboy…, before you heat up your branding iron to claim this stray, how about a name or, or, maybe the name of the spread you work for at least. Before I get burned by someone's red hot poker, I like to know who it belongs to, is all!"

"Nope! No names. I am travelling incognito. For your information, I am a spy!"

"A spy you say…, ah c'mon Mr. Incognito, just a little, itty-bitty first name. Larry, Moe, maybe Curly, or some other stoogey name like that will do. It won't blow your cover as a spy…, and, and, exposing yourself to me won't create a cop-call situation either. Trust me, I've heard every name in the book. Real or rococo ridiculous, trust me, my lips, will remain sealed. Get it…, lips sealed… ha, ha,"

"OK. If you insist, Oh cloistered one. This is going to be grim though. Very grim. You see…, my first name is…, my first name, is Grim."

"Bullshit! What can be grim about a first name! Maybe you were sent from Heaven just to look after little, old me. Maybe you were sent by Saint Christopher, you know, the bloody patron saint of travelers.

Where were you when the ass-hole baggage handlers in Freeport put my bags on the wrong flight? One measly drink in a bar on some other small dot in the Caribbean Sea, a dot that masquerades as a country, will not compensate for the inconvenience that I have suffered. Trust me! Those morons will pay for their sloppy mistake!"

"No, not grim as in sinister and joyless, Grim as in Grimley, my first name. My mother's maiden name actually."

"So Grim it is then. Well, Grimley, named for your mother when she was a maiden, before her garden had ever been hoed..., thanks for...,"

"No, no. My name is Grimley Reaper. You know the harvester. Bringing in the sheaves, bringing in the sheaves..., we shall come rejoicing, bringing in the sheaves. Sunday school and all of that. You remember. Or were you one of the fortunate ones who escaped the partial purgatory of Sunday school.

"No, but I was pardoned early. Maybe it was for good behavior, but I doubt that. May I sit down at your table Mr..., Mr. Grim. I know, maybe we could talk about some of the stories for kids that you and your brother collected and published. Maybe we could talk about the true meaning of Snow White and Cinderella in the context of a post romantic world. Maybe we could do something, anything, to avoid shit-talk about the present, trauma inducing world, the one which is filled with so many, in your face, stupid people."

In an attempt to escape from the conversational quicksand she had just created for herself, Connie stopped talking. She chose instead to blink coquettishly in mock, child-like innocence. The strategy worked. Her facial contortions delivered the diversion she desired.

Her successful maneuver was made easy by my disinterest in both her take on 'post-romanticism' and her pet peeves about certain people. Postponing her pedantic memory spill from some sophomore class attended years earlier would, as our amateur hour lurched forward, I hoped, prove to be permanent.

"Join me at my table? Of course you could. It would be a pleasure for me to share my table with you. You noticed, of course, that the place is full. Tables and chairs are all at a premium. But enough of this Hansel and Gretel crap. My name is Michael, Michael Campbell. Pleased to meet you, Miss…, Ms…,"

I half rose from my seat and shook the hand of the smiling Ms. Francis. She appeared to be quite intrigued by our silly banter. The disclosure of my name seemed to merit a slight nod almost of tabulation, as though a deposit was being made to her memory bank. I was probably reading more into her response than was actually there. I had a tendency to do that when I was bored. It was probably no more than a part of the bonding ritual of sorts between people in bars everywhere, people who both belonged, and wanted to be, somewhere else.

"And this good, this very good little girl, this little girl who knows her nursery thymes, this girl who is now politely sitting at your table is Donna Jean. But her friends call her DJ. So if you want to be her friend, you have to refer to her as DJ too! Careful with the consonants though Mister Michael. That's DJ with a 'D' not some other two letter label that also ends with a 'J' but begins with a 'B'. Got it!"

From a Connie of the concert circuit to a DJ, the decision maker as to what graced the radio turntable most often. Shades of Wolfman Jack! Stardom through saturation of the airwaves with a particular song. Performance and payola. Not mutually exclusive terms way back when and no contest as to which mattered more.

"Were you in Freeport too, I mean, before you came here. You don't fit in this out-of-the-way, well, this backwater. You don't look like the other pathetic, boiled lobsters scuttling around in the lobby, is all."

Perversely, I decided to satisfy the young woman's curiosity with the truth. I wondered if I could sustain the weave of its loose strands with the same dexterity I had perfected with its Siamese twin. Joined at the head, the truth and its creative counterpart had, all too frequently, served the same purpose.

Thread the needle and sustain the stitch that fastened two people and their illusions of reality together. For fleeting encounters at least.

"Actually, I flew in a couple of weeks ago from Bali."

"Bali, hmm, Bali. That's in Indonesia, right! A sort of Aussi North for some loser, low-life Australian types from down under as well! That's what I hear anyway."

DJ definitely got marks for geography. Most people thought that Bali was a country and Indonesia merely one of many islands that swam, close by, in some unheard of sea or other.

And she knew about the social blight that had marred the streets of Denpasar in Bali for years. Shirtless, white trash Australians, stoned and drunk, by turns, who survived by defrauding their national government's workman's compensation and welfare system to live as slum dwellers on the periphery of paradise.

On a weekly basis at least one of the cretins was sent home via air freight because of misadventure; motor cycle accident, deliberate food poisoning, or violent altercation over money, sex, but usually drugs. According to the Jakarta Post, since machetes were a favored method of settling street disputes, outcomes were usually less than favorable for any foreigner involved.

DJ could only have known of the phenomenon well enough to comment on it had she witnessed the mayhem first hand, at street level. Or…, or, if she were privy to dispatches…, regular, restricted releases which related to the deaths of foreigners in regions of high interest.

But interest zones for whom? And what agencies, American or otherwise, would dig that deep or be that sensitive to potential, flashpoints of social discord?

Best to continue to play the suit that was my strongest. Honesty mainly…, but with a catch basin, a safety net, of lies at the ready, if needed, should I falter and fall!

"Yep! Bali as the working set design for a remake of the movie, 'South Pacific'. This time with Australians hired for non-speaking roles only…, walk-ons, or maybe in crowd scenes. Tokenism, to be sure! So, yes, Paradise in South East Asia. That's what all the travel brochures claim at least."

"Paradise lost then, based on your experiences there? Paradise lost, just like in every other goddamn, former pristine place in the world."

More marks for DJ. No one used that expression without at least having heard of the poet from another age, John Milton. Adam and Eve, the serpent, aka Satan, and the eviction notice served by a wrathful God to all who attempted to quench curiosity with knowledge.

Christ, this woman was worse than Jonathon. Iceberg tips both, floating in seas of intrigue, deception and deceit. Play on, I thought, just play on. This was not the deck of the Titanic, nothing was in danger of sinking and any music ensemble on deck would not be delivering their swan song for anyone soon.

"In a word, Yes!. Never mind the fact that everything in Bali is ready to burst. Everything, from the daily tidal wave of people who clog the streets, shops and beaches, to the enormous size and sheer number of look-a-like hotels that clutter every beach front property, everything delivered in extra-large size only, makes the place a victim of its own success. The place is about the size of Rhode Island. But it surpasses all the tourist traps in the Caribbean, in terms of clutter and confusion, combined.

And the result of course is that real estate in Denpasar, the tourist mecca of Bali, is at a premium. I would bet that the going rate per square foot rivals that of anything to be found in lower Manhattan.

And that is another similarity that Bali shares with Manhattan…, and Brooklyn and Coney Island too. Imagine, human waste, including hospital discharge, washing up on the beaches in both parts of the world almost daily. Syringes, needles, many used to treat patients who are HIV positive, along with all manner of synthetic waste, from containers to condoms, everything that is symptomatic of our 'throw-away' society, litters the beaches around the Big Apple and Bali as well.

So, while you are here, enjoy the twelve mile stretch of pristine beach that is just beyond the patio stones outside because its days, I am sure, are numbered."

DJ seemed to be, if not enthralled, then certainly entertained by my story. She sipped at her drink and never looked away from the face that was motor mouthing about the man-made monster that was both very close and also very far away. Maybe I should try the truth more often, I thought as I finished the remaining scotch in the glass.

"Will it be more of the same poison for you DJ or would you prefer something else?"

DJ seemed startled by the question. She had had a front row seat at some improv stage production and there had been no expectation that the lead actor would step out of character and address the audience directly.

As she stared unknowingly at her empty glass, I circled a victory sign above my head toward our latent, although sometimes loquacious, barman.

"Wow, you are quite the story teller, Michael. I'll bet that skill works like magic with most of the unbranded heifers who hang out in places like this. Good for you. So what were you doing there? In Bali, I mean. It must have been more than just a holiday."

DJ did not want my take on the troubling tale from 'down under' to end. Tough broad bravado was replaced by little girl longing. She was listening to a ghost or goblin bed time story. She fought to find the fewest words needed to prime the pump, to get Daddy to tell her more before the lights were turned off.

"Yes, well I work in Jakarta. You know, the capital of Indonesia. Business took me to Bali because the company I represent had a client who resided there. And that's why I am here in the Turks and Caicos Islands actually. The gentleman died, unfortunately, and I am acting as the executor of one segment of his estate.

Boring stuff really. Money transfer from Singapore to the Turks and Caicos, and then on to Bali for its final disposition."

The drinks arrived. DJ benignly starred at me while she absently stirred her emulsion with the swizzle stick. Her free hand remained completely wrapped around the base of the glass. She reminded me of a neophyte drummer trying to maintain a steady, soft back beat with the foot pedal while coaxing a seductive, soothing sound from the taught skin in front of her with a raked wire brush.

Had her leprechaun-like body been possessed by a lyric at that, 'scotch and soda' moment, it could have been – 'Dry martini, jigger of gin, Oh what a spell you've got me in, Oh my, do I feel high…,'

A small, mischievous spirit from Irish folklore, or a student concentrating on cramming final facts into her head in anticipation of the cold indifference of the examination room, which was she?

I glanced at the enigma across from me as I tasted what I knew was my last drink of the day. I decided to shift gears with my new-found drinking buddy.

"But enough about me…, let's talk about you…, what do you think about me?"

I waited for the Bette Midler line from the movie, 'Beaches' to sink in. I knew that I had not delivered the short epistle on ego with the same panache, the same spontaneity as did the buxom star with the voice that could bring the stoic to tears, but the resulting laughter from my audience of one proved that my timing at least was right.

"Well sure as hell you're definitely not Indonesian, no, I don't think so. Blue eyes, egocentric, no, not Asian at all. And I can't place your accent either. New England, no, not even Vermont. I live there, not Vermont, Boston actually, and I've heard every accent there is up and down the Atlantic seaboard. Maybe California, northern California, San Francisco maybe…., there is a certain condescension in your voice…"

"Well, you're getting closer. One more stab at it before I tell you!"

"OK, let's try a little logic then. Here you are in the Turks and Caicos Islands. They are a British protectorate. Maybe you are a Brit."

"Pas du tout. Je viens du Quebec. Je suis un ancien Montrealais."

DJ grinned widely at me. With a smirk of self-congratulation, she mumbled a few words under her breath that were barely audible.

"Bien faites… l'equipe. Notre client…, cible…, est proche.

"Mon Dieu, Oh my God! Vous venez du Quebec et…, and…, You are from Quebec and…, and…, you speak French too!"

Too little was said by DJ to get a fix on the source of her knowledge of the language of Napoleon. Was it mimicry of the dialect spoken by the locals in the towns along the northern coast of Maine acquired during her summer vacations as a kid or was it something more sophisticated than that! Did I hear the echo of post-graduate work done, 'en-Francais', in some suburb of Paris. Who knew! Did she know what she was saying or was she only rhyming off dialogue, no, merely disjointed words heard on some televised kid show while she completed her morning toilette. Who knew!

Don't read too much into anything, I cautioned myself. I barely knew the woman. Time was on my side. And as was usually the case, more would eventually be found out about the woman than I really wanted to know anyway!

I was always hesitant about divulging my nationality to an American. It was like telling a more affluent neighbor that you had just purchased a Chevrolet Biscayne.

The listener, of course, owned a Chevy Impala. It was all about the amount of chrome trim and the light clusters above the back bumpers. The former sedan was always outfitted with two tail lights on either side while the latter was adorned with three. A conspiracy by Detroit to keep people in their place I thought as I chuckled to myself about the mechanical metaphor for pride and prejudice I had just manufactured.

But the Quebec part, being partially French carried with it a certain cachet. It meant that I might possibly own a Citroen, Renault or Peugeot as antidote, almost, to the dorsal fins from Detroit.

Any trace of DJ's capacity to speak anything other than American English, completely disappeared.

"Well, OK, so what the hell am I doing here all by myself you might ask."

"Yes, I might just ask that very question. So…,"

"Simple! I am rewarding the best person I know. Me! And why not! I made a promise to myself that if, at the national sales meeting of my company, I was voted the best Regional Sales Manager for the year, the best without having to bed some guy to buy recognition, I would splurge and pamper myself with a three day vacation. You know, booze, sex, sex on my terms, and rock and roll. Not necessarily in that order either! Ha ha.

And the Jack Tar Village close to Freeport was the right place at the right time for me. I won the goddamn award and so, here I am! The lady of the year but wouldn't you know it, the queen has no fucking clothes!"

The rude, crude surface of the woman notwithstanding, DJ did possess a natural candor which made her quite ingratiating. She possessed, as well, an equilibrium that was visited only upon those who knew and were satisfied with whom they thought they were. Her self-deprecating humor was both refreshing and disarming. It spoke of those who possessed the magic which made others march to the tune that they chose for them.

And I loved women who used the word, 'fuck', during their first conversations with me. Almost as much, that is, as the women who dispensed with propriety, those who took the best verb in the English language to denote perpetual motion and made poetry of it with their bodies before our first encounter came to a close!

"And what magic in a box are you married to that makes you such a star."

"What! What did you say? You don't believe me. You think I am lying to you about Jack Tar and the prize? Oh, oh…, sorry. You are asking what my company sells! Is that it?"

Shit, I thought. Contain your cynicism. Circumlocution was probably seen by this woman as an attempt at entrapment. Maybe she was not from American Bandstand at all. Maybe she was from another popular time waster on the tube, "What's My Line?'

Promotion and sales of pharmaceutical compounds had been my forte in both the North American and the South East Asian markets long before DJ had even been given air time on the turntable of life.

So I knew the ropes in the marketing and sales game all too well.

Those who were most successful in the enterprise of bonding 'want' to 'need', exhibited strong family values. Not of the home, hearth, and human nurturing variety but more a total fixation on their products and services and how best to direct their efforts at target consumer markets.

They became parents to their precocious products. Personal gratification and ultimately self-definition were derived through their efforts that recognized no time constraints. They were '24-7' voices for their host companies. And the recipient firms of the focused evangelism eagerly responded to their windfall wunderkind with a certain largesse and in so doing, gave the apostles of commerce a rationalization that worked.

Financial reward was heaped on star players, and by extension, their families, in large doses. Trophy houses, cars, boats, country cottages, and private schools stood the Calvinistic cautionary tale concerning individual reach and grasp on its head.

And their number had included, for a time at least, me!

"Yes, but more precisely, what do you do that makes you such a paragon of business virtue…,"

I was about to call DJ, 'Little Miss Goody Two Shoes', but thankfully, thought better of it.

"Yes, OK, well, what do I do! Yes, what the hell is my bloody function…, First of all, yes, first of all, I am the District, the District Sales Manager for a company called, Penthesilea. Have you ever heard of it? Pen-the-sil-ea, Penthesilea. No!

Well, I am not surprised. Why would you have heard of a company that sells fake tits?

But in all seriousness, the company is real and…, and so too are its products. Penthesilea creates breast prostheses for women who have undergone radical mastectomies. You know, breast cancer survivors for example. Our products allow women to resume a normal life style…, everything from feeling comfortable around the home to wearing elegant evening wear…, and even lounging by the pool. All of the products are non-invasive. They are affixed to the exterior chest wall with a patented, non-allergenic adhesive tape. Easy to position and adjust and just as easy to remove."

Compelling promotional copy repeated, no doubt, verbatim from the sales brochure. But DJ had piqued my interest. How was it that I had never heard of the outfit? Was it that they were a new player in an established prosthetic market? Did they not see the value in medical journal advertising? Or had my interest died along with my career when I decided to pull the plug on it all. Crossing a bridge meant leaving what was, behind. And what was, was never more than imperfect memory. It was bereft of knowing, or caring, what came after you were gone.

"How very interesting DJ. You must find the work very gratifying."

"You've got that right, mister! The company is very young. It was started only five years ago by a group of doctors in San Francisco. I just got lucky. I entered their elevator of success at the ground floor and have enjoyed the ride straight up ever since. Yep, just a lucky decision for me and…,and…, nothing. That's it!

Oh yes, and just in case you didn't know this, Penthesilea is the name of a woman archer from Greek mythology. She fought against men in many battles, fought in defense of her homeland, fought against all who were her enemies and she won…, always, she won! She even had one of her breasts removed so that it would not affect her ability to use a bow and arrow. Hence the company name that the doctors in San Francisco came up with. Pretty powerful stuff, don't you think?"

DJ made it all sound as though she was truly in her element. She was in the Turks and Caicos Islands because of Penthesilea and she was in her comfort zone talking about the most recent incarnation of the Greek woman of war. She had done her homework, if indeed it was merely homework, well!

Nodding was all that was needed to keep the geyser going. But was I witness to the personal rush of individual success in business or was I acknowledging a well thought out, well-practiced rouse?

"So what exactly do I do on behalf of Penthesilea? Well, I am responsible for sales in the New England states. I have six sales reps reporting to me…, let's see…, in Maine, New Hampshire, Vermont, Connecticut, Massachusetts and Rhode Island. I don't touch New York. It's too big. We have two Regional Sales Managers there. One just for New York City and one for the rest of the State. And, and I have eight major accounts of my own, scattered all over the place. They are big and they are all mine.

I got the award not because of the highest sales in the country. How could I compete with New York, or San Francisco or even Miami for God's sake! No, I got the award for having the greatest sales increase over last year. That's only fair. Right!"

A field management mantra among those in pharmaceuticals came to mind. Better to look good dancing in small shoes than to look foolish drowning in boots made big by 'loading in' and over stocking. Easier to grow a sales territory that was new or had been neglected than to achieve success with one that had been coddled and then corrupted.

And the product itself, a fake tit! Originating in San Francisco and sold mainly in large, urban centers. Transvestites, cross dressers, the whole gender bender population would have been prime, albeit silent, subscribers.

Just as with certain psychotropic drugs, sales would have been boosted considerably by addictive street use.

"Yes, of course. That shows sustained commitment and effective entrepreneurial and leadership skill."

DJ grinned widely at me.

"Wow! That's almost exactly what our president, John Stevenson said when he presented me with the trophy and, best of all, the award cheque at the banquet dinner! Are you sure you and John aren't brothers. You two are very much alike. You are a cool customer. There is no doubt of that! You seem, at least, to be a real gentleman, and, probably best of all, you are calm and you make people around you calm as well. John is good at doing that too!"

DJ leaned forward and clicked her glass against mine. I knew that my time with her was running out but I wanted to give her a few minutes more to bring closure to our discussion about her recent coronation as Queen of New England.

"Listening to you DJ, I can tell that you would have changed nothing you did for Penthesilia even if they had not awarded you the prize. People like you do what they do to satisfy a little voice that is inside. It always tells them the truth about themselves."

"That is so true, Michael! No matter what the cost. I know that I made a lot of people jealous. They think that Mr. Stevenson has a soft spot in his heart for me and that he was playing favorites. And that is fucking bullshit…, just not true! They don't know about the fucking snow storm that stopped everything on the interstate except me when I had to make a special delivery to Bangor. They don't know how many times I had my reps practice their presentations at my place, at my expense, on my time. They cannot even guess how many days did not finish for me until well after nine o'clock at night. I think that I am the only one in the company who says, "TGIM', Thank God it's Monday!"

Maybe I should have been a lawyer, a criminal lawyer. I had fallen into the habit of asking people questions that, when answered, held no surprises. I knew her answer before the question had even been asked!

"You are a rare breed young lady. A breed apart. May your tribe increase!

Now, I am afraid, I have to go. I have to pick up my daughter from school. She, like most females, does not like to be kept waiting."

More of the truth, I thought, from the man who managed, most of the time, without it. But this time the truth had teeth. Christina was still in dire need of whatever I would be able to devise and deliver to assuage the recent psychic blow she had sustained.

I could feel the fan that was feeding DJ to me abruptly get switched to the off position.

"What the fuck…, can't her mother do that! Can't you wear the goddamned ring on your fucking finger to show that you are married? Christ! What a son of a bitch you are."

DJ slouched back in her chair and stared out at the ocean.

I deliberately counted ten steamboats before I answered her. It worked playing touch-football. It gave the offence time to make their play. And I was going to make it work for me to counteract her aggressive attempt to gain yardage at my expense.

"No, on both counts, DJ. My daughter, Christina, does not have a mother and therefore I do not have a wedding ring. Sadly, they never even met each other. A road accident, a simple, avoidable road accident that …, that was just meant to be, I guess. But that was four, almost five years ago now and, and life, like the sea out there, answers to no one. Both are obdurate…, and both must be obeyed."

She rolled her eyes in response to my platitude and frowned as I wiggled the fingers on my left hand in her direction.

Rubbing at her eyes angrily, DJ alighted from her seat. She reached out toward me with both of her arms and cradled the butterfly that my outstretched hand had become between her own. She nudged and kissed at the creature she had overpowered and, with a shudder, held it gently to her cheek.

I had been with big game hunting parties in Alaska more often than I cared to remember. At great expense to the hunter, bears, both brown and grizzly, as well as sheep; Dall and bighorn, and Rocky Mountain goats had been targeted, tracked and ultimately trophied.

The death scene on the side of a mountain was, always, turned into a photo op. The dead creature had its body hair brushed to rid it of brambles, debris and blood. The corpse, I say corpse because the animal was made to appear almost alive, alive with a clump of grass in its mouth, was positioned so as to appear in the best light and at the best camera angle. And the hunter, the victorious gunman, the dispenser of death from almost one mile away posed, magnanimous in victory, hugging and kissing the unblinking, sightless beast.

Was I prey, or merely pariah to this huntress who was hovering above me?

"I am sorry Michael. I am so, so very sorry. Christ I can be so fucking stupid sometimes. So, so, goddamned stupid! Forgive me and my comments that were dead wrong. That's not the way I usually operate. No, I never do things, stupid things like that. Maybe it's all the excitement of the trip catching up with me…, anyway…, "

Was I witnessing sorrow for my loss and contrition for her initial outburst of anger? Was it empathy masking embarrassment or its mirror image? A moot point perhaps. Strangely enough though, I felt that a bond of sorts had just been forged between us, a bond that would make any future meeting matter.

"Tomorrow, if you are willing to play the role of Lenore, I can be your Raven and together we can become the Gothic stars in the Edgar Allen Poe poem."

"Yes…, yes, oh sure, Michael…, Poe…, The Raven…, yes, we could play gothic roles together. Sure, sure, that would be fun…, yes, that would be lots of fun."

"OK. Same time and same place then and together we can further explore the land of Nevermore!"

"Nevermore…, yes…, Nevermore then, nevermore…,together."

I leaned over, dryly kissed the forehead of the huntress turned parrot and was gone.

Chapter 3

Christina swam in the solitude, the safety and the sun baked simplicity of the Turks and Caicos Islands. Relative to the tumult that had been her lot in South East Asia, this was, to her way of thinking, just perfect. It was heaven. We were alone, just me and her surrounded by the slow motion magic of the sea and the sound of soft kisses as salt water and sand celebrated their perpetual embrace.

Because of her verbal skills, and her capacity to read quite well from the dog- eared grade one classroom books that were more cartoon than copy, she was admitted to the Princess Margaret School. A one room school house, it was situated about ten minutes away by bicycle from the small dwelling we occupied. Between Grace Bay and the Bight Settlements, the Princess Margaret, in dire need of make up in the form of fresh paint, was just off the Leeward Highway. Its shabby appearance was masked by mangrove thickets that grew dense and undisciplined in all directions around its foundation.

Twice daily, we had settled into a routine that had my daughter perched on a small cushion which straddled the handle bars. Her feet fit perfectly into the utility wire mesh basket which rested above the front wheel mud guard. It was supported by struts that were affixed to the axel and brackets clamped to the handle bars ensured its rigid integrity no matter how heavy or unstable the load.

Secure yes, but for a little girl, precarious, because her balance became a blessing bestowed only by the weight that went with the voice behind her. And the seemingly, yawning chasm between her and the moving ground below her feet grew in direct proportion to the speed we attained. But like a rider on the back of a motorcycle, she quickly learned the knack of shifting her weight as we negotiated the twists in the road.

Curves in the road were one thing, but my constant sharp turns to avoid pot holes close to where the edge of the road was being eroded by the relentless incursion of gravel and sand, caused initial shrieks of fright. But they were always followed by full blown frolic.

Christina would lean back on the bars when she knew that the road ahead was rough. This would render her neck vulnerable to a lip attack accompanied by fierce growls. The unseen monster behind her would only relent when it felt that the fair maiden was on the verge of letting go of her tight grip on the handle bars.

Our laughing could have been heard by the hearing impaired at least a mile away on either side of the road.

My daughter perched precariously in her aviary early every week day morning and I provided the motive power to ensure her punctual arrival at school. It was ten or fifteen minutes of sheer joy for both of us.

Her arrival at the school was always in advance of that of the teacher. I would lift her from the basket, watch her as she joined her new found friends and then I would appear to strike off back down the road. But instead, I would hide in the mangrove bushes until the schoolmarm arrived. A dozen or so unattended children would have been a cause for concern anywhere in North America but not, it seemed, in the Turks and Caicos Islands.

I was thankful that the ride home was along the Leeward Highway. Most days I needed the prevailing north wind to dry my tears. Christina, years younger than most of the other children, had taken it upon herself to assume the role of surrogate teacher once I was out of sight. She would see to it that everyone was seated in their proper places. She would ask all of her classmates to have their homework assignments open and ready for inspection.

And then, almost as a reward, she would regale her rapt audience with embellished, animated tales of her adventures in far-away Jakarta and Bali. She spoke at length of the bigness of both places. The buildings, the size of the trees, the crush of too many loud people everywhere and always.

The tone inside the room tumbled the moment that the teacher, Miss Glover, arrived. I left for home often humming the opening lyrics to the Paul Simon song, Kodachrome.

'When I think back on all the crap I learned in high school, it's a wonder I can think at all…'

The same delicious interlude was revisited each day when school was let out at three o'clock.

The trip home was even better, from Christina's perspective at least, than the morning run. Frequently we stopped along the way at Uncle George's general store. More a rickety old shack that was in worse shape than the Princess Margaret, Uncle George carried staples like flour, cooking oil, cereal and seasonings. But he also had a confection counter on top of which was a glass case which contained a variety of Cadbury chocolate bars. Christina would select one and we would share it during our journey back home.

Initially the eight squares were divided up evenly between us but, by the end of the first week, I found that my share had dwindled to two, little pieces. I was told by Christina that it was because she was a girl, she was younger than I, much younger than I, and she needed more because she was still growing.

I could not mount a persuasive argument against any of the three rationalizations she had manufactured. I could not have mounted any comment, no words, only nonverbal compliance. The moment I stared into the face of my daughter, my darling daughter, I was lost. Christina was the duplicate of her departed mother.

The day before I met DJ had been different though. Much different!

Christina never walked anywhere. She danced and frolicked her way between destinations. That day, however, with her head bowed, like a person in mourning, she had trudged over to me, lifted her arms in anticipation of being basketed, and, once atop the bike, just slumped forward and stared at the ground.

I had seen Christina like that only once before. She had witnessed our housekeeper in Jakarta, Siti, lying lifeless in the empty tub of our hotel bathroom in Singapore. They had just come back from an afternoon of shopping and the two were in love with the world and their place in it.

Christine had been told at the time that her best friend, her surrogate mother was just sleeping. But she never saw the young woman again. In fact, Siti had been murdered. And the death of the innocent, young girl was little more than a small piece in the bazaar puzzle that had prompted Christina and me to be in the Turks and Caicos Islands. There was a financial matter, a large financial matter, that had to be attended to there and that had provided the convenient cover needed to nest among the nettles in that far flung place.

Not a word was spoken between us on the trip home. Christina did not even look up as we passed by chocolate George and his outpost of opportunity.

My daughter did not look at me as I had helped her off the bike. She just made her way up the four steps to the front door of our temporary lodging and disappeared inside.

Our abode, which was perched on an outcropping of rock, more resembled a camper trailer than a house. It was nestled tightly among other dwellings of similar construction. All were inhabited by large, loud families. The only real living space in the place served as both living room and bedroom. Everything had been fitted to fold into something else. The washroom and kitchen, like after thoughts, post construction, more resembled walk-in closets. Privacy was at a premium. Personal space was not part of the rental agreement. There was nowhere to hide.

I left her alone for fifteen minutes, fidgeting and feigning interest in the spokes of the bike.

When I finally entered the house, I found Christina huddled in the fetal position in the corner of the divan. She was sobbing. Quietly, I walked over to her side and sat down. I gently placed my hand on her back.

"Christina, we are best friends you know. We are partners together, you and I. And we love each other more than anyone else in the world. And, you know what? Best friends who love each other like we do, share everything together.

We laugh together when we are happy and we both know that we have each other when we become sad or upset. You know what! We are even more close than two pieces of chocolate from the store of Uncle George."

I stopped talking and winced at the stupid analogy I had just drawn. But my analysis was wrong.

Upon hearing my last words, Christina jumped up, scrambled over to me and buried her tear streaked face in my chest. It took what seemed like minutes to calm down the wailing little creature. She clung to me like a baby monkey who knew only mother's bosom as safe refuge.

"I never want chocolate again. Not ever, no, never, not for ever and ever!"

I remained silent and just stared out the window at the spindly tree in the front yard.

"Miss Glover said I am bad to eat more chocolate than you. She said that is sin and Jesus is mad at me. Is Jesus mad at me Daddy?"

"No, Jesus is not angry with you my darling, little girl. Jesus loves young people like you, Christina. It says so in the Bible. In many places in the Bible Jesus told his followers to bring the little children to meet him so he could talk to them.

Jesus said that all people who wished to go the Heaven had to become just like little children all over again. And that's because Jesus knew that children were the best..., the best behaved, the most pure of all of the people on the earth. And you and your friends at school are the most deserving to go to Heaven. There is no doubt about that. Jesus said so!"

A little spontaneous, revisionist theology seemed to be the best offence possible to surmount the sanctimony of her simpleton teacher. She had succeeded in compounding the primitive concept of God that my daughter had acquired at the side of our maid in Jakarta. Siti's concept of the world and the role of Jesus in it, was real, albeit rudimentary and, it was wrong.

"But we played with paper today in school and Miss Glover said that me and…, and everybody, everybody in the school, did sin against Jesus."

"Was it a fun game with paper, Christina?"

"No, no, it was not a fun game Daddy!" Christina hit my chest hard with her clenched fist.

"So, tell me how this not-so-fun game worked."

I fought hard to maintain a straight face. I wished at that moment that my daughter was ten years older. My response to Christina would have been one of dismissal coupled with a derogatory comment about the teaching qualifications of the perpetrator of the classroom witch hunt.

Ironically, the silly and misguided Miss Glover had committed the worst sin of all. She had sought and achieved an ample measure of personal vengeance. To her way of thinking, my upstart daughter had usurped her dominant role in the classroom. And she had reached into her limited bag of adult tricks and had come up with sin, a concept over which the hapless children had no defense, as her retributive response. And all because of her lack of punctuality. And all because of the bullshit that had been fed to her as a child.

Christina's days at Princess Margaret were numbered. And our stay in the Turks and Caicos Islands would enjoy the same sort of truncation.

"Miss Glover gave everybody a piece of paper with a big 'X' on it. She got very angry with me right away. She told me I had the paper with the 'X' the wrong way. She said it was not a 'X', it was a cross. She said it was to show the cross of Jesus.

Then she said for everybody to close their eyes so they could remember all the sin they had done. And…, and when they remembered they could open their eyes and say, 'I am sinner, Miss Glover'.

Then Miss Glover got mad at me again. She yelled at me again too. She said, Christina, open your eyes. You are the last one. Do you think you have no sin!

Almost Daddy, almost I started to cry. I did not know my sin. But, but, then, then…, I remembered the chocolate bar all the time from the Uncle George store. Maybe I took too much so you have only a small piece to eat. Maybe that made Jesus mad at me. So I said, Yes, Miss Glover, now I know what is my sin.

Miss Glover got a big smile on her face and then she said to all the class to put a sin sticker on the cross…, I forgot to say Daddy that everybody had stickers too, sin stickers for the cross…, to show that the sin of everybody must go on the cross and then Jesus will for…, forgive the sin and be happy."

I hugged the little girl beside me. I hugged her for her honesty in the face of confusion, I hugged her for her bravery when confronted by adversity and I hugged her tightly for all the Miss Glovers her future would hold.

The idealist would say that God helped those who helped themselves. Life on earth demanded that the singular personal pronoun, 'I', dominate. 'I' will do well in school. 'I' will work hard to carve out a career for myself. 'I' will provide for my family. 'I' will strive to ensure that my life benefits others. Self-imposed limitation based on fear of transgression, of offending a force looking over one's shoulder was counter-productive at every way station alone the road of life! The sin of self-sufficiency was so, only when not practiced.

Maybe the concepts of 'sin' and 'win' were not in opposition to one another at all. Maybe they were the same. Maybe their difference was merely one of degree. Both were manifestations of ego. Personal success and possession of a soul. The former was limited to the finite planet earth, while the latter was thought to be infinite and of the universe.

Maybe the Jews had it right. Maybe they were God's chosen people. Maybe their book, the Old Testament, a text rife with human sacrifice, defined the relationship between God and his son, Jesus. Maybe Jesus was sent to pay for the transgressions of mankind. Maybe he died on a cross and maybe he stayed dead. Maybe it was God following his commandment to Abraham concerning Isaac. Only God followed through on what he had demanded, then rescinded, of His devoted follower.

Maybe Christ was merely a sacrifice made by God to His people. Maybe one could still call oneself Christian, but only as a memorial to the fallen flesh of God.

"You know what Christina? This has been a long day for both of us, and I think that we should celebrate being together again. I think we should go the restaurant in the hotel for supper. They have your favorite you know. Pizza. But not just any old pizza. Pizza with what you like best on top. Pepperoni, mushrooms, pineapple and extra cheese. What do you think…?"

Christina had heard enough. Without waiting for me to continue any further, she sprang from the nest she had made beside me and pounced at the one person in her little life who was not mad at her.

Almost as though the run-in with the evangelical had not happened, we played, 'I spy with my little eye', during the bike ride to the hotel. We laughed as we ate our meal and flush with the food and her new found hope, Christina summarized her ecumenical encounter within the walls of Princess Margaret.

"You know what Daddy? I think that God and Santa are naughty. And, and…, I don't like them very much. Not very much, no, not very much at all!"

As was the case with an ever increasing number of pronouncements that issued forth from my daughter, I had to stop analyzing implications and start reacting more quickly to face value meaning.

Fascinating though. God and Santa in the same thought. Santa usurping the role of Christ. How very Western in focus. The victory of the role of the Magi over that of the Messiah in the commercial pageant that Christmas had become.

"And why is that, Christina?"

"Because we are learning in school how to sing a new song, 'Santa Claus is coming to town'. Do you know this song Daddy?"

"Some of it, I think. Let me give it a try. 'He sees you when you're sleeping, he knows when you're awake, he knows if you've been bad or good, so be good for goodness sake. You better not pout, you better not cry, you better not shout, I'm telling you why, Santa Clause is coming to town."

I looked at my daughter expecting approval of my lyrical trip down memory lane. Instead, I was met by a face that was contorted into anger and frustration.

"You see. You see! Santa is bad. He is looking at me when I am in the bathroom and he is looking at me when I am getting ready for bed.

And…, and…, God is like that too. Miss Glover said to us that God sees everything, all the time, we do too!"

The genesis of self-consciousness and shame, I thought as I stared at my distraught daughter. The ubiquity of it all, right down to childhood songs about a fat guy with a penchant for naked children.

"Never mind Christina. We will have plenty of time to talk about Santa and about God too. We can't figure out everything in one day you know. The world is complicated. I mean there is a lot to figure out and to understand. That's why everybody has to go to school for many, many years. It takes a long time to figure everything out. But you know what? That's part of the fun. Every day we learn something new. And that's exciting.

Now, you know what? I have a surprise for you. I took it from the fridge before we came here. Do you want to know what it is?"

"Oh yes, yes. What is it daddy? Will I like it? Show me what it is. Show me what you brought from the fridge for me. Pleeease."

I placed the Cadbury chocolate bar in front of my daughter. She looked at it, then up at me and then back at the beckoning dessert.

"Oh, all for me, all for me. Do you want me to share with you, Daddy?"

"Nope! This chocolate bar is all for you. Just for you. You can have some now and maybe save some for tomorrow. It is your decision Christine."

Without taking her eyes off the blue and gold wrapper, Christine's response forced me to grab my napkin and, feigning a cough, bury my face in it. I knew, at that moment, that my daughter was leaving me. As a needy, dependent child, she was leaving me. To become a better person than I could ever hope to be, maybe.

To try her hand at the life skill, essential for daily survival, of placating those in power through the dispensation of possessions which were of transient value, definitely!

"Umm, I love chocolate, Daddy. But not today. Today is different Daddy. I am going to give this chocolate, all of it, to Miss Glover. I will give it, all of it, to her tomorrow. When I see her tomorrow I will give it to her. Chocolate makes me so happy Daddy and, and, I want Miss Glover to be happy too!"

Christine's juggling act to secure personal safety through the appeasement of God or His emissary with sweetness was worthy of St. Ignatius of Loyola and all of his Jesuit minions combined.

'Give us your young children in their formative years and we will give you compliant adults, forever.'

Chapter 4

We did not return home that evening after our meal in the restaurant. It was too late and I wanted the luxury of the large, comfortable bed in my room. We both needed a sound sleep. God only knew what the following day would hold for both of us.

With the little glass soldiers from my favorite Scottish regiment at parade attention in front of me, I sat back in the miniature chair on the balcony and starred out beyond the hotel grounds toward the darkness that had created an ink black sea.

Upon my initial arrival at the hotel, I had unscrewed the balcony light bulb so as to not contribute to the low voltage gaiety that management hoped to project once night fell. The room was meant for periodic escape not permanent residence. No sense in advertising what was not meant for public, curious or combative, consumption.

My little girl was wrapped up in some corner of the small farm that served as a bed and her gift for Miss Glover occupied the space in the mini bar that had been vacated by my Scottish comrades in arms.

As the rim of the ice filled glass of blended fermentation lingered long under my nose, I chuckled to myself at the recent olfactory antics of Elithia. Her seemingly spontaneous gesture had, in no small way, contributed to the mathematical certainty that the right one plus another right one always equaled a bigger and better, splendid One. 'White on White by Black'. It always made for great sport when, on the playing court of consent, both players knew and followed the rules of the game.

I downed the first half of my drink, swallowed hard, and then finished it. I was in the process of drafting another soldier into service when I heard the muted sounds of a man and a woman in heated discussion somewhere in the bushes to my right, just beyond the main grounds.

Silence ensued as they both emerged from the dark foliage. They followed the narrow path that led from the corner of the property up to the hotel and bar area. Both had been walking very closely together, perhaps because of the thick foliage, but both instinctively moved apart when they reached the manicured lawn that led to the lobby. Both attempted to straighten out any creases that might have been noticeable in their clothing.

The woman wore long, Bermuda-like shorts that made it impossible to discern her age. She could have been in her thirties, forties, or fifties. If in her thirties she was wearing an outfit, deemed appropriate for the tropics, that only her mother would have chosen. If the woman I saw was old enough to have a twenty-five year old daughter then she was ludicrously dressed and doomed to fail at imitating a female one generation her junior. The loose fitting top made the woman, regardless of her age, look like a trollop.

Their behavior was reminiscent of my own when in the company of someone with whom I was not supposed to be. Prudence, that usually welled up too late, was thought to be the best defense against wild and irresponsible tongue wagging. It almost always became the precursor to disaster for both players.

I leaned back as far as I could against the sliding glass door and gently put my glass down on the table. Slowly, I craned my neck forward to get a glimpse of the couple whose apparent coupling was best kept quiet.

It was Connie Francis! And she was reunited with her aging beau, Bobby Darin. That made as much sense as DJ and Mister Jonathon did sneaking out of the bushes together! But there they were, just three stories below me, making their way toward the Mahi-Mahi bar.

The friend of all fish stopped at the edge of the grass, allowing DJ, unescorted, to enter the bar first. He waited a minute by untying his shoe lace and then retying it tightly. Then he too disappeared inside the 'meet the meat' market.

I quickly poured myself another drink. Think, you crazy bugger, think, I half said out loud.

What were the possible, what were the probable explanations for their clandestine meeting?

DJ was horny. And any father figure, what was his name…, Stevenson, a company President Stevenson surrogate, cock of the walk, would do. No, that wasn't it. She was not even close to being a player in life's little game of Hearts. The concept of throw away trump cards was still far away down that road of choice. A dead-end travelled most often by those blamelessly bereft of gaming skills. No, DJ was more, much more, than that! But built to satisfy whose bidding?

The two of them were related. That was it! A brother, a half-brother, a step-brother, some biological or legal connection. No! No reason then for a cover up. The two of them shared something in common. Maybe. They both purportedly hailed from New England. Perhaps she was a former student of the man on sabbatical. Maybe they had been lovers way back when and their meeting in the Turks and Caicos was for old time's sake. No. Only in Broadway plays did that happen. Bernard Slade and "Same Time Next Year'. And Jonathon was no Alan Alda.

A common connection. A common connection. Jonathon was no more on sabbatical than I was. If his interest and focus were on whales and their breeding habits, a common pastime or professional focus for foreigners in the Turks and Caicos, then he had positioned himself on the wrong side of the island chain. If his real interest was, in fact, sub-aquatic, then the movement and tracking of naval behemoths, of both friend and foe, was a more likely explanation.

DJ could maintain her prosthetic posture with her eyes shut. Maybe her real focus was in deep water as well. She struck me as the type, all stars and stripes, who would have jumped at the request of Uncle Sam to contribute to national security, the defense of the land of the free and the home of the brave.

Maybe DJ was his assistant. Maybe not. Maybe she had just innocently poked around the hotel property, chanced upon Jonathon's shack, been invited inside and merely talked, over coffee, as any two nationals would in foreign territory.

Who knew! Who the hell knew!

All the more reason to get away from the Turks and Caicos Islands and return home to South East Asia as soon as possible.

The remaining twelve year old warriors, those still equipped to do battle another day, were returned to their dark, air-conditioned barracks. Quietly closing the miniature fridge door, I tip-toed over to the lump on the far side of the bed.

Christina had, as usual, buried her face in what resembled a fouled jib sail. No bed sheets could withstand the pitching and heaving of my daughter in the minutes before sleep becalmed her.

I quickly brushed my teeth to rid my mouth of the foul taste of scotch and, in the darkened room, made my way over to the far side of the bed.

I prided myself on my stealth. But as is the case with most human pride, it was dashed almost immediately by the sleep warm, slayer of sails who noiselessly nestled in beside me. She searched for and found my Adam's apple. Then she gently rested the palm of her hand over it.

We both fell into a deep sleep. We were both at peace with the world.

* * *

"Good morning Mr. Samuel. I very much appreciate your seeing me on such short notice. I will attempt to be brief so as not to interfere with your personal time away from the office in Cockburn Town."

"Yes, well, your call was certainly unexpected. But here you are! So what can I do for you, Mr. Campbell?"

The less than enthusiastic response from the man in front of me was expected. Whatever had motivated him to travel, by sea or float plane, the fifty odd miles from Cockburn, pronounced by a Brit as 'Koh Buhn', to Parrot Cay was his own affair.

A tall, somewhat corpulent man, he sported a graying moustache and goatee. He could have been a stand-in for Burl Ives, the sometime singer and actor in 'B' grade adventure movies.

Thank God, I thought, that the man who had been chosen to assume stewardship of the funds, some twenty nine million, nine hundred twenty-four thousand in total, on its tax avoidance journey from Singapore to his outpost in the middle of the Atlantic, before the final transfer to Bali, did not appear to have a single bone in his body that was bent. Gray was his color and propriety provided his only spots.

"I want you to know Mr. Samuel that knowledge of your whereabouts was not divulged to me by your office secretary. She merely indicated that you were out of town and not expected back for three days. I merely guessed at your location."

"But…"

"How did I know about this residence that is off the beaten track? The same way I know that the first name of your wife of twenty-five years is Cynthia. The same way that I know that your only child, Jennifer, is enrolled in a private school for girls in Canada. In a suburb of Toronto to be exact. She is, I believe, in grade eleven."

"But, but, why would you wish to know all of this about me?"

"Do you think for one minute Mr. Samuel that the people I represent, the people behind the funds you are currently holding in a suspense account chose you by accident? By merely searching through the local telephone directory? You were thoroughly vetted my good sir. You were chosen because of your history of competence and discretion in matters involving the financial affairs of your select, albeit short list of clients. My people prefer quality over quantity in all of their financial transactions."

I now knew that I had carte blanche with the man's time. Cynthia was not with him. He would have introduced her to me straight away. But someone was. I could smell the lingering scent of a woman in the room. The tantalizing fragrance was French in origin and I guessed not too long off the shelf of some duty free shop.

And besides, Christine and I had awoken to a rainy day. She had been sent to school in a taxi to avoid the downpours that I knew would punctuate the entire day.

Mr. Samuel was trapped. He had nowhere plausible to go.

"So, the original question remains, Mr. Campbell. What can I do for you?"

"The estate of the late Mr. Albert Edward Tan of Singapore, the portion of it that has been entrusted to your Firm for appropriate disbursement, needs your immediate attention. Please see to it that the sum of twenty-four million dollars US, is transferred to the branch of the Standard Chartered Bank in Bali, Indonesia, to the account of PT Bali High Art Enterprises. Make it to the attention of a Dr. Rajawane, the principal of record who is domiciled there.

Further, you will transfer the remaining funds also to a branch of the Standard Chartered Bank. But this time to the one located in Cockburn Town. Just around the corner from your office actually. Two million is to go into a trust account in my name and the remaining three million, nine hundred twenty-four thousand is to be deposited in my personal chequing account. Your transaction fees should be deducted from the sum that will be placed on deposit in this latter account. Both accounts were opened, in anticipation of the transference of the estate funds, about one week ago. That, in a nutshell, Mr. Samuel, is what you can do for me.

Let me apologize for the lack of forewarning but, as is perhaps the case with your own professional life, issues do arise that require immediate attention. I am needed back in Jakarta within the next couple of days."

"That could prove to be problematic Mr. Campbell. There are regulations to be followed you know and legal documents requiring certification. You understand."

Why was it, I wondered, that the professionalism which people possessed on paper perished when they were pushed into tight time envelopes and deep pools of money!

"Perhaps you could offer me a drink from the well-stocked bar that is sitting forlornly over there in the corner."

"Of course, how gauche of me, of course. Please excuse my lapse in manners. What will you have Mr. Campbell..., a glass of sherry, a white wine perhaps?"

"If you don't stock Chivas Regal, then a double, single malt on the rocks would suffice."

"Certainly. Would Glenfiddich do? It's the only scotch I have at the moment. I'm a rum man myself. Any one of the local blends from Jamaica…, when I have the time and inclination to get it."

Captain Morgan clumsily placed the drink on the beveled glass that perched on a large piece of driftwood in the center of the living room. The primitive, hackneyed piece of furniture undoubtedly served, more often than not, as the focus of polite conversation with neophyte guests. A piece prompting pap that is, when the gushing guests were in need of neutral subject matter.

Mr. Samuel had chosen to seek refuge in a glass of port.

Deliberately, I lowered my voice to the point where Mr. Samuel had to lean forward to hear what I was saying.

"Regulations and a paper trail you say, Mr. Samuel. Well, as you can appreciate sir, that is not my area of expertise.

By any measure, we, you and I, are discussing a substantial amount of money. Money that, most certainly, was not acquired by religiously depositing funds in a savings account as reward for a life time spent working for others in some factory or office.

So, Mr. Samuel, let me tell you a little about what the people who surround me do, indirectly, that reaps such rich reward.

We are talking about creativity, Mr. Samuel, financial windfall based on the wizardry, if you will, needed to exploit the human condition. I am going to cite just one example of what I mean. But there are many others, believe me. The story I am about to tell is not for your amusement or entertainment. It will however, for a discerning, analytical man such as yourself, convey a message, the meaning of which, you would be wise to heed.

This tale involves individuals who are in the business of arranging marriages. Bizarre at first blush, I know. But unlike you and I who factor love into life time commitment, vast numbers of people throughout the world follow their ancestral, traditional values and mores. They allow their families to find suitable mates for them.

Let's take Sri Lanka as a case in point. Young women of marriageable age who live there, not much older than your Jennifer actually, say between eighteen and twenty four, rely on the intervention of their fathers. And of course, in the case of Sri Lanka, fathers there do not want their sons or daughters to remain in their country of birth. The Tamil Tigers, the civil war and all that. Murder and mayhem have been the norm there for years. No place to settle down and raise a family.

So, through family contacts, the fathers locate single, male, former Sri Lankans living in Europe. Let's say in France.

For a fee of, oh, maybe, fifteen thousand, the father enlists the aid of a trusted family friend in Sri Lanka who guarantees that the young woman will be united with an eligible male candidate she has never met who lives in France.

In the airless hold of a boat, tramp steamers you and I would call them, the young lady, along with close to twenty others, is first transported to Thailand. The trip lasts more than two weeks. The Indian Ocean, the Strait of Malacca, the South China Sea and the Gulf of Thailand have one thing in common. Never do they offer calm sailing waters. By the time the girls arrive in Thailand they are exhausted and many are sick.

Nevertheless, our young, soon-to-be bride and her fellow passengers fit in well with the other slum dwellers on the outskirts of Bangkok because they look Indian in ethnicity. There is a large Indian population that permanently resides there.

The girls remain in captivity in Thailand for about two weeks. They are warned never to go outside because the place is teaming with robbers and murders and the police, if they catch them with no passport, will put them in jail. And their families will lose all the money they spent to get them to their marriage partner.

Two weeks is enough time to create fake passports to replace the real ones that are destroyed when they arrive at the secret Thai safe house.

Any comments so far Mr. Samuel?"

"No, no, go on. Do go on. Your story is fascinating. A version of human trafficking you say. And each shipment grosses about three hundred thousand dollars!"

I couldn't tell whether Mr. Samuel was, if not appalled, then at least taken aback by my story of human hardship. Or was it that he identified more with the machinations of the criminals. Had my story merely appealed to his entrepreneurial spirit!

Loose an arrow into the heavens and know that all power to control is relinquished to capricious fate.

"Ok. So, the women are eventually trucked from their hiding place to the Bangkok airport. Then they are put on a flight to Amsterdam, or Berlin maybe…, and then, usually by rail, on to Paris. They are instructed, when they arrive at the first European airport on the itinerary, to mill about in the baggage claim area for thirty minutes or maybe even an hour. Long enough for an international flight, ideally one from India, to arrive. Then, and only then, do they go through customs along with the crush of the other newly arrived refugees and regular tourists.

Once outside the airport they are met by a relative of the future husband, in most cases the man's brother. The perspective bride stays with the brother for about one week and then is introduced to her future husband. They marry within the first month of her arrival and stay in France for anywhere up to three years.

The new husband, usually a French citizen, sponsors his new wife as a landed immigrant. No suspicion is aroused and all the documentation they need to travel anywhere is acquired legally. Then the couple, if they do not want to stay in France, picks another country where they do wish to settle down permanently. And that's it. From oppression to opportunity. All for a price."

"Yes, yes, I see. Some people just don't worry about possible negative consequences, do they! What you just outlined as a business plan does have weaknesses though. It could very easily fail. Someone could step out of line or get caught. But then, as you implied earlier, they would be left for dead where they fell on the battlefield of life. That takes a lot of intestinal fortitude on the part of the men who engineer the whole event. A lot of logistical challenges. The women too are brave, of course. Must not forget them."

"Some might put it that way, yes. But the story is not finished. The three hundred grand gross profit that you calculated is just the tip of the iceberg."

Time to add a little more luster to the lure, I thought. Old fish were old fish for a reason.

"The young women in transit are always accompanied by matrons who speak their language. Older women who, depending on your point of view, are either adjudicators, women do have issues, periodically, if you know what I mean, or jailors.

Prior to arrival at any of the numerous customs stations, all of the women are given tampons and instructed to insert them just as a precaution. They are told that any trace of blood will cause the guard dogs on patrol to attack them. Remember, these girls are exhausted, frightened and disoriented. They will do whatever they are told to do. Remember also, they are always surrounded by people who speak a language that they do not understand. The tampons are retrieved by the matrons once they clear customs."

"I don't understand. Why the need for all of that fuss if the woman is not menstruating?"

I sat back, rolled my scotch around in the glass and took a number of soothing sips. I had Mr. Samuel where I wanted him.

"Think about it Mr. Samuel. Think about how that process would generate a profit that would render the three hundred thousand mere icing on the cake."

"Oh my God, drugs in the tampons! But…, but…, the dogs would sniff them and the, the girls would be arrested. Or the drug containers would rupture while inside them and the girls would die."

"All true. Your premise is correct but your product choice is not. No drugs…, for the reasons you just outlined. Plus the fact that tampons are too small to accommodate kilos of product, whatever it is. But you are on the right track. Keep going. What else of value would fit into a tampon?"

"I know. I know! Jewels…, precious stones…, diamonds!"

"You said that, not me, Mr. Samuel. I'm just telling you a story about the transport of young, Sri Lankan women that was told to me.

That's all. Embellish the story to become one of wretchedly poor people possibly carrying precious bling on their person if you wish."

"Amazing, absolutely amazing. Are you ready for another drink Mr. Campbell?"

I could not believe Mr. Samuel's reaction to my tale of dread and deceit. Instead of instilling fear for his own safety and that of his family at the hands of my ruthless associates, he chose to feel honored that I had sufficient respect for him to bring him into my confidence.

My job was done. I knew the money would be sent both around the corner from his office and around the world to far-flung Indonesia. Compliance was guaranteed because Mr. Samuel's sleepy little life had been given a shot of adrenalin albeit anecdotally and accidentally. He chose to believe that he had been treated almost as a player. Ego trumped trepidation every time!

He even offered his new found friend and honored house guest a second drink. Clearly a drink to celebrate his own, new found celebrity status.

Arrows loosed toward the heavens!

"No, but thank you very much for the offer. I have taken up enough of your time already Mr. Samuel. A busy man such as yourself needs some 'R and R', rest and relaxation, just to recharge the cells.

It has been a pleasure to have had this time alone with you sir. A real pleasure. Know that I will be in touch with you again in the not too distant future. More business perhaps. And if you ever want a guided tour of any corner of South East Asia, just call me. It can be arranged. I know I can come up with an agenda that will be pleasing, very pleasing, to your palate.

My boat is waiting so I shall bid you adieu."

I chuckled to myself as I walked the short distance to the dock where my rented boat bounced, heaved and strained against its mooring lines.

Mr. Samuel's lady in waiting upstairs would certainly benefit from our conversation. Armed, as he was, with a new found sense of 'player' status, I was certain that he would more than rise to the occasion of counterfeit connubial bliss.

Chapter 5

The speed boat run of about ten miles back down the coast from Parrot Cay to Provo was completed between rain showers. But the sea swells exploding on either side of the bow as it cut through the water, provided more than enough spray to be baptismal. The sting of salt water on my face was just what the doctor ordered. Success made one impervious to the hostile capriciousness of mother-nature. For a short time at least!

Both the hotel lobby and the Mahi-Mahi bar were packed with what looked like stranded refugees from a land where at least two of the four horsemen of the Apocalypse had stopped to graze their animals. War and famine came to mind.

Sullen, anxious faces told the story. Most were ready to do battle with the elements that had become the enemy. They had to validate their birth right. Sun starvation, at great financial cost, was not going to be tolerated. Sandaled, shabby, but sun-lotion ready, they resembled high school students impatiently awaiting the arrival of the school bus that would take them to the fair grounds.

The more adventurous backpacker set frolicked on the wet sand outside almost taunting the shelter seekers to join them in their make believe fun. Most glanced surreptitiously at the wet hospital bed arrangement of beach chairs coveting the one that, by squatter's rights, was theirs. Most grinned their commitment to its acquisition once the treasonous sun broke through the clouds.

"Well, well, well, Mr. Michael Campbell I believe. The man upon whom everything hinges, so to speak. We meet again, sir. Our small world of yesterday seems to be shrinking even more now that the rain clouds have decided to take up permanent residence over our heads."

The voice came from a perky little creature who, at first, I did not recognize. It was DJ. But not the Donna Jean I had met the previous day. No, this was a completely new DJ.

Gone was the rumpled grey business suit. The frumpy shorts worn the previous night had also been packed away in the suitcase reserved for dirty clothes. In their stead, were fashion threads that captured the image of what Caribbean vacations were touted to be all about.

A bikini top, which was more string than stitched material, was covered by a loose fitting, flimsy beach poncho. It trailed down to just above her navel. Her shorts were short, very short and the outline of the bikini bottom underneath was evident to all who merely glanced in her direction. Leather thronged sandals and a bandana of red, blue and turquoise formed parentheses around the perfect, little, fashion statement. A pair of large, designer sun glasses sat, regal like, on the top of her head.

DJ's breasts were too large. More like melons in an open air market, they were both incongruous and unsightly. They succeeded merely in diverting one's attention away from the rest of the woman's otherwise perfectly proportioned body. And they exacerbated, in no small way, her already diminutive frame. But, her radiant, unblemished face was as American as apple pie. Her attempt at Miami Beach chic had worked. She made the other women in the lobby look positively dowdy.

Talking to DJ was, initially at least, like conversing with an articulate offspring. I had to guard against committing the crime of condescension. Physical size and maturity were mutually exclusive terms. I knew that. But without her high heels, DJ could not have been much taller than most grade six students.

"Would I be correct in assuming that your lost luggage was found DJ?"

"Yes, those ass holes in the Bahamas finally got their shit together. They even threw in a hundred bucks to compensate me, they said, for the logistical shortfall, imagine that, they called it a fucking logistical shortfall which created little more than a temporary inconvenience.

Imagine that. No admission of ineptitude or responsibility. And not much of an apology either. Oh well…, Ben Franklin will come in handy. I am sure that one hundred bucks is as easy to spend here as anywhere else. Right."

"No doubt. Take your windfall as a stroke of good luck. It might prove to be the only good fortune anybody sees today. I'm afraid that Lady Luck might have written the rest of the day off. Like you said, rain clouds seem to have become permanent fixtures. Maybe, unlike your fellow hotel guests, she, the Lady with all the Luck, likes wet weather.

Look around DJ. In our land of Nevermore there is absolutely no place to even sit down. This raven needs a place that is quiet and secluded, you know, away from the maddening crowd. Even the dead fish on the wall agrees with me!"

DJ had, apparently, forgotten my parting remark from 'Poe' of the previous day. She looked around the Caribbean equivalent of the O'Hare Airport in Chicago during a summer rain storm and then stared up at me.

"Well, what the hell, we could go to my room. No black bird perched on the window sill there but at least we could sit down. As long…, as long as you don't ask me, with a kid's smirk plastered all over your face, the bullshit question, the hackneyed, not so funny double entendre, 'Can I come inside', once we reach my door.

So, now that we have an understanding, what do you think? Should we go to my little box of a room or not Michael?"

"Yes, definitely we should. But there is, however, just one condition that must be met before we proceed…, the notion of 'coming inside', notwithstanding. Before we go any further I insist on paying you one hundred dollars up front, before I set foot in the little place that you call home."

"What! What did you just say! You want to pay me one hundred dollars for…,"

"For what I will do once I am there, in the room, alone with you. Yes. One hundred dollars. That should cover it."

"You mother-fucking, arrogant prick! I have never been so insulted in my life. Michael, what the fuck do you think I am anyway! Some cheap, easy slut who…"

"Expenses DJ, merely expenses. Once we are in your room, I will order lunch from room service, for both of us, of course. I don't know about you, but I am famished. And…, and, I plan on raiding and pillaging your mini-bar more than once. And there is no way that you are going to pick up the tab for any of that, even though you are a Benjamin richer now than you were when you woke up this morning."

"You really do take some getting used to, you know that Michael Campbell! You remind me of durian fruit from Indonesia. It smells like shit…, like dirty feet but, over time, you can develop a taste for it. Has anyone ever compared you to dirty durian fruit before, Michael?"

"No, that is a first. I remind you of a 'prickly pear', durian fruit. That is definitely a first. Thank you. I must admit that I quite like the creamy, caramelness of the damn thing. It fits. Despised by most and loved by a select few! Me, Michael Campbell, a 'just dessert' for the moveable feast that is life. Yes, I can live with that!"

I smiled and winked at the visibly perturbed young woman who was shaking her head back and forth in disbelief beside me.

Dj's room had already been made up. I chuckled as I looked at the towel with the twist that was squatting in the middle of the bed. No raven to be sure! The nesting bird from my room had found a new home. Ignored for just one day, it had flown away to nest with DJ. It had Elithia, my favorite artist who specialized in works done in black and white, written all over it. Only she could coax terry cloth to reincarnate.

"Wow, what a great view of the ocean you have DJ. This is penthouse living, girl! Even on a cloudy day, like today, it's enough to bring out the poet in anyone."

"If you bloody well think so," she responded flatly.

"Excuse me, Michael. Give me a minute to change into something more comfortable. That is the hackneyed phrase isn't it? I don't think we will see the sun at all today. I won't take long."

"Sure. But just before you go, what would you like for lunch? I'll order while you are changing, if that's OK."

"Oh, just a fruit plate for me. And a large glass of fruit juice..., anything, it doesn't matter..., orange, mango, pineapple..., whatever they have..., but definitely not durian!"

"Done," I said to the bathroom door as it was closed and locked.

What did I really want from this woman? Never mind that. What could this woman possibly know that would be of any interest to me! I peered around the room to determine where my second scotch of the day was hiding. Forget the first drink and the success that had attended it. That was then and now..., now..., there was a little lady hiding from me in the water closet.

I would have settled for mere polite conversation. Maybe we were just two disparate people with enough experiential threads in common to weave, for a few rainy hours at least, a tapestry that would be informative and perhaps even mutually entertaining.

Malevolence or even innocuous mischief on her part would not be the order of the day. Both could be dismissed as the paranoia which afflicts the imaginative..., the somewhat creative types who sometimes have too much time on their hands! Even if she did curl up and attempt to strike like an immature rattle snake, I felt confident in my ability to out maneuver any evil she might try to manifest.

I picked up the phone on the night stand to place our order. As I listened for the dial tone, I heard the click of the other phone in the room. The one in the bathroom! Had DJ just finished speaking with someone on an outside line, was she merely curious about my call to the restaurant or..., was she in the process of making a call to some acquaintance, no, some accomplice, outside!

Never mind her fear of being alone with me in her room. The wheel had turned and now I was the more fearful one. What did I know of her, her friends, and her real reason for being in the Turks and Caicos Islands!

I looked around for something that could be used as a weapon. I managed to shove the mini-bar cork screw into my pocket just before DJ unlocked and opened the door.

With new found confidence, she strode into the room

"So, how did your little girl, your daughter, how did Christina get to school this morning in all the rain?"

The question was almost accusatory. Its inflection suggested doubt as to the validity of there being a daughter at all.

"You're right. Too wet for a bicycle ride today. Today she took a taxi. She would have used a taxi today regardless of the weather though. I had an early business appointment on one of the Cays north of here. Just a fifteen minute boat ride away. It got wrapped up quicker than I had expected. Always a pleasure to deal with people who know what they are doing. Hence my return, before midday, to your hotel."

"But isn't it too bloody rough out there…, in the ocean…, on a day like this. I mean…, in a small boat?"

"Not really, because the sea, when restless, produces long, rolling waves that are easy to navigate in a reasonably sound, fast boat. Unlike fresh water…, large, inland lakes that get churned up into short waves…, choppy water that is far more challenging…, to one's navigational skills…, and one's stomach! I know, after we eat I could take you out for a spin. You might find it exhilarating."

"No, I think I will pass on your kind offer, Michael. Death by drowning makes for good copy in a newspaper, but something quicker, something on dry land, something like hanging, would be more to my liking."

"Well, if you change your mind…, about the Boston Whaler, the fast boat…, anyway, as you can see, I am about to follow through on my threat to raid your fridge. Can I get you something…, anything that would be in keeping with your new fashion statement? The hundred dollars, by the way, is beside the phone on the night stand."

"Yes you can. Let's see, what would go well with Jordache jeans and a matching, denim top. I know, a smooth gin and tonic. The laid back casual kissed by a cold as ice sophisticated lady."

"See, I told you. Weather like this brings out the poetry in a person. Great imagery DJ. Your elixir of life is coming right up."

I made quick work of her unsophisticated, drunkard's drink and with mine in hand, proposed a toast to our captivity. Some of the hostility in DJ's demeanor dissipated as the first sips were swallowed.

Her apparent readiness to spring at her tormentor, me, like some small trapped animal, disappeared. And in its place, tentative signs of contentment, the step-child, in human discourse, of control.

"So, let's start with macro issues and then move to more interesting micro ones later on."

"I'm not sure I understand what the hell you mean, Michael. Sorry."

"Yes you do. Big issues in our lives first and then personal ones…, ones that we are comfortable sharing with one another. For example, as an American, I would love to hear your take on the upcoming presidential election. Democrat or Republican. Which party will hatch the next occupant of the White House. What does New England say?"

DJ shifted in her chair much as I envisioned a Masters candidate would, when asked to defend, verbally, her final thesis.

"Well, the Republicans have been in power now, in the Oval Office, for two terms. And eight years is long enough. Our constitution says so. Thank God! Ronald Reagan's words have not been matched by his actions. The only place where he is still liked is the UK. God knows why, but Margaret Thatcher still loves the man. Memories of his movies as a handsome, leading man maybe. Who Knows. Who the hell cares!

But…, I can tell you…, from a national security standpoint, his blundering stupidity, or was it his actual foreign policy, anyway, by the end of this term I'm not sure whether even he knows the difference, international political stability seems to have been bolstered…, in the Middle East…, South East Asia…, some, if not in most of South America…, but enough said about that! Reagan's complicity in the Iran Contra affair will prove to be more than enough to sink him and his party, for a long, long time. Yes…, as they say in Texas, you can stick a fork in him because he is done!

He has no support in the Senate or the House of Representatives. He, and his party, are lame fucking ducks right now. Nothing, legislatively, is getting done.

So my money is on Michael Dukakis and the Democratic Party to win big this time around. And everyone I know feels the same way."

Since even Cher's shadow, Sonny Bono, could get himself elected mayor of Palm Springs in California, there was hope, it seemed, for the political aspirations of all and sundry in the land of opportunity, I thought sardonically.

"OK, but does that mean that your Democratic candidate of choice is merely less damaging for the country than the current President. What, from your standpoint, does Mr. Dukakis bring to the national political table that will move your country forward?"

I found myself using every hackneyed phrase employed by the media to keep the lady seated across the room from me, engaged.

"Michael Dukakis is a man of integrity, a man who is honest and a man who has the energy to follow through on his commitments. He is the opposite of Ronald Reagan, the man he will soon replace. In a word, he has balls! Imagine that. A man with balls!"

"Another man with balls, a Republican presidential candidate, Barry Goldwater, back in the sixties, coined the phrase, 'Virtue, taken to extreme, is not a vice.' He lost the election back then, in part, because he espoused and proposed acting on that philosophy. Mr. Dukakis will, if elected, abolish the death penalty. Did you know that DJ? He would not execute anyone…, even if that 'anyone' was convicted of raping and murdering his own wife!"

"How the hell do you know so much about what goes on in my country. You know more about America than most Americans do."

"Empire DJ. The study of empire. Right now, America is the political, economic, military, and I might add, cultural center of the world. America has out spent the Soviet Union militarily and now it dominates the globe. In fact, it is the most powerful empire the world has ever witnessed.

Did you realize, for example, that between 1960 and 1968 there were about ten, B-52 bombers, all nuclear armed, that were permanently airborne, two or three at a time, somewhere in the skies over every region of the world!

They were ordered, 24/7, to follow three different, overlapping flight patterns. Deployed from bases in various locations in the continental US, their sole purpose was to keep a watchful eye on the arch enemy of freedom, the Union of Soviet Socialist Republics.

Aerial surveillance by the military began during the Khrushchev era and it was sustained for nearly a decade. You know, keep a watchful eye on the Godless bad guys who pounded their shoes on the desk tops of the world with impunity. Code named, 'Operation Chrome Dome', the same three routes were flown, like I just said, 24/7, for more than eight years. And they represented just one of many costly adventures engaged in by your military machine!"

"My God! I didn't know that. Why did I not know that! I mean I have heard the code name. By now everybody has! But not the description you just gave. Why have I never even heard about any of that! Chrome Dome! Why was I never briefed about that! I mean…, your version…, I mean…, Goddamn it, what else have I not been told, I mean what else and…, and who else do I know nothing about!"

I dismissed DJ's outburst as anger over one-upmanship. Americans did not like hearing of the skeletons in their closets, especially from outsiders.

"Think of the logistical expenses incurred by just that one military exercise alone! Air and ground crews, planes; both storage and maintenance and, of course, fuel and armaments. Think of the wealth of your country of birth that allowed it to sustain such an expensive, defensive action.

And remember, that's only one military initiative. On top of that there is a nuclear submarine fleet, a flotilla of aircraft carriers…, and, and ground engagements requiring soldiers and supplies in just about every far flung corner of the world. No other nation on earth could shoulder the financial burden that America does DJ! That's a fact."

My polite attempt at condemnation of the excesses of the military-industrial complex, a phrase that now garnered a groan of over familiarity more than the gasp that Ike had intended, seemed to be completely lost on the lady from the make believe land of Penthesilea.

"Fucking right, Michael! I could not agree with you more. America is the watch dog, the…, the bloody conscience almost, of the world. It isn't fair, you know. Why should we bear the entire financial burden as the world's policeman, the peace keepers, the only real champions of democracy!"

I was completely taken aback by DJ's response. For the second time in one day, for the second time in less than four hours, my ramblings had been completely misconstrued. Mr. Samuel had embraced the role of cardboard cut-out gangster in response to love and marriage, Sri Lankan style and now DJ was playing the jingoistic, Jordache-girl with her realpolitik response to raw aggression and provocation.

Maybe it was time for me to enroll in some Dale Carnegie course which had a focus on plain speaking.

"Did you see the recent AP photo of Michael Dukakis confidently smiling from the turret of an Abrams, M1 tank? It was in all the papers a few weeks ago."

"No, but I just know that he will talk the talk softly with our allies and he will carry a big stick and damn well use it, should the need arise, against those who oppose us."

I thought, how about the use of both soft talk and a hard stick with all players on the political chess board. This woman was no rough riding, Teddy Roosevelt. And San Juan Hill would not have appeared on any mental map she possessed. Realpolitik, the reality of Machiavellian misadventure and, as a consequence, the potential need for Presidential plausible deniability was, in all probability, beyond her capacity for depth perception.

Buried beneath an army helmet borrowed for the occasion, the Presidential candidate for the Democratic Party had looked like a hirsute Elmer Fudd. Michael Dukakis had three strikes against him before the electorate even went to the poles. He would not be a chameleon on the complex issues that all chief executives would have to face. Maybe! He would have agreed with those who felt that only dogs had the right responses to poles, opinion or otherwise. Maybe! And he was a photo-op failure. Definitely!

He was not Presidential material. He was not Presidential material for all the wrong reasons. That was the reality, within the echelons of power, of the greatest empire the world had ever witnessed! That was the reality of a super power in decline.

The name, George Herbert Walker Bush, never came up during our conversation. That was another reality of a super power in decline.

Lunch arrived. Our plates of food, once arranged on the small table that was close to the balcony doors, were a study in contrast. The heaping mound of freshly cut fruit was visually appealing but my layers of toast covered protein surrounded by fries just oozed odor that was irresistible.

The look of envy on DJ's face gave me my cue.

"You fruit plate looks absolutely irresistible DJ. So I have a proposition for you. You get half of my sandwich and fries and in return, you give me some of that great looking fruit, especially some of the pineapple. Is it a deal?"

She deftly made the trade between plates without saying a word and only after swallowing the first mouth full of fries and chicken breast did she proffer a comment.

"You handled that very well, you know. You are one smooth operator. I like your style Michael. I like it a lot."

"Sorry. Now it's my turn to say that I don't know what you mean, DJ."

"Yes you do, you sneaky little prick! You know exactly what I mean. I wanted what you ordered, once I saw and smelled it. And you knew that. I know. You could tell by the way I looked at all that greasy food on your plate. But instead of going, ha, ha, look what I've got that you haven't, you made it sound like I was doing you a favor by sharing my fruit with you.

I'm going to remember that gambit when I visit some of my other operatives…, you know, some of my difficult clients in New England. Trade on a fake favor to you that plays to their actual need. Not bad. What else can I say? That is a first for me. Not bad, not bad at all Mister Michael, sir!"

I hated it when people saw through me so easily. I hated it just as much as DJ hated being upstaged by what she saw as a lesser being.

"Can I ask you a personal question DJ? You don't have to answer it if you don't want to. You can just tell me to go to Hell and mind my own business."

"I know what you're going to ask me, Michael. I am a successful business woman, a very successful business woman, and I can look, when I choose the right clothes, I can look pretty damn sexy. That's not boastful…, it's just bloody true is all. So you're going to ask me why, based on all of that, why the fuck then, am I still single. Am I right?"

"Yes, that was going to be the question. You are a beautiful, engaging, young woman and those facts have nothing to do with what you decide to wear."

"Thank you Michael. Those are very kind words. Kind words do not come my way very often. Anyway…, well, I have had boyfriends, quite a few in fact, but all of them fell short of the mark. Seriousness, aspirations, commitment, or more precisely a lack of it, missing sense of adventure, even less capacity for humor, it was always something…, There was one however, one a few years ago who seemed to fit the bill…, a keeper. But, believe it or not, the poor, misguided, cock-sucker, no pun intended, turned out to be homosexual, or bi-sexual, or whatever it takes to attract other men. Anyway, who cares! It's his soul that is in jeopardy, not mine!

We were already living together, sharing the same apartment and…, and…, well, instead of kicking him out, that's what the bastard deserved, along with an unkind cut to his manhood, to the thing he enjoyed putting in all the wrong places, I thought about doing that…, many times…, too…, but I decided instead to continue living under the same roof with him because…, because his just being there gave me a convenient cover, I mean…, we looked like a couple and that kept all the prowling wolves at bay…, and…, and…, well, because safe, reasonably comfortable places in Boston are hard to find. And the rents are ridiculously high too.

So I have been living with my former lover, now brother, going on three years now. Better than being with another woman. That would drive me crazy. Just imagine two women and one bathroom every morning. That would really be purgatory with no possibility of parole! Definitely not for me!

That's my story, my story of straight, Christian love and forbearance and I am sticking to it. Does it shock you Michael? The living arrangement I have, I mean."

"Well, you certainly get full marks for adaptability. You just said that your place has only one bathroom. After showering, doesn't the impulse to revisit what was between the two of you occur?

"No, James has turned into a finicky, little old lady. He's definitely, what I think is referred to by his crowd as, a 'receiver'. Believe me, there is no erotic impulse there."

"Coffee DJ," I said to my table mate, wishing the dissection of her personal life to end before the cuts became any deeper.

"Yes, just black, black as my history with men, please."

DJ sat back in her chair and stared at me like someone who had just finished an adolescent game of show and tell with her body. She had given her all and now she expected a response in kind.

The general to the specific and back to the general. Go there, go there now, I said to myself.

"Sorry for the 'dead-end' men in your life so far DJ. For what it's worth, I could give you my take on the male of our species. Men and their relationships with women to be specific. It would be more anecdotal than scientific…, bar room banter, reading at length on the subject and of course, observation of the creatures at close range. I have been able to define three specific groups of guys, based on their interactions with women.

All very different. All with one trait in common. And what is that commonality? All are never what they seem to be. And all inevitably alienate their partners of the opposite sex."

"Sure, shit, why not! It's still raining outside and I don't think that it will stop anytime soon. Like you said in the bar yesterday, I was the most beautiful woman in the place because I was the only woman there. Well, you are a great conversationalist for the same bloody reason! Touche, oh silver tongued orator!"

"Stop me DJ, whenever you get bored. Either with the tale or the teller. This snapshot of the male animal will not take long to develop. It is, as I said, short, very short. And I must caution you, it is also not very long on generating optimism about the likelihood of finding a Mr. Goodbar!"

"You mean the chocolate bar with lots of nuts or the lots of guys who went fucking nuts with the teacher in the movie?"

"Neither, but a good guess. Actually, I label the first group after another fictional character. I call them the 'Walter Mitty Missionaries'.

They, like Walter Mitty, inhabit worlds of their own creation. They 'moat' themselves away from reality by constructing castles, complete with mental draw bridges, which keep the real world at bay.

Day-dreaming is their antidote to a dreary, monotonous, unrewarding reality. They live in make believe worlds in which they play the leading roles. From their castle parapets, they become the staring characters in heroic, adventure stories. Great, modern day, delusional, James Thurber characters to be sure!

They are the antithesis of brave, forthright, individuals. In reality, they are men who lead unexceptional lives. We all know them very well. They give new meaning to the expression, 'silent majority'. They are the types who are motivated to complete, on a daily basis, all of the soul destroying, repetitive tasks that low end jobs entail. They live to ensure that the safety net provided by their employer, the medical and dental insurance and, of course, a guaranteed pension plan, is never jeopardized.

They live in modest, little abodes. They stay in a loveless marriage to the same woman forever, just as their dear old dad had done, and they are always 'just around', just around, usually in front of the television set, while the two children of the passionless marriage mature, usually into clones, if they are male, of the 'old man'.

These men come alive, somewhat, only at night, only once a week, and usually on Saturdays. While in the missionary position with their wives, this is where their name comes from, they bury their faces in the pillows beside their bedmates and commence a masturbatory rhythm and maintain it until they reach their frenzied finishes. Whether their wives ever achieve sexual fulfillment, is irrelevant to them.

As I said, they imagine that they are someone else and that they are with someone else, as well! Quite a feat, actually! Their make believe bed-mate could be a secretary in their office, a woman on the same commuter train, a talking head on TV, a smiling miss, only partially clad, grinning down from a calendar that hangs on a wall in a gas station or barber shop.

These missionary men fantasize that they are with anyone other than the women to whom they are married. And why, because they imagine that they are powerful, dominant males, males with prestige and influence who are idolized by the receptive woman who is panting, more imagination at work, below them. They are ensconced in castles which are of their creation.

These 'quiet desperation' groups of men are reliable providers but they strike out even before they step up to the plate in the real baseball game of life.

Comments, criticisms, come-backs. What do you think DJ! Do you know the type?"

"Do I know the type! Do I know the goddamn type! I think you just described most men. Pathetic losers and prissy little pussys to a man! That's most of the males I know and work with anyway. Ass lickers on the job…, total ass-fucking-holes…, almost all the time and almost to a man. Dream of conquest, maybe, but do nothing requiring balls or brains to actually achieve it!

Good start, Grandpa. I like your story so far. It is good and…, and.., maybe, just maybe, if it continues to entertain, it will be your ticket to get your brains fucked out tonight. And then, for the rest of our scheduled interlude together, whether measured in hours or even days…, I will be able to sit and stare at your crotch and know what lies, in wait, behind the zippered curtain. I could have a post-coital, dream fuck-fest of my own…, a little bit, maybe, like what your Mr. Mitty does!

You know, maybe this Mitty mother-fucker helps to explain why so many of my girlfriends, the ones who have been married for a long time to the same men, complain about what lugs, what fuck-ups, their husbands are around the house but how frisky they become, you're right, about once a week. I always thought that they were bullshitting me about the once weekly bedroom bang because…, well, how could anyone, not living under the same roof, ever know!

Not much of a reason to stay with anyone, if you ask me. But thank God that most women do. Think about it. By keeping their idiotic husbands, those who suffer from permanent adolescence, off the street, they spare the better half of the human population, the female half, the grief of having to put up with them.

Anyway, this is all very interesting. Don't stop. Tell me more about the men who populate and copulate in the world as you see it. You are at least bringing some light, albeit artificial, to an otherwise very dreary day."

"Look, women are just as guilty of sex partner transference as are men. Both sexes have told me that they have to caution themselves, remember, both men and women have told me this. They consciously guard against screaming out the wrong first name, that of a fictional or an actual other lover, just as climax is about to occur."

"Very funny Michael. That is just too bloody funny. A reason maybe, to date only people with the same first name as your marriage mate, ha, ha. Go on, do go on. I want to hear more from your amateur socio-sexual study."

"So the Mitty Missionaries are as regular as clocks. If life were a bowel movement, they would be glycerin suppositories. But they are not present in the here and now of their lives, nor in the here and now of the lives of those around them."

"You do have a flare for analogy Michael. I'll remember that one…, glycerin suppositories."

"Next are the Cupcake Casanovas. These men are very successful in their chosen lines of work. They are good providers. Time, energy and resources are committed to all members of their families as and when needs arise. When they are at home, that is. They fully support and participate in the social functions that their wives deem to be of importance…, BBQ's, church socials, visiting relatives, the works…, Also, the school sporting events and academic pursuits of their children…, theatre, debates, public speaking events, are rarely missed.

Notice I said, when they are available. When they are at home. They are men who invariably travel a lot in connection with their jobs. Another city or another country, it doesn't matter. Their periods of absence are measured in weeks during every quarter of the business cycle.

These men embrace the supposed logic that a direct relationship does and should exist between professional performance and personal reward. Life for them is a catwalk, a place where stars strut their stuff.

They will point with pride to the fruits of their labor. A house in the right neighborhood, private schooling, late model cars, cottage, boat, country club membership…, even the academic performances of the kids get written up on Christmas cards which they send out annually to all and sundry."

"Shit! You just described a lot of the senior men I work with and report to now! Strutting peacocks who are full of themselves…, just give them a gun and…, I mean, men I have worked with in the past. Men not connected with Penthesilea. Ah…, men, just men. That's all, just bloody men! They still outnumber my gender in many work places across the country ten to one, you know!

God, they are insufferable. Their sense of self- importance is larger than life. They create false reputations and then they cloak themselves in their own mystiques. Their importance in the world…, their actual worth…, to anyone…, even their bloody dick size…, never measure up to a reality check."

We appeared to be on a roll and I did not wish to lose the momentum so I chose to ignore DJ's faltering disclosure about the actual men in her 'other reality' work place.

"I will say no more. You just described my second group to a tee. The gentleman, for example, the gentleman with whom I had the business meeting just a few hours ago is a perfect example of a Cup Cake Casanova at work. Hiding upcountry in a chalet which overlooks the sea, he and his girlfriend will while away the day together, dreaming of what the other cannot ever provide.

Now, to fit him and his tribe into the spousal matrix that has been fashioned. As I said, these men travel a lot. And true to their credo, they demand of life a fitting reward for everything they do. The TV in their hotel room is rarely switched on.

They are too busy searching the 'personals' in the local paper or the hotel magazine for escort services. They feel that they deserve not only a cup-cake treat as a reward but gobs of icing on top as well. Gushing young things, who are practiced in the art of telling men what they wish to hear are, of course, the sweet gobs.

Yes these women, young women whose profession it is to accompany the men of means to the restaurant, to the theatre, to the bar..., to anywhere that the men deem safe and secure from knowing eyes, are the icing on the cake. That, of course, includes the hotel room. These men and their appetites have created a thriving cottage industry in every medium to large city in every western country I have ever visited.

Reduce an escort to her moving parts and it will come as no surprise that she charges most, on an hourly basis, for her brain, for her mental ability to stay in synch with the middle aged dream weaver by her side.

Young women, in many college towns and most cities, are able to put themselves through university in style, live in up-scale apartments, dress in the latest fashion, even take trips to the sun while still in school, and all, all, as a direct result of these self-styled studs who behave like little gods on their own clouds of self-deception."

"Sure, that's why so many of them come home almost dancing on air. I have seen them, the grinning fathers of my girlfriends. Full of energy and ready to light the BBQ, for anybody and everybody, with their big Bic lighters which are cradled confidently in their hands. Dis-fucking-gusting!"

"Maybe that's why so many of them come home walking the walk and talking the talk of conquering heroes. They see themselves as a latter day, Ponce de Leone. Theirs was, while away from hearth and home, a respite at the fountain of youth.

So our Cup-Cake Casanovas are active and attentive and generous at home. And, to their way of thinking at least, they are loyal as well. But, of course, they are frauds."

"Yeah, you are right on the money, Michael! I remember, some time ago, reading an article published in the New York Times about the Alfred Kinsey research study, 'Sexual Behavior in the Human Male'. The article, actually a letter to the Editor about the study, was old, very old. I must have been a student doing research at the time.

Anyway, the author of the piece, a woman, an artsy-fartsy broad of some consequence, a woman I had never heard of to be honest, was bemoaning the fact that the Kinsey researchers had spent so much time and money only to reach the conclusion about men that every thinking woman has known since the dawn of time. Namely, that they all think and act like goats…, all irrational, fixative, self-centered and opportunistic in the extreme.

Your little story of the puffed pastry Ponces from wherever, reminds me of what some of my girlfriends have told me they have done to these guys, these sugar daddies. What they did when they realized that they were about to be dumped by them for a newer, younger model, that is.

They neatly folded and hid their soiled panties in a suit jacket pocket of their lame-ass, soon to be former lovers. Their thinking being that the loquacious mother-fuckers should be afforded an opportunity to demonstrate their verbal skills in front of an audience which would be less sympathetic to their ramblings than the hired one they had just dumped! Ha, ha, ha, a scene, I know, that would be just too incredible for words!

So much for the 'what' of these men, Michael. What about the 'why'? Seriously though, for just a minute. Why do you think the Missionary Mittys and the bloody Muffin Men are like that? Why can they not just step back and look at what they have and be grateful and appreciative of what life, or God, or nature, has provided? Is the problem innate to the nature of the beast or do you think that men are bent the wrong way by the social pliers that are usually wielded by their always mothers and sometimes fathers. Ha, ha!"

"Ah, the crux of the matter. Why indeed! Strictly opinion now, DJ. Strictly my opinion. I use biology as their excuse. Back to basics. The basics of biology! Male ejaculate, all ten cc's of it, normally, is alive with sperm. Millions of them, wiggling this way and that. Whereas, most often, when females ovulate, only one egg is involved.

Females of the species are built by disposition, let's subtract women's liberation and political correctness for the moment, no, let's just fuck both movements altogether…, to, to nurture, to sacrifice for the one. Men, on the other hand, who are subconsciously conditioned and motivated, since the dawn of homo erectus on the earth, to propagate the species, see multiple mates as the copulative imperative in order to ensure that their seed survives and thrives.

I know that the view of the world which I am espousing is anathema to the water-walkers, the religious zealots whose differing reality is crystal clear only because they, and they alone, formulated it. But for argument's sake, let's just suspend incredulity and go with the notion that at least a smidgeon of truth is contained within my supposition."

"Sure, if you insist. I'll give you a pass. But most women I know would say that your Mitty and Muffin men are weak, pathetic 'crocks of shit' excuses for thinking, responsible adults. And I would side with their opinion. But, for the moment, what the hell, let's just go with it. Just know that you will need a full head of steam because from now on the conversation is going to be headed uphill. You have been put on notice mister-man. So straighten up, keep your eye on the prize and stay on track!

Redeem yourself, go ahead, redeem yourself if you can. Tell me about your next group. Group number three. I have never heard anyone fabricate such a fantastical story in my life. You manage an interesting weave of seduction and pseudo social science, you know. Yes, quite seductive…, But never mind, tell me about the next group of losers, your third group of men. I mean, what type of moronic male is left to describe?"

"Mitty and Muffin men – merely an alliterative crock of crap or, Mitty and Muffin men - a crock of the misguided with mighty machinations? Never mind. It doesn't matter. Anyway, here goes.

The third and last group of men I shall describe are anything but members of just another legion of 'losers'.

I term this group the Misanthropic Magnets. These are individuals who have little or no time for societal strictures and even less for the slugs, as they would call them, who slavishly adhere to man-made constraints which diminish personal freedom. These men are loners. These men have talent that is exceptional.

Whether it is in the arts, politics, business or even religion, they possess greatness. Not necessarily greatness on a global scale, but what they do is noticed, be it in their small villages or throughout the world. It doesn't matter.

They chart their own courses and usually develop followings, almost in spite of themselves. Castles and catwalks are built in their honor by an adoring public. They are the men who get written about in the history books. Picasso comes to mind as does Napoleon, Kennedy, the one who was married to Jackie, and maybe even Jefferson and…, and, men such as Martin Luther King and Gandhi.

Men who qualify as Misanthropic Magnets embrace all aspects of life. They possess over active libidos to be sure. Remember two of the last three gentlemen I just mentioned. They had a distinct penchant for members of the opposite sex and, for what was and still is in America, the opposite race as well. Their appetites are considerable and their need to engage…, to engage always…, all of their physical and emotional senses is, well…, constant! But the details of that discussion will have to wait for another time. Suffice it to say that all of these men make enemies and they create a following with almost equal equanimity.

They view women primarily as motivational manikins to be fawned over, to be idolized for a time, but when spent, summarily discarded. Trophies to be trumpeted in season, not equal partners who merit patience and praise.

But even though they are forewarned, women flock in droves to the power of this type of masculine presence. Power that tends toward the perverse in many cases, I might add!

The upside for women who bond with this M&M group of men is that they are granted exposure to the blinding light of greatness. A walk, even a short stroll through a chapter in life with these men, sharing the rarefied air that they breathe, defines a woman's life forever afterward. But everything that follows greatness is, well, less than great.

The downside for these consorts, these catalysts for creativity, comes with the inevitable realization that they are merely fuel to stoke the fire, for a time, of the famous. Always in the shadows, they bask, in the warm, reflected glow of greatness. But their stay is usually brief and the banishment back to the land of the mediocre and the banal is final and forever."

"And all because these men, these fucking men possess the ability to put pen or paint to paper in a way that pleases a fickle world. What fucking bullshit! Maybe though, just maybe though…, maybe it's time for these high and mighty men, these callous users and abusers of others, including women, to be brought down from their exalted perch to the real world. The world that is inhabited by us mere mortals. What if their human frailty was exposed! What if they were made mere victims of circumstances as well!

Forget the Mittys and the Muffin men. They are too bourgeois…, too…, too…, commonplace, and too numerous to deal with. But your Magnets, their numbers are relatively small. They are a force that can be confronted. Remember, you said so yourself, they exploit and take advantage of those around them, especially women, so why not become proactive. Why not give them a dose of their own medicine!

Murder maybe…, or…, or…, microbes, or, perhaps, murder by microbes!"

"I am not sure that I follow, DJ. What do you mean, murder by microbes?"

I knew exactly what the wench meant but I wanted to hear it from her own lips. I needed to almost taste the venom, the vitriol, that this sea creature that had washed up upon my shore, was capable of excreting. I needed to see through her inverted looking glass, to witness the other side of her that lurked just below the surface of civility. Did she actually believe that by diminishing the great she could effect an elevation of the mediocre? Maybe yes, maybe no. Or was she just a run- of- the-mill man hater. Definitely yes, I thought to myself.

No matter. I now knew her secret. She was only one fish among many, one with teeth however, whose task it was to wrest Bali High Art from its rightful destiny. Of that I was now certain!

Finally, I thought to myself, finally, the fish I was trolling for had taken the bait! I had her because, unlike her paramour in salty shorts, my hooks were barbed.

Time to play with the scaly monster that was tugging on my line, the fish that was all prickly spines and pent-up pugnacity. Time to tire it out with a taught line, with a differing type of truth. One which was fixed to not founder or fail because the drag on the reel had been set too tight. Time to exhaust the catch, time to ready it for easy gaffing later…, for another time and another place, but for gaffing just the same.

"STD's Michael. You know, sexually transmitted diseases. Infect the bastards and then see if their greatness is any match for the result. Chlamydia, gonorrhea, you know, the clap, herpes…, all are treatable with strict drug regimens but most stay with the host forever! Never mind syphilis or HIV/AIDS. No need to kill the pricks, just hobble them and their 'free-style' lives. Just make them miserable. And make their conditions obvious so that their misery and despair would not so willingly be accepted and shared."

"And how would you accomplish that exactly?"

"Oh, there are ways! Believe me there are lots of proven ways. Not very sophisticated perhaps but effective just the same…, nefarious ways…, injections, pedestrian collisions on the street, hand-shakes, ingestion, why I know…, yes, well, let's just say that I know. I know that there are ways…," DJ looked away self-consciously much as one would who had gained a rapt audience with commentary which was contrary to deeply held religious beliefs.

"OK, but how would you factor into that equation of retribution the fact that sometimes the king and his consort are very much in love with each other? Mutual love for various reasons; father figure fulfillment, Pygmalion personification, mutual magic of newness, youth through association, wisdom through the same process, reasons that are as multifaceted as the players themselves, reasons that are stranger than fiction and more crazy than the world is crazy. One plus one can, sometimes, be a marvelous, bigger ONE. That's all!"

"Nonsense. We are talking about mutual usury, mutual, emotional masturbation. We are talking about coerced consent to feed insatiable ego. Period."

DJ folded her arms as if to signify that the conversation was over. Time, I thought, to push her over the edge of rational response.

Chapter 6

"And we haven't even broached the subject of the oneness that embraces the oneness of gender."

"From a distance you know, you actually look normal. What the fuck is the matter with you. To add insult to injury, now you are advocating homosexual liaisons. All in the name of art and creativity. Are you insane? Have you ever thought to pick up a Bible and read it. You are advocating, among other things, sodomy and that particular devil will keep the gates of Heaven closed to you for eternity. I am sorry Michael but you are damned. Damned for all eternity."

Visibly shaken, DJ looked down at her lap and began to mumble the portions of the Beatitudes served up by the remnants of childhood memory. Blessed are the meek, the poor in spirit, the merciful, those who hunger and thirst…

The woman had to be actively serving in some branch of the American foreign service. She was a walking personification of the credo that that they all shared.

Subscribe to our values, accept our dominance in the world, comply and don't argue for dissent is treason and treason will be dealt with harshly.

Time to back off. The poker had been held in the fire long enough. Back to Huey, Louey and Dewey. Back to the three musketeers. Back to Larry, Moe, and Curley. Back to any trio, other than the Christian one, that would get us on track to move forward.

"OK, Mitty Missionaries, Muffin Men and Misanthropic Magnets. Such a motley crew of characters. Any favorites DJ?

"Nope, shit is always shit, but, if I may ask Michael, in which group do you think you are a card carrying member!"

"Well, I could fall back on Shakespeare as an escape you know…, 'All the world's a stage, and all the men and women merely players, they have their exits and their entrances, and one man, or woman, plays many parts.' But I won't.

No, instead I will say, only half factitiously, that I am, ha, ha, merely a child cradled and maybe cajoled by nature. I feed on the same force that forms the wind. I gather energy from whatever the conditions are that surround me. Also, I might add, from those with whom I associate as well. By accident or design. Mood swings maybe. I run hot and cold. I can be dry, very dry, a desert sirocco, and also very wet. Like the weather outside right now. Annoying for some, but beneficial to others.

Maybe, unlike the three walking chemical compounds we just visited, the men from Machination, I am in a fourth group. A very small group. Statistically unimportant. Maybe I am just a free radical. Sometimes I get involved in changes to people's lives, but only rarely am I changed by the experience myself! Now, how is that for clarity!"

I had no idea where the personal charter of liberty, my private Magna Carta had come from. In truth, I had been a prancing little goat in each one of the little boy's clubs. The first two, for too long, for far too long. I had worn out my own welcome. But I was not about to provide a summary of my former intimacies. Too long ago and too, too banal! Just too, too bloody boring!

I was tiring of the room, of the shades of gray outside the window and the shades of gray inside as well.

DJ just stared down at her lap and mumbled something to herself.

"Well, DJ, maybe you've heard enough for one day. I think it is time for me to…,"

"No! No…, I don't want you to go Michael. Not now. Not yet. Please…, I need you, no, I want you to stay…,only a little while longer…, please!"

With that, DJ sprang from her perch on the far side of the table and lunged toward the bed. Mid-flight, she seemed to pause, mid-air, like some small raptor about to swoop down on a hapless mole. She gave me a quick peck that was aimed at my neck. It missed and landed on my forehead.

"See, look Michael, see, I'm almost ready for you. I am almost all yours!"

Almost ready…, almost all yours! Had I missed a reel from the afternoon matinee…, a movie in which I had a major speaking role? This woman might have been faster than Elithia was at jumping to conclusions and then acting on them, but her reasoning skills, the wellspring of creative thinking and the formulation of logical conclusions, were nonexistent!

Her deductive capacities, if formally tested in a controlled environment, would never have passed muster with anyone, anywhere. Certainly not within US government agencies whose job it was to 'out fox' the foxes which they felt were lying in wait everywhere. Not even as a neophyte could she have passed the thorough, exhaustive testing that was the hallmark of the CIA, the National Security Agency, or any of the other 'cloak and dagger' organizations that operated below the awareness level or the scrutiny of the general public.

The woman appeared to be just too stupid to be involved in espionage. Too stupid therefore, for me to continue to worry about! Maybe! Or, was her foolishness contrived. Was DJ merely just too smart…, just too, too smart…, too smart by half, for her own good!

Lying ram-rod straight on her back, she struggled with her jeans and managed to get them down to just above her knees. As she stared up at the ceiling, her fingers found and fumbled with the two crotch snaps that held her elasticized Teddy in place. Successful release of the snaps allowed the black, lacey material to pop up toward her tummy and expose her pubic patch.

"There you are Michael. Now you can see all of me. Do you like what you see, Michael. Am I making you hard? See, my pussy, my pussy is purring for you Michael.

But one last, little thing Michael…, Michael darling. Would you please pull the curtains shut. I like it better when I am in the dark."

I looked out beyond the window at the rawness of nature and the turmoil it had created. I knew, at that moment, I knew where I wanted to be. Out there in the turbulence. I wanted to boat my way back to my new found colleague with the single malt whiskey. I wanted to be there, to be anywhere, anywhere other than where I was.

Reluctantly I complied with my room-mate's request. The sheer curtain was drawn across the full length of the track.

"The other curtain too, Michael. The heavy one. I like it best when it is like night time."

The supine figure of DJ was reduced to little more than a shadow. What was the matter with this woman? She looked like a cross between a cadaver partially stripped for post mortem examination and a high school student who was frightened to death of the 'puncture and pump' assault she had decided to inflict upon herself just to get rid of the stigma, impose by her peers, of still being a virgin.

What had DJ chosen to leave out of her history of intimacy. What other monster male Goodbars had she encountered. What brute had traumatized the young woman to the point where sexual intimacy was akin to painful debauchery!

Or was it that she had a penchant for, a predilection toward pussy. Was she on the roster of a team from the other, parallel playing field of life. Was she also banned at the Gate in perpetuity by St. Peter?

I went over to the side of bed, found DJ's hand, and sat down beside her.

"DJ, listen to me. I think we both know that what we are about to do is wrong. It would be morally wrong. Morally wrong because we do not know each other well enough to make love. Not yet. We would just be using one another. And that's not making love at all! Just a minute ago, you said so yourself. Remember."

I winced at the sound of my own words. I hoped that the thin web of sanctimony I had just spun for DJ, a loose weave to cover my growing revulsion at the very thought of intimacy with her, was not too threadbare.

I looked down into the face of the inert woman beside me. Only her eyes were alive. They glistened, even in the dark, as the tears rolled down both sides of her face.

"Michael you are making me feel so…, so…, vulnerable and exposed! Exposed, and ashamed and…, and, abused. You are making me feel like a tramp. All your talking has made me want to give myself to you and you…, you…, are saying, No to me. You are just like John Stevenson all over again. He said almost the same thing to me in the Jack Tar Village in Freeport.

I want you, Michael. I am so wet for you, Michael and…, and…, I want to see you again after we both leave here. I want both of us to have a reason to meet again.

And, and time is running out for us, for both of us! My plane leaves early tomorrow morning."

Funny I thought. When cornered, DJ lost all capacity to 'potty mouth' her way out.

As I squeezed DJ's hand, the noise of someone fumbling with the room door lock dissolved the impasse, no, the morass, that yawned between us. I stood up and grabbed what I needed from my pocket in anticipation of confronting the intruder.

DJ did her best to re-hoist her clothes that were bunched together at half-mast.

"I believe that you are in the wrong room, sir," I half thundered.

"And I believe that you are with the wrong woman," was the equally loud reply.

It was the man I knew as Jonathon!

Angry and distraught, he lunged at me only to trip over the shoes that were scattered along his unlit path of attack. He fell, hitting his head against the corner of the mattress. The jolt caused the framed picture above the headboard of the bed to fall noiselessly into the pile of pillows below it. The print of coconut palms arching over a beach toward the sea, just like the one in my room, proved that some art work was easily bettered by a blank wall!

As he attempted to regain his balance, I turned the flustered man around, quickly felt all the way around his belt for a weapon, and then pressed the tip of the cork screw into his neck.

"Perhaps sir, you have at least a rudimentary sense of what the carotid artery is and its approximate location in the neck. If you don't regain your composure now, right now, your neck will become a cork in a bottle. And it will not be red wine that will flow. Do I make myself clear?"

To add emphasis to my threat, I punctured the man's skin. A thin trickle of blood appeared and slowly ran down to his collar. I held the chromed instrument in place and waited for his reaction.

DJ went berserk. She started to scream and frantically dance around both of us.

"DJ! Stop it right now! Stop right now and listen to me! We have already caused enough noise and commotion. Someone will call the front desk and the person on duty will call the police.

That will not bode well for either you or your gentleman callers. Fornication is illegal in the Turks and Caicos Islands. Just like being topless on the beach and sunbathing in the nude. Think girl! This is your room and should a constable arrive, what will he see! Two men fighting over the same woman. The same woman who is only partially clothed.

If that happens, you can forget about going back to Boston tomorrow. You will be remanded in custody. The charge could be either solicitation or prostitution or both! Look over there, on the table. The one hundred dollar bill is all the evidence the constable will need!

And you can dismiss any notion of a promising future with your company as well. Most firms take a dim view of an employee, no, a manager being involved in something, anything, that hints at scandal. Go, go right now and open the curtains, and then sit down and, above all, control yourself and just shut up!"

Christ I was good, I thought. Give me the right circumstance and I could bullshit 'best practices' protocols with the best of them. The best, even the self-styled paragon of virtue with Penthesilea, whose profession it was to be persuasive, make believe mammary glands, notwithstanding, could be moved!

DJ more than moved, she complied. Her voice and composure revisited her partially clad body with a vengeance.

She acceded to my suggestion, no demand, concerning the window curtains that covered both the picture window and balcony door. With no adjustment to her state of undress, DJ slowly and deliberately waddled back toward us and then paraded back and forth like a model most at home on a cat walk.

"There is a discrepancy between me and both of you, my gentlemen callers, an expression which you, Michael, have either borrowed or stolen from Tennessee Williams, if I am not mistaken. Further, I do not believe that any progress can be made regarding the presentation of individual agendas let alone the settling of individual differences, should any arise, until this imbalance is addressed.

I am assuming, of course, that you two gentlemen have more than just me to squabble over.

Anyway, imagine, for a moment, that all three of us are Ford Mustangs. I like Mustangs. Very sporty lines, don't you think? Well, maybe not anymore. A friend says that the new ones look like fat rubber duckies! She's right. Original Mustangs…, that's what I mean. The original ones…, the ones from the sixties.

Anyway, not only are we going to be unbroken, wild horses, but, even better, we are to be Mustang convertibles to boot. See…, my rag-top is down and I think that both of you should be 'rag-topped down' too!

I am referring, of course, to the positioning of my jeans relative to those that both of you are wearing. I want you two to lower your Levis to match the position of my own. That way we will all be on the same page and reading from the same text, so to speak. There will be fewer secrets, far fewer secrets, separating us. Less of each of us to hide under the table, right! And we will be able to concentrate completely, if not exclusively, on the issues at hand.

Oh yes. One last thing. Protocol. Let's exhibit a sense of decorum while observing the rules of protocol which are the hallmark of all civilized societies, in particular those which are ruled by democratic principles. The British system of parliamentary government could be fun and instructive for us to follow.

So both of you are to be members of the House of Lords, the upper house of government…, like our Senate. A dress code will be in effect. Pretend that you are in formal attire; suit, no wigs, but white shirt and tie. When needed, I will serve as Lord Chancellor. Not the Chancellor of the Exchequer, no, that would be the finance minister of the UK, you understand. No. My function, as Lord Chancellor, will be to ensure that your assets, got that, your assets, are open, always open to government scrutiny.

To that end, each of you, when you wish to speak, will stand to address the legislative body and when finished, and only when finished, will face me, bow, and then will sit down.

I will occupy a seat that is slightly elevated above your own. That is in recognition of my authoritative role in the proceedings which are about to commence."

DJ grinned as she moved the large end table lamp to the bed, mounted the bare piece of furniture and sat cross legged, Indian style, on her throne in front of us. Bemused, she folded her arms much as a mother might when, in the presence of her adult children, she announced that she had acquired a younger, much younger, lover.

"Why…, why, that idea is ridiculous. That makes no sense at all, DJ. I will not do it. No, I will not! Why, that is the most preposterous suggestion I have ever heard you utter. You should be embarrassed…., you should be ashamed of yourself."

"Stand please, to address the Upper House of Parliament."

The befuddled man complied.

"What has come over you? Why are you acting like an unruly child at a birthday party! What makes you think that anyone wants to play 'show and tell' with their private parts? No, this is absurd, all this nonsense about the Brits and their government and…, and…, I will not stand for it…,no, no, I…, I…, will not do it!"

"If you are finished, then bow please, in recognition of the Lord Chancellor, before you take your seat."

While Jonathon was in the throes of enunciating his sanctimonious rant on personal freedom and responsibility, the removal of the corkscrew from his throat had given him a renewed sense of purpose, I stood up, unbelted and unzipped, and lowered my jeans and jockeys to approximate the position of those displayed by the lady Chancellor in front of us. The same lady who had just divined, with a majestic sweep of her arm, that the room should be not only one of light but of parliamentary privilege and protocol as well.

DJ's move was brilliant. Pants down to knees guaranteed that the fettered combatants would not run very far, either at each other or along some spontaneous escape route. We would all be trapped by our designer threads and worse, our own irrational traditions. Clothes would be the ropes and Judeo-Christian beliefs about nakedness, the scaffold.

We would be forced to dialogue, to debate, to rely on the facts at our finger-tips and through the verbal expression of those facts demonstrate how persuasive we could be. Each of us would have to write the right words to the rhythm that reverberated only within our own grey matter..., and present it as paean to attract partner participation.

What claptrap, I thought. A rationalization of the ridiculous! Poetry of the absurd. But I was game for it.

In one fell swoop DJ had leveled the playing field and positioned herself as moderator, the one to be emulated and hence followed by the other two players. Had she just been lucky with a spontaneous, half-baked, adolescent idea or was the ruse well planned in advance of the meeting? The latter grew more plausible with each thrust and parry of her quixotic sword.

Admittedly, men became unruly when left to their own devices. And they crowed like cocks most often when their offending, protruding organs, were concealed and cradled in cotton. Then, dimensions could only be guessed at.

And males with any coital experience at all also knew that the vagaries of ambient room temperature and conversational timbre and intellectual triumph could and would, in nano-seconds, reverse any 'David and Goliath' contest involving two or more strutting and posturing peacocks.

I knew better, but, for some reason, I allowed size to matter. I felt confident that I would make a good showing at the spontaneous county fair that was about to have its opening ribbon cut. I was well fed. The half fried chicken sandwich had been delicious. I had not had my neck punctured by some ruffian and I had just been treated to a viewing, for the first time, of a comely, young woman's crotch. I was as ready as I ever would be to face the judging committee of two!

"Two against one Jonathon. See, Michael has already voted yes. A strong, definitive 'Yes', I might add. True democracy in action, one might say. Majority rules. C'mon Jonathon, your turn. Be magnanimous in defeat!"

Jonathon looked away from both of us as he slowly got up and even more slowly complied with the Chancellor's command. My God, I thought, he could almost have gone fishing without taking his fly rod along at all. Long and thin, like a large night crawler, his appendage seemed to never end as it was unsheathed and allowed to dangle in the languid light of the dreary day.

How patronizing of DJ to suggest that my offering was "strong' or 'definitive', I thought.

I think his private part might have required the amount of erectile tissue normally allocated to two men who wished to perform their weekly bedroom duty. It made my appendage look like it had been cropped to scale to accommodate a very small picture frame.

I looked at the face of the man whose body was now bathed in the harsh Caribbean light. His skin was leathery and blotched below the eyes but he wore the badge of his indolence well. Thin, with good muscle tone and a body tan which looked like it had been applied expertly by someone with a brush, he looked very fit for a man who was probably five years my senior. His complexion however, remained ashen grey. And he looked sullen and spent.

I made my way over to the sliding door, opened it to the ocean air, turned and bowed and returned to my position at the corner table.

Silence. My fellow parliamentarians had turned silent. I could almost hear their gears frantically grinding out credible alibis, stories that would be flawed because circumstances would not permit collaborative communication.

"Well, this British-like, stiff upper lip, this three-some vote of no confidence is becoming boring and ridiculous. One of you, say something. One of you could start with the short-pants romance that involved both of you appearing on the path from the sugar shack last night. You know, it ended by staging, with the help of a loose shoe lace, separate times to enter the Maki-Maki bar like two, naughty teenagers."

"Next time you speak Michael, don't forget to stand and acknowledge the House, the Chancellor, when you finish please."

I pursed my lips and half kissed the 'House' air between myself and the lady Lord Chancellor.

Jonathon stood up and tried to speak but he could only manage a hoarse croak. He cleared his throat and tried again.

"You…, you are needed back in Jakarta. Your boss, Colonel, what's his name…, Satu, Colonel Satu, he has got himself into a lot of trouble with people, powerful people who want his head. You should not have hidden yourself away in the Caribbean for so long. Your people in Indonesia are frantic to get in touch with you."

"Stand please when you address Parliament. Thank you."

"Should I continue to call you Jonathon…? OK, Jonathon it is. Jonathon, back up a little bit. In fact, back up a lot. How do you know anything about that particular country or that specific man? Now, don't try to bullshit a bullshitter."

"Do you think we could dispense with the confrontational…, the Spanish Inquisition approach to this interrogation? I am beginning to feel a little nauseated. High blood pressure and…, and, I left my meds back at the shack."

"You can't use that tone of voice with my fiancé. Look how much you are upsetting him! Tell him Jonathon. Michael can't do that to you. You, you are the Manager of Field Operations for the Central Americas and the Caribbean."

"DJ, your job is done. Your mission is completed. You got the man here and you kept him occupied. Now back off. Back off, please, and let me do my job. Let me do my job my way. Please!"

"For God's sake you two, let's stay focused. Neither your lover's spat nor your bloody matrimonial plans, nor your sense of protocol are relevant right now.

So, the two of you concocted this little piece of theatre, with me in one of the starring roles, so that you, Jonathon, could interrupt a steamy little drama with your betrothed just to tell me the latest gossip from Indonesia! Are you kidding me?"

"The walls have ears Michael. Even in the Turks and Caicos. Even my shack…, but never mind. I needed a secure place to meet with you and since DJ has no connection…, no connection with me professionally, none whatsoever, her room was the only place I could think of that would be safe."

"OK, I'll buy that. But maybe, just maybe…, You might want to consider, in the future, concocting a better story for yourself than a sabbatical which involves fly fishing and whale watching as your cover. Few are as naïve and accepting as the barmen downstairs. You and your idiosyncrasies stand out like a sore thumb.

What are you again? Field Manager for the Central Americas and the Caribbean? What three letter moniker goes with a title like that? FBI, ATF, no, they're both domestic, the CIA, some branch of the National Security Agency, the DEA maybe?"

"I am afraid that I am not at liberty to divulge that information."

"Do you have any idea who you are talking about? Even from his perch in what you might view as far away, primitive Indonesia, he could have you 'Offed' before the cock crows thrice!"

"Are you threatening me, Michael?"

"Are you this myopically miss-informed all the time Jonathon, or is this a command performance just for my benefit. Have you ever heard of a 'Gypsy Murder'? Probably not! Ignorance is bliss…, for some of us at least!

You don't know what kind of Pandora's box you and your organization have just opened. Maybe you and your colleagues spend too much time along the banks of the Charles River contemplating your collective belly button lint."

"Look! Documents, sensitive documents have gone missing from our strategy session held recently in Kuala Lumpur. And Asian Security Systems, the Company owned and operated by your Colonel, had the contract to ensure that everything would go smoothly. Security was breached and we believe that your boss was complicit in, or was at least cognizant of, the plot to commit the theft."

"And you want me to go home, get to the bottom of the situation with the old man, retrieve the dossier and return it to you or your nameless South East Asia counterpart. A man who works for the same, no-name, generic outfit that seems to have you on the payroll. Is that about it, Jonathon?"

"When you get back to Jakarta you will be contacted by, yes, by my Asian associate there. His name is…, Mr. Law…, Mr. Brian Law. More information will be given to you by him. I must allow him to expand upon what I have said as he sees fit when you two meet face to face.

I know that I am not giving you much to go on. Just contact your people in Jakarta. They will verify the urgency of the situation.

Let me ask you Michael, have you ever heard of 'Decision Dooms Day'? News of our think tank operation got leaked to the New York Times a few weeks ago. But the editors decided, based on, what they determined to be unreliable sources, to bury the item a few pages after the op-ed section and await further corroboration before going front page. And we do not want that to happen! It cannot be allowed to happen!"

"No on both counts. Missed the article and have never heard of your 'D-CUBED' board game."

"Well, you mentioned Gypsy murders earlier. I have no idea what that means but I think you will find the word Gypsy to be relevant. My organization, like Gypsies, gains credence by attempting to look, analytically, into the future. The future and what it holds relative to national security issues. American national security issues that is. Suffice it to say that we are very interested in the San Francisco Bay area and the

Strait of Malacca. And the missing documents are very germane, hence sensitive, to a number of 'what-if' scenarios in both regions.

I can say no more Michael. In fact I have already told you too much."

An impartial observer would have been impressed, I thought, not so much with the quality of the information exchange as with the rapid adjustment to prescribed protocol both parliamentarians had exhibited. We had popped up and down at our seats, like two animated pistons in an engine block and we had bowed, in turn, Japanese like, to the lady Lord Chancellor. We had, as well, both stolen looks at the table-top prize which was wantonly displayed in front of us.

We had become, it seemed to me, the antithesis of the CIA, the agency that had, probably prompted our meeting in the first place! We had all been laid bare by our mock parliamentary antics in the Turks and Caicos Islands. Our 'post-lunch' nakedness had prompted an immediate honesty. And as was true of any efficacious cathartic agent, we had all been made better by the process!

What an effective antidote to the legislative disease of 'filibuster', I thought to myself. Prolonged exposure of private parts to public, sometimes televised, scrutiny would dissuade even the most rabidly loyal Democrats or, or, even Republicans from slavish adherence to the party line!

But the fetish for secrets, the hallmark of those in command, those who sustained the perpetual need to create novel and perverse misinformation concocted and promulgated solely as a means to destabilize indifferent, unfriendly or hostile regimes, the raison d'etre of the Agency, could not be 'play acted' away.

The paranoid drive by the CIA, by the State Department, by all agencies operating, legally or otherwise, on the international stage, to patrol and protect against the invasion of foreign ideas which could be deemed 'un-American' by the descendants of Senator Joseph McCarthy, was relentless.

Jonathon was the McCarthy protégé and the Turks and Caicos Islands, a British Protectorate, was the perfect geographical locale for the big snoop. Together, they were a perfect fit! America was spying on one of her most feared enemies, the one that was, ironically, one of her most trusted allies!

I fought to maintain my composure. But I was defenseless. I had no idea what Jonathon actually knew about Col. Satu or Asian Security Systems. Don't burn bridges! Just don't burn bridges out of spite. Especially with your pants down, I reminded myself. I surreptitiously glanced over at the resident night crawler and then at my meager contribution to the late afternoon lawn party and, voicing a conclusion was the only option that made sense!

"Thank for the information Jonathon. I hope that, should we meet again, a corkscrew will be put to better use in accordance with the purpose for which it was intended.

And good luck DJ, good luck in the future with your difficult clients who are served by Pentheselia. I hope your new found strategy of reverse benefit proposal works well for you with them."

I did not wait for a response from either of them. I remained standing, hitched up my pants, slipped into my shoes and walked directly to the door. Without looking back, I quietly closed it behind me. I patted the purloined, chrome corkscrew that was buried deep in my front pocket…, a silver medal showing, of sorts, for my entry in the just concluded garden party exhibition.

Strange, I thought, once the rules had been established, DJ had sat through the verbal serves and volleys between Jonathon and me without uttering a single word. Her attention, it seemed, had remained exclusively on her betrothed. It was as though I had ceased to exist other than as a mechanical ball server.

It was like she was adjudicating a Pentheselia practice selling session with one of her junior sales reps! Jonathon's verbal thrusts and parries did not seem to be viewed by the woman who remained stationary on the night table as sophisticated, foreign concepts at all. Nor was there any evidence suggesting respect for the man who opposed me. His professional rank and his pending change in marital status simply did not contribute to the woman's demeanor.

DJ outranked him! That was it! That had to be it. She was his superior! Jonathon was being tested by DJ. She was his coach, and mentor. My God I thought, she had to be his commanding officer as well!

Chapter 7

Luxury was a great insulator against the jolt that travelled the copper cable of crisis. And one had merely to ascend the tight, spiral staircase and occupy a seat in the First Class cabin on a Boeing 747-300 to acquire it. The gold braided cord that hung loosely across the wrought iron stair railing separating the officer material upstairs from the seat-sale, Stalag prisoners down below was a better barrier against trespass than the Berlin Wall had ever been.

The passenger seats located in the bulge of the upper fuselage behind the cockpit, were arranged in groups of two, with six such clusters on either side of the aircraft. Each double set of seats was tilted slightly back from the windows on either side of the cabin. A spacious corridor separated the port passengers from those on the starboard side. A large, stationary service station filled with magazines and newspapers, occupied most of the corridor space. It further distanced the travelers on one side of the plane from those on the other. Privacy was what had been paid for and precious personal space, albeit premium priced, was what those in First Class got.

I had reserved the two corner seats that were nestled between the port side of the fuselage and the bulkhead at the back of the cabin. That location afforded Christina and I an unlimited view of whatever was going on in the entire cabin. I did not want her to miss the frequent rounds of snacks nor any of the meals that would be served.

Royal Dalton reigned supreme in First Class. Even through young eyes, the pageantry of perfectly positioned gleaming glassware, porcelain plates and polished metal cutlery made every offering of food a regal celebration.

Yet, when our movie screens were lifted from below the arm rests and positioned in front of us, we were cozily cloistered away from the hubbub that played out in the rest of the cabin.

And once my daughter got into the rhythm of the routine in the First Class cabin or got bored or overwhelmed by all that was going on around her and fell subsequently fell asleep, I knew that she would be blissfully content in the comfort provided by her oversized, cocoon-comfortable chair.

She would not need me. I needed me. I needed the luxury of time alone with my thoughts. I needed both the time and the space to digest the events of the last few days. I had to learn my lines from a script that was still a work in progress. Before I made my entrance, center stage, in the drama that was enfolding in Jakarta, I needed some opening lines. After that, I felt confident that I would be able to wing it.

I had deliberately lingered long in the Turks and Caicos Islands, for the better part of a week, following my 'Strange Interlude' with DJ and her bungling beau, Jonathon. Regardless of his dire pronouncements concerning the fate of the Colonel, I knew that the turf battles and internecine warfare that defined American espionage efforts world-wide would always remain a constant. I had time, plenty of time, on my side.

Christina, following my slight bow of invitation, took the seat closest to the window. Grinning widely, she scrambled up into the plush, dentist sized chair, stretched her arms and legs, flexed her toes in sheer delight and exclaimed, "Oh Daddy this is perfect. This is really, really, just, just very, very perfect!"

I grinned my complete agreement with the sentiment she had just gushed. But Christina did not need my endorsement. She was completely absorbed in pulling and poking at the myriad of gadgets and recessed trays and cup holders that her comfortable throne commanded.

And all of these moments of sheer Christmas-like magic were ours for a mere five times what the cellar-dwellers had paid for the same, trans-Pacific flight! Money didn't talk, it whispered seductively and allowed one's imagination to fill in the rest!

Singapore Airlines did it right, especially with premium paying passengers. Prior to take off, a saronged, young creature floated over to our corner, bowed toward Christina, and held out a cellophane wrapped box with a beckoning Barbie Doll inside.

This Barbie came complete with multiple wardrobe changes; Barbie at the beach, Barbie at work, Barbie at home in her lounge wear and a set of combs and brushes to ensure that Barbie's long, golden tresses were coiffed for every occasion in her busy little life.

Christina, with her mouth agape, did not know whether to get up and hug the stewardess or immediately tear into the package to become the close confidant and best friend of the girl from the Mattel mansion on the hill.

She chose instead to wrap her arms around the boxed present, rock back and forth in her chair and talk soothing to the smiling plastic figure inside much as a mother would with her first born child.

I was given a handsome travel kit. The imitation leather carrying case and the faux tortoise shell brushes inside hinted at a luxury that would prompt many recipients to save it, unopened, and mentally place it at the top of the Christmas gift list for that special someone who was not special at all!

To the polite query as to whether I would like a pre-departure glass of Champaign and orange juice, I responded, with a knowing smile, that a double scotch on the rocks would be appreciated. I knew that it would be Johnny Walker Black, or Chivas Regal or a single malt offering. Quality scotch paved the way for a smooth road to reverie regardless of the label. Effervescence in a glass, on the other hand, effectively eradicated the enjoyment of the 'King-for-a-day' experience.

My child quickly succumbed to the overkill of her first experience in First Class. With the half grapefruit earphones askew on her head, the screen in front of her alive with animation, and her newest friend back in her box, Christina basked in blissful sleep. The wheel had turned. I chose to believe, with stretch sufficient to make my reverie match that of my daughter, that her decision to gift Miss Glover a few short days before our departure was being rewarded ten-fold over.

I deeply inhaled the air above the rim of my glass and sipped contentedly at the cold surface.

Colonel Satu's situation would not be a problem. He needed me. Sure. He needed my command of the English language to give him the buoyancy to stay afloat in the angry sea of American vitriol.

Nothing more than a 'tempest in a teacup', I thought dismissively.

The Colonel and I were very close. We had shared a lot, some would say, too much, together. We had been blood brothers in crime. We knew all there was to know about each other. We trusted each other implicitly. And there was no room for others in our club. And that obviously annoyed the American puppy dogs who were nipping at our heels!

But what had the Colonel done! Had the 'Decision Dooms Day' working dossier simply been lost? Had it been thrown out by mistake along with the other waste paper at the end of the day? Was it in his possession and was he holding out for some sort of ransom? No! Impossible. Was the man being blackmailed into its forfeiture? Had his past history, what some would view as a descent into debauchery, finally caught up with him? No. That was too much of a stretch as well.

The Colonel saw himself as a military man. And as such, he always honored his commitment to the person in charge from the sponsoring company. He saw that individual as his commanding officer for the duration of, what he fancied, a campaign composed of coordinated military maneuvers.

The Colonel was not for sale! The Colonel was fastidious to a fault regarding his personal life. His secrets were his secret. He was, I thought, unassailable.

So what had gone so terribly wrong?

That would have to wait until he and I were alone somewhere other than in his office. A safe house. I would need a safe house or at least a safe place. One that could not possibly be bugged. Maybe Sari, the Colonel's secretary, would be able to supply one.

Sari! Sari! The private secretary of one man, the Colonel, and the personal, very personal, secretary to another. Me!

My one telephone call to her had been troubling. Very troubling!

"Salamat pagi, good morning Sari. This is Michael speaking. Apa kabar. How are you?"

"Oh my darling Martin. It is so good Martin to hear from you. You are away for too long, you know. Everybody is very worried about you. But do not be concerned. Everybody here in Jakarta is fine. Only Uncle Samuel is giving us trouble. But only a little bit. You know he is very old.

I will be very happy when I see your smiling face and your big brown eyes when you come back Martin. When you come back from your trip to Thailand and China. You will come back soon, yes! I hope the answer is yes. I will be very happy when you come back to Jakarta to see me, Martin. See you soon. Yes, see you very soon! Bye. Good bye for now my dear, darling Martin. Bye."

Sari had hung up the second she had finished delivering her message to me.

The office phone was bugged and what she had just delivered was, only perhaps a credible, coded message. There was no doubt in my mind that she had prepared her monologue in anticipation of my call.

Her message had been short. Maybe just short and gushing enough to have thwarted the snoops who were listening and recording all incoming calls of interest.

Martin, my darling Martin…, I grinned at the game within a game that Sari had chosen to play. Under the guise of a coded message she had given vent to her true feelings about me. A smart little cookie that one!

Sari might have felt that way about me but she would never have uttered the sentiment in public. Darling…, darling…, a Western term of intimate endearment…, from her lips though, a term of concern for the personal welfare of the listener…, a warning to beware…, a warning to not call the office number again.

Everybody is fine. Just leave out the negatives. The message was clear. Everybody was not fine!

And only Uncle Samuel was causing trouble. Uncle Sam could be like that sometimes, I thought sardonically.

Everybody will be happy when you come back. Back from Thailand and China. Back from 'T' and 'C'. Of course! Back from the Turks and Caicos Islands! You hold the key to the predicament we face. You will know what has to be done. And we know that you will do what has to be done too! You with your smiling face and you with your bigger than beautiful, brown eyes!

In my absence, the Colonel would have had no one to whom he could have turned. The only other male friends he had were his boy toys and not one of them had ever thought of leaving the isolated island of narcissism that they called home. His other male associates were mere soldiers. His private army, that numbered maybe a dozen, was composed of doers, not thinkers. And to confide in a woman would have been, to his way of thinking, akin to seeking the advice of a child regarding some complicated litigation that had been brought against him.

My ruminations were abruptly interrupted by what I thought, at first, was a large rodent crawling up my leg. Christina had shed the half grapefruits that had covered her ears and her boxed friend had been left to occupy her chair. She had decided to forego the pleasure of her exclusive perch in favor of the warm lap that loved her.

"Daddy, I think I ate too much the delicious desserts. I feel sick."

"So you only come over to see me when you feel sick. Is that it?"

"Noo, oo, oh! Only I want a story Daddy. Tell me the story of stallymites and stallitites again. Tell me story of the big waves and the big caves when we are there not yesterday but other day ago."

Exhaustion and halting language skills still enjoyed a direct relationship with Christina.

I did not have to search for and then press a ding-dong, 'Avon Calling' button to get the attention of a stewardess. Nor settle for a long term interlude prior to satisfying an immediate need.

The young lady had noted my daughter's migration and, with a folded blanket at the ready, grinned down at me and my nesting offspring.

"Thank you. Thank you very much. You are very kind and considerate. I wonder…, would it be possible to get a soda water for my daughter and a refill for me, please." Cabin staff proficiency and politeness, mine, enjoyed a direct relationship in the First Class cabin.

Both drinks were placed on the table beside my arm rest before Christina had stopped squirming into my chest. Two loud, soda water induced, burps were followed by light slumber. I had only to add my whispered voice to the mix to put her out for the count.

Our trip to Middle Caicos had proved to be the highlight of our stay in the Turks and Caicos group of Islands. Neither planned nor properly provisioned for, the normally grueling, seventy plus mile open ocean trip by speed boat, from the Bight Settlement to the Conch Bar Caves, had completely eclipsed our eventual tour of the limestone caverns. The latter provided sensory overload, to be sure. But the former was the stuff of shared serendipity that time could never erase.

As expected, the roofs of the caves, the gray, brooding, distinctly threatening, natural counterparts to the Sistine Chapel creations of Michelangelo, had lost none of their capacity to produce a certain religious wonderment. And the Greek columns that were the stalactites in permanent vertical embrace with the stalagmites, prompted every person present, to just gawk upward in disbelief.

That day however, with its conspiracy of brilliant sunshine, light ocean breezes and a somnolent, rolling sea, was owned by our thirty foot Boston Whaler sporting twin, two hundred fifty horse power Mercury outboard motors.

That day, exhilaration trumped awe.

We became star trekkers and the mile of water between us and the shore was the only heading we heeded. Christine handled the wheel with a dexterity that was beyond her years. We laughed at ourselves, at each other and our spontaneous, foolish, antics, and most of all we laughed at the wonder of being alive, truly alive in a world seen at sea level. Even with the throttle pulled back to three-quarters, we achieved a blistering thirty-five miles an hour. We went faster than the 'sharky-fish' which Christina feared were waiting to ambush us just around every spit of land. The two hours and change required for the trip there and the subsequent return had been all too short. We both instinctively knew that the magic moments we were sharing in the full embrace of life would not, for either of us, occur again anytime soon.

First on and first off. If only that feature of air travel, for the chosen few, could be transferred to the world outside the airport!

We were home. I knew exactly where I was and I was immediately content with the fit! The hot, humid air in Sukarno Hatta Airport was comfortable backdrop to the discordant symphony that was the human condition careening around every corner of the place on only two of its four wheels.

I was prone to losing myself in novels during my spare time, no matter where I was. The Turks and Caicos Islands had been like a long afternoon spent with Santiago and his prize marlin. I had been the little bird resting on the gunwale of Santiago's small boat. I was the audience and confidant he had had while ruminating about baseball, about the weather and about 'salao', his very long run of bad luck. The story was short on sentiment and sensuality. It, like the Caribbean Protectorate, was all about survival. 'The Old Man and The Sea', was Hemingway, and his reliance on lean prose, at his best.

Jakarta, on the other hand, was a veritable tome that could have been written by James Joyce himself. Jakarta was a stream-of-consciousness place in its most raw, unpunctuated, unedited form. Everyone in the capital city seemed to be on a personal voyage to somewhere.

Some were Ulysses-like in their undertakings but most were merely fulfilling the quotidian pursuit of the trivial, trite and transient in their lives.

Leopold Bloom and Stephen Dedalus could have been the role models for the chain smoking, boisterous, ever accepting denizens of the capital city who lived, loved and laughed through whatever fate flung their way.

Chapter 8

I chose not to return to our home in the city after we cleared Customs. Better in the daylight and better to have my neighbors awake should assistance, police assistance, be needed. Instead, we checked into the Raja-Laut Resort Hotel. It was only minutes away from the international arrivals terminal.

An unlikely place to stay, if my American thought processes served me well. The spooks would never think to look for me there. The hotel was cheap and it was in plain sight. It was not buried in the sprawling barrios that made up the city of ten million people and therefore not likely to appear on their 'fugitive-find' radar screen.

Also, hospitals situated close to the airport had reported a troubling increase in the number of patient admissions suffering from demam berdarah, Dengue Fever. Some of the cases seemed to have been traced back to the mosquitoes that inhabited the foliage around the Raja-Laut Resort garden restaurant. A false-positive test result no doubt. The biting little bastards were everywhere in the city. And they did not differentiate between local and foreign blood. Only the press did!

Christina's singular focus, between the plane and the peppermint pillowed hotel room bed, had been for the safety of her new, best friend. Both she and Barbie, who was outfitted in pink lounge wear to herald her first visit to the capital city, fell into a deep sleep the minute their heads hit the bed.

The only viable plan of action I could think of to get Colonel Satu alone and in front of me required the aid of a hotel based taxi driver who spoke reasonable English. The man I chose had considerable difficulty understanding my instructions at first. But, by the end of my fifth attempt, his lights went on. His lights were switched to high beam when I presented him with a fifty dollar bill, in advance, for a successful return with his passenger. I had not had time to get any rupiahs. To the taxi driver, a fifty was a month's pay. But to me, a fifty was cheap payment if he successfully completed his assigned, clandestine, potentially dangerous task.

With the TV switched on to some sort of quiz show, something with loud talking and even louder audience reaction and commercials, I busied myself at the mini bar. A double scotch for me and a double cognac, at the ready, for when or if the good Colonel came knocking at my door.

I had chosen a suite of rooms on the top floor and at the end of the corridor. Christina was removed from the deliberate noise in the living room area and conversation between two people close to the balcony door, I reasoned, was more likely to travel upward than in any other direction.

I sat back in my chair which was positioned so that I faced the open, but screened access to the balcony. I lit a Marlboro Light and blew the first puff at the screen. The wire mesh seemed to swallow the smoke and then share it with the evening air outside. Good start, I thought to myself. Hurray for advertising. Second hand smoke had not yet been invented as a health hazard when Lady Nicotine and I had first been introduced to each other more than a generation earlier.

Let the Colonel do most of the talking. Listen, just for a change. Listen to what he had to say. Listen for what he chose not to say too but, above all else, be supportive. Innocent and able to vindicate himself, victim, or volunteer in crime, it didn't matter. Be supportive. There would be ample time to criticize another day. Play Joe Friday in the old TV series, Dragnet. The facts man, just the facts!

I was half dozing in my chair with my second scotch when I heard the light rap at the door. Three knocks in quick succession followed by a pause then two more. It was the Colonel's, cops and robbers, secret code. And only he and everybody else knew it.

I opened the door and the grim faced, stout man in uniform brushed me aside and rushed over to the chair by the balcony. He pushed it back into the corner away from the sliding door, sat down and stared past me at the far wall.

"Michael, everything happens like they say in their plan. I rent the Huey they wanted for two days. The big one with the big doors on the two sides. Like the ones just like in Viet Nam. Only now they are white color. I told them in Kuala Lumpur, I told them in Malaysia, I told the people with the Hueys at the airport in Kuala Lumpur that they were land developers, just like they said I should do. Yes, I told them that my clients were land developers. They were land developers who were looking for good ocean property with a view, yes, with a view, for…, for hotel resort possible location.

They fly from Kuala Lumpur down to before Singapore and also on Indonesia side of Strait of Malacca from almost close to Jambi to close, very close to Medan. And they do this three times. On day one and on day two too! I know. I know because pilot after the trips tells me this. Even he tells me only they make movie with big camera of water and boats in Strait of Malacca. Never do they make movie of good land for high quality hotel."

The Colonel gulped down the double cognac and held the glass out in my direction for a refill. The man had decided to come out of the gate at full gallop. And the only riding crop needed was the one kept in cold storage on the floor beside the TV cabinet.

I had never seen the man so distraught. His demonstrated capacity in the past for a certain grace under fire was what had initially endeared him to me. And it, among other factors, factors of mutual need, had sustained our relationship. But someone or something had shredded his protective armor. His onion layer of steadfast decorum, which, like the epaulettes on his shirt, was donned daily for public consumption, had vanished.

"And Mr. Brian Law was your contact man in Kuala Lumpur," I intoned flatly, as I handed the Colonel his refilled glass.

"Yes! It is Mr. Brian Law who is the boss of the meeting in Kuala Lumpur. But, but, how do you know this, Michael?"

"The Turks and Caicos Islands…, remember…, I just came back from the Caribbean with Christina. Remember! I am home because you wished me to come home to help you. A man who works with Mr. Brian Law told me this. Here, wait a minute. I have something for you. From Christina and me from that far away place. Wait."

I retrieved the small conch shell that was buried among the clothes in my bag and handed it to the man.

"Now, Col. Satu, now you will be able to blow your own horn whenever you want to! See, like this."

I held the empty shell up to my lips and, with bulging, Louis Armstrong cheeks, went through the motions of how to coax a mournful bleat from the fortress that had protected the creature inside from all threats save those posed by marauding, manta rays and man.

The Colonel looked at me blankly as I placed the shell down on the table beside his drink. He neither understood the humor in my remark nor did he attach any significance to the present that Christina had chosen for him. Somewhat annoyed, he continued with his story of implied innocence.

Now I knew that it was only a question of 'what', not 'whether', he was guilty of some transgression in the eyes of his American masters.

"Yes, it is Mr. Brian Law. He is boss of group in meeting. He is very much like snake, Michael. He is very friendly many times when many people can hear his words but he is snake when he is alone with me and nobody else can hear his words. And he is dangerous too! He is, what you call, he is bully! Yes, very big, very evil, bad, bully."

He says to me that meeting must have high security and men, nine is total, no, ten with Mr. Law, must have high protection after meeting too. And…, and this is what I give to Mr. Brian Law and to nine other men. Even when he says to me that if security is bad then I will pay high price for mistake! I know he talks about using knife or guns to hurt me and my men. I know this. He is bully. But never mind.

Even when they go out after meeting, it is always to same place at same time. Same place, a bar with restaurant to serve food with name, 'Artful Dodger'. I hire extra people to make security certain. It is not difficult job because all men in group are not genit. All men do not like

Asia ladies. Only they like American ladies. They say so, I hear them, when they eat together in Artful Dodger. And only they go to Artful Dodger at night, like team, to eat or they stay in hotel, like team, after meeting. Never there is kupu-kupu malam to visit the rooms of the men of the team. Never!"

Only a guilty man could deliver such a detailed, linear diatribe that divulged nothing that even hinted at the disaster, I thought to myself.

The Artful Dodger! What a perfect name for the backdrop to the piece of theatre that the American men on a mission had chosen as their nightly nest. Charles Dickens characters right out of Oliver Twist to be sure.

But which one of the players in Kuala Lumpur was the Artful Dodger? Satu, dressed up to be someone he was not just as the Dickens character was a child pickpocket masquerading as an adult. Or was it Brian Law on a quest to snoop on and then steal sensitive and hence valuable foreign military data. A theft that was secretly sanctioned by the State Department perhaps! Or was he merely a modern day pickpocket, an opportunist operating on his own, using his persuasive guile to stay just one step ahead of the law! Brinkmanship among the morally bankrupt!

Art and life, not so much in imitation of each other as intertwined in insidious, incestuous intrigue.

And the butterflies of the evening, the kupu malam. What man who defined himself as a mobile, marauding testosterone machine would not, could not have at least flirted with the women of the night in Kuala Lumpur. They were as thick as the mosquitoes that hovered everywhere. And the human crush at the entrances to the expat watering holes, like the Artful Dodger, made for a bountiful hunting ground for the more adventurous, sequined searchers for a better life.

They were all beyond beautiful as they waited and watched under the forgiving street lights that created languid and inviting pools of promised pleasure at every street corner.

Only a man whose mission was all consuming would be immune. Only the obsessed. Only men whose agendas, self appointed or otherwise, were bigger than they were. And it was only men like that who would stop at nothing to achieve their mandate. Nothing and no one would be allowed to stand between them and their Decision Dooms Day goal. It was their promised land of milk and honey which, they believed, encompassed all three of the dimensions in their delusional, definitely paranoid lives!

"So tell me Col. Satu, why is this bully, Mr. Brian Law, so upset? The security measures that you put in place obviously worked well…, as always. Was something lost or stolen while the ten men were in the hotel?"

I had to cut to the chase. It was getting late and I was tired. Tired of the true but truncated story and tired of the teller as well.

"No! Nothing is stolen from the big room for the meeting and nothing is stolen from the sleep rooms of the land developers. I know because I had my soldiers everywhere, in all the places in the hotel. And they gave me good reports every day. No, nothing…, nothing, no nothing, nothing is stolen from these men!"

The Colonel folded his arms across his chest. The gesture was almost a dare. I was not to continue my current line of questioning.

"OK, it all sounds good to me, Colonel. You know, I think you can do the job of security for companies that have meetings in Indonesia and all over South East Asia for that matter, without me. Maybe I should retire…! But not right now. No…, I enjoy too much the work that I do with you at Asian Security Systems.

But one last thing before we stop for tonight, Col. Satu. Do you think that maybe it is possible for me to meet this Brian Law maybe tomorrow or maybe other time soon? I am sure he is busy man. Maybe he has already gone home, gone back to the United States to do other, new project."

"I do not know about this Mr. Brian Law and where he is right now. Maybe Indonesia. I do not know. But I will verify this for you. Tomorrow Michael. I will verify this for you tomorrow."

"Good! How about we meet for lunch at the Hotel Indonesia. Is one o'clock a good time for you, Col. Satu?"

"Is good time for me, yes one o'clock. Michael…, Michael…, only it is to say…, I am, I am happy…, I am very happy you are home…, you are here together with me in Jakarta. Yes, it is good. It is very good. Together we are team. Yes! Oh yes, you must thank Christina for present of dead sea shell for me. It is very nice."

The Colonel strode over to the door, turned as though he wanted to say something further, thought better of it, and departed. I knew that he could handle the trip home. The taxi would stop one block from his second apartment. It was buried among the markets and mayhem in the somewhat notorious part of Jakarta known simply as Block M. He would make his way to the roof of the building adjacent to his own and descend the fire escape to the structure that contained the little cubby hole that he sometimes called home. And no one, it was hoped, would be the wiser.

Chapter 9

I could not coax more than six new, four letter words from the most ubiquitous one in the world. The one that is printed in white, capital letters, on a red, octagonal background. The one that commands attention anywhere that two roads meet. One of the new words began with an 'O', two began with 'P', two more began with 'S', if 'sopt' could be used in place of sopped, and I could think of only one that began with the 'T'.

I was not cut out to be a cop. Definitely not a cop on a stakeout assignment. Road signs as a center of attention, would not be allowed to occur more than once.

"Mas, Mas, ikuti mobil itu."

We had been parked one block away from the address that the Colonel had given me. Kindness and compassion had not worked with the old man the previous night. He had danced with no music and no dialectical rhythm.

The taxi driver, who was just as bored as I was, gleefully followed my instructions. He put the car in first gear and raced after the white Lexus that had emerged from behind the iron gate.

I did not care who was in the white car in front of us. Following was better than lying fallow.

I tried to quell my mounting frustration and agitation. I was chasing someone in a car. Someone or a group of people in a car whom I had never met. A person or persons whose destination was as shrouded in mystery as they were.

Control! I needed to regain some measure of control. Christina! At least Christina was being well cared for I thought. That was comforting. It was clear from the moment that we had returned to our home in Jakarta that my daughter would not, could not, stay there.

The place was empty. But our former, now deceased pembantu, little Siti, who had been surrogate mother to Christina was, like a living ghost, everywhere.

Our recently arrived, next door neighbors, the Lee family, were from Houston. They proved to be our salvation. At least Renee Lee, the matriarch of the family, did. The product of strong, steadfast, rural stock, she seemed to be ever cheerful, brimming with common sense, and very witty on the few occasions we had met across the fence or at neighborhood expat barbeques.

She did not appear however, as was so common among her sisters in a foreign land, to have been bowed, like a standing shaft of wheat, by the harsh winds of solitude imposed by the nature of her husband's work.

Jim, her high school sweetheart, was an oil man. He managed more midwifery to the nascent oil derricks along the coast of Kalimantan, still referred to by some as Borneo, than he did the husbanding and fathering needed back home. Nothing out of the ordinary in that, I thought. Nothing except for Renee's apparent ability to fly with ease over the silence and the solitude that surrounded her.

I hoped that Renee's budget would accommodate the purchase of a Barbie doll set to match that of her newest house guest, Christina. Otherwise, her daughter, Jessica, a spoiled little brat who knew how to play one parent off against the other in her ceaseless quest for attention, would eclipse her standing record for anger induced mischief. One issue at a time, I thought to myself. Do one thing, one thing done well enough to work, at a time.

Why was I in a taxi playing sleuth for the Colonel? My own fault, I guess. I had known from the outset what the old man's problem was. And I had decided to cut through the fog that had shrouded his better judgment. Even if it meant running roughshod over his self-fulfilling fears.

"Col. Satu, it is too late for more games like we did yesterday at the hotel. This is dangerous situation. You know that. So we must find solution right away!"

"Already I told you all the story about Mr. Brian Law and the nine men of him and the helicopter, the white one, for video in Strait of Malacca, and the meeting of the men from America in Kuala Lumpur in hotel."

"Yes, I understand all of that Col. Satu. And thank you for the detailed information you have given me. It is a real help for me to understand the situation. But I need to know more Col. Satu. Now we must move on to other situation. Now I need to know something from you, Col. Satu, something very important. Now you must tell me the name of the Dukun who talks to you before this meeting. Before this meeting with the Americans, before it starts in Kuala Lumpur."

The expression that visited and filled the vacancy on the Colonel's face was a twisted swirl of trepidation and terror.

Dukans were to Indonesians what Medicine men were to early North Americans, what the Shaman represented to those in northern Asia at one time and what Voodoo priests represented to every resident of Haiti since time immemorial.

All were self-appointed, all claimed direct communication with some god or other and therefore all could see the future and the role of the supplicant, for better or for worse, in it. Some were admittedly insightful or just lucky guessers, and all were committed to the 'truth', their 'truth', to gain personal recognition and reward.

The Indonesian incarnation of men with magic, the Dukuns, was downright ludicrous. They preyed on and prayed over the weak and superstitious in mainly urban areas. Large cities provided an easy escape once their deeds of deceit were done.

All Dukuns, from the personal accounts that had been shared, teary-eyed, with me, were men. So it was only natural that a favorite target was young women.

There would be clandestine meetings during which, between wails and incantations, the young business woman, maybe a sales representative for a multinational company or an employee of a bank or insurance company or a travel agency, anywhere that offered full time employment, would be told that she was spiritually unclean. And her lack of cleanliness was all that was holding her back from promotion.

To rectify the situation she would be instructed to collect flowers from eight different plants or trees and bring them to the hotel where the Dukun was staying. A bath would be drawn for her and the flowers crushed so that the petals formed a blanket of purification over the surface of the water.

The Dukun, following much wailing and gesticulating, would, post purification, help the girl dry off, and, just to complete the cleansing process, suggest that coupling would be smiled upon mightily by the Gods.

Often, to add insult to injury, he would 'borrow' the girl's motor scooter, just for a few hours he would insist, to complete an important task. Once away from the hotel grounds, he would promptly sell it to the first buyer he could find.

And, like any self-respecting carpet bagger, he would promptly vacate his room without paying and without leaving the hotel with any recourse. The credit card he had used at check- in had been stolen!

With male clients, those who were players in some enterprise that was bigger than they were, the more sophisticated Dukuns employed a very different strategy. Rituals to achieve greater success in business, their bread and butter, were replaced by issues of the psyche. Grave concerns about the physical health and spiritual wellbeing of the 'pilgrim' were voiced. Stern warnings were given about his current behavior and its invitation to Satan to draw near. The very soul of the man was said to be at stake.

The Dukun would, of course, be able to help the man to save himself and his immortal soul. The vulnerable dupe would be told, in a very stern manner, to either cease certain activities for a set period of time or initiate actions that would alleviate the harm that had already been done.

Rarely was the call to action by these Dukuns initiated by them. They played marionettes to other, more powerful puppeteers. The conspiracy became air tight in the eyes of the wretch who had been wicked because the credibility of the Dukun would never be questioned. No financial gain for the man with vision was ever requested nor, if offered, accepted. The Dukun would graciously decline any financial offer made to him. Bigger bucks came from elsewhere.

"Michael…, I know nothing of this.., of this Dukun that you talk about! I know nothing, no nothing of this."

"Col. Satu, you need to be strong and you need to be honest with me. Your life might depend on it and mine, maybe, as well! Think…, think, my brother in arms. Think. Already we know 'what' has been done because of the meeting in Kuala Lumpur. Mr. Brian Law and his men were there for military reasons. They did reconnaissance in Strait of Malacca. We do not know exactly what they look for but we know this. They do not look for good location for new hotel. You and me, we both know this.

We must think about the reason, the 'why' that they do this operation.

It is because South East Asia and South China Sea are important to them, to the Americans. That's why! The enemy for them and maybe for you and me too, for everybody maybe, is in China.

Now there is Dukun who talks to you maybe many times. He is not your friend, he is your enemy. Think! How does he know to talk to you about what is the work of the Americans. Somebody told him. Somebody who wishes to maybe stop what they do. Some people who think that they can use you to help them…,

And I know that somebody who thinks like that is wrong, very wrong, about you."

The truth serum that proved to be efficacious was forty percent alcohol by volume. Three doubles of Remy Martin had done the trick!

The sparkling white machine with its tinted windows which was in front of us came to a stop at the main entrance to the Hilton Hotel. It belonged there. It looked like every other means of conveyance that was parked nearby. Whereas my little, rusted Bluebird taxi looked like a forlorn transient that had lost its way.

The only passenger in the Lexus got out only after the driver had walked briskly around to her side of the car and opened the door.

She placed her hand on his and alighted into the klieg light that the late morning sun provided. The expression on her face seemed to acknowledge the staccato clicking of camera shutters and the noisy adulation from the gathered throng. Her regal bearing suggested a silver screen siren whose stellar arc had not quite reached its apogee.

The Walter Mitty complex was apparently not gender specific. A few words of direction were given, as she alighted, to which the middle aged man in uniform knowingly nodded.

The woman was not Indonesian. Young, tall, and very self-confident, she ascended the stairs and disappeared into the hotel lobby as if she owned the place.

She was dressed in 'good Muslim girl' chic. The flowing folds of fine, colorful, filigreed cotton that she had allowed to embrace her body were capped by an equally elegant head scarf, the hijab.

Follow the rules of social, political and religious protocol, I thought, but project, when your psyche screams capability, that you are more than the sum of your moving parts.

The Hilton Hotel, located just off Jl. Sudirman in the heart of the business district of Jakarta, was a Mecca for those of means. The spacious, well treed and meticulously tended grounds, its courteous, competent staff, and first class, live-in-luxury lodging afforded guests ample opportunity to rub shoulders with others of privilege. And more importantly, they could revel in their perceived birth right, the use of perpetual passports of plastic to ensure limitless earth-bound pleasure.

The Komodo Bar was nestled close to the expansive entrance. With its dark interior, like the lair of the large lizard after which it was named, it always delivered drinks that were never measured in a tumbler. Metal gamelan gongs sat in wooden framed readiness beside the foyer entrance to the bar. The musical masters of the instruments would arrive each day at noon. Dressed in elaborate, traditional garb, they would, mute and expressionless, bathe the hotel 'portal to pleasure' with the haunting, somewhat lugubrious, music which was old, centuries older, than the country itself.

A profusion of oversized potted plants bowed and seemed to almost propel the visitor in the direction of the main lobby.

On this occasion however, the sensuousness of the place slide into mere, painted backdrop. The woman! I could not lose sight of the woman. She was the only thread to the weave, the weave that I had committed myself to unravel.

As I rounded the corner and entered the check-in area, I caught a fleeting glimpse of her tresses as the bank vault, elevator doors closed behind the precious cargo that she had become.

I sat down in a lobby chair and picked up a discarded copy of the Jakarta Post. Automatically I went through the mechanics of folding the daily journal so as to appear to be burying my nose in the news of the day. I watched the red, single digit as it changed above the elevator door. Eight was the highest number reached before the number paused and the count-down commenced for the cabled cube to begin its descent. The lady had a rendezvous on the eighth floor. Maybe!

I was not going to content myself with the Jakarta daily rag. It was too light on real news to last more than five minutes anyway. It was too early for the Komodo Bar to be open and its cloistered comfort would rob me of my strategic observation post.

Think, you silly bugger. Think!

Your assets. What operational assets did I possess! The man I was looking for went by the name, Saladin. The Colonel thought that he was from the Middle East, and he spoke bahasa Indonesia very well. He was about forty years old, thin, and he sported a goatee. Each time he had met with the Colonel, he had been dressed in traditional Arabian garb. The neck to ankle white, loose fitting robe, the thawb capped by a square cotton scarf with a checkered pattern, the keffiyeh, must have made the man look like a stand-in for a young Yasser Arafat!

He had given Col. Satu his address, but only after persistent pleading, and, undoubtedly, after quite a few rupias had changed hands. That was where I had gone fishing. But the only catch of the day seemed to be the puffer fish who was, basking or spawning, on the eighth floor.

The only other player I knew of was Brian Law, the supposed brains behind the cloak and dagger operation in the Strait of Malacca. I would be able to recognize him immediately. The Colonel had managed to take a photo of him while he played stand up presenter to his group of nine pins in Kuala Lumpur.

While committing his facial features to memory, from the small, laminated photo taken at the far end of the meeting room as the man stood, with felt pen poised at the top of a pad of flip chart paper, I had chuckled out loud. The man leading the seminar on sabotage could have passed for the twin brother of Dan Quayle.

DQ, the paragon of permanent perplexity, had been chosen by the George Bush handlers, the Republican Presidential hopeful, as his running mate. Bush aspired to follow in the somnolent shadow of his boss, Ronnie 'Bonzo' Reagan. And Mr. Dairy Queen was thought to be a sound albeit submissive choice as his running mate.

Brian's blank face, dominated by big blue eyes, was perfectly proportioned and his well-coiffed hair was a dirty blond color from a box. He looked like a Mel's Drive-In extra from 'American Graffiti' with no lines to recite. There was an honesty, no, a sublime naivety to the face of the man in the picture.

The fast food outlet and the man with the baby face had something else in common, apart from the same initials. Both were vacuous. The former was a statement of empty calories while the latter seemed to be, like a radio era vacuum tube, both bulky and brittle possessing insufficient amperage to activate, let alone broadcast, thought.

It was easy to connect the dots when there were so few of them on the game board in front of me.

There was one other asset I possessed. Personal recognition in the hotel. Use it. Just use it, I said to myself as I approached the front desk.

"Excuse me, Ahmed, I am Michael...,"

"Yes, of course, Mr. Campbell. What can I do for you today, sir. Will you be checking in for another short stay with us...,"

"Actually no, not today. I wish I could but..., well, you know..., business, always business must come first."

"Yes, of course Mr. Campbell..., then..., then, tell me sir, how may I be of help."

"Well Ahmed, I am a little bit embarrassed to ask you but..., I have an appointment with a guest who is staying with you here at the

Hilton..., on the eighth floor. But unfortunately I forget his room number. His name is Mr. Brian Law. I wonder...,"

"Just one moment please..., let me check our guest registry. Yes, yes, here he is. Mr. Brian Law, room 837. He will be with us for the week. But Mr. Campbell, I must warn you, Mr. Brian Law left strict instructions with the desk that he is not to be disturbed for the next two hours. We received his telephone call here at the front desk less than thirty minutes ago. But if you wish, I can call him and tell him that you are waiting...,"

"No, no, that's alright Ahmed. My friend Brian..., Mr. Law, is a very busy man. Perhaps I got the exact time for our appointment wrong. I will just wait here in the lobby or wonder around a little bit and then check back with you later. Would that be alright?"

"Yes, of course. As you wish Mr. Campbell. It is always a pleasure to see you and..., and..., do come to visit us anytime. There will always be a room, one of our better rooms of course, waiting for you."

"You are very kind Ahmed," I said, as a folded ten spot quickly changed hands.

"Oh, one last thing Ahmed, please say nothing of our conversation to Mr. Brian Law. I feel terrible. First I forget his room number and then I cannot remember the time of our appointment."

I winked at the young man who obviously enjoyed being a player in a small conspiracy.

Thank God, I thought to myself as I walked away, that all Hilton staff members wore polished metal name tags.

The steps in the stair well were taken two at a time. No sense stretching Ahmed's capacity for complicity. Red numbers were nice but not as a signal to the man on front desk duty that the naivety of his disclosure was being exploited.

Sixteen landings and one hundred ninety-two cement steps later and I was not out of breath. Lady nicotine continued to graciously accept my habitual liaison with her. I was emboldened.

The corridor on the eighth floor was deserted. As I tip-toed up to the recess that housed the two doors, 835 and 837, I realized that stealth was not needed. Even though the wall indentation created the illusion of exclusivity and privacy, and the teak doors looked impregnable, to both external threat and the escape of the noises from within, I had no trouble interpreting the muffled sounds that came from the room of Mr. Law.

Grunts and moans, the unmistakable guttural sounds of two people in the throes of coupling were audible even from the center of the corridor. I was listening to people who, though physically united, voiced their occupancy of two, separate and distinct worlds. Worlds which were not necessarily mutually exclusive, but worlds, nevertheless, in which self-gratification reigned supreme.

Whatever happened to words, I thought. Heart-felt words, happy words, words of tenderness and affection, words which would, if nothing else, add fuel to the ardor of the other. Maybe Mr. Law was just as inept at love making as he seemed to be at everything else he touched.

Or maybe that was not the nature of their tryst. Maybe it was engineered to be nothing more than mutual masturbation. Just one person using another. Maybe the Muslim maiden was merely plying her time honored trade. Maybe the client, before big, blue eyes, had been Saladin! Maybe, but my bet was, decidedly not!

The mechanical, drum-beat thumping of the bed frame against the far wall, like the sound of a washing machine during the spin cycle, was not exactly what my lawyer friends would have called, exculpatory evidence. It was more than just a little suspicious. It almost seemed unnatural. But mystery it must remain, for the moment, at least. No more snooping, I thought. Why temp fate and risk exposure.

Two of the dots had been connected. But what did that mean? Never mind. For the moment, it was enough. Regroup, get out of there and rethink the possible ramifications of this new twist to the weave.

I skipped down the clockwise staircase and went back to my new found friend at the desk.

"I'm sorry, Mr. Campbell, but there has been no new message from Mr. Law. Would you like to write him a note. I will see that it is delivered to his door immediately."

"Thank you very much Ahmed, but no, that will be fine. I will call Mr. Law myself later today and book another appointment with him.

But I wonder, might I borrow your desk telephone? I need to make an urgent business call. A local one in Jakarta. And the call will be short, very short."

"With pleasure Mr. Campbell."

"Renee, it's Michael. I'm just checking in to see if everything is alright. I…,"

"Oh Michael, I'm so glad you called. I have been trying to reach you at your office but the lady, Sherry, I think, said that you were out. Listen, there is nothing to get upset about but Christina and Jessica got into a squabble over the Barbie doll and, and, I am sorry to say that Barbie has been beheaded."

"Well Renee, I must say, that this is a first for me. I know that Barbie was molded to make male heads spin out of their sockets, perfect, plastic beauty and all that, but I had no idea that she was prone to losing her own the same way."

"Well Michael, when I go to the shopping center later on today to get Christina a new Barbie doll, will I be able to find a Michael doll too. One just like you that I can talk to and well, just keep in the house and fuss over? Oh, sorry Michael, I didn't mean that the way it sounded. Sorry."

"I don't want your sorrow ma'am and no on both counts. No, do not buy a new doll for Christina. Dolls, like people, sometimes get broken. This is a moment I want to share with my daughter. And no, there is no Michael doll. There better not be. I will sue the company for past royalties owning.

Now listen, I will be home in about twenty minutes. I will bring the wine and we will drink it at your place or, you will have the wine and we can drink it at my place or, we can both just whine and that can happen anyplace."

"Well, based on those options, maybe Jessica and I will break more dolls!"

The taxi ride home gave me the time I needed to think. The puzzle of the two players at the Hilton would only gain focus when the relationship between the lady in the Lexus and Brian was understood. The man, who had claimed at the Artful Dodger that Asian females did not appeal to him, obviously made exceptions to his 'born in the USA' rule about the opposite sex. One women at least, one of Middle Eastern descent, was a very real exception.

Was that woman related to Saladin? Sister, lover, boarder, fellow countryman, spouse. Or was she just a 'walk-on' in the stage production that I was witnessing.

One of the ten dossiers containing the details of the Malacca misadventure had gone missing. I knew that because the whale watcher in the Turks and Caicos, Jonathon, had said so. Col. Satu had purposely and steadfastly remained evasive on the subject even though all American fingers pointed at him. So, what really happened in Kuala Lumpur, who instigated the whole farce, and to what end!

I already knew who was going to bring clarity to the situation for me. And broken Barbie had become the catalyst needed to make the necessary rendezvous a reality.

"So Christina, tell me the whole story about what happened to Barbie when you were at Jessica's house."

I had said my 'hellos' to the two thirds of the Lee clan, assured both of them that I knew it was just an accident, even though I knew differently, and whispered to Renee that I hoped that we were still on that evening to share my bottle of excellent, not to be missed, red wine.

Barbie, still clothed in her lounge wear, lay on the kitchen table between us. Her head lay nestled, face up, in a hay stack of blond hair. The disconnected appendage smiled stupidly up at the ceiling.

"Daddy, it is not my fault that my Barbie is dead. It is Jessica. She is mean to me and she is very bad too. She breaks my Barbie dead. Look my Barbie is dead just…, just like my Siti is dead. Both are dead because the neck is broken. See, look at my poor Barbie."

"Yes Christina, you are right. Siti is dead and in Heaven because her neck was broken when she fell in the bathroom. I remember and, of course, you remember too…, when we had finished our shopping together in Singapore. We talked about Siti many times when we were together in Turks and Caicos Islands too. When we were on holiday together, remember?

And Barbie is hurt right now. I can see, she is hurt very badly. But…, but, it is not too late to make her better. She needs our help Christina. Right now too. It is too late to blame anybody. That will not help Barbie. Right now we must give all of our attention to Barbie to make her as good as new. Will you help me try to do that!

I think that, together, like two doctors, like two very good doctors, we can make your Barbie better. We can make Barbie as good as new. Shall we try to make Barbie better again Christina?"

Christina rubbed angrily at her tears. Brightening somewhat, she looked up at me.

"We can make Barbie better again Daddy? But how? Look, her head is broken off from her body."

"Well OK, chief assistant doctor, let me take a look at our patient. First I will make my examination of your friend, Barbie, and then you can make an examination of her as well. Then we can decide what will be the best procedure to follow. OK?"

I picked up the doll's head and peered into the hole in its base where the skinny neck had been seated. Noting the means by which the neck plug connection between the two body parts had been made, the inch long piece of plastic did not appear to have been damaged. The simple, 'snap-on' connection allowed for little more than limited head movement even when the doll had been fresh from the factory.

The only real sign of violence was a small, quarter-inch, rip in the plastic stretching from beneath the chin to the edge of the neck where the head had been jolted from the torso. A skill acquired when I was no more than a few years older than Christina, honed behind a closed bedroom door to avoid the meddling of my mother, would, I knew, make the mending of the doll seem like magic.

"OK Dr. Christina. You examine the patient and then tell me what you think we should do. Tell me your diagnosis."

My daughter picked up the two disconnected pieces and mimicked what I had done. She peered into the open wound, looked carefully at the two separated parts with unknowing eyes, and then gently placed them down on the table.

"I agree with you Doctor Daddy. I think you can make my patient, Barbie, be saved. But I think it will be hard work. I want you to start and I will watch, OK."

"I'm glad that we are in agreement Doctor Christina. Shall we get started? First, I want you to talk to Barbie just to make her calm. She trusts you, you know, more than anybody. She needs to be relaxed before we start the procedure."

Christina aligned the head of the doll immediately above the torso. She leaned forward and placed her right hand on Barbie's chest and her left on the doll's forehead. She relaxed her comforting grip on both parts only when she was sure that they would not roll off the OR table. As an after-thought, she gently brushed a tangle of blond hair away from the face of her favorite playmate.

"Everything will be alright Barbie. We will take care of you. Me and my Dad will make you all better. You just wait and see. Yes, we will make you better and good as new."

I picked up the two pieces of the doll and tried hard not to wince. Plastic had a tendency to break when elasticity was needed most. I positioned Barbie's head above the body, and making sure that both pieces of the doll were facing in the same direction, slowly but steadily pressed the two pieces together.

I was rewarded by the 'popping' sound of the two pieces of semi-pliable plastic as they snugly reconnected to one another.

I gently lifted the intact doll up and away from me, much I thought, as an obstetrician would a new born infant. Gingerly, I twisted the head from side to side and even more gently, back and forth. The neck plug had not lost its integrity. Only one other 'medical' problem remained. The facial laceration under the chin, the tear caused by the deliberate assault of Christina's former, next door friend, was both practical and aesthetic. The successful operation would quickly fail if the rip were not closed. And Barbie would face social ostracism if her scar were not 'face lifted' away.

"Here, Doctor Christina. You hold the patient, but hold her gently, while I get another surgical instrument. We have one more procedure that we must follow to make Barbie completely well. And you must help me with this. So you can put Barbie down, gently, on the table and come with me.

I knew what I needed, I knew that we had what I needed, but I had no idea what Siti had done with it.

The third kitchen drawer which was searched contained the sought after prize.

"Well, Doctor Christina, we have been successful so far with our reconstructive surgery but one more intervention is needed. The patient has a deep laceration, do you know what a laceration is Doctor Christina?"

My daughter, with eyes as big as saucers, could only shake her head slowly from side to side. She was in the OR and she was assisting in a major surgical intervention. And she was enjoying every second of the experience.

"No, well, a laceration is just a fancy word for a cut. Doctors love using big words to describe small things. Don't you worry about it. Here is the medical instrument that we need. Do you know what this is Doctor Christina?"

"Yes Doctor Daddy. That is a meat ther…, thermo…, thermometer."

"You are right, but only on special occasions, like Christmas when we use it in the turkey right? Right! But today, because we are surgeons helping our patient to get better, the meat thermometer will be used to allow us to cauterize, 'cot-er-ize', the cut just below her chin. That way Barbie will be able to move her head just like always. And…, and, she will look as beautiful as ever too.

'Cauterize' is just another fancy Doctor word for seal shut, to close something that is open too much to be healthy.

Go and get a stool so you can stand up beside me in front of the stove. We will get our new, surgical instrument ready."

Christina was standing on the stool between me and the stove before I had twisted the knob that controlled the front element.

"Now watch. The front electric element will become red as it heats up. I have put it on high so we do not waste any time. See how red it is getting. That's why you must always be careful around the stove. But you already know that, right Doctor Christina!

OK, now watch as I place the pointy end of our instrument on the element that is now very hot. That will make the pointy end hot too. Now here is where you must help me, Doctor. You watch the dial at the far end of the probe…, of the thermometer, and tell me when the needle inside points to 300 degrees. Are you watching? Good. Just let me know when the needle points to 300."

"It's there Doctor Daddy. It's there at 300. The needle says 300, 300 degrees!"

"Good! Now get down from the stool and together we will complete the medical procedure on Ms. Barbie, OK!

You put one hand on her forehead and the other on her stomach. That way Barbie will know that you are very close to her and you can help keep her calm and steady while I finish the operation procedure. OK!"

Funny, I thought, how the hobbies of youth came back to either haunt or hand-hold decades later. I had become very proficient with a wood burning tool. It had been used on all of the plastic Revell warplane models my parents had bought for me. They had all flown, albeit via fishing line, for a time, in deadly aerial combat around the ceiling sky of my bedroom.

The heat from the tip of the metal tool, when correctly applied, allowed the propellers on the warplanes to spin. By melting the end of the plastic shaft when placed in its housing, as opposed to simply following the printed instructions and gluing it in one fixed position, I was able to achieve greater realism. Plastic as practice for and precursor of Proud moments. Parentless moments. Moments when proficiency prevailed. Repairs to broken pieces of the fuselage and wings became child's play. Melt the crease between the two broken pieces and smooth over the operation with the adjacent plastic material which melted to the touch of the magic heat. And avoid inhaling the acrid smoke of the burning plastic!

Barbie became the beneficiary of my boyhood, Walter Mitty, flights of heroic fancy.

"Now Doctor Christina, remember that your patient has just undergone major surgery. So she needs to rest. She is not ready to play with you just yet. Time is a great healer, remember that.

And as for the little scar that Barbie has below her chin because of our successful surgery, remember that all surgery patients are left with one. Barbie is still very beautiful you know, and if you want, you can cover her little mark with a top that comes up around her neck or, or, you can put pearl jewelry on her. As a fashion statement, sure, you can adorn her neck with fine jewels like maybe even diamonds. But I think pearls would be just fine. Yes, I think pearls would be best."

I waited for my daughter's response. I feared that she would now see her newest friend as 'damaged goods'.

Christine played therapist as she knowingly moved the doll's head back and forth and up and down a few times. She gently touched the scar with her forefinger in an effort, it seemed, to concentrate all of her healing power in the tip of her outstretched digit. Then she carefully placed Barbie on the table as if in readiness for repose.

She shrieked and made a gleeful lunge at me.

"Oh Daddy, you are the bestest of all. This is the bestest day for me ever! You made my Barbie better. Always, you know, I will remember this special day. How you…, how you and me, how we made my Barbie-best-friend all better."

She disengaged herself from my upper torso, gathered up her patient and skipped down the hall to her bedroom.

Laceration, probe and caut…, cauterize, laceration, probe and cauterize, were the vespered words she chanted. They were caught and made to dance in the vortex of air which was left in her wake.

Bali, the surprise destination for Christina the following day, would, I knew, soon relegate the doll to the status of background dust collector. Old friends there and frenetic activity everywhere there, would ensure it. The same fate had befallen my B-25 bombers. Only they had suffered a worse fall into oblivion than Barbie ever would.

They had been obliterated by my subsequent adolescent fixation, a B-B gun.

Chapter 10

Renee seemed to be the kind of woman for whom intimacy felt right only if the marriage certificate hung, in a sturdy, glassed frame, above the bed. Prolonged abstinence and resigned acceptance of the occasional tsunami rush from her dutiful husband, seemed to be viewed by her as a woman's lot in life.

Accommodate and adapt through personal fulfillment elsewhere. That seemed to be her credo. Child care, charity work, meeting the girls at the club, house cleaning done daily with religious zeal, they all had one thing in common. Their end point was eventually reached and with it the realization that they were all merely time killing, Band-aids. They were bereft of intimacy, of grand release, of providing fulfillment to a bona fide player in the game of life. They all failed miserably. They merely masked the empty maw in her gut that needed filling.

I had never seen her fresh, handsome good looks marred by make-up. Relegated to the side lines, there was never a need for blackened skin above the cheek bones because the glare from the Sun didn't matter. She was never, apparently, on the receiving end of the thrown football.

Red wine and wishful thinking were the co-conspirators who made the promise of 'paradise regained', or more likely, first gained, come tantalizingly close.

Christina was asleep in our bed and Jessica was also somewhere asleep and I didn't care where. The latter slept with the satisfaction of having vented her frustration with the world and my daughter reposed, content in the knowledge that she had helped mid-wife her reincarnated friend.

Renee and I met at the gated fence that separated our two rented properties.

"Oh, Michael, it's you!"

"Yes, it's only me. I live here, remember."

Seeing that Renee had a bottle of wine in her hand, I lifted mine over the fence gate toward her.

"Salute neighbor. Great minds think alike."

"And we both know what fools do, don't we," she retorted as the two bottles clinked together.

"Well, will it be your place or mine?"

"Let's start with your place, Michael. Believe it or not, I have never set foot in your back yard. Either you're away somewhere, or the pool parties are at my place…, when Jim is home. Sure, when Jim is home. He is becoming just like you, you know. Never home!"

"Wait…,listen…, is that a violin I hear somewhere off in the distance. Is it the strains of 'Oh, Lonesome Me', the plaintive cowboy song or maybe, "Rhapsody In Blue', the Gershwin tune from the early jazz era?"

"OK, OK, you win."

"No, not if we assume that actions, sustained actions, are a consequence of intent. We both arrived at the gate, the gate which separates us, with fermentation in hand, at exactly the same moment. I think we both win. Sainthood gets acknowledged because of a singularity of purpose, you know."

"So does criminality. Sorry, but I am not comfortable doing what I am doing right now. This is not me. No, this is just not me at all! I'm sorry Michael."

"And, if I may be so bold, what is it exactly that you think you are doing right now. The casual observer would say that two adults, two neighbors, are meeting to greet and embrace the evening air. They are having a drink of wine and they are conversing with one another. I'm partial to that point of view. What about you, Renee, what do you think we are doing?"

"You are a crafty little bugger, aren't you Michael. I wonder though, why was it that you seemed so…, so, unobtrusive at the back yard cocktail parties we have attended. We met and we exchanged brief pleasantries. That was it. You seemed to be content to get sloshed, really sloshed, and then just fade into the woodwork."

"Literature, my good woman, literature. You will find the missing piece, in the puzzle that is all about 'I', in future, published prose. I think I'm going to write a book, a novel, about what expats do in South East Asia in their spare time. I am still collecting data on that particular sub-set of our species. I am fascinated, not so much by their hunting and gathering techniques as I am by the rituals that attend their social gatherings. I think the title of the novel will be, 'Lascivious Interludes'. Do you think it will sell?"

"I think maybe I should have had a power snooze before I came to your door. What were you Michael, I mean, what did you do before you became a globe trotter doing God knows what?"

"I was a drug dealer!"

"A what!"

"A drug dealer, you know, pharmaceuticals. I was a Country Manager for a European pharmaceutical company in Manila until, well let's just say, until there was a difference of opinion as to what I should and should not be doing on their behalf."

"And why does that not surprise me about you, Michael. I mean, what I mean is…, iconoclast, I had to look it up to remind myself of the meaning of the word. No other person I know could wear that moniker as well as you do. That's what I meant to say…,"

"I will take that as a compliment Renee. Most people consider me to be nothing more than just a run-of-mill, pain in the ass. Wait, while I go fetch the cork screw and something to nibble on from the kitchen."

I had the sneaking suspicion that, had her house been chosen for our rendezvous, not only would the odor of potted pot-pourri been present, but a simmering, savory, pot-au-feu as well.

The mechanics of cork popping, glass filling, and the scattering of trays filled with sugar or salt things from glass bottles or oblong boxes took mere seconds.

"Renee, now that you have surveyed my luxurious estate and you realize that it is vastly superior to your own next door, c'mon in here.

Join me inside the sun room. Those biting little bastards out there everywhere will rudely interrupt any conversation we might have, regardless of the topic we choose."

"I like where your pool is located more than mine Michael. Yours is placed well back in the lot. It makes your patio a lot larger than mine."

"Envy, you know, is considered one of the seven deadly sins."

"Along with pride, anger and lust, I might add!"

"So let's drink to some of the virtues of the soul then, shall we. To altruism, to happiness for others, but let's forget temperance for the time being. It's vastly over rated as a virtue anyway. Remember the period of Prohibition in your country of birth."

"No, let's just drink to us and our sometimes outcast state."

"Right, a toast to the Bard. Well said."

A moment of uneasy silence fell between us. We both sipped at the surface of our wine and looked away with feigned interest in the darkened walls of the screened enclosure.

"Michael, how is that someone with your obvious charm and no shortage of spontaneous wit, is…, is…, well, unattached…, single?"

Renee took a large gulp from her wine glass.

"I'm so glad you asked me that, Renee. And I suppose you are going to tell me that you have a twin sister, or a sibling at least who is also 'free' at the moment and that I possess the 'must have' attributes for inclusion on her potential candidates list.

Just joking with you Renee. Just joking.

Well, I am single now because of circumstances. Circumstances, some of which were of my own creation and others…, well others, which were beyond my control. Simply put; one divorce and two deaths."

It was my turn. I emptied my glass.

"Oh Michael, my dear, unfortunate man. How did you ever manage to cope. Divorce and death! That makes my life seem absolutely bland and banal in comparison."

"No, normal might be a better choice of words.

Lydia, my first wife, and I, had two sons. They are both in their late teens now. I think that all three of them live in a suburb of Toronto. I'm not sure because, well because, we all have new lives now and, I guess, we have just gone our separate ways.

Wife number two, Viven, was from Manado. You perhaps know, that's in northern Sulawesi. Viven was the mother of Christina. She died in childbirth. That's why Siti, remember little Siti, was with us. She was surrogate mom to my daughter. And she is with the angels too, or so the comforting story of the dead, by the living, goes."

Sometimes virtue lay with the lie. Sometimes masking the monstrous was less cruel than cradling the contemptible.

Did the details of Viven's demise really matter to anyone! Anyone other than myself!

"And wife number three was from Singapore. Her name was Victoria. She died as a direct result of injuries inflicted by…, well…, by her own mother. As difficult as that might be to believe, it is true. Her own mother, who is now, also deceased.

Victoria and I had no children. We were not together long enough for, for anything of consequence to happen."

"Oh my God. No wonder you are so introspective. You are carrying one heavy emotional load on your shoulders, Mr. Michael Campbell. I don't think that I could manage it.

But…, but, where was the father, the father of Victoria, in all of this tragedy. Was he just not around, was he already dead…, I'm sorry Michael, that's none of my business…, sorry…

Thank you. Thank you so much. Thank you Michael, for being so candid with me. I feel like I am looking at a completely different person than the one I knew, or thought I knew, before today."

"It's easy Renee, it's easy to say a whole lot without telling anything. The difficult part is the backfill, the fleshing out of the story, the parts that give form and substance to the skeletal sketch I just provided. Victoria's father was a player in the Agatha Christie piece to be sure. But all of that will have to wait for another day. Here, let me refill our glasses."

Renee moved forward in her chair to grab some of the nuts which were closest to her.

"Ouch, ooh, God that hurts."

My porch mate grabbed at the back of her neck with both hands and tried to massage where the pain had erupted as best she could.

"Sorry Michael, it's just my neck. Sometimes, when I move too quickly the wrong way, I get a stabbing pain in my neck. It doesn't last long but it hurts, really hurts for a minute or so. Don't worry, it will pass. Just leave me alone with my problem for a moment."

"How long has this been going on Renee?"

"Oh, just a couple of days. I was lifting the end of the chest of drawers in my bedroom, something was stuck there, I don't even remember what, and bang, the pain hit me."

"Would liniment help? I have some in the house...,"

"No, no, it will be OK. Thanks for the kind offer anyway."

"What about your family doctor here in Jakarta? He or she could write you a script...,"

"No, really, it will pass soon. It's OK. Really, when I think about it, I know that this and every other ailment I suffer from right now are all just symptoms of a larger issue. And the issue is me! I really need to start to live a different life. I need to be on my own. No! I need to be with someone, some loving someone, who is there for me all the time, someone who cares about what happens to me. Someone who can be attentive... can offer advice... like, like, you just did..."

"Well, Ms. Walking Wounded, or should I call you Ms. Pain In The Neck, ha, ha, you are in luck. Let's tackle one ailment at a time, shall we? First the neck pain, OK. It just so happens that Mr. Michael here, is a fairly accomplished masseuse. It's true, he will tell you. Just ask him."

Renee stared evenly into my eyes before she spoke.

"Well, Mister Michael, we both know that I am new to the little 'bored' game, bored as in sick of paradise, that we are playing, but wouldn't what you just said qualify as a gambit in chess? You know, initial risk of piece or pawn to gain positional advantage. You enjoy taking chances, don't you?"

"Tut, tut. I will have you know, Ms. Lee, that I am a professional. I concentrate only on the areas of the body stipulated by my partner, I mean, client."

I grinned the guilty grin of a youngster who had been caught looking for Christmas presents in the closet. But I was damned if the moment would be allowed to turn maudlin…, maudlin because of transient pain or because of someone lost to trepidation over paths not taken!

"The discomfort is in your neck, so I will massage only that area, as well as your shoulders of course. And I will finish with a brisk rub down of your lower legs, below your knees. I'll bet you stand most of the day. Stand on rigid ceramic tiles. Right! That means that your lower leg muscles, your calf muscles, are probably stretched, you know, probably sensitive and stiff."

"Do you play Michael? Do you play an instrument? You have the hands of a musician. Your finger tips are nimble and their touch so very delicate but, when needed, they do have the power to really strike a chord. Ohhh! Like you are doing to me right now."

Renee had tentatively accepted my invitation to lie, face down on the couch. She made sure that her top was pulled down tightly to her waist and that the pleated tennis skirt experienced the same attempt at enlargement of its store rack size.

Renee had a body that was fit and firm. Very firm. Almost masculine, I thought. She obviously used the workout equipment at her club as much as she partook of the gab-fests and the finger food feasts of her friends.

The combination of finger-tip kneading on and around the point of pain, palmed pressure on and above her shoulder blades and forearm presses on and down both sides of her spine bore fruit.

Occasional, muffled 'popping' sounds were audible as I pressed deeply along both sides of her backbone and the knotted muscles in her neck gave way like lumps in kneaded bread dough to the practiced pads on my finger-tips. The promise of Protestant reward for persistent effort, I thought to myself.

"Half way there Renee. Have a sip of wine with me before I tackle your legs."

"Michael, what did you just do! The pain is gone and look, I can move my neck like nothing had ever happened to it. Where did you learn how to do whatever you just did?"

"High in the mountains. I made a pilgrimage to a guru high in the mountains and he taught me everything he knew. Well almost. Actually, we both descended from the mountain heights and we visited the sleaziest bar he could find. The masseuses in there taught both of us everything we know."

For the first time during our strange interlude, Renee laughed. She laughed so hard that her eyes watered. Her laughter came in waves. She would no sooner wipe the tear drops from her face than another gut laugh would erupt and she would wet herself anew.

I was witnessing, I thought, the metamorphosis of this woman who had chosen to seek refuge under my roof. Pupa to adult, she was flexing her newly formed wings, ridding them of their wetness and she, subconsciously, was preparing to fly.

As her laughter subsided, she found her legs, walked the two steps over to me, cupped my head in her hands and kissed me on the forehead.

"I'm going to recommend you to the girls at the club. You are simply wonderful."

"Well two issues come to mind, Renee. One, I will have to charge them. A bottle of wine for each will run into big money. And two, I will only accept those whose muscle tone matches your own. You are in splendid shape."

"You mean splendid shape for an old broad...,"

"No I mean splendid shape for a young woman who has not even begun to plumb the depths of what is waiting inside. Now assume the position you silly wench so I can continue to demonstrate what I have learned in the bars of South East Asia."

Deep, upward, pencil eraser strokes with my thumbs and finger raking returns to her heels prompted initial, 'hurt so good' gasps as her kneaded calves flexed and accepted their needy touch. Renee's soft groans soon subsided as her lower body rolled ever so slightly to the sea-wave rhythm of the massage. The muscles in her legs surrendered to the persistence of the padded bones that played across her skin.

"Renee, this is what you should build into your visits to the club. I am sure that the staff in there could recommend someone for whom massage is a calling. Not just a hobby. Reward yourself girl. Yours is a tough row to hoe. Physical exertion all day, every day…,"

No response.

"And check out a good shoe store. Arch support and all of that. Walking around barefoot on the tiled floors in your house is cool to the bottoms of the feet but a real 'killer' to the rest of your legs…,"

Still no response.

I leaned forward toward Renee's face. Her breathing was deep and relaxed. Soft snoring accompanied every inhalation. I sat back, flexed my fingers to free them from their lock of tooled contortion and refilled my glass.

I sat and sipped and stared at the inert figure of the woman in front of me. The muted porch light softened everything that surrounded her. Lithograph-like, her skin was a study in pastel shades of gray and brown.

The bottom of a woman was where the mating ritual began. Fashion said so, it screamed it, seasonally, with flare. The female form, seen from afar, said so, replete with implied dare, and the font of female fecundity was its twin with mere centimeters to spare!

Doggerel be damned! It was the Holy Grail which, once found, doomed the male to descent!

The French had it right. Foreplay was meant to be 'totalement formidable' and that, of course, made fornicating with one's face, 'de rigueur'!

Tonguing around and under the back side of Renee's narrow, lace covered panties was a voyage worthy of Columbus. Billowing Atlantic waves were replaced by taut, becalmed expanses of skin. Descent down the slot formed by her pillow perfect, full sails, made the decision to seek safe harbor seem more a delight than a dangerous undertaking.

I stopped midway down between her steep, majestic promontories and revisited the ship's stores. A forty percent barrier against microscopic malevolence was best, but, in its absence, a six percent solution was better than none at all.

My concern about roaming, indigenous, microscopic bugs was ill-founded.

The Bay of Renee, as I had just christened it, was awash with the delightful residue and odor of bath oil.

The woman, the woman of reticence, the woman who talked of the worst, had prepared herself for the best!

I resumed my journey of discovery and decided to linger long in the shallows created by striation. Imaginary whirlpools were created by swizzle sticking my tongue up and down and around her indentation and by punctuating the process with tentative, tongue tip, probes.

Mother earth moved. Not a violent upheaval caused by knee-jerk reaction to assault, but more the nursery rhyme rocking seen when boats adjust to the incoming tide, boats, that is, which fit the water.

Renee groaned as her lower torso took on an animated life of its own. Her bottom rose in response to the slow arching of her back, and with her legs spread wide, she smothered my face with the deft deliberateness of a mother hen preparing to settle on her clutch of eggs.

Disengaging myself from her warm, wet nest, I gulped in some much needed air. I allowed my left forefinger to play with the passion slurry created by my tongue and the excess droplets, following the law of gravity, provided the lubricant for my right thumb to slide into her vagina. The web between my lost appendage and my forefinger filled her crevice and allowed the tip of the digit to rest on her clitoris.

"Oh Michael no, stop, please stooop! Please, please…,No, no, don't stop. Just a little bit more. Oh, oh there, yes' right there…, God, oh my God…, oh no, I'm coming. Oh God no, I'm coming."

Renee froze for a moment as if commanded by a photographer to stop fidgeting.

"Get out of me, Michael. Get all of you out of me! Ohhh. Just give me a minute. I'll be alright. Just a minute. Just give me a minute."

She tried to right herself but the muscle spasms that ruled her body made her first few attempts futile.

Heeding her request, I had backed off and undone the front of my shorts. I even managed to finish the remaining wine in my glass.

I grabbed her by the shoulders, turned her over on her back, pulled her panties aside and entered her. All in one unscripted, maniacal move. I wanted to, no, I needed to look into her eyes at that moment, but she was having none of it. Instead, her head was turned as far to her left as she could manage. She was biting her lower lip, not in pain but, it seemed, in anguish and embarrassment.

I stopped abruptly. I stopped deep inside her and remained motionless.

Her face told the story. It was the picture of someone who was doing wrong, who knew she was doing wrong, who knew that she had instigated, or at least been complicit in, the wrong doing and was guilty, guilty, guilty, on all counts. She was guilty of a crime for which there was no redemption. The spilt milk, the loosed arrow, the hurtful word spoken, the promised body to another, given to a stranger in momentary weakness, Renee was the fallen woman. And the sentence for her willful crime of passion, came with no hope of parole.

I wondered at that moment, if Renee would actually contemplate telling Borneo Jim about her sin as a means of expunging the scarlet letter that, otherwise, would be forever hers to wear, emotionally at least, in the public arena of scorn.

Renee blinked, turned her head and stared past my eyes. Something had happened. Something deep inside her, like some tectonic plate, had shifted. She groaned as the wave of release rose up and washed over her. Her midsection seemed to buckle and heave as though it belonged to someone else. She wrapped her arms around my back like someone seeking protection from typhoon force winds. She clambered over my chest like a dazed creature clinging for dear life to the trunk of a tree.

In the tumult, I came. I tried to disengage myself from the maelstrom but only partially succeeded. Gushes of what looked like stem stained water in a thin necked flower vase, one which had been accidently knocked over, spurted out and pooled above her pubic patch. Her Richter scale event completely eclipsed my social faux pas contribution to the upheaval.

"God..., shit..., hell! Michael, shit Michael, this is not supposed to happen. Not today, not ever..., not with you, no, not with you..., ever!

But..., but..., something, this something force just grabbed me and it would not let go! That has never happened to me before. No, not like this. No, never like this at all! I don't know, something, something so strong, so, so, strong, just took over. It…, it grabbed me and just would not let go. Something just…, just would not let go of me. I could not control myself. It just would not let go of me!"

"I was with you Renee. I was with you in the same storm. And, and I got all wet too!"

"Oh my God, you didn't! Tell me, please, tell me, you didn't come inside me too! Did you?"

Thinking that her body had been scrubbed but not made secure, I readied my profuse apologies.

"Michael you did. Oh my God, you did! You came inside me! You came inside of me and all over me! I didn't know. Why didn't you say something, anything…, anything so we could have stopped. Michael, we can't be doing this. This will not work between us. It can never work between us. There is so much…, too much that…,"

Renee seemed crushed. Her crestfallen face spoke volumes. She was like a child who had seen the doll of her dreams in a store window. She had been allowed by the store clerk to hold the make believe baby in her arms. But, on the day of purchase, the toy had disappeared. It had been purchased by a stranger. It was gone. Never really hers. Taken. Gone forever!

Schizophrenic; retreat from meaningful social interaction, schizophrenic; experience trouble with the marriage of thought to action, the woman was truly schizophrenic. She was, at once, the killer at the keyboard, Jerry Lee Lewis, and his cousin, the pussy pastor, Jimmy Swaggart. And each persona was envious of the other.

Surmising that nervousness, the shadow cast by novelty, was the root cause of her anguish, I plowed ahead.

"Never mind Renee. I can make amends right now."

Foolishly, I disengaged myself from my partner in crime, crawled down along her torso and crouched between her legs. Slowly and deliberately I kissed and sucked at her salty wetness. I slithered up to her navel, pulled her skirt down slightly and dripped some of the prize in my mouth into the deep end of the empty swimming pool that was perfectly located on her property. Patio placement notwithstanding!

My voyage due north was interrupted by Lewis or Swaggart. I had no idea which one uttered the request.

"Michael, you are so…, so…, I don't know what, so…, so…, attentive. Yes, yes, that's it, attentive. All the men in my life have seen hibernation, once they have finished, as a fitting finale. But not you. Not iconoclastic you."

Renee pinched my nose to accentuate her break through analysis of my behavior.

The word, 'all' in her disclosure was not lost on me.

"Yes Michael, I want you to make another deposit for me. I want you to make my nipples big, big and erect, just like they were when…, just like they used to be."

I pulled both her jersey top and bra up toward her neck and played nursing infant with her breasts. Even though Renee was lying flat on her back, their pudding perfect form remained full and voluptuous.

Tongue, lips and teeth contributed to the result that the lady desired. The finishing flurry was to bathe both brown pop-ups with the magic elixir which remained in abundance in my mouth.

As I ascended toward Renee's face, I entered her again.

"Oh my God! You…, again! But you already came for me! What are you doing, Michael? Oh…, oh…, yes, yes…, stop right there. No, a little more. Yes, that's it. Ohhh, so, so, good. Ahhh, Michael, Michael, I'm coming again. You are making me come again.

Quick, kiss the you…, the you from me…, the you in your mouth from me…, into me! Please, I want it. Yes, kiss me Michael. Kiss me hard. I want all of you."

As my former mother-in-law had counseled me, when we were still on speaking terms, watch what you wish for, you…,

"Ahh, Renee, I'm ready too. There is, ahh, music in the magic, yes, magic, magic, when our two worlds connect, magic when our two worlds collide."

Mortar in pestle, train over trestle, always to wrestle with one who seems special.

Mortar in pestle, train over trestle, always to wrestle with one who seems special.

George Orwell's, 'Big Brother' must surely be watching. Where was his hiding place this time? Nowhere and everywhere. Oranges and lemons say the bells of St. Clement's. Oranges and lemons say the bells of St. Clement's. Winston and Julia cannot remember the remainder of the rhyme. The past erased. Julia cannot even remember what a real lemon is! The past replaced!

Live long enough, as the saying goes, and you get to experience everything. For the first time ever, I had executed what the German army had perfected, namely, the pincer movement. Simultaneous attack from two directions. My two pronged pincer movement was, to be sure, composed of squirming little soldiers. And their deployment had proved to be deliciously pleasing to both me and to my new found lover!

Spent, we both fought to regain some semblance of normal respiration. Then, suddenly, without speaking, we disengaged from one another and hastily rearranged our clothing as if we were preparing to catch the commuter train that would shuttle us to work. And the clock on the wall proclaimed that we were running late.

We kissed each other perfunctorily. Our children had come back into focus and maybe they were waiting in the wings of the other stage upon which we were pivotal players. As Renee disappeared behind the gate, I heard her giggle. It was not the smug laugh of someone who had just beaten someone else in a contest.

No, it was not that!

Granted, she had not ventured to wear her heart on her sleeve, or even recite a chronology of personal catastrophe, as I had done for her. No! But her muffled, little titter of a laugh took me aback.

It was, at once, arresting. It sounded inclusive. Her wordless whisper said that she knew me. She now knew who I really was. It seemed to be, as well, a self-conscious, almost embarrassing, realization that she had enjoyed what she had just done with me. What we had just done to each other…, with each other…, together.

The sound that had emanated from her throat, no louder than a whimper, was of celebration. It was exclusive. It was inclusive. Her shared intimacy was her badge of accomplishment. It was metamorphosis at work. She was proud, she could fly on her own and she had the 'right stuff', to alight at will, as well!

Our tryst had occurred in a public world of hostility squirreled away in a private corner of wishes and whispers. It was hers and hers alone to savor and digest.

The life force had triumphed over moral and legal trepidation. She had sallied forth and had reconnected with her own self-worth. Probably not, in a very long time, but definitely not for the last time either!

The woman needed to know, like everyone who comes to the realization that their time is ticking and that the bell would eventually toll, that she could still attract, and perhaps sustain the attention of a man of her choosing. Renee had enjoyed the gambit she had engineered. She had renewed her faith in her ability to see three or four moves ahead on the chess board of her choosing.

She must have had, she would have to have had, an inkling as to what her husband, Jim, did during his down time in Kalimantan. The stupid, insensitive man had bragged about his conquests to his male friends during the two or three drunken back yard parties I had attended. Bragged about his fuck-fests when he thought his wife was busy elsewhere.

Truck loads of silly, rapacious, ignorant, little girls who were easy. Little creatures who saw foreign men as money making machines, for themselves and their village dwelling families, machines which needed little more than periodic 'servicing'.

The Bard came to mind again. All the world's a stage and all the…, blah, blah, bloody fools, blah, blah, made bastards, blah, blah, or bozos, blah, blah, of themselves, blah, blah, blah, or both, blah, blah, blah, blah, blah, blah, blah!

Chapter 11

"Well Dr. Rajawane, did you ever think, in your wildest dreams, that you would end up being crowned King of Paradise? Here we are, sitting beside your Olympic size swimming pool looking down into a lush valley which is punctuated by a pristine lake, Lake Batur, and both are framed by majestic, limestone cliffs to our right and far off on the horizon."

I grinned widely at the man of medicine beside me. A sublime comfort warmed the space between us whenever we conversed. There was a male meshing of sorts that dovetailed him to me and the mitered fit made both of us all the more strong.

"Michael, I know that you are getting on in years, so tell me, are you considering a mid-life crisis career change? Writing copy for travel brochures or composing passionate prose for greeting cards comes to mind. Your gift for hyperbole would break the best bullshit meter on the market!"

"To bullshit and its measurement meters, Dr. Rajawane…, and to the minions out there whose actions make the meters necessary."

We laughed loudly, clinked our first glasses of the day together and savored the downward scorch that a large gulp of scotch always delivered.

"Dismissing the King of Paradise notion, I must say that I do wake up most mornings wondering how fate and fortune, good or otherwise, put me here. I think that it is your fault completely Michael. Your bloody fault! I have made a pact with myself, you know, regarding my future. I must become more discerning regarding the friendships I allow to infiltrate my world and adversely affect me!"

"Well, better paradise, I think, than the postcard prose career you just proffered."

I replenished the ice and refilled both glasses, as we settled into our lounge chairs more comfortably. We both knew that there was much to discuss but we each came at the new creature of our creation with decidedly different agendas.

"So shoot, my learned man of medicine. What is looming large on the horizon of Bali High Art, as we speak?"

"I'll get to the mundane mechanics of the operation later. Let me start Michael by suggesting to you that the news of our new enterprise has not remained ours alone to savor for very long.

Mr. Tan's deteriorating health was monitored not only by you and me, but by others whose interest in the man was not humanitarian in nature. Case in point. Just yesterday an offer was received, the third one to date, to purchase the property. Most are addressed simply to 'The President', but reference is always made to you as the reigning decision maker. Just shows how far behind the times some people are, ha, ha! The point. The point is that the most recent proposal is for three times the amount bequeathed by the man who wished to cultivate and celebrate Asian art forms."

"Seventy-two million dollars! Are you kidding me, Dr. Rajawane?"

"The offer to purchase is on my desk. I'll show it to you later. Remember, it was you who told me, not that long ago, that Mr. Tan bought the place, way back when, for thirty cents on the dollar. Yes, from some shrimp farmer in Kalimantan who went bankrupt. I have asked around in Denpasar and seventy-five to one hundred million is quoted as the current market value of this property."

"Real estate developers. Men and their insatiable machines who want to establish a Bali North along the shore of a pristine, fresh water lake. They want to sub-divide the whole thing into postage stamp lots and build enormous houses on each one. A new millionaires' row in what is left of paradise. Is that about the size of it?"

"In a nut shell, yes. But it doesn't end there. Opportunists, whose pockets aren't quite so deep, are also perched near our window. Some are proposing just water front development while others see a hotel and condominium complex, over in the shadow of the cliffs as a fitting compliment to what they think we are all about.

All suitors, are, of course, suggesting that their projects will benefit Bali High Art through sustained revenue flow from the flood of interested buyers their projects will attract. So we could get on with our little artsy-craftsy fantasy in the alley ways that remain after they have finished!"

"Well, isn't that where artistic endeavor has always sought refuge and flourished in the past!"

The doctor looked at me askance.

"I have got to fly to Jakarta and soon. This fish we just landed has got to be secured to the deck. Tied down legally that is. It has taken on a life of its own, a new life that could prove harmful to others…, others who venture too close. Do you know what I mean, Michael?"

"People who are prepared to bribe are also prepared to bully. Yes, I think I do understand what you mean. Doctor, you are coming back with me to Jakarta. Tonight. I leave on the last plane out of here and you and I will be on that flight. And you will be staying in my house. It's empty and, ha, ha, I want, no, I need, trust me, I really need your company…, and your considered opinion on a rather important issue that has recently arisen."

"OK, no more of this. Let's not hold the knife to the grindstone too long. The blade is sharp enough. We are both in agreement then, as to what Bali High is all about, art for art's sake, and our modus operandi has been clear from the outset and it is not about to change either. Incorporation with all operational, including financial decisions, rendered by committee action exclusively. Right Michael!"

"I never argue with the professional opinion of a doctor, Doctor. Not in a hospital, nor here and not at my place of residence in Jakarta either! You're safe from censure with me, Dr. Rajawane! Just make sure that Indonesian law blesses everything you set in motion and that a well-marked paper trail follows in your wake."

I leaned over and gave the man beside me a nudge on the shoulder.

"OK, the soft issues in summary then. Well, from my standpoint at least, it is all roses. Mr. Tan's secretary, his former secretary, Rebecca, his only remaining daughter, is blossoming under the tutelage of my good wife, Edith. I do believe that she is enjoying her new found independence. Independence from me that is. We are both flying by the seat of our pants you know. And this time, I cannot protect myself from her by hiding behind medical jargon either!

I feel exposed and vulnerable. But that's what I signed on for. I wanted to see if this old man could still dance. Even though it's only a two-step shuffle, still, I am happy with the progress, our progress, to date.

Rebecca will be happy, by the way, to have someone under her, someone she can direct, someone to be her friend and confidant, someone like your Christina. Let her stay here as long as she likes Michael. The experience will be beneficial for both of them."

"Thank you Doctor. I will tell Christina that she is going to be able to help Mr. Tan's dream become a reality. She will like that. She will like that very much. She tried flapping her wings in the elementary school she briefly attended in the Turks and Caicos Islands, but was shot down in flames by the teacher. Another story for later on tonight, perhaps.

What about Siti's dad, Rocky. Dare I ask about him? I know I was enthusiastic, no, effusive in my comments about him to you...,"

Dr. Rajawane shifted slightly in his chair and looked straight at me.

"Well, you were wrong about Rocky. He is not cut out to be a project manager on a construction site. No, that did not work out to my satisfaction...! He is so much more than just that! He has been appointed to the position of senior project manager, let me stress, the man who is in charge of all the construction needed to make Bali High Art a reality.

He is competent, more than competent, and he is a people person in the best sense of the term. He has been instrumental in contributing greatly to the camaraderie that has come to define the players in our little enclave. And he is tireless in pursuit of his objectives. And his focus on the job at hand is contagious!

He is what this country, if it were just left alone, would be all about. He makes me proud to be Indonesian."

Even our drinks seemed to smile as our robust toast to the man caused the tawny liquids to slosh around wildly inside their crystal containers.

"Interesting Dr. Rajawane, that you should bring up the concept of Indonesian self-determination and the foreign meddling that thwarts it. Never mind the two military juntas that followed the Indonesian independence movement in 1946. I already know your opinion of those events; international financial interests, American, Middle Eastern and, I might add, Soviet, all aimed at the then President Sukarno. Remember, his invasion of East Timor? Successful only because of American complicity. More on that sensitive issue some other time too, maybe. No, the influence and interference of outsiders that is going on right now in Indonesia is what I need to talk to you about."

Dr. Rajawane's practiced medical mind raced ahead of my comment to potential implications. His placid face morphed into a mask which molded the deep creases in his cheeks and forehead into a frown. It was as though a patient had just inadvertently disclosed a symptom which, if not treated immediately, could prove fatal!

"You possess a certain capacity, you know, to put the issues of others in neat little word bags. Then you tie the top strings. And then you shunt them off to the end of the conversational table. And then, and then, you clutter that same table with your own, usually messy agenda. I think the current expression for someone like you is, 'a piece of work'!

So go ahead, Mr. Piece of Work. Go ahead and make my current issues seem almost paltry and pedestrian in comparison."

The Doctor smiled thinly at me knowing full well that I only gave him national barometer readings when immediate action, defensive, or restorative, was required. Implied calls to action that entailed, if not a degree of personal danger then certainly a strong element of discomfort.

It took mere seconds to give the good Doctor an abbreviated version of the problem facing Col. Satu and my darkest fears about him. My run-in with Jonathon in the Turks and Caicos, my knowledge of Brian Law and his helicopter safaris over Malacca and the maybe mysterious woman from the Middle East who seemed to be connected to the Dukun, Saladin, the man who had so devastated my security business partner, completed my pen, less paper, sketch.

I poured both of us fresh drinks as he pondered what I had disclosed.

"Not much patient history to build a diagnosis upon. Let's look a little closer at the two areas of sensitivity you mentioned. The San Francisco Bay area and the Strait of Malacca. Interesting. More so I think, if we reverse their order. What danger real or imagined, lurks in the waters between Indonesia and Malaysia that would be of concern to the Americans?"

"About forty percent of the world's commercial shipping uses that forty mile wide stretch of ocean to move bulk and container cargo. That's straight from the horse's mouth, the late Mr. Tan. Remember, he was the king of container transport with his now defunct Good Earth Distribution Company.

And just to loosen the strings on one bag of words over there, in the corner of the table, he was the gentleman who wished to buy his way into the kingdom above the clouds by infecting us with the Bali High virus. Just to keep the medical metaphor alive and well. Ha, ha!"

"Smart ass! Anyway, the Strait of Malacca. A choppy piece of salt water, as I recall, one that is shrouded in fog much of the time."

"And clogged with ships operating under every flag of convenience…, every Third World country that issues maritime registration certificates."

"The ports of call, the ports of call, to pick up or discharge cargo…, before entering the Strait from the west…, possibly the Middle East; Saudi Arabia, Yemen, Iran, maybe Pakistan, India, Bangladesh, with two of the last three possessing nuclear weapons…,"

"A nuclear devise detonated in or around San Francisco Bay would obliterate the whole region! And…, and I think that it could be even more devastating than that! Could such an explosion rupture some weakness in the San Andreas Fault and wreak havoc up and down the whole Pacific coast?"

"Not necessary. Destroying the Golden Gate Bridge would suffice. The American press and its shrill cries of impending Armageddon would register higher on the societal Richter Scale than any dislocation to the earth's tectonic plates that have created the so called, 'ring of fire'.

Remember, Americans are no more free than any other national group of people whose laws fill whole libraries. But Americans do have icons attesting to their freedom, liberty, and their pursuit of individual happiness."

"You are right, and the Bay bridge is only one of them. An individual or a group so inclined could attack any number of empty crosses scattered across the country and then wait for the social implosion that would follow.

Georgie, Tommy, Teddy and Abe, the Mount Rushmore boys could be on the list of icon irreplaceables. The Hoover Dam, the Statue of Liberty, with the broken chains of oppression at her feet, The Lincoln Memorial, even the White House, could be on an 'A' list!"

"And an attack on any or all of the structures you just mentioned could commence its final run out into the Pacific Ocean from the Strait of Malacca!"

"Christ. Do you know what time it is? We have got to go now Dr. Rajawane. Now, within the next twenty minutes, or we will be S.O.L., shit out of luck, for the last plane flying to Jakarta tonight."

While my friend scrambled back into the house to fill a suitcase and provide his wife with the list of needed 'musts' to bridge his three or four day absence, I searched around for Christina.

"Daddy, daddy look. I have my very, very own hard hat. See, yellow! Even it has my name on it, on the front. See. CHRISTINA! It is for me every time I go with Rebecca to where the men do the work. Rebecca is my bestest friend, you know. My bestest in Bali. But you…, you are still my bestest friend at home.

I gave my daughter a fist full of Indonesian rupias and some American money as well, just so she could treat her new, 'bestest' friend when they went to the nearby village. I reiterated how happy Mr. Tan would be to know that Rebecca was helping to make his dream on earth come true. And I added, with a wink and a nod, that he would be overjoyed to know that Christina, my daughter, was helping too!

We hugged briefly and she was gone. I watched her as she rejoined Rebecca and skipped away down toward where the water front condos, if some had their way, were to be located. The location that was lusted after by those nameless, faceless, others…, others with deep pockets…, others with deep motives as well!

The portent of my progeny, I thought. Christina would need less and less of me and more, so much more, of the stuff of the world which would make her, not merely my equal, but, sans my cynicism, my superior.

I allowed Dr. Rajawane to sleep during most of our flight. He needed his rest and the plane cabin was not the right venue for the continuation of our conversation.

"Michael, I can't thank you enough for your hospitality. Your guest room is marvelous, big, and with a view of the garden out back. Even has its own en suite bathroom."

"Well don't be intimated by the dust bunnies that have probably bred copiously during my absence. Are you hungry or will these cashews be enough?"

"Cashews will do just fine. I managed to eat whatever they served on the plane. Right now it's sitting like a bolus, lumpy mass in my stomach. I feel stuffed."

"Cognac, or will you stick with scotch on the rocks?"

"Scotch is fine, but only one. I have to have my wits about me tomorrow when I meet with the lawyers and the accountants. Why is it that the tort tellers and the bean counters always hide behind jargon. They're almost as bad as doctors!"

"You said that Doctor, not me!"

"OK, enough of this social banter. One last topic I want to talk to you about before we retire for the night and then go our separate ways tomorrow morning. Michael, what do you know of the Dukuns in Indonesia?"

"I have lived in your country long enough to know of their existence. I know what they do to young, impressionable girls. They, teary-eyed, have told me. And I know what they can do to superstitious, old men who should know better. Their modus operandi is very reminiscent of what I have read about snake oil salesmen and circus tent evangelists in North America about one hundred years ago. All smoke and mirrors. Exploitation of the weaknesses inherent in the human condition.

But remember, the man, the Dukun we are talking about, this man, Saladin, is not Indonesian by birth. He speaks the language but he is from somewhere in the Middle East. Hence my reference, when we talked earlier by the pool at Bali High, to foreign interference."

"What you just said stole all of my thunder. You know as much about that particular human sub-species as I do. All that is, except for one important fact.

You remember, I'm sure that you remember, the medical conference we attended a few years ago in Miami. Remember, I was a guest presenter and you were the representative of the sponsoring pharma house. I don't remember what I spoke about, some surgical procedure perhaps, and I don't remember who you represented either. Anyway, none of that matters. Excuse an old man and his ramblings.

Miami, yes Miami. We chartered a fishing boat during one of our 'off' days and the captain of the vessel took us far off shore claiming that the best fishing was in deep water. We both got terribly seasick and between us we managed to catch just one, eight pound dolphin. We took it back to the hotel and one of the chefs prepared it for us. Great meal!

The point, the point in all of this is, remember, we were told repeatedly, once the fish has taken the bait, do not allow any slack in the line, otherwise the only catch of the day would be our story of the one that got away.

Dolphins and Dukuns share that in common. So, whatever you plan to do with this Saladin character, once he knows that you have your hook in him, do not let him loose. Give him no wiggle room. No slack, until you succeed in getting from him what you want. Men like your Dukun are more slippery than eels. And some are very well connected in certain circles of power. Circles over which we, you and I, have no influence or control. Circles which could easily turn us from the hunters into the hunted.

Do I make myself clear Michael? Fishing or big game hunting, they are both the same. The easiest part of both is the kill. The hard part is what to do with the quarry once it is down, once it becomes a trophy."

"Like a woman, Dr. Rajawane. The easy part is the seduction. The hard part is the subsequent dislocation and necessary adjustment."

"Trust you to come up with an analogy that involves women! Seriously Michael. Be guided accordingly. Now, it is time for this old man to bid you adieu for tonight."

"Thank you Dr. Rajawane. I will not forget your advice. Oh, your house key will be on the kitchen counter in the morning. Come and go as you please and do avail yourself of whatever you can find in the fridge or the bottled fermentation vault just beside it.

I might be joining you tomorrow night for super but that cannot be guaranteed. If not, be neighborly, and call on Renee, my next door neighbor. I think that the two of you would enjoy each other's company."

The Doctor, shaking his head in paternal forbearance, disappeared down the hall.

I sprawled out on my bed and stared at the ceiling. Faint whispers of moon light danced off the surface of the pool outside creating a miniature, simple-silver, Aurora Borealis in one corner above my head.

God, how I missed my daughter cuddled in beside me. I missed her warmth, her even, contented breathing, even, her occasional twitches. Fetal-like, with her little hand cupped over my Adam's apple, she was my lightening rod, my safety blanket, an appendage that affected every nerve ending of my being.

I was in my 'there' and she was in some other 'there' that was very far away.

Chapter 12

The lizard kings of the world are Komodo dragons. Native to only a few, small islands in the Indonesian archipelago, they, like sharks, have survived every upheaval and natural disaster since the age of the dinosaur. Adaptation has not been necessary. They have, almost from the dawn of time it seemed, sat comfortably atop the food chain in their chosen environment.

Komodo dragons did not share space with other living things, they subtracted it from them.

And they were immune, more immune than most creatures at least, to human encroachment as well. Their skin, unlike that of the crocodile, alligator and snake, was laced with cartilage which created a chain-mail like weave over the entire body. It afforded the creatures protection from attack in the wild and it gave them a failing grade for the fashion industry.

Almost immune. Zoos in the tropics and those with temperature controlled environments, prized the beasts. They were crowd pleasers and with a life expectancy of twenty odd years, they were seen as a good investment.

One of the holding compounds for the captured reptiles, most were strategically positioned on the island of Java, was located close to Carita. A two hour plus drive, west, south-west from Jakarta, it was a sleepy little place in the shadow of the infamous resident of the Sunda Strait, the volcano, Anak Krakatau.

While there, the animals were fed, observed and medicated, as the need arose, for about a month. Then they were shipped off as comatose cargo to the highest bidder.

The Carita Komodo compound was a rectangle measuring approximately seventy feet by one hundred feet. And it was surrounded by uninterrupted, fifteen foot high, cinder block walls. It was topped by the ubiquitous Indonesian finishing touch; broken glass and barbed wire anchored in concrete. It kept what was inside, in, and the curious outside, always outside.

The only access to the enclosure was through two, heavy timber, locked doors which were hinged to open outward on to a rutted, dirt road. A pathway cut through the dense brush would have been a more accurate description of the connection to the outside world.

When unlocked and with its doors swung open, the visitor was treated to the dark, tunnel-like interior of a discarded ship container. It was foul smelling and cluttered, like a suburban garage, with all manner of rusted and grease covered junk.

A narrow gage set of steel tracks ran the full length of the container floor and continued out into the pen for a distance of about fifteen or twenty feet. A platform made of planks was affixed to a metal frame to which miniature railroad wheels on axles had been attached. The Keystone Cop vehicle rested astride the rails, at the ready, to run a new arrival into the jail or usher an established resident out to continue its long life of incarceration somewhere else.

The container had been positioned snugly, at right angles, to the wall which ran along the edge of the road. The end of the steel box that jutted in toward the middle of the compound was outfitted with two, padlocked doors composed of vertical steel bars welded to thick hinged metal frames. They provided what, at first glance, appeared to be scant security against the roaming scaly residents with the lethal jaws.

Also at the entrance to the fortress, a second derelict container of the same size had been secured. It was perched atop its brother, at right angles to it. From the end sections and along both sides of the elevated container, rectangular, window sized torch cuts had been made.

Crude, irregular awnings had been fashioned for each window by heating and hammering the flaps that remained attached along the tops of the window cuts. Bent up and away from the container walls, they provided, in turn, shelter from the tropical sun and a modicum of protection against the torrential, seasonal rains.

Water would have pooled everywhere in the rocky compound during the rainy season. But to ensure that the beasts had adequate drinking water during the four or five months of near drought, an orange, sun bleached, one thousand five hundred liter water tank sat at the ready.

Perched along the top of the wall in one corner, it was supported by two, parallel metal beams which put it out of reach of the creature inside. When needed, the tank spigot was set to drip continuously into a shallow, cement basin which was positioned directly below it. It was about the size of a child's wading pool.

The upper container served both as office and observation post. A tight, metal, spiral staircase provided interior access to this guard tower, to view the roaming refugees from a different planet who, periodically, rummaged about down below. Night light was provided by multiple, glass chimneyed, kerosene lamps and a few flash lights.

A chemical toilet replete with a curtain for privacy was nestled in one corner of the top container. Irregular cleaning, I was told, merely involved deftly walking along the foot wide side wall to a corner, usually while the beast was asleep, and dumping the contents of the 'honey pot' over board. Maybe on unsuspecting passers-by or maybe not!

Two mature, almost skeletal, fruit trees, avocado perhaps, or guava, and a crude, brush covered wooden lean-to completed the stage setting.

The place was macabre. It looked like it had been fashioned by an adolescent, one who had decided to create a world taken from the pages of a novel by Stephen King.

Given my intent, the place was perfect.

The two custodians of the single Komodo dragon that was currently in residence, had been asked to visit the town of Carita for a few hours. Sufficient rupiahs changed hands to ensure that their stay would be longer than requested.

We paid them double the going rate for the yearling goat they had tethered inside the lower container. It saved us the time and the trouble of going back to Carita to purchase one from a farmer.

The two locals, overjoyed by their serendipitous good fortune, were told that we wished to take a few camera shots, for promotional purposes, of the animal held in captivity. We implied that we were complying with a personal directive from the leader of the country himself, President Suharto. The bigger the lie, the more credible it was, it seemed…, in some circles at least!

Saladin had been easier to capture, subdue and transport to Carita than any of his reptilian counterparts had ever been.

All I had done was make one telephone call to a man named Perulian. All I had said, to push his start button, was that the life of Col. Satu had been placed in danger by the man whom I wished delivered to me in Carita.

Perulian was a man in his middle to late thirties. He was, what I termed, the director of field operations for Colonel Satu.

He, and the rest of the men in the platoon sized outfit commanded by the Colonel, felt that their leader had provided them lives, lives of adventure that were worth living. To a man, they also believed that the Colonel had saved them from certain death on multiple occasions. Their analyses of events however, never went to causation. To their way of thinking the Colonel never made mistakes. He was revered, almost worshiped by his followers. They subscribed to the same tradition enjoyed by Napoleon and Robert E. Lee. Waterloo and Gettysburg notwithstanding!

Perulian's strong suit was tactics and, like anyone holding a fist full of spades, he was devoid of any inkling of the 'heart' of most operational matters in which he assumed an active role. The man possessed no strategic sense whatsoever. The 'how' always trumped the 'why' in his mind. Once he received a command however, not only was it completed smartly but with a high degree of creative flare as well.

The word 'Perulian', had too many syllables, so his friends and associates, including those who reported to him called him Mr. 'P'. Only the Colonel and I used the moniker 'Pearly' when speaking with him. It was a nick-name which, when delivered by either of us, prompted the man to visibly swell with pride.

I had given Pearly the name and description of the man I wanted to be delivered, unhurt, to Carita. I provided his address, and a request for one of the man's finest, traditional Middle Eastern, dress outfits, a white one preferably, that a quick search of his closet would provide.

No harm was to come to the man and that rule applied to anyone else in the house, especially the pembantu, the maid. Stealth, speed, and a clean crime scene were, as always, paramount.

The car containing the prize stopped abruptly in front of the compound. Supported on each side by men dressed in jungle camouflage, the hooded hostage, whose hands were tied behind his back, was hustled into the lower container. In one fluid motion, he was lifted onto the rail carriage and his legs and chest were buckled to a spindle chair by three inch wide freight straps. Only then was his hood removed. Only then did it become clear that his silence was not based on surrender but on a pink sequined dog collar that held a red ball, about the size of a plum, securely in his mouth.

Saladin squinted and blinked as his pupils fought to adjust to the spotlight in the sky. All five of his captors, including myself, donned nylon stocking masks.

'Did you get a good look at any of your captors?'- 'Could you identify any of them?', would be met, should a police interview occur, with the same blank stare.

Pearly gestured to his associates to release the young goat into the compound, close and lock the gates behind it, and railroad the flat-car up against the vertical bars.

"This show is for you. This show is just for you. You watch this show very carefully." Pearly spoke slowly. He delivered the message much as one would to a child or to a neophyte student of bahasa Indonesia. He loomed over the man until he received a nod of comprehension from him. Pearly stood up, winked at me and silently made his way back to watch the event from the safety and relative comfort of my vantage point.

"Mr. Michael, I will explain the thing in the mouth of the crazy man later. It is part of crazy clothes costume we find in the closet of him when we got the special ones you wanted of him. I know that you do not want him dead. I have plan to make him better than dead. You will see later. Yes, this Mr. Saladin man will be better than dead. You wait. You will see. More than dead. You will see."

Pearly grinned widely at me. It was the perverse smirk of a high school kid who had figured out a way to sabotage the car of a teacher for whom he had a particular dislike.

Almost as an after-thought, Pearly took in a deep breath and tugged hard at something stuck behind the belt holding up his trousers. The bent dossier that he quickly shoved in my direction prompted me to wrap my arms around the man, lift him off the ground and kiss him through the nylon mask on both cheeks.

"Maybe this is good for you Mr. Michael. Always I look under the bed of target prisoner when I visit his house."

The circle containing the profile of the scowling head of a bald eagle positioned above a rendition of the compass rose was all I needed to see. Pearly had just handed me the prize that I sought. For a moment I considered calling off the continuation of the plan. Who needed to witness a man voiding himself! Who needed the pending theatre of a man, dressed like a lost soul who had found himself while roaming through the wilderness, in a hotel room with the Colonel, in parade perfect, faux uniform!

The sooner I returned to Jakarta, armed with the ammunition that I now possessed, the sooner I could settle accounts with Mr. Brian Law.

But the Colonel, alone and badly wounded on the battle field, could not be abandoned. Particularly when our gagged clown was the sole possessor of the field dressing he needed. The play became the thing!

"Pearly, I trust in your judgment to complete this operation perfectly. I know that Col. Satu could not have chosen a better man to guarantee his personal safety. Now look, here is what you have to tell Mr. Saladin after he has seen the show with the Komodo dragon.

You were very effective to talk to our prisoner. You waited until you got him to give you a sign that he understood what you said to him.

Make sure that this time before you take him to the hotel in Carita that you get the same signal from him. He must understand what you want him to do completely. This time, make him repeat back to you what you told him he must do. Our success with this prisoner, our success to save the life of Col. Satu will depend on that.

OK! Now here is what you must say to him…"

The kid goat jumped and frolicked about the compound in unbound ecstasy. The animal's every fiber celebrated its new found freedom. I was reminded of a calf when first let out of the stall in a barn into the unbridled pleasure of brilliant sunshine and the Spring fed, abundant, green grass. How macabre, how poignantly poetic I thought, given the inevitably of the events that were about to unfold. The final meal of a condemned man came to mind.

Pearly was a quick study. I had only to repeat the message twice to get the grin of comprehension that I needed.

'Better than dead!' I was intrigued by what the man had in mind for Mr. Saladin.

A lifeless man would have been a liability. A shallow grave close by the compound, disposal at sea, both carried the risk of being witnessed or discovered. Both carried the potential for dots being connected.

Death in Indonesia and the subsequent burial rituals that ensued were as diverse and drenched in drama as the country itself. Disposal of the deceased required strict adherence to the religious doctrine that had defined the individual while he or she had been more quick than dead.

Muslims were buried within twenty four hours of their passing. Not unlike Jews in the rest of the world. Both the Koran and the Old Testament of the Bible endorsed, in fact, demanded adherence to that holy directive. It was the only way to thwart the rapid onset of rot in very hot, almost always humid climates.

And, for faithful Muslims, at least one pilgrimage to Mecca during their life time provided the assurance of one opportunity to traverse the seven layers that separated them from Allah. Women were equal players in the game of 'eternity' but only with the help of the steroid, progesterone. Disqualification was the price they paid if menstruation got between them and Mohammad.

The more frequent the hajj to Mecca, the greater the chance of celestial reward. A sort of lottery to liberate the soul! The more you played the greater the likelihood of winning! And the rich, the frequent flyers in life, enjoyed, as always, a favored position.

Hindus, especially on the island of Bali, were all about samsara or rebirth, and escape from worldly desire. They strove to attain maksha or salvation. They sought the Devine force as their ultimate reality. They had their remains, amid flowers and burning incents, committed to a funeral pyre. When their financial circumstances, or those of the family, permitted.

In rural areas, shallow graves, marked by small stone borders, temporary plots which always attracted frenzied, barking dogs, kept lower caste members under wraps, so to speak, until a wooden set design of death could be purchased.

Christians, whose faith was based on the embrace of a loving God through His hybrid Son, were the least inclined, it seemed, to have their remains depart the pain and sorrow of this world.

The Christian residents of Sulawesi, were, more often than not, drained of all bodily fluids and pumped full of formalin to defeat, or at least deflect the universal law of nature to reclaim its own. This allowed for two or three days, perhaps even a week, of viewing the remains by relatives and friends. The nostrils of the deceased were plugged with balls of cotton and the mouth along with the other end of the digestive tract were corked. This was done to thwart the odor which would attend any seepage of the corpse's final fixative.

Some even had large, white, almost garden sized gloves fitted over their hands as they rested in permanent slumber. For the same reason perhaps, that the Queen of the World, at one time, not the Virgin Mary, not even the Virgin Queen of England, that was Elizabeth 1, no, Queen Vicky Victoria herself, had the salute of her sailors changed from an open palmed check to the side of the head to a palm raised to the temple parallel to the deck.

Apparently she, like the heavenly host, did not wish to view the callused hands of those who had toiled ceaselessly in her service, more precisely in servitude, as they fought God's good fight against sin, manned her ships of war and, in that duel process, gave brutal meaning to the hymn, 'Onward Christian Soldiers', in every corner of the world.

One final fact of life, not unlike an epilogue, followed many Christians, especially self-styled blue bloods, the old aristocracy in Indonesia, even in death. Central Sulawesi was a region pockmarked by limestone caves. The interior of the caves was always cool and dry save for occasional rain seepage through the mountain of rock above. Over time, many shelf or platform like indentations had been created inside the caves and they afforded the dead, an exalted, mausoleum-like final resting place. They also created conditions for a final and permanent traffic jam.

Coffin chaos resulted when too many of the flimsy, balsa wood or veneered cardboard boxes were forced into too limited a space. As with auto bumper benders caused by impatience and speed on fog shrouded roads, the ends of most of the coffins suffered similar fates. Their dented and smashed condition was due to the desire of the pall-bearers to reach their destination, deposit the departed, and then withdraw as quickly as possible.

Multiple collisions occurred every time a new box was added to the cluttered, dead space. This caused many of the coffin lids to separate and fall away from the box containing the deceased.

Anyone who visited the caves, in remembrance of the departed or as part of a tourist trek, was confronted by a scene that prompted a certain gallows humor. All denizens of the caves, dressed in their best, Sunday-go-to-church clothes, were decidedly dead. Their sunken facial features and leathery skin left no doubt as to their condition. But they, especially the men, had had their chests festooned with cigarettes and rupiahs of various small denominations by relatives and friends either prior to or during the funeral service.

It seemed clear, to some of the living at least, that the deceased, before reaching the Pearly Gates, would encounter vendors of cheap food such as nasi goreng, fried rice, or chicken sate perhaps. Presumably the implied logic was that one would best be able to mount a persuasive argument concerning one's eligibility for inclusion in the select coterie of saved sinners on a full stomach!

And to further assist the departed prior to pleading their cases before the stern St. Peter, it was thought to be prudent, or at least practical, to have a cigarette or two, at the ready, to pluck up one's courage.

If being undead was not the same as being alive, as one wag put it, then being stone cold dead did not necessarily dampen all desire!

The beast emerged from its 'lean-to' lair at the far end of the enclosure. It was large. As it approached the ship container it became very large. Its serpentine, after-birth, like tongue forked the air like a divining rod. Flies, green bodied flies, the kind attracted to decaying flesh, buzzed around the animal's mouth which was slightly ajar.

The playful kid, oblivious to the appearance of its fellow inmate, raced around the yard, stopped abruptly and frequently nibbled at the clumps of grass below its hooves. It jumped straight up and kicked its hind legs out much as any exuberant creature in love with living might. Then it resumed the race against its shadow following a route that only it recognized. The animal could not get enough of its new, its very own play pen.

Initially, the adult male Komodo, looked like some mechanical monster featured in a 'B' grade, sci-fi thriller. But only at first. The giant lizard not only demanded its own space, but it almost seemed to annex the space of all else, living or dead, which was in the enclosure with it!

As it approached the containers, its low slung, flat skull, like that of a crocodile, seemed to be framed by disproportionately massive shoulders and legs. One leg swung out and forward, as though it was tracing part of the arc of a circle. Slowly and deliberately, in true reptilian fashion, the one leg was then followed by the sweep of the other. The creature appeared to be controlled by some fiendish puppeteer who had not quite mastered the fluid motion of regular leg movement.

Three elements dispelled the notion that we were witnessing the display of some ill adapted, plodding, innocuous land creature. Sharp, black claws, measured in multiple inches, limply folded back as the animal shifted its weight from one leg to the other. They automatically returned to support the beast at the last instant as the animal moved forward.

Viscous, whitish drool hung in long, lethal, glutinous strands from both sides of the beast's mouth. It was clear that the dragon had no control over the constant flow.

Every few seconds the pinkish, gray protrusion would appear between the upper and lower jaw. Looking more, when close up, like a portion of an internal organ harvested at autopsy, the devil-like divining rod gave the animal the ability to sense…, to feel the presence of the prize it sought.

Saladin squirmed in his chair and looked away in horror.

One of the Colonel's men jumped up between the man and the beast beyond the bars. He slapped Saladin across the face and screamed, 'lihat', watch! To emphasize his command, he pinched both nipples of the man and did not let go until the squealing, squirming prisoner complied.

At first, the kid thought that it had been joined by a playmate.

It scampered about in front of its new found friend almost daring it to a game of tag. The monster was unperturbed, even by the noise that had just come from inside the darkened metal box. Its forward advance quickened until it was within a couple of feet of its prey. Then it stopped.

The young goat, not knowing the game that the dragon wanted to play, attempted to leap away to safety. The Komodo swung its head at the moving target but missed the youngster as it bound past him. The beast missed the main target, but won the contest all the same. The dragon's teeth penetrated the lower part of the goat's hind leg, breaking it immediately with a loud snap.

The short, happy life of the kid goat, just like that of Hemingway's, Francis Macomber, was at an end. The big game hunter was shot dead by his wife after affirming his manhood in the face of a charging beast while the innocent yearling was doomed to defeat by the same poisonous force of a capricious nature.

Whether the poison was from the mixed cocktail of the fifty or so bacteria, some virulent, in the monster's mouth, or from a neurotoxin contained in its slimy drool was a moot point. The stricken animal, robbed of its speed and agility, was defenseless. It would lie down, paralysis would set in and it would be devoured.

The Komodo would wait. It knew that dinner, or at least the hors-d'oeuvres, would soon be served.

It turned its attention to the bleating creature that inhabited the darkened space on the other side of the metal bars. It, unlike the kid goat, smelled of fear, it seemed to be immobile and, best of all, it was tantalizingly close.

The lizard rammed its snout into the steel bars causing the whole container to shake. Everyone inside, save Saladin, grabbed at something metal for support.

Its darting, tentacle-like tongue came within inches of the strapped down man in the chair. Unsuccessful in its attempt to simply barge through the barrier between it and the prize, it tried to scale the annoyance that stood between it and food.

Supported by its large, long tail, it deftly mounted the end of the container. Our view of the yard and the small, stricken animal in it was completely obliterated. Only the weight of the beast kept it from climbing any further up the end of the container. The smell that assailed our nostrils from the spread eagled creature above us was as pungent, as choking, as any that came from the slime which bloomed in an unattended fish tank.

What I was witnessing, I knew, was a major factor that contributed to the survival of the species. Young Komodo dragons lived high up in trees and ate whatever climbed or crawled up and along the seemingly protective limbs.

Adult Komodo dragons were cannibals. Komodo dragons would eat their young if the opportunity arose. Only their mature weight kept them from climbing up and consequently bringing down their own species on the planet.

Finding no easy access to the distressed creature inside, the dragon slowly descended from its preying-mantis position. The climb and subsequent return to earth worked on the animal's digestive tract. Like a cat gagging up a fur ball, the reptile coughed clear the black and white casting which was composed of recent victim's three, distinctive 'H's'.

Hooves, hair, and horns! The remnants of the beast's previous meal. The resulting odor which filled our airless enclosure was worse, far worse than that of a child's vomit in the family car. Much worse!

Everyone, save the prisoner, scrambled away from the bars which seemed alive with the gastric discharge.

The creature ambled slowly toward the kid goat. The yearling had chosen to, or, more likely, partial paralysis had forced it to lie down in the middle of the compound about twenty feet beyond our protective bars.

The beast stabbed its tongue out toward its young prey and, without warning, lunged forward and snapped its jaw shut on the soft underbelly which was exposed.

The kid blinked once or twice at the enemy as its head and upper body twitched and fell back toward the ground.

The teeth of the dragon were such that no escape was ever possible. Triangular in shape, the anterior portion of each tooth was set in the jaw at right angles to it and the posterior edges, with about a sixty degree slope, were razor sharp and serrated from top to bottom.

And like a shark, the beast possessed multiple rows of teeth buried below the gum line that were at the ready to replace broken or missing ones.

The dragon allowed the portion of the first bite that contained the lower bowel and its fecal contents to fall to the ground in a fountain-like spray of grey, gluey saliva. Then it gulped down the remainder of the first torn piece of flesh. Not more than a half dozen raggedly ripped bites would be needed to completely devour the goat.

The Komodo dragon was the perfect killing machine. It was even better positioned in nature than the great white shark. The salt water predator had to avoid the frequent menace posed by killer whales and drag-net, floating fisher factories of humans. The Komodo knew no such enemies.

The goat would soon disappear without a trace and it would disappear as well without ritual aimed at its reincarnation or redemption. How fortunate for the young kid, I thought.

I gestured to Pearly to follow me back to the front door of the compound.

"It is not necessary for our prisoner to see everything the Komodo will do to the goat. Maybe, he has seen enough to be effective. Remember, he cannot be nervous when he talks to Col. Satu. Only he must be effective. Very effective. This is something for you to decide. I will go now because I have very important meeting in Jakarta with the man who wishes to have the papers you find under the bed of Saladin.

You do very good job with this operation, Pearly. I will say this to the Colonel when I see him tomorrow in Jakarta. Yes, I will say this to him about you!"

I lifted the mask to expose my mouth, feigned a snarl, and imitated the first bite of the beast on Pearly's forearm. I stood back, grinned at the man, shook his hand and embraced him. Then I was gone.

Chapter 13

It was a relief to remove the nylon stocking from my head. The stale air in the container had conspired with my own expired breath to create a miniature global warming effect that was more than just a little uncomfortable.

After leaning my head out of the moving car for a few minutes, like some car-sick kid, I wedged myself in the corner of the back seat with my newly acquired reading material.

"Mas, mas, cepat, cepat!" It was the only expression in bahasa Indonesia that I knew to get the driver to develop and deploy a lead foot.

There was something wrong with the dossier that I held in my hand. Dead wrong! The Duo Tang cover was made in the USA. The brand name and the country of manufacture were stamped into the back cover in the lower right hand corner. Credibility ended there.

Everything printed on the cover and on the inside pages was mere mock up. A crude rendition of the circular emblem of the CIA adorned the front cover. But it had been photocopied and an attempt at color enhancement of the bald eagle had been done by hand. It was a crude caricature of the real thing.

The gobbledygook on the twenty or so pages inside had been lifted, randomly, from various journals and monthly publications. Mastheads and page numbers had been scissored away prior to photocopying.

The Economist, with its penchant for dispensing with 'ed' in favor of 't', misspelt its way through the first few pages of the hoax. Their prognostications concerning the North American housing market, religious strife in the Middle East, and insurgent activity in the Balkans might have been of interest to self-styled erudite audiences but it was definitely not the stuff of CIA confidential reports.

Pages from a tourist brochure touting the scenic pleasures to be experienced on the island of Sumatra had been included as well. Irrelevant bar and line graphs had been taped over the photographs which had pock marked the article.

Even a few pages from an article published in The National Review were included. Pages professing the rightness of the American presence in Viet Nam, post French occupation, as the bulwark against the spread of communism, had Bill Buckley written all over them. Ironically, the man's preference for slouching, almost slithering, in a seat rather than sitting on it, when being interviewed, became a metaphor for the sloppiness of thought that his circumlocution and pedantry projected.

Great hegemonic mumbo-jumbo, but decidedly not part of a CIA blueprint for a covert operation either.

It was obvious that any print material lying about in the creator's hotel room had been incorporated into the jumble of thoughts and ideas contained in the Colonel's precious portfolio.

This was not code for anything. There had been no need for a coded blue print of the South East Asian adventure. The operatives were few in number and their task, as I understood it, was exploratory, hence innocuous.

It was bait. And it had worked. They gambled that the Colonel would not even have bothered to open the Malacca memorandum. And they were right. He had simply followed Saladin's instructions to secure and deliver the rubbish to him for safekeeping.

As I flipped through the last few pages, a thin, white piece of paper fell to my lap. It was a sales slip. It was in the amount of twenty-four thousand rupiahs, about twelve dollars, and it was dated one week prior to my run-in with Jonathon, the cork screw, king fisher, in the Turks and Caicos Islands.

The sales receipt was from Media-Asia, a chain of stores with formidable square footage which operated across the Indonesian archipelago. All large population centers had at least one outlet occupying space on their commercial landscape.

The company specialized in stationery supplies, photocopying services, and books: fiction, non-fiction and school texts. Always a beehive of activity, the buzzing drones it attracted seemed to be mainly students and secretaries. The latter group was regularly charged by their companies with procuring copious copies of professional looking sales brochures, business proposals, minutes of executive meetings, as well as training manuals. All with rapid turn-around times.

The former, moneyless, group spent most of their time aimlessly walking the aisles. Media-Asia was the most popular, highest volume, book store in the country. From the technical to the trite, from the language of Shakespeare to the word spoken on Indonesian streets, it catered to all tastes and abilities and budgets.

Media-Asia was a constant source of consternation, particularly among the foreign, self-styled intellectual elite in attendance at back yard yawns or restaurant rendezvous. The disconnected and discontented wives of expats, those who reinvented themselves as star reporters on human interest assignments in South East Asia, felt that they had been summoned by fate to release the creativity that had remained dormant within them for too long. They believed that their Bachelor of Arts degrees in English Lit, or History, or Psychology, or Sociology from some liberal arts factory back home, equipped them to write knowingly and convincingly about that which they knew very little.

'How-To' booklets for new arrivals in Indonesia, and dilettante dabbling into 'quaint' customs and mannerisms of the indigenous populations, abounded. Once vetted, to ensure that no slight could be construed regarding the reign of President Suharto in particular and the Imams, the religious men who controlled the Holy Koran, in general, an agreement was struck for the publication of an initial run of a few hundred copies. The commitment was made for a second run if and when the initial printing sold out.

Payment, at a buck a copy, was made in advance, to the author for the initial trial run. No more money ever changed hands. Media-Asia management claimed that client interest was insufficient to merit a second run of the booklet. Without spotters in centers like Surabaya, Bandung, Medan, Ujung Pandang, Denpasar, and Yogyakarta, the hapless authors had no grounds for argument. Sales, less payment for intellectual property rights, almost always remained brisk and lucrative long after the initial print run.

The Colonel claimed to know two characters in Jakarta whose financial focus and success, was predicated on book theft. Nothing so simple as spiriting texts from the shelves of retailers, however. Nothing that primitive.

Twice every year, so his story went, the young men of his acquaintance would travel to Los Angeles where they maintained an apartment. They would buy the Sunday edition of the New York Times and, in the literary section, consult the best seller lists. One would focus on fiction while the other specialized in non-fiction. Armed with a suit case filled with purchased copies of their selections from the published lists, they would, after playing tourist for a few days, return home.

Some of the thinner volumes in their cache would morph, via poor translation, into local offerings. But with the majority of the works, nothing would be changed. The books would just appear on the shelves of Media-Asia and the claim, 'Best Seller' would always occupy a prominent position on the dust jacket. Profit, less mere production and distribution costs, so the Colonel's story went, was the hallmark of the business model used by both supplier and retailer in the cozy partnership.

Intellectual property rights and patent protection were foreign concepts in a country where one's final academic standing could be enhanced considerably through the purchase of a course text book in Singapore. That island state knew only Western notions of the high road to academic achievement.

The text book would be presented to the school lecturer in Indonesia, as a 'gift', to replace the crude photocopy he or she, and every student in the class, was using. And that exercise in largesse would land the gifting-but-not-so-gifted student a 'B+' rather than a 'C-', the grade which was deserved, based on actual academic performance.

Media-Asia was the perfect place to have a mock-up of any print material reproduced. Clean, crisp copies could be printed quickly. Clean, crisp copies could be printed without any evidence of actual origin.

Brian Law's booklet had been bait. And it had worked. And I felt the distinct embarrassment, the anger, the discomfort of having been the one who had struck at and been hooked by it!

Mr. Law and his little lawless gang had had no interest in Col. Satu whatsoever. They had hired him as their security wall just as a means of getting to me. They had known that any danger that befell the old man would prompt my immediate return to his side, regardless of where I was or what I was doing. My special relationship with the Colonel was common knowledge in some circles.

CIA interest in me was, however, another story. It had been created, no doubt, by the prompted, no, the paid for ramblings of old man Whitehead. He was the illusion dwelling, Walter Mitty lawyer in Singapore, the lawyer in Singapore who had a very well-developed taste for the 'S and M' side of life.

As a trusted friend of the family, he had been engaged as executor of the Tan estate. He believed that he had a vested interest, an intimate vested interest, in not only delivering the details of Mr. Tan's largesse to the waiting recipients, but of being included in that select, 'beneficiary' group himself.

The poor man believed that he was the biological father of Geoffrey Tan. Geoffrey was Mr. Tan's only male child and sole heir to the family fortune. Mrs. Tan had pre-deceased her husband by mere months. A complicated situation to be sure, but commonplace among the wealthy in South-East Asia.

One step at a time, I said to myself. Stay focused on immediate issues. At least the Colonel was off the hook. I knew that Pearly would ensure that the Colonel returned home safely and that some degree of normalcy would ensue. That was something at least!

Attention had to be paid to loose-lipped Whitehead on the other side of the Strait of Malacca. Pearly's pronouncement about Saladin came back to me. Better than dead, I will make him better than dead! The red ball gag in Saladin's mouth! I knew exactly what that meant and I knew then that Whitehead would be made to suffer a similar fate to that of the Dukun from the Arabian Peninsula.

Taste buds, a person's taste buds, a person's ability, a person's desire, to savor and celebrate life, render the physical senses inoperative through head games, and you render your quarry, defenseless. You reduce your victim to a level of despair such that willingness to truncate their life holds the most meaning.

Retribution would have to wait though. Brian Law was too far down the food chain to pose any real threat. Saladin was dead a thousand times over. The dragon and the pink and red ball gag had seen to that. I needed those who were still waiting in the wings. I needed those whose promptings from the sidelines propelled others. I needed the big fish, those that swam in the depths.

I was beginning to develop an inkling as to what it was that these yet unseen, shadowy players were really after. I shuddered at the thought of the potential they represented for poisonous impact on the fledgling enterprise called Bali-High Art.

* * *

I decided to busy myself in a corner of the Hilton hotel lobby that was far removed from but still within view of the elevators. Thirty minutes of watching the vertical game of slow motion, people tennis served up no sign of Howdy Doody, the wooden headed marionette from Malacca. Don't wait for Mohammad or the mountain, I thought. Go and get both of them, yourself!

The name of the front desk person whose smile banished all boredom with the forty-love elevator game I had been a spectator to, was Leni. Her pinned name, which was affixed to the lapel of her blue blazer, said so.

Leni's call to Brian Law's room to politely indicate that a gentleman with a file folder was waiting to see him in the lobby, was met by a voice which was hostile in the extreme. Somewhat shocked and taken aback, she instinctively held the receiver away from her ear to avoid the discomfort of the decibel assault.

"Tell him to wait. Tell him just to…, to just wait in the lobby. Tell him I will meet him in the lobby. I will be down stairs in about thirty minutes. Do you think that you can manage to tell him that! And do not, I repeat, do not bother me again!"

"Leni, this is for you. I heard what just happened and you did nothing to deserve the bad manners of Mr. Law. Let me apologize to you for his unnecessary outburst.

You handled it very professionally. Congratulations young lady. You are made of the right stuff. I am going to tell your boss, Mr. Haryanto, that you are very good at the front desk of the Hilton Hotel."

I grinned widely as I shook her hand and passed a folded US twenty dollar bill into her palm. I turned and walked away before the woman had a chance to respond to me or the money.

The little piece of theatre which I had just witnessed triggered my memory of the strategy which had been chosen many times for opening day of deer hunting season when the big game tag I had in my pocket was valid for buck or doe.

Antlers would have to wait. They were the crown signifying woodland royalty, no doubt, but sinking one's teeth into a delicious roast of venison, one which a young doe would provide, would make for a much more gratifying experience. And a doe, forced out in the open by the ever weary male, would appear first. And the doe I was expecting would know more about the buck and his habits than he probably did himself!

I was not disappointed. Saladin's house mate came striding out of the elevator, alone, as though her name had just been proclaimed by a liveried town crier in the midst of a phalanx of trumpeters.

Feigning total concentration on the cover of the Duo Tang folder held in front of my face, I collided with the woman as she wove around the empty conversation clusters of chairs which were positioned between her and the front doors.

The force of the impact sent her sprawling into one of the cushioned chairs. Great timing on my part, I thought, as I rushed to her assistance.

"Maaf Ibu, so sorry. Are you alright?"

Before the woman had a chance to respond, I leaned forward and, within licking distance of her face, recited the lines that had come to me seconds earlier.

"Salah ad-Din, the first sultan of Egypt and Syria died with only one piece of gold in his hand.

The wealth of this world remains with no one.

We will meet again to talk about your Sultan of Egypt, Mr. Salah ad-Din."

I was out the front doors before the woman had a chance to completely right herself in the lobby chair, let alone digest what had just been delivered to her face. I knew that all she needed to hear was the non-Western pronunciation of the name of the Sunni Muslim warrior and leader who had lived in the twelfth century.

For the second time, in the space of thirty minutes, I gave away a crisp, engraved likeness of Andrew Jackson to another Indonesian of merit. The Bluebird taxi that had just disgorged its revelers at the front steps of the hotel, had provided my perfect getaway. The skinny, chain smoking driver had known every short cut to the address I had given him. He broke the land speed record that previously had belonged to Pearly and the Colonel's gang of speedsters.

The front gate had been left unlocked and the looming, two story, house at the end of the driveway, was in total darkness. It appeared that no one was home. Maybe the abduction earlier that day had been enough to prompt a temporary evacuation of the place.

I hoped that my short history lesson, delivered in the lobby of the Hilton, would change that!

The occupants were probably Muslim so there was no need to worry about a barking dog. But the presence of a maid, whose quarters would have been at the rear, would have been problematic. No sense traumatizing the poor creature twice within the same half day. Maybe she had been given the rest of the day off to be with friends. A little thin on likelihood and too thick on hope I thought as I scanned the ground level windows which were situated on both sides of the door.

In their haste to get away from the Saladin crime scene, I hoped that no one had thought to activate any electronic security system the place might have had. Why lock the gate after the horse has bolted, my mother used to say.

One of the shuttered windows responded to my gentle push and I was inside. Perched on the window sill, I removed my shoes and slowly lowered myself to the floor.

With the folder in my belt, Pearly style, and my shoes dangling from my forked fingers, I stood and waited for my eyes to adjust to the dark interior of the place.

There was no need. The head lights of a car entering the property bathed the interior in more than enough light to easily make my way from the study, to the main foyer and up the stairs to the bedrooms.

I chose the second room on my right just as the lights downstairs came on and the conversation between a man and a woman ended. The choice was a lucky one. Ladies underwear thrown in a heap at the side of the door and cosmetics that littered every flat surface which stood on legs told me I was in the room of the woman of interest.

I closeted myself in the walk-in apartment which was reserved for satin and chiffon from every corner of the fashion world. The air in the garment grotto, was awash in a sea of sibling rivalry fragrances. French and Italian in origin, all, and fortune makers all, for the Houses that held their patents, no doubt!

The woman who entered the room was very distraught. It was Brian's bedmate to be sure. My quarry paced back and forth anxiously as she shed and trampled on her layers of social identity. It had taken her mere seconds to morph, sullen and self-absorbed, into a model waiting for her cue to pose for a Victoria's Secret lingerie collection shoot.

It took me the same amount of time to fumble and feel for an appropriate piece of clothing. I removed it from the hanger and stepped out, with a terry cloth robe in hand, from behind the door.

"It's time to talk. Now it's time to talk about your friend, Mr. Salah ad-Din. But first, you need to put on more clothes."

The woman grabbed at her chest and shrieked in abject fright. She glanced over toward the table beside the bed seemingly in an attempt to take note of the time displayed on the digital clock. That was the signal I had hoped for. The bling time piece which adorned her wrist could have provided the same mundane service.

I threw the kimono at her head as a distraction and quickly moved between her and the night table. Never taking my eyes off the woman, I slowly opened the small drawer, felt for, found and withdrew what I knew would be there.

Stamped with Arabic characters on both sides of the black receiver with a warrior emblem on the grip, was a standard issue Helwan. Parented by Walther and Beretta, it was a 9mm, eight or ten shot, military grade, semi-automatic, hand gun.

I pushed the lever that released the magazine, which was full, into the palm of my free hand. Then I pulled the slide action back to ensure that a round was not already in the chamber. I squeezed the trigger and with my thumb, I released the hammer and firing pin so that they came to rest, harmlessly, on the frame.

"Now that we are on an equal footing, why don't you cover yourself up. Then we can compare myths about each other and the man of the hour who seems to have gone missing."

"What, what did you say? Who are you? What do you want? If it's money, I have none in the house, so I think you should leave."

I just stared at the woman, leaned against the wall, and smiled.

"We have a lot to talk about Miss…, whoever you are. Money is irrelevant and this house is not a safe place to be in anymore. For either of us. Within the next thirty minutes I expect that the Indonesian police, maybe even the military, will be here, along with your sometime friend Saladin, to collect his passport. Believe me, he will be on the next flight to Singapore and then he will be placed on a plane headed for the country that issued his travel document.

You, in particular, do not want to be here when he, when they, arrive. Mr. Saladin's transgression in this country, in any country, cannot be contested.

Regardless of who you are or who you think you are or how many guns you have lying around the house, you are vulnerable right now, very vulnerable.

So, what's it going to be, Missy? You, with me, in a restaurant…, or you, alone, trying to explain to the authorities the harmlessness of a crime against nature, as they will see it, committed by a foreigner residing of this house!

Just say the word and I am gone. I have bigger fish to fry than you anyway. Do you understand what I have just said to you or shall I attempt a simpler explanation of what is about to happen to you if you stay in this house! Time is running out for both of us!"

The woman looked blindly at me. Her manikin-like pose more resembled plastic than one in possession of a pulse.

"Time's up. The rainy season that is about to arrive will, without doubt, drown you and whatever mission brought you to South East Asia! So don't say that you were not warned."

I had given up on the woman. If one yells at someone standing in the middle of the road, warning of an approaching, out of control truck, and the only response is frozen transfixion, then death becomes merely part of a just dessert.

As I walked briskly down the road that led toward lights and vehicle activity, an arm slipped behind mine and held on to my bicep tightly.

"Take me away from here. Whoever you are. Please, just take me away from this place quickly."

That was all the woman could manage between gasps for air.

As we were about to turn the corner at the end of the street, I stopped, with the woman still clutching my arm, looked back and waited. Mere seconds elapsed before my Nostradamus stab at the tense that follows the present, came true. Three cars turned into the open gated driveway. The first and last had small, flashing red lights that slowly rotated inside their roofed bubbles.

"A first class grade goes to the lady with superior common sense…, the kind of common sense that is not so common," I said to the air in front of me. I turned and grinned at the woman and gave her a dry peck on the forehead. She snuggled in even closer to my chest as I raised my hand to hail a cab.

I knew that what I was doing was tantamount to sleeping with the enemy. But what choice did I have? I needed to know what only she could divulge. Being a Bogart in the situation did have its limits though. I was spent and just as frightened as she was!

As the woman moved to the far side of the back seat of the taxi, she opened her mouth to speak. I quickly leaned over and covered her lips with my forefinger.

"Faites attention! Le petit copain devant nous parle l'anglais et il possede deux oreilles si grand q'un elephant. Attendes le restaurant."

My warning about loose lips coupled with the snide comment about the size of the driver's ears, caused the woman across from me to giggle and snuggle even further into the crevasse created between the door and her seat. She never took her eyes off me.

I just knew that, unlike me, she would be perfectly fluent in French. Parisian French. The bearing of a French speaking woman, her stride, her posture, above all, the mimicry of her mouth which was trained, tailored to the sound, the order, the rhythm, and the meaning of the language of Napoleon, was unmistakable.

French was the most sensual of languages when spoken well. The tenses which spoke to time and intent, the singular and plural forms of the nouns that doubled the size of the dictionary, and the discipline demanded to differentiate between the masculine and the feminine notwithstanding, it was the perfect medium for an Aznavour or Brel or Piaf melody of love lost.

The taxi came to an abrupt stop outside what looked like an abandoned warehouse. It was a relief to get out of the Bluebird. It had transferred every bump in the cobble stone road, common in the old port area of Jakarta, to the bottoms of the back seat passengers.

"Welcome to my home away from home. We will be safe here. It is off the beaten track, you might say."

"Here! You think that I am going to accompany you into a place like this! Why didn't you just shoot me when you had the chance back at the house?"

"If you have ever fired the 9 mm that I found in your bedroom you know that it makes enough noise to wake the dead. Hardly a welcoming sound for your neighbors to hear and…, and just very bad form in the rich-bitch area you call home.

Just joking with you. Thrust me, you have so far. C'mon. You will not be disappointed."

I took her by the hand, walked up to the bolt studded door and pounded on it two times. I waited five seconds and thumped it again. Three times. I stood back and waited. A slot at eye level clanked opened.

"Salamat malam Om…, ORANG UTAN!"

The slot slammed shut as the large door swung open.

"Salamat malam sir, always good to see you. A table for two?"

"Yes, terima kasih, Emile. A pleasure to see you as well."

With the lady in tow, we were escorted down a poorly lit corridor of rusted steel and dirty, limp cobwebs to a second set of doors. The lady tried, somewhat half-heartedly, to escape my hand cuff grip on her wrist.

"Always darkest before the dawn, young lady. Match your common sense with a dash of curiosity. Believe me, this experience is reserved for a select few in Jakarta and will, in all likelihood, for you at least, never be repeated.

As the second set of doors opened, I released her hand and stood back so that she could witness, unobstructed, the spectacle that beckoned beyond.

Twenty feet below where we stood was a highly polished, kidney-shaped dance floor. It was about the size of an outdoor swimming pool found in any top drawer suburb of a world class city. Spot lights in the ceiling bathed the stained mahogany slats in brilliant light. Everything else in the cavernous room, beyond the glistening floor, was in near perfect darkness.

Once the neophyte's eyes had their fill of the creation in richly worked wood, a galaxy of dim lights shrouded in little red lampshades could be discerned. They adorned tables which were warmed by a host of wrap around, deep red brocade, seats.

At first, one's eyes supported the illusion that most of the cozy nests were suspended, like fish net floats on a calm, night, sea. Sustained focus, however, on the massive area which was enveloped in a cave-like quietness, quickly dispelled the illusion. A series of raised ledges came into focus. University lecture hall like structures ringed the stage. The platforms, each connected to an adjacent one by wide, shallow steps, created a series of personal islands of intimacy in a sea of, what appeared to be, a large school of little red, reef fish.

"I think that I will start with a double Chivas Regal on the rocks. What will your poison be, oh fairest of the consorts of the lounge lizards this evening."

"A Remy Martin, a double Remy Martin on the rocks please, Mr…, Do you have a name or shall I just refer to you as Mr…, Mr. Abductor."

"Done! Some people call me Michel. You can call me Michel, if you like. How about you. What would you like me to call you? A first name, any first name, will do."

The woman seemed to be fighting to get her head around the dichotomy created by the sight of the corrugated metal structure squatting among the smelly, seedy docks of Jakarta outside, and the visual overload which was the sensuous island of self-absorption inside.

It was a pearl, as big as the world, a pearl resulting from the secretions of an ugly metal oyster. And this pearl of the Orient was, even for the intrepid, mere baby steps of faith away from the other, the lesser, more mundane, reality. All that was needed to gain access was to take the first step.

In her defense, it must be admitted that the woman had been challenged. A frightening encounter in the lobby of the Hilton hotel, an intruder in her bedroom, being disarmed so easily while so naked, forced to trust a stranger, a nameless stranger who seemed to know too much about her present and her future, forced to suspend rational thought and accept the notion that some guy off the street would be less lethal than the authorities who had her associate in tow, and then having that same arrogant interloper give her instruction, in French, to keep her mouth shut was, I knew, disconcerting, disorienting, and somewhat defeating to say the least. And the sustained assault had occurred within a period of less than one hour!

The whole interlude with the woman who favored hand guns had not gone well. I could feel it in my bones. Too, too much of me and not enough, not nearly enough, of her.

"Lilith, you can call me Lilith. My real name is Lilith." The woman looked at me in practiced expectation of an incredulous response.

"So, you are named after a sexually wanton woman, a demon of the night, who stole babies away from their mothers. A killer of infants! I think that's the description of your namesake found in Jewish myth! Who gave you that name, your mother of your father?"

"Neither. I gave myself that name. Lilith was the first female on earth. She was made, as was Adam, from the earth. She was his equal. She was not his rib. She was not his servant. She would not submit to any subservient role. All of the claptrap that you just listed is character assassination perpetrated by those scribes and religious leaders of the time, whose task it was to give the scriptures a self-enhancing, misogynistic slant."

I snickered to myself. As I remembered it, the myth of Lilith had gone on much further. She left Adam because she refused to accept his demand to be on top of her during copulation. The woman of lore was no missionary, by position or disposition it seemed, at all!

"Pick your mythical, your metaphysical poison, I guess. Commit it to parchment, and then, over time, come to revere and worship it as the truth. All belief systems, particularly religious belief systems, take flight on gossamer wings, don't they!

Let's talk further shall we, about a mutual acquaintance who trades in the belief systems of the vulnerable, trades in and tricks them into despair. Tell me about Saladin."

"Why should I. According to you he has been caught and is about to be dealt with harshly. What would be the point. You have already got what you wanted."

"The point, the point! Stupid does not fit you very well.

See, I have this friend and he came to me with a problem. The problem was his girlfriend. She had been seduced, literally and figuratively, by a man claiming to be a medicine man, a Dukun. Your Mr. Saladin. He not only had his way with her, such a quaint expression don't you think, almost Biblical, he not only fucked her face off but…, but, he stole her jewelry valued in the thousands of dollars.

And that is only one story in the scriptures according to Saint Saladin.

Undoubtedly there are others. You know that I was the one responsible for having the cretin kicked out of the country. You just said as much. Would you like to hear any of the details? They are amusing, to say the least."

I hoped that my story of vengeful retribution would fly, fueled by curiosity or, failing that, at least by her need to know what to report to others. I was wrong!

The muzzle of a .25 caliber hand gun is about the diameter of an HB pencil. But when seen mere inches away from one's chest, it appears to be enormous.

"Enough of this nonsense. I have heard enough. You are just a bloody nobody. Do you know that! A nobody…, who just got in the way, that's all. I want to leave this whore house now! And you are going to be my ticket out of here. Do we understand each other…, Mr., whoever you are…, Mr. Michel?"

"But we haven't even finished our drinks. Couldn't you at least be polite. No! Well then how about demonstrating some prudence at least. I have something in my pocket that belongs to you. It has your finger prints all over it. If you shoot me here, even a cursory examination, post mortem, will reveal your complicity in the crime. No matter how fast and how far you think you can run.

It's right here in my front pocket. I will slowly remove it and give it back to you. I am not leaving here any time soon and you are not going to fire that gun."

I placed the ammunition clip, taken from the Helwan pistol in her bedroom, on the table. As I did so, I thumbed the top bullet out of the magazine and held it up between my thumb and forefinger.

"See, your thumb prints are all over the casing. Tut, tut. Soyez prudent Mademoiselle Lilith. Be more careful in the future."

Like the arc traced by the released arm of a mouse trap, I picked up and threw the rectangular, metal clip box at her face. Her knee jerk reaction to the assault on her cheek bone allowed me the time needed to slip the bullet from the magazine between two of the fingers on her left hand. And with all the force I could muster, I squeezed those fingers together.

Before the invention of "the bully" as boogey man in elementary schools, it had been common practice, in my circle of friends at least, to use the 'pen and two fingers' maneuver on friend and foe alike. When pressure was applied to the two fingers supporting the pen or pencil between them, the recipient of the vice-grip attack was immediately reduced to paroxysms of unbearable pain. A rounded, foreign object achieved greatest effectiveness when positioned between the intermediate phalanges, the second set of bones in the hand counting down from the finger tips.

Care had to be taken to not squeeze too hard or for too long. Broken fingers did cross the boundary between a prank and possible expulsion. Even in the dark ages of my formal education.

Lilith dropped her gun on the carpeted floor as she writhed and squirmed frantically to get away from the pain. Like some innocent wretch caught up in the Inquisition, one who had just begun to pay the price for heresy, she would have done, she would have said anything to get the torment to stop.

I did not relent. She was complicit in the conspiracy that prompted my abrupt departure from the Turks and Caicos Islands. She, along with others, had made it necessary to hide Christina away from her home and away from her father. She was a co-conspirator in the nonsense which resulted in Col. Satu almost foundering on the shoals, the psychic shoals of demented, self-deception.

"You're right Lilith, I am your ticket out of here. Find yourself a three star hotel and stay there. Or don't stay there. Who cares! Try the Hotel Ibis. I think there is one somewhere in Jakarta. The locals would call it Hotel Iblis, you know, Devil's Hotel. Small rooms, very small rooms and no amenities. You, more than most, might be very uncomfortable there. Cheap has a price, you know!

Emile will see you to the door, without the weapon of course. A taxi will be waiting. Don't worry, your fingers will feel better by tomorrow. If not, use splints. Popsicle sticks or chop sticks work well I am told. And should your taste in partners ever go contrary to what is now, the

'Law', or should you stray into the realm say, of the perverse, just as was the case with your Mr. Saladin, know that my best wishes are with you. But maybe you should stick with the mundane. Remember, as with any pretty, little slut from a pick-up bar, bound fingers are purported to be a great penetration device."

"You, ahh, you have no idea, God Damn It, no idea who you are dealing with. You will pay for this Mr., MR MICHEL. I have friends who…, God almighty that…, You will pay for this…, Believe it! You will regret that we ever met!"

"Well should we meet again Lilith, it will be a pleasure for me to share any pain I experience with you."

The woman stumbled away from the table cradling her damaged hand. She obediently followed behind my rotund Asian associate and disappeared at the end of the corridor. The inner door shut quietly behind her.

Emile knew the drill to follow when a gentleman's escort, a 'kupu kupu malam', a butterfly of the evening, became unruly. A member of staff would accompany her in the cab and see to it that the lady's head was hooded. A long, circuitous route would be followed before she would be dumped some distance away from her desired destination.

Lilith was, what would be termed by most, a trophy female. She was that rare breed of gorgeous woman for whom men of means would readily forsake the Gods of their fathers just to sustain her presence in their present perfect worlds!

Nefertiti, Cleopatra, or Elizabeth Taylor playing Cleopatra, they all possessed the same, je ne sais quoi! Their bearing, beauty, and their brains, were wired to wantonness and witchery. And even practiced male eyes provided an inadequate defense. Their iridescence was irresistible.

There were only two sources of male disillusionment capable of dethroning them. When these regal beings assumed the crown of conceit, a self-awareness which produced petulance, getting what they wanted…, always…, or when they travelled down the road of deceit, the tangential traverse to the transgender, only then, and only sometimes, did they risk the fall from grace which would be permanent.

When the roles were reversed, my female friends never tired of repeating, in lugubrious, eulogistic tones, those usually reserved for accidental, youthful death, to any and all who would listen that, as a result of being in the company of and basking in close proximity to the splendor of maleness at its apogee, the maleness of fastidious dress and demeanor, but the maleness which beckoned and belonged to other, like minded maleness, the spectacle of biological miscue which was visited upon them was as traumatic as it was tragic. And through a thinly veiled mask of dismissive distain they would mutter, 'What a waste'. What a bloody waste!

Chapter 14

From the balcony of our villa, Dr. Rajawane and I were serenaded by the chirping of the sparrows, the canaries, and the forever fidgeting, whitish-grey wrens as they heralded the new dawn. Was it that stimulation of their retinas by the promising light of day prompted an involuntary instinctual chirping response or was it just their spontaneous celebration of life? The latter, of course, being the purview of the poet with the former, the more mundane, the more likely. A Chinese proverb probably had it right. A bird does not sing because it has an answer. It sings because it has a song!

The song birds of Puncak, pronounced Poon-chuck, seemed to have anticipated our nesting among them. They gave us a full-throated recital.

We both just sat there with our cups of coffee cradled in our hands. Daybreak in the mountainous islands of Indonesia was always sweater summoning cool.

We just looked out at the sylvan countryside, listened to the sounds it harbored and inhaled the air which was rich with the tantalizing aroma of cloves.

Cloves triggered the right clicks to unlock the memory vault that was all mother, all festive occasion, all fondness for family almost forgotten.

Christmas was turkey, as was Thanksgiving, but Easter was ham. And not just any plain old ham. No, the mound of meat presented to us by my mother became the centerpiece of the festival of food which ushered in the new season of Spring. Baked and basted in honey and brown sugar, the entire surface was festooned with browned pineapple slices. And in the center of each slice was a clove which just managed to poke its head above the sea of solidified sugar. Just the head, but their contribution to the meat was exquisitely exotic.

My mother, both creator and caterer, did it all. I knew, from an early age, that 'all' included the silent saving and scrimping for weeks to purchase the expensive piece of meat and the requisite trimmings.

Feast from fastidious thrift.

Parental words to a child are worthless. What parents do, silently, out of sight, without thought to personal sacrifice, creates the vault that houses inherited values.

There was no need for talk. Together, the Doctor and I had already played the game of word warrior the previous evening.

I had rushed back to the Hilton immediately after the disastrous rendezvous with Lilith. She might have chosen to seek solace in the comforting arms of the 'Law'. But I doubted that. She looked like she had been mugged. And she was dangerously close to the border of the hamlet called Hysteria. It was very unlikely that he would have been seen by her as a hospice of help. Theirs appeared to be a relationship which was based solely on fair weather, mutual usury.

I had wanted to unload the dossier that the Colonel had given to Saladin as well. That would end the trumped up turmoil and besides, the damn thing was becoming very uncomfortable cinched against my skin behind an already too tight belt.

At the front desk, I quickly penned a note, ostensibly from Col. Satu, folded it up into an absurdly thick wad, and sealed it along with the folder in a hotel envelope to be delivered to Brian Law's room after I left the lobby.

I snickered at the silly game that was in play. I had scrawled the note with the pen held between my middle fingers. Phrasing like, 'I found special document of you for maybe new hotel in Sumatra…' and folding it like a love note created by some elementary school kid, I hoped that the package would prompt Brian Law to gloat on and snicker at the success of his baiting plan.

I no sooner finished my Romper Room antics and handed the package to the smiling clerk, than a hand forcibly descended on my shoulder. I turned sharply, with my fists clenched, to meet my unknown assailant.

"Michael, thank God I found you here! We have to get out of this place. We have got to get out of this city. We have got to get away from here right now!" The hissed plea came from Dr. Rajawane. At first I did not recognize the man.

Everything about him, his face, awash with anguish and his body, almost cowering, spoke of someone who knew that he was being hunted.

"What's the matter Dr. Rajawane? You look like you have seen a ghost. Or is it just that you have grown tired of my humble abode." Talking, talking too much, always seemed to help when my body needed to come off an impending adrenalin boil.

"Yes, the house Michael. It is your house and there is a…, a problem. Someone, some people have been inside your house and they have…, they have…, not made a mess, but they…, they have moved everything. I even went to your neighbor, Mrs…, Mrs. Lee but no one seemed to be home. Someone was there, in Mrs. Lee's house, but no one would answer the front door when I knocked. Michael something is wrong. Just very wrong! We have to leave Jakarta right away, right now!"

My most trusted friend, Dr. Rajawane, had taken his share of strolls on the wild side while in my company. But our peccadilloes, planned and paid for in advance, had always been predictable. Time, location, the purpose and comportment of the other players, all were understood prior to the commencement of the games which were played out in the dark.

This was different. This was not part of a prolonged celebration with friends and colleagues. This was muted malevolence. This was intentional intrigue and we had been targeted.

Welcome to the real world of 'finders keepers, losers weepers', I thought as I drew on my dwindling energy reserves to assuage the frayed nerves of the medical man at my side.

"You are right Dr. Rajawane. Best that we leave right away. C'mon let's grab a taxi at the stand outside. We can decide on a destination once we get moving."

With my arm over his shoulder, we exited the hotel and crossed the roundabout to the herd of taxis that seemed to be grazing among the palm trees.

A small crowd of drivers had gathered at the front of the line of taxis. They were loudly discussing the lottery winner in their midst who had been given a crisp, one hundred dollar bill by someone in need of a ride who was in a very big hurry.

The generous passenger had been a beautiful woman who spoke bahasa Indonesia well but with a foreign accent. Even though she was wearing large sun glasses, the drivers agreed that she was trying to cover up a black eye. Also, one of her hands was wrapped in bandages and it was supported by a neck sling. She paid the man, in advance, more than two months wages, to get her to Puncak as quickly as possible.

That was all I needed to hear. Even my limited command of the Indonesian language gave me what I desperately needed to know. Lilith had won the race to her Hilton home. Obviously, once hooded and in the car she had negotiated with her captor and was victorious. The club by the docks was staffed by those whose sense of allegiance was predicated on the offer of bank notes. The greater the denomination of the note, the greater the allegiance!

Lilith had come to the Hilton but had she actually spoken to Brian Law? More likely, that had been her initial intent, perhaps, but upon arrival, she had thought better of it. She knew that time was not on her side. The man who attacked her might not be far behind.

The run-in with a stranger hiding in her bedroom, the disclosures made, which proved to be true, concerning Saladin, the bazaar venue for drinks would best be enumerated when she felt better. Tears, resulting from physical pain and emotional disequilibrium, would not help. She needed to regain her composure, to be more in command of her wits. I was counting on the woman's innate intelligence to favor a plan of action that focused on a regrouping strategy.

"Dr. Rajawane, we are going to visit Puncak for a couple of days. Just some R&R that we both desperately need. But first I have to make a quick stop at my house. It's only about ten minutes away. It will be OK because the storm caused by our unwanted guests has already passed.

I just need to pick up some new clothes and a few odds and ends. And then, yes then, we'll get lost in an oasis of pre-colonial Indonesia that is waiting for us upcountry."

I did not wait for a response.

Funny how a house ceases to be your home after illegal trespass. Sanctuary suffers. Not one room had been spared the groping hands of strangers. The layer of dust which covered almost every flat surface in the place had new squatters in residence. And the resulting dustless bald spots, where things had been, looked embarrassingly incongruous. Clothes that refused to settle back into their drawers after having been rummaged through seemed to drip down, limply, between the front carcasses of the chests of drawers and their un-closable compartments. Books which had been regimental and in spine perfect order looked like they had been routed by a superior military force.

What had the team of thugs been searching for? What paper trail did they believe ended at my door step? What possible information, written or otherwise, would suggest that I was a person of anything more than passing curiosity to them?

And who had the power to order the orderly disorder? And where had Renee gone? Was her place really vacant? An exterior light was on at the side of the front door and the back patio lights were ablaze as well. Perfect signs for any practiced prowler that the abandoned place would be easy pickings.

Pearly, wonderful Pearly, true to his reputation, had set the table of entrapment well. He had served up the fool who was the food, with flare and had thought to finish the evening with a perfect, parting gift. A white, unmarked envelopment stared up at me from the floor as I had opened the front door. I could tell what was inside by the feel of the stiff, cardboard backing on the three or four items inside. Later, I thought, look inside later.

The resort in Puncak probably required a reservation. Call the place from the house. It would only take a few extra seconds. No, not likely. The break-in artists might have been better at installing wire taps than finding non-existent incriminating evidence. Better back at the Hilton. I would stretch the patience of Dr. Rajawane just a little bit more.

A Dick Tracey radio wrist watch would have been just the thing to have. But the technology employed by the comic strip character was far in advance of the heavy, cumbersome, war time, walkie-talkie boxes which were currently available. Minutes of talk time secured by hours of recharge time made them more trouble than they were worth.

One of the joys, for me at least, of living and working in South East Asia was the splendid isolation the region afforded. Even when the noise machines improved, who wanted or needed every Tom's dick when harried, calling and interrupting one's personal, private schedule!

The contents of my over-night bag clanked as it came to rest at our feet in the taxi.

"Just a few bottles of olive oil, extra virgin, vinegar and lemon juice to make salad dressing while we are 'roughing it' in Puncak, Dr. Rajawane. Ha, ha, ha! Good thing we are taking the scenic route to Puncak and that the weekend is just beginning. On Sundays they close the road in the direction we want to accommodate the traffic returning to Jakarta from Bogor."

I hoped that my bullshit remarks would assuage the man whose patience, I knew, had run out.

"You and your salads! I know all about you and your salads. But never mind any of that. What I have to tell you will trump any report of a traffic jam, Sunday or any other day, believe me. Are you ready for the better than best news possible?

Ok, but bear with me Michael. I want to go slow. I want to savor this moment…,"

The doctor was almost overcome with emotion. I had never seen that side of him before. I decided to remain silent, to just let his story play itself out. And in the process of being carried along, like a stick in a swollen stream, by it, enjoy the moment that, I knew, was the signal of his rebirth as the rightful leader of Bali High Art.

"So…, the birth of our baby, Bali High Art Limited, and its legal status to date. It's going to be a long drive and by the time we get there we, or at least I will be spent. Well, not too spent, I hope. Maybe some salad dressing will be appreciated! Yes, we must save a little of ourselves to enjoy some of your salad dressing. I know that I have your concurrence on that point."

Dr. Rajawane winked at me and smiled. Good to have him back on track, I thought to myself. I knew that my house visit and the return to the Hilton would have been seen by the man beside me as a maddening, colossal waste of time.

"Good news or otherwise, Dr. Rajawane?"

"You will be happy to learn that it is all good news, better than good news, great news in fact. And, believe it or not, it is all because of some gentleman in Jakarta whom I stabbed in the gut early on in my medical career!"

"I didn't know that you were prone to violence when you were young, Dr. Rajawane."

I knew perfectly well what instrument was used in the stabbing but I wanted the doctor to give 'simple me' an elaboration. I wanted Dr. Rajawane's exposition pump to be well primed.

"I just wanted to assure myself that I had your full attention, Michael. The man who is now in charge of domestic corporate affairs for the government of Indonesia is a Mr. Abdul Prawata.

When we met in his office I had no idea who the man was. But he certainly remembered me. After receiving a big bear hug from him, he reminded me that I was the surgeon who had given him a new lease on life twelve years ago. A bowel obstruction is what he claimed to have had. Colon work; ascending, transverse or descending, I have no idea. But the man felt that my presence in the OR had been the work of God. And the blessing that was my presence beside him then, was calling on him, some decade plus years later, to respond in kind. Time to repay providence, so to speak.

The man has obviously enjoyed much success in the political arena since our hospital meeting and, judging by his current girth, he has more than made up for the limited diet that victimized him for years subsequent to his surgery.

Here is the document of Incorporation. Normally the contents of this folder take months to complete. But Mr. Prawata saw to it personally, that it arrived, in finished form, in my hand, within two, short business days. And that's with no envelopes being slipped under the table to anyone! What does that say to you about the relationship, the direct relationship that exists between high personal motivation and task completion that is marked by superior results?"

It says, I thought to myself with a sardonic grin, that the net of fear cast over Col. Satu by the con-artist Saladin had required a similar, all-consuming motivator, in that instance fear, not gratitude, to be as successful as it was in weaving a web of dread..., of psychic death, that would have remained active in the man forever.

Know the enemy, cloaked usually in enigma or ignorance, and 'carrot or stick' that player to performance. Business building behavior, 101!

"So our baby is born. She has all of her fingers and all of her toes and, best of all, her birth certificate will follow her where ever she goes."

Dr. Rajawane chuckled, sat back in his seat and let the night lights that flashed by his window become the backdrop for the dream machine that was Bali High Art.

The file folder that Dr. Rajawane dropped in my lap had the weight and feel of a proclamation of an irreversible event. A new entity had indeed been born. The salmon pink, embossed cover was a solemn piece of work. And true to Indonesian officialdom, it was immediately suspect as well.

The national emblem of Indonesia, the Garuda, a mythical, eagle like bird, occupied the top of the cover page. With wings spread and clutching a banner in its talons, it proclaimed the heady time in the country's history, 1945, when independence from the Dutch seemed imminent.

Blazoned across the chest of the bird was a shield. Symbolic to the point of absurdity, it depicted a star, a bull, a tree, a chain, along with stocks of rice and cotton. Religious tolerance, social cohesion, diversity of cultural roots, justice for all, and prosperity, were symbolized respectively.

The scroll in the bird's claws proclaimed to motto of Indonesia, Unity in Diversity.

Immediately below the bird was, in large, capital letters, ABDUL PRAWATA, SH, followed on the next line by a slightly smaller,

NOTARIS. The man was both a notary and a lawyer as well. The address of his personal business office and the telephone number followed in very small print.

Obviously, no conflict of interest was perceived by anyone relative to the man's governmental position and his penchant for personal business. Personal business that would have been enhanced through his professional profile as a senior business representative of the Indonesian people.

Or maybe he had just made an exception for the magic doctor with the scalpel. Maybe he merely wished to have his name in bold, black letters as a sign that he too was capable of marvelous feats. Exemptions to any regulations concerning conflict of interest were more the rule than the exception in the nation of islands that straddled the equator.

Even the stamp had the Garuda depicted on it but looking the other way.

Below that, the name of the newly formed company appeared, in its Indonesian incarnation. Bali High Art Ltd. became Pt. Bali-Hi Kerajinan Tangan, Bali High Creativity by Hand. Better than no title at all, I mumbled under my breath.

Heavy stock paper formed the interior of the document. Composed in Indonesian, I was certain that most of the articles had been lifted from Malaysian sources. Given the fact that the languages of both countries had the same Malay origin and, in the case of the former British colony, that attention had been paid to the expression of civil law long before the territory had become the nation across the Strait of Malacca from Indonesia, I was certain that my assessment was accurate.

The 'whereas' and 'further to' ramblings were of no interest to me. I could not read Indonesian very well at the best of times and the weak light provided by the little ceiling light in the cab made the exercise impossible.

I became intrigued by the actual construction of the corporate birth certificate. Nine pages, measuring about sixteen inches by twelve inches had been folded vertically creating a document containing eighteen, 8x12, pages. Each of the pages, printed on both sides, seemed to have been divided into three equal vertical sections.

The first section on the left of each page was blank save for a red colored stamp of the Garuda at the top. The remaining two thirds contained the copy.

At some point in the construction of the legal document, someone had drawn vertical lines, with the aid of a ruler, beside the entire length of each paragraph. The sequential numbers of the articles in each section also had lines drawn beside them as well.

The lines, I assumed, like levees, were meant to keep any flood of fraud from inundating the original intent and integrity of the document.

The pages, all with vertical lines, like bank regulation rule books, were born of necessity. The necessity of curtailing previously exposed fraud committed by former, financial players.

The pages were neatly stitched to the cover by thin, white thread the ends of which, were flattened against the inside front cover and sealed in place by another representation of the ubiquitous bird. A colorful stamp, the size of a postage stamp, immediately followed the last paragraph on the last page like some psychedelic caboose. Written across the stamp were the generous initials of Mr. Prawata himself.

Ironic, I thought, that the artisanship of the legal document in my hand, was a fitting precursor to, what would be, the formalized company mission statement.

"Well done, Dr. Rajawane. This is more than merely a legal document. This is a work of art. Now all we have to do is follow through on the shores of Lake Batur in like manner.

"Yes, the whole exercise to date, has been very gratifying. And I have confidence that with effort and expertise, it will continue."

Feigning interest in the darkness outside my door window I half mumbled to the lights that flashed by. 'Keep thinking like that, my dear Doctor friend. Try hard to keep thinking like that when your board members mature into independent, enlightened, self-interest advocates. And when the outside world comes not so politely knocking with agendas that differ from our own. Both events will, without doubt, occur much, much sooner than later!'

"Dr. Rajawane, have you found the time to consider the executive element needed to give form and direction to Bail High Art?"

"Michael, that is one of your more endearing traits. Sometimes, when you are at your best, you think just like me."

Dr. Rajawane gave me a sharp elbow jab to the ribs.

"Our Board of Directors! Yes, well, let me tell you what has been done to date in that regard and then I want your roses and reproaches. Remember though, I am a sucker for roses. Just like my wife!

Seriously, as I see it, Bali High would best be served, particularly during its teething stage, by a small group of individuals, six to be exact, plus a chairman of course, and that would be me. All Board members will possess specific areas of expertise which will reflect those of greatest importance to the fledging organization.

In no particular order, here is a rundown of those candidates whom I have approached, individuals who have proven track records in their chosen fields, that's what a business man like you would call them, I think, who will assure us of open, frank, and actionable dialogue.

Let's get my first choice out of the way right away. My wife, Edith has been approached and has agreed to sit on the Board of Directors for a period of two years. That time frame will be true for all candidates who decide to serve. I am confident that she will consistently bring her no nonsense pragmatism to the discussion table.

I know, I know, that screams of nepotism but remember with her in attendance, there will always be the 'sometimes' benefit of pillow talk, another one of your expressions I believe, to get both a formal and not so formal take on the group dynamic. Also, the female staff of Bali High will be reporting to her. She will be their voice and best represent their interests in the Board Room. Comments? Criticisms?"

"There would have been the latter had that sterling lady not been at the top of your list, Dr. Rajawane." I gave the man a playful nudge on his forearm.

"Next on the proposed roster is yourself. You are, after all, the causative agent of this whole enterprise and you, above all others, are one hundred percent committed to the enterprise envisioned by the late Mr. Tan. I dare you to argue with that choice!"

"Despite being a Bole, pronounced 'boo-lay', a white guy, and most comfortable speaking in English, I accept the appointment with the greatest of pleasure Dr. Rajawane, or is it King Arthur." I leaned over, like a knight of the round table, and kissed the man on both cheeks.

"I certainly hope that your reaction Michael is not repeated by the rest of the potential appointees, Edith, notwithstanding.

The next candidate for inclusion on the Board of Director team is Siti's dad, Rocky. During his short stay with us at Bali High, the man has proven himself to be a paragon of virtue. And, with some tutelage, I know that he can blossom even more fully, especially when in the company of those he feels are his superiors. He is a builder..., he shares our vision, and he is a man with no pretention. The physical plant and infrastructure as well as cohesion within the group will all benefit from his presence.

Next on the list...,Michael, have you ever heard of the artist, Emilio Ambron? No! Well he was an Italian painter and sculptor who visited Bali more than three generations ago, fell in love with the place, and never left. This, I believe, will be of particular interest to you. His artistic focus was almost exclusively devoted to the female form, nude or otherwise. His sketches in charcoal and his erotic, arresting sculpted works are on display not far from here, in the Klungkung museum.

I will take you on a guided tour of the town sometime soon, very soon. You need to see his work. Klungkung is less than a two hour drive from Bali High.

As an aside, the king of the region at the turn of the nineteenth century was Ida Dewa Agung Jambe. A monument of sorts was erected in his memory. Erected is the right term to use in his case. He, along with his one hundred or so willing wives, populated the region way back then with hundreds and hundreds of new citizens. His monument is a huge, erect phallus. Carved from stone it stands more than thirty feet high. It is positioned in the town square just across the street from the local museum. Blackened with age and pollution, it still stands proudly as the symbol of a long departed man and a long departed era which was both pre-women's lib and pre-political correctness. Ha, ha!

Anyway, the point. Let me get to the point. Emilio Ambron had a number of protégés who studied under him at his studio in Denpasar. One such man is, Agustino Nilawati. Balinese by birth, he has, in the minds of many, surpassed the master both in terms of output and individual artistic expression as well!

Agustino has stated, more like gushed, great interest in the Bali High Art concept and the founding role he might play in it. His concern is his professional agenda that has him working on almost every continent on earth, well, maybe not Antarctica ha, ha, at least once or twice every year.

He is definitely not motivated by the stipend that such a position will command. The amount I have in mind for annual board participation is twelve thousand, US. He does see the big picture however, and he does have a well-developed nationalistic bent. He might prove to be a bit of a handful to keep on the Bali High track, but I believe that his ability to attract neophytes and national attention as well, will outweigh his sometimes peevish temperament. I expect to receive word of his decision by the end of next week. I am optimistic.

Your thoughts…,"

"Well, we are not at the stage, and I hope that we never get there, when plough horses will replace unsaddled mustangs. I like the choice you have made and the profile that you provided seems to suggest a good, albeit sometimes larger than life, fit.

Who is next on your list Dr. Rajawane?"

"Keiko Hartono, that's who. If you have never heard of Mr. Nilawati, then she, in all likelihood, has never been a blip on your radar screen either. She…,"

"She is a lady of Japanese origin who, at age ten or twelve visited Bali with her parents, fell in love with the place, in particular Balinese dance, studied assiduously at home and in Bali and became world renowned as a master practitioner of the art form. I have seen her perform many times. All eyes, neck, wrists, fingers and hips, she transports audiences to where she, artistically, lives."

"Is there anything about women, in the arts or elsewhere, that you do not know, Michael?"

"Everything!"

"If you say so, man of many guises! Keiko, by the way, agreed, with great enthusiasm, to join Bali High when it is deemed appropriate.

Now, my last choice for membership on the Board. Abdul Kohar. Abdul Kohar is the gentleman's name. Recently retired, he was, for a long period of time, measured almost in decades, the Governor of the Lake Batur Region. He remains well connected in the corridors of power in Bali and in Jakarta as well. And he knows where all the political quicksand and lizard traps are located in the area surrounding Bali High.

He is well versed in achieving results via committee combat too. His presence on the Board will serve not just as a channel marker, but more pragmatically, as a conduit to current authority. He is a man whose reputation for tenacity precedes him. He can be counted on to champion the presence of Bali High Art.

He too will let us know his decision by the end of next week."

"Unity in Diversity, Dr. Rajawane. The banner held by the Garuda on our Charter says so. Well Done."

"Yes, and all will be paid the same amount, 12K, US, annually, plus expenses, with initial meetings held monthly, unless major issues arise, followed by quarterly meetings once administrative stability is achieved."

"I can't wait to get my first Bali High pay cheque Dr. Rajawane. I am going to save it in a newly opened bank account here in Bali. Then, I am going to double the amount on deposit at the end of the first year with my own money. The entire amount, twenty-four grand, will serve as the commission awarded to the artist who best responds to the profile I will create of the late Mr. Tan.

I am talking about a statue of our benefactor which will capture him ruminating over the Horace Mann musing, 'Be ashamed to die until you have won some victory for humanity'. The statue, maybe not as large as the one you just described of the king of conception in Klungkung, but an arresting visual statement, just the same."

"Another one of your endearing traits, Michael. You pluck out of nowhere, what needs to be said and then act on it. You are one of a kind young man. Yes, one of a kind!"

"I'm sorry Doctor, what was the verb you used just before the word, 'nowhere'? You can speak more clearly than that with me. I will understand."

The doctor was perplexed by my seeming non sequitur. He mouthed from memory what he had just said, paused, then shook his head and burst into laughter.

"I don't know how anyone, female or male, could put up with you on a daily basis."

"Yes, well, many have tried and many have…, have had the good sense to just give up. And in that same vein Dr. Rajawane, we are almost at our destination so why don't we just let our favorite mythological bird of prey flock off for a while. We can poke through the other details in his droppings later on when we get settled in Puncak."

"Could not have said it any more succinctly myself, oh fellow low road warrior of high art!"

Chapter 15

Scotch created the certainty that clarity of thought was waiting just around the next curve along the stream of consciousness road. And all it took to come into view were the words of a comrade who was tippling from a similar tumbler.

It was the passing vista provided while someone else was at the wheel. Focus on my friend's words only required recognition of the subject matter. The remaining time was lost in the luxury of contemplation and energy conservation for later on when Dr. Rajawane had retired for the evening.

Puncak was a destination waiting to happen. Majestic hills and verdant valleys as far as the eye could see, all turreted by towering pine trees, the location was a developer's dream. That would be, I was certain, the unfortunate future awaiting the sylvan splendor that assailed and assuaged my every sense. It was mere minutes away from the town of Bogor and its burgeoning BMW populace. They believed that theme park water slides made of aqua-marine blue and orange plastic would be kid perfect. Their perfect kid, perfect! Such structures would give lasting form and function to the work which had merely been initiated by God.

My hasty call to the Lembah Bukit Raya Hotel from the Hilton front desk in Jakarta had borne results. That was mainly because my memory had served up the right name when it was needed.

Claiming to be a close friend of Mr. Harold Burr, had resulted in the good Doctor and myself being chauffeured by electric golf cart to one of the executive cabins which was nestled among the trees at the far end of the resort grounds. The grand view from our second story balcony was dominated by a sea of peacock turquoise and green, peacock colors to be sure, but without the squawking bird that usually lived amidst the colorful plumage.

Our Walden Pond abode was, less a statement of sumptuousness than a Spartan replica of a Swiss chalet. The no nonsense, utilitarian ambiance of the log cabin interior did not, however, compromise the creature comforts it afforded its guests. Everything was spotless, the bathrooms were well stocked with necessities, the couches were conversation comfortable, and the TV which normally sat perched ready to spread its blue hue at the press of a button, was discretely hidden behind a closed credenza door. The accommodation was more than any one booking a last minute reservation deserved, the contemplative Henry David Thoreau, notwithstanding.

Harold Burr, the name that still opened doors, and I had worked for the same big pharma outfit in South East Asia. Harold and I had been on a parallel collision course with destiny. I was the country manager in Manila and he had been, for a short time, my counterpart in Jakarta.

He had fallen in love with the Lembah Bukit Raya. It was both a weekend getaway for him and his wife and their two daughters while he was stationed in Indonesia and the site of choice as well for almost all of the company sponsored events from new med-rep training to quarterly management meetings to company sponsored doctor symposia. Harold's endorsement of the place had been, during his tenure with the company in Indonesia, a major contributor to the reputation and success of the property.

I had committed the corporate crime of insubordination by refusing a new posting in Europe, a demotion actually. That had been a mere misdemeanor in comparison to Harold's felony crime of being at the helm when the gross sales in Indonesia faltered and failed over four consecutive quarters.

I quit and Harold was fired. We both moved on. Moved on, but decidedly in different directions. I went the entrepreneurial route while Harold, so the rumor mill had it, joined a competitive company back home. He lasted about nine months before the enemy realized that he had no more trade secrets, products in the pipeline and their launch dates, to divulge. He had then foolishly jumped into bed with a medical instrument outfit in New England. A desperate move, given that he knew nothing about the products or the people who drove that particular machine. Consequently, within six months of his appointment, he sought solace in the company of a hand gun. He committed suicide in his corner office.

The game of life, snakes and ladders: the snakes being understood and never underestimated while the ladders, precarious steps to the pinnacle, proved to be the more treacherous because of their untested, their unreliable rungs.

Burr proved to be better as a memory, than he had ever been as merely undead and waiting!

A generous fruit platter and tall, tropical delight, iced drinks, replete with little umbrellas, were waiting in readiness on the living room coffee table for the Doctor and me. We tentatively took a sip of our ruby red cocktails, winced, scooped the ice out of the sugary, Singapores-in-slings, rinsed them off and let them fall noisily into two empty glasses commandeered from the bathroom.

We made our way to the balcony with our glassed treasures in hand. I carried the best salad dressings known to man under my arm while Dr. Rajawane managed the large platter of freshly prepared fruit.

"Not bad, Michael. Not bad at all. For a spur-of-the-moment decision, for an effective action plan, and for this marvelous result. Congratulations! You should consider a career in business you know. I am sure that many firms would benefit greatly from your expertise. Ha, ha."

"Maybe, but my efficacy comes with rather severe side effects. Ask anyone who has seen me in action! And ha, ha, yourself. And speaking of poison Dr. Rajawane, what will yours be, Scottish or French? Glenfiddich or Remy Martin?"

"I consider both national groups to be suspect. Too emotionally involved in politics for my taste. But, this time, I think the nod will go to the Scots, if you don't mind."

I drowned the rocks with generous doubles, just to take full advantage of the rapidly disappearing medium that gave our fermentation the right feeling as it was about to commence the descent to our depths.

We clicked our glasses together and smiled in anticipation of new moments together in conversation and camaraderie.

"Well, to us Michael, to the team that has been assembled and, and, to the success of Bali High Art. Great things are about to become a reality you know!

I stared at the two bottles that stood between us on the table.

"Cheers, my fellow pilgrim. May our new Jerusalem be filled with wonderment, awe and, of course, a reasonable return on investment!"

"Good segue, Michael. Money is as good a place to start as any. Your Mr. Samuel in the Turks and Caicos Islands proved to be very prompt. The funds for Bali High Art were waiting in a suspense account with Standard Chartered in Bali before I had arrived. The transfer of funds between Bali and Jakarta was mere child's play using the bank's inter-branch telephone connection."

I grinned as I thought of the man so far away whose whole world had been turned upside down by the notion that tampons were the ticket to the illicit diamond trade.

"While in Jakarta, I had the Standard Chartered people set up a current account for Bali High into which I deposited two million dollars. That should be sufficient to at least get us started on the new construction projects and see to operating expenses as well. The remaining funds were placed in an investment portfolio that is low risk. I insisted on that. And, if past performance is an indicator, we will be guaranteed a minimum of about eight to ten percent return annually.

The investment is both safe and, at the same time, good for Indonesia. I instructed the bank investment manager to focus on the natural resources sector.

You know, PT Freeport in Irian Jaya, INCO in Sulawasi, and Pertamina throughout Indonesia. Gold, nickel and oil! Sure bets, wouldn't you say?"

I nodded and grinned at the man and his perceived, new found investment acumen. All good bets for the Companies mentioned but only marginally beneficial for his country. Long term contracts and percentages being what they were for raw material extraction all over South East Asia. Welcome to the compromise that attended high stakes gambling, no matter how low the risk factor was purported to be, I thought.

"A wise, investment approach Dr. Rajawane. And your decision to use Standard Chartered as the financial institution of choice is prudent as well. They, unlike their Indonesian competitors are somewhat more resistant to the vagaries of Asian markets and national politics."

"Yes and what is more...,"

The two bottles of alcohol, standing so close together on the table between us, loomed large once again. I was no longer on the island of Java. I was in Lower Manhattan standing at the base of the South Tower of the World Trade Center.

I was the guest of Simon Blanchard, my Investment Advisor with the Company, Dean Witter. An annual event, he saw to it that I was given a 'Cook's Tour' of their facilities somewhere in the clouds. Fitting for a client with a low seven digit portfolio, no doubt.

Dean Witter prided itself on its 'client first' philosophy. It seemed to say that a man's word was his bond. Anachronistic perhaps, but comforting none the less. Somewhere above the forty- fourth floor all elevator travelers had to disembark, like train commuters, to connect with another bank of elevators, a corridor away, to continue their ascent to high finance.

No place for anyone with vertigo, the narrow windows in the Dean Witter offices stretched from the floor almost to the ceiling. The Statue of Liberty, the Hudson River, Ellis Island, they all competed with the jaw dropping spectacle of helicopters and light planes going about their business at elevations which were floors below where we sat and sipped coffee.

During one of my frequent Phillip Morris moments down at street level, smoking was not permitted on the premises, I stared up, and up, and up, as I inhaled the sensuousness that was Lady Nicotine.

I squeezed the solid rubber ball that Simon had given me. A little smaller in diameter than a tennis ball, it was a miniature globe given to all neophyte, IA's who were in the throes of coming to grips with the myriad of governmental rules and regulations which drove the legal acquisition of wealth in America.

The oceans were blue and the continents were green. A stress reliever, it also suggested to the owner that the world was within his grasp.

I had just gawked up at the sheer grandeur, the statement of accomplishment, the marvel of the human condition that had produced such a spectacular thrust toward heaven.

I hoped that the same conditions would prevail on the site of our marshaling of the same human spirit. Maybe my misgivings were ill founded. Maybe my fears of rapacious monsters looking over our shoulders were pure fantasy. But my gut told me otherwise.

"...and I believe that the position of Chairman of the Board for Bali High Art should receive a salary commensurate with the responsibilities that attend that position. I was thinking that a starting salary of eighty thousand dollars, US, would be appropriate."

The Doctor looked up at me. He seemed to almost be expecting an objection to the amount he had suggested. In that regard, he was not mistaken.

"Well, Dr. Rajawane, I certainly agree with you that the position, Chairman of the Board, is of the utmost importance. The man..., or woman, who occupies that post will give direction to and be the 'Mission Statement' force behind the whole enterprise. So...,"

"So..., you think the amount is too high?"

"No, not at all. In fact, it is too low. Look, even Country Managers stationed in Indonesia who represent any of the multinational companies doing business here make at least 120K. One hundred fifty thousand when you factor in the danger pay and the isolation pay. Imagine, Indonesia as a dangerous or an isolated place. Never mind, don't look a gift horse in the mouth, right! And..., and that is before you add on the generous client entertainment budget. And all of this time you actually believed that my generosity came from my own pocket. Tut, tut, Dr. Rajawane."

I refilled both of our glasses and drowned the slivers of ice that remained which were forlornly swimming around, like dying minnows, on the surface.

"I think I will be seeking your advice more often, Michael. I like the perspective you bring to the discussion table. I like it a lot! I will take your comments about remuneration under advisement for serious consideration later."

We clicked our full glasses together once again.

Dr. Rajawane did not, could not know some of the people and their circles of influence with whom he would soon be dancing. But when the music began, I was damned if he was going to be under dressed for the music or the dance floor!

"Oh, one last thing, Michael. The property deed transfer. That has been put to bed, as you might say, as well. The PT Good Earth Distribution ownership of the Bali property is now an asset of PT Bali High Art as per the article in the will of Mr. Tan. A bona fide copy of his will, coupled with your notarized letter of intent made the ownership transfer child's play. That and the shepherding process overseen by my friend Mr. Prawata."

Dr, Rajawane winked at me. A comfortable silence ensued. We sipped at the surface of our drinks and stared out at the darkness that was alive with the sounds of the small creatures of the night. The small inhabitants of the place who, I knew, would be able to adapt to whatever transformation caused by greed might befall them and their timeless abode.

"Dr. Rajawane, allow me to play devil's advocate with you for just a moment, if I may."

"Yesss, but don't be a party pooper. Is that the right expression, party pooper? Such a strange language to have dominated the world!"

"Before we retire for the night, could I get from you the list of companies which have expressed interest in the Bali High property? You mentioned, when we were chatting together beside the pool, what seems like ages ago, that written proposals have been received. I…"

"Under no circumstances will the property of Bali High be sold to anyone, regardless of the proposed uses they claim…, in part or in whole! There, is that statement clear enough for you and the hoard of opportunists who have or will come knocking!"

"But what if Bali High receives an offer which it cannot refuse. You remember that line from the 'Godfather', don't you? What happens if a Marlon Brando character, or a series of Marlon Brando characters come knocking at the gate!"

"Violence, you mean violence and coercion as a means of wresting the place away from us. Why, I would call the police…, the military, if necessary. I know many powerful people in authority. I know…,"

"And what if some of those people in authority were in league with what you termed, the 'opportunists'. What then!"

"Michael, what are you intimating? What do you know that I do not! During most of my rambling this evening, your mind has been elsewhere. What's going on in that grey matter up there, the thinking part of you that is between those ears of yours?"

"Just a premonition Dr. Rajawane. No proof of anything sinister…, yet. It's just a feeling that all is not quite right! The list of suitors would help me get to the bottom of anything that is suspicious and, and probably dispel the apparitions that have taken up residence in this damn suspicious mind of mine."

"Sometimes Michael, you become your own worst enemy. Do you know that! Your own worst enemy! But, to placate you and your ghosts, I will rhyme off the short list of would be suitors to date. Let's see…, well there is, The Battleford Group, Rubicon Incorporated, the Ramparts Group, and Playfair Enterprises. Maybe more will be waiting for me when we return to Bali High. I don't know and I…, well you know the rest of it.

Interesting though, they all played the same game. It was as though they had all been trained in persuasive technique by the same coach, no, theatre director!

First there was the telephone call no…, telephone calls. All had persisted until they got me on the other end of the line. I remember male voices mainly, but in the cases of Rubicon Inc. and Playfair Enterprises, the voices were female.

Regardless of the gender, they all, in essence, said the same thing. First and foremost, they wanted to know if I knew where you were. Then they congratulated me on my decision to leave medicine and join the team that would give direction to the wishes of Mr. Tan. They implied that Mr. Tan had been a close friend and associate of theirs. Implied, because how else could they know about the man and the particulars of his will.

But of course. Your lawyer friend in Singapore! The gentleman who was executor of Mr. Tan's estate. Mr…, Mr…,. whatever his name is…,"

"Oh yes, Mr. Whitehead. That man is no gentleman. He is guilty of utter betrayal. The man is also guilty of breach of professional conduct. The man would do anything for money. Soon, very soon, that man is to be justly rewarded for his transgressions.

Maybe more about that later…, Right now, give me, if you will, the modus operandi of our suitors to date. Just how have they tried to ingratiate themselves to you. And what have they proposed which would allow them to gain inclusion in the creative impulses and processes that will be at the essence of Bali High Art."

"Fine, so, after the smooth introductions, they all had TV commercial voices which dripped of self-assurance, honesty and conviction, they stated that the organizations they represented had great interest in associating, just like you said, with you and me relative to the new, cultural enterprise on the shores of Lake Batur.

In every case, the telephone calls were followed, in less than a week, by letters. But not just ordinary business type missives. Oh no, all were printed on fine, almost parchment like paper. Through the mumbo-jumbo of their supposed history of supporting only those enterprises which showed genuine promise, did they state that a meeting between us, or among us, would prove to be handsomely, that's the word they used, handsomely advantageous for Bali High Art.

And our 'marriage' with them, if you will, would result in even greater benefits for us as our relationship 'blossomed' down the road. That was their word as well! Nothing specific though, was mentioned. That, I suppose, would be divulged at our meetings. That's why I said to you earlier that under no circumstances would I consent to the land holdings of Bali High Art being divided up. They can take their fine words and sticky sentiments and go to…, just go to somewhere else!"

"So you did not respond to any of their letters. Is that right, Dr. Rajawane?"

"Definitely not."

"Very good, no response, excellent!

Of course, we must acknowledge that, in that list of suitors which you just rhymed off, at least a few probably did know Mr. Tan in his prime. When he was at the helm of Good Earth Distribution. At that time, he had his fingers in a large number of entrepreneurial pies. And although most were decidedly sweet, some were less than savory.

But, in terms of the final disbursement of the Tan estate, only Mr. Whitehead in Singapore could have supplied those people who are hiding behind shell companies, with the added pieces to the puzzle which enabled them to target us, me specifically, and Bali High Art enterprises.

But it's too late for all of them. Bali High Art is a done deal! And the gentleman that you carved new life into so many years ago, Mr. Prawata, made magic happen by creating our new reality almost overnight.

Obviously they must have been counting on my reticence to follow through on Mr. Tan's final wishes. They thought that I would be seduced into inaction or dissuaded to act in good faith on the strength of the personal fortune to be made by selling the property to the highest bidder."

"Remember Michael, remember! We even joked about that very thing happening, and how rich we both would be…, before, before that is, dismissing it utterly as legal and moral claptrap."

"The universally held notion, in some circles at least, that fraud is a legitimate stepping stone to success. Greed as the ultimate good! They think that everybody thinks and acts just like they do! And that's why some of the people who are hovering nearby are so dangerous! Monsters dressed as Machiavelli himself.

I will meet with the man whose loose, ship sinking lips placed us in this sticky situation. Within the next couple of weeks, actually. And I will need your professional help in order to ensure that the outcome to our little rendezvous in Singapore will be richly rewarding for both of us.

Now, give me just half a minute. I want to show you something that might cast some light on at least one or two of the suitors who are almost in our back yard."

Travelling lightly had its advantages. I was back in the company of the Doctor in the time allotment I had given myself. I placed the envelope left at the house in Jakarta by Pearly, in front of my companion.

Dr. Rajawane opened the envelope flap automatically as he stared at me with a quizzical expression on his face. He allowed the four Polaroid photos to fall in his lap. His jaw had dropped as the glossy shots came into focus. He shot an accusatory look at me that seemed to imply that I was responsible for what lay before him. Murdering the messenger could have been the caption under a photo taken of his face at that moment.

Good, I thought. I needed his disbelief, his disgust, as catalyst for decidedly criminal behavior.

"Michael, where…, how…, where do you meet people like this. Why, this is absolutely disgusting."

The Doctor tossed the offending shot in the direction of our slender glass replicas of the World Trade Centre towers and proceeded to almost lasciviously devour the remaining three photos on the table. They too were soon discarded in apparent disgust. He returned to the first shot and studied it more closely.

I agreed with his choice for detailed scrutiny. All four had been taken along an abandoned stretch or road somewhere between Carita and Jakarta. All four were of the man who had almost been a meal for the monster inside the container compound.

The Doctor's photo of choice had revealed the subject at his best. The mouth gag, red ball and pink belt, was tightly buckled in place. An abbreviated, pink Speedo swim suit was the man's only wearing apparel. Abbreviated because it contained three, red sequined, capital letters; M, O, and W. Between the 'M' and the 'O', a letter had fallen or been ripped off, probably during the dressing ritual which would have occurred despite the protestations of the wearer.

The outline of the letter 'E', in caps, was visible as a darkened shadow on the stretch, nylon material. The shadow completed the intended, four letter word.

It was, in some semi-secret circles, the language of a sissy. It was "Pussy talk"! I chuckled to myself!

But the abbreviated dress parade uniform entailed more. Much more. Protruding from the rear of the Speedo was, what looked like, a horse tail. I could only conclude that the foot long cascade of black hair was attached to some sort of butt plug. The probe had either been forced through the bathing suit material or a reinforced hole had been stitched into the garment to accommodate the addition.

The wearer had been rendered incapable of extracting the equine appendage. A stout piece of cord ran through the pink colored handcuffs he was wearing behind his back and it was knotted to the neck chocker. It was impossible for the man to reach down to his behind to extract anything that might have been lodged there.

"So what do you think, Dr. Rajawane? Would you like to have a gentleman such as the one in the photos as part of your family tree! No, never mind that! How about as a sitting member of the Bali High Executive Committee?

"Decidedly not! What kind of preoccupation with self or perversity prompts people into such foolishness? Dr. Nuriana, my ENT man at the hospital, has carved out, and there is no pun intended, a lucrative side line for himself, by attending to patients, much like this man, who present with problems at the far end of their torsos. By default, he has become the hospital resident proctologist for perversity.

Everything from children's pliable toys, Disney characters are a favorite, to kitchen items such as salt and pepper shakers, not necessarily empty at the time of insertion, to house hold items like thimbles and erasers and candle stubs, anything which goes in much easier than it comes out, has been 'excavated' and 'notated' by him, so to speak!

All of the play things which turn treacherous are revealed only when a self-retaining specula and forceps arrive, like the American cavalry in the movies, to rescue the embarrassing, uncomfortable day. And, let me supplement the story with an addendum. Many of his patients learn little from their experience bent in two over the proctology table. They seem to suffer from a complete lack of self-control or shame, for that matter. The result is that their voluntary, or involuntary condition becomes chronic. Great recurring, lucrative business, he jokingly admits, whenever I meet him in the doctor's lounge, post, local anesthetic surgery!

And the cause! I have no idea! Latent homosexuality, I somehow doubt that. Anal caress to assuage or sustain the shame of late toilet training, I know even less of that, mere prostate stimulation, well, maybe. There are pliable products on the market for that very purpose, you know. Dr. Nuriana finds them, pushed in too far, all the time. I suggested to him that he should start a re-cycling business because, I am told, they command a high price at the retail level. Before they have been test driven, of course. Ha, ha!"

I could not allow the Doctor's discomfort to dissipate through diatribe.

"Would you like to know who the man in the pink is, Dr. Rajawane? The name sake of the Sultan of Egypt about eight hundred years ago? The man named after the Sunni Muslim military and political leader, Salah ad-Din? The man in Polaroid pink is Mr. Saladin!

You remember, the man of magic, the Dukun who wove his black magic to snare Col. Satu. The man who was hired to prompt my unscheduled return to Jakarta from the Turks and Caicos Islands. The catalyst, I believe, used by those with hostile intent, to get to me, through the Colonel. Get to me to further their goal, namely, the acquisition of the Bali High property.

They must have been led to believe by our Mr. Loose-lips in Singapore that Mr. Tan had bequeathed the place to me, me alone, with no strings attached. They must have thought that I could do with it whatever I deemed appropriate, or more likely, personally advantageous. That would have included selling the place to the highest bidder! That is exactly what the Singapore lawyer would have done."

"What happened to our quiet little respite in the country side? What happened to our moment of sober reflection and civilized discourse? Are the Philistines really that close, Michael? Are they really at our gate?"

Dr. Rajawane was back on the emotional track needed to move the train forward, and in the right direction. This was not the time, I reasoned, to tell him of the real reason for choosing Puncak as our reality escape. The 'Genesis' story of Lilith would have to wait. Her reality would be for another day. After our 'little engine that could', crossed the great divide between naïve aspiration and nerveless acquisition of the prize.

"Tell me, Dr. Rajawane, how difficult a task would it be for you to concoct a document attesting to the paternity of Mr. Tan's son, Geoffrey? Such an official looking piece of evidence, viewed only once by our legal eagle in his Singapore aviary before it was destroyed, would serve to ensure that my mission with the misguided, malevolent man will succeed.

"I don't even want to know why, Michael. I trust you enough to be confident that a larger good will be served through the use of such a ruse. And since you deem it necessary to help get that particular foreign object out of our corporate behinds, then so be it! Let's do it. The forceps and speculum and the hinged table and…, and even the anesthetic…, be damned!"

"Listen, if you find when you wake up tomorrow morning that you are the last man standing…, that you are holding down the fort all by yourself, just know that I am not too far away. I will be attending to a few small details that relate to the smooth launch of Bali High. Details, only small ones, which are best dealt with when I am alone. And if need be, make your way back to Bali when you deem it appropriate without me. I will not be far behind."

"Small details you say…, more likely details that have very rough edges. I understand you Michael. I understand you all too well."

"D'accord, cher Docteur. Alors, nous avons beaucoup de choses a faire demain. Many, many issues remain for tomorrow all of which will require our prompt, our focused attention."

"All in good time, Michael. Mountains are mastered one step at a time. It said so in the last fortune cookie message I read. Well, in spite of the heavy clouds on your horizon, on our horizons, tomorrow will temper what we have talked about tonight. I believe that it is time for this nearly, no, newly rich Chairman of the Board to call it a day. Alors, cher Michel, jusqu'a demain, mon ami…, mon frère."

The good doctor was a better man than I was by half. And the better half that made the man who and what he was, sat squarely above the water line, in Bristol condition, for all, who were knowledgeable of form and function, to see.

I had raided one of the two cartons of chocolate bars which had been slated for distribution among the Bali High staff. Of course, Christina would be the distribution agent for the cornucopia of confection. Whether she was Santa or merely knew him well, albeit with great apprehension, was a moot point.

Neither Dr. Rajawane nor I had eaten anything other than a few nuts and some fresh fruit from the complimentary platter. The pineapple, mango, bananas and the red, spiny replicas of scuttling sea creatures, rambutan, had been fresh but far from filling.

He strode off to his bedroom with a Cadbury barbell in each hand. And I, feigning retreat to my room of rest, looked like I had visited the same work-out gym and had acquired the same heavy calorized, exercise equipment!

Chapter 16

The rhythmic rumbling of a spent man at rest was not long in coming. Now! How to find a needle in a haystack? A needle in a haystack and, a haystack in the dark! Well, not entirely dark.

As I squinted to ensure that I remained on the darkened foot path which wove through the compound, I was guided, in part, by the flickering, electronic light, like lightning on the distant horizon, which emanated from the half dozen or so occupied chalets. Like electronic monitors in the OR, they seemed to be recording the vital signs of the people who were cocooned within.

The numbing dumbness of the pastime, I thought. Not only was the image on the screen vapidly innocuous but the constant camera angle changes, aimed at retaining viewer attention via retinal stimulation, had the opposite effect. The kaleidoscope of changing colors and forms did not, in fact, allow for any viewer concentration at all! Pablum for the proletariat with the promise of an ever decreasing attention span to boot!

Lilith would have been in one of the miniature, gingerbread houses. I just knew it. She would have been compelled to seek the privacy, the isolation which one of them would provide. The rooms in the main hotel building were too small and too exposed. She needed to regroup after the series of traumas caused by her unplanned encounters of the day.

Her collisions with a meddlesome, snide, foreigner, her suffering from the undeserved pain which he had inflicted, the inescapable conclusion concerning her own ineptitude when attempting to demonstrate necessary force against him, all were out of keeping with the self-concept which the woman possessed. All spoke to her inadequacies in the face of the demands of her job. All would make her handlers, Egyptian or Israeli, Mukhabarat or Mossad, it didn't matter, less than pleased.

And to add even greater insult to her injury was the admission that other members of her team had also fallen short of the mark. Saladin was no longer part of the Jakarta equation. And of course there was the cartoonish character, Mr. Brian Law, her very own 'Thumper' from the Bambi story, who unfortunately, seemed to be her main, maybe only connection to the CIA.

Her vulnerabilities had been brought into sharp focus by her encounters with me! I was undoubtedly seen by her as the devil incarnate. And she didn't even know who I was! But like anyone who blames misfortune on what is outside, what was inside her would fester in the dark and blossom full bloom during our next encounter. Like a lioness with an infected tooth, her pain would erase all caution and conditioned, rational response. Lilith would be, as was the case with the angered Biblical God of old, a fearsome, irrational force with which to contend!

Daniel Boone, a contemporary of Davy Crockett in colonial America, had been quoted as saying that a neighbor was residing too close to him if the smoke from that neighbor's chimney could be seen from the frontiersman's front porch.

An Indonesian 'blue-blood', a member of the former noble class in central Sulawesi, a man whose regal bearing was now bestowed primarily upon a lame dog and a tethered rooster, held court in the middle of his mountainous jungle domain each day regardless of the season.

Once, while visiting the region, we had serendipitously met. People and the parade of events that had shaped him were, his regal bearing notwithstanding, all from the distant, indistinct, past. He had told me, through translation, that, if the crowing of the neighbor's cock could be heard, the man who owned the bird and his family were residing too close to him and his kin for comfort.

On the other side of the Pacific Ocean, bar room wags with whom I sometimes tipped a jar or two, observed that if a roll of toilet paper could be borrowed from a neighbor by reaching out between open bathroom windows of adjacent dwellings, then maybe their wretched abodes were too close together!

Relativity, the favored child of situational analysis, perhaps!

I didn't find Lilith so much as a distinctive sound that seemed to follow in her wake, found me.

Barely audible at first, the muffled, regular, somewhat monotonous thumps could have been mistaken for the distant garage drum beats of a suburban, wannabe rock band.

The ground level window of the bungalow, the one which was host to the sound usually reserved for those in possession of a stethoscope, was framed by off white, sheer curtains. An undetectable, tip-toed approach to the window casement was easy. Any view of the inside of the room was however, decidedly more difficult. The lower, horizontal portion of the window frame was home to a phalanx of books aimed at, no doubt, guests who preferred 'old-style' entertainment through exercise of the intellect. A complement, perhaps, to the silent, sylvan surroundings of the secluded abode they had rented.

Beyond the books and their pressed pages however, a pair of naked, adult feet could be seen. Poised in the air above the head of their owner, the position they assumed was reminiscent of that achieved by Christine when, as an infant, she had been fascinated by the number and variety of toes she possessed.

The upper torso of a woman could also be seen. It was positioned between the two outstretched legs. The woman to whom the body belonged appeared to be in the throes of making the upstretched appendages oscillate like the arms of a work-out machine. Her sole focus seemed to be to flex the muscles of her lower back. 'Fuck your way to fitness', came to mind as a suitable title for the image which was framed by the open window.

The woman's breathing was even but somewhat strained. She possessed the rhythm of a sculler who had fought to gain the right response in the quest to marry wood with water. Tightly grasping both elevated ankles for stability and for leverage, she absently looked everywhere about her other than down at the recipient of her energy expenditure. I ducked down quickly before the uninvited voyeur in their midst interrupted, what I assumed would be, her impending, simulated coital climax.

The woman in control of the artificial intimacy being played out in Puncak, the woman from Hilton 837, the woman who was man to the woman-man below her, was Lilith!

Frequent exposure to the perverse, rendered its impact, on me at least, marginal. I became the unwilling viewer of a summer re-run on television. Commercials for the plastic products used would have been of greater interest than the silly sit-com itself. But, I had to admit, the woman was a quick study. She knew how to play the tune well with her plastic paraphernalia. And at least one client, one regular client, made muffled sounds to suggest that he shared that view!

My mind wandered to the mechanical. How had Brian Law managed to get to Puncak as quickly as he did. There was no doubt in my mind that the hairy legs which were attempting to toe paint the ceiling belonged to the man from the Straits of Malacca, the man who was the spanner in the gears of Col. Satu. The mechanics of course, didn't matter. His presence, upright or prone, did!

I slowly backed away from the chalet, crossed the path, and sat down beneath a large tree that was perhaps fifty feet from the front door. There was no other exit from the place other than to disturb the window library and jump into a dense, dark growth of prickly shrubs.

I settled in for the 'big wait'. The same suspect, same modus operandi, same strategy to intercept. Too bad there wasn't a stop sign nearby. I could have concocted some new words to go with the six I had already squeezed out of the word while on stake-out in Jakarta!

This time, the wait was not long. Lilith came out of the darkened chalet and descended the steps toward the pathway. At the bottom of the third and last step, she abruptly stopped and grasped at the railing.

Like someone who was receiving body blows from an invisible assailant, she gasped, doubled over, and crumpled into a groaning heap on the bottom stair.

My first impulse was to go to her assistance, but instead, I waited. Too many variables - her reaction, the response of the person or persons inside the suite, assistance or interference from one or more persons who were also lying in wait somewhere in the dark nearby..., even an innocent passerby..., benevolence be damned! This woman was no friend of mine anyway.

Nothing happened. No noise, no new players, nothing. Lilith got up slowly. She let go of the railing, ran her fingers through her hair, rubbed consolingly at her lower gut and took a few tentative steps in the direction of the main building.

If she was having a gall bladder attack or if her appendix was acting up, both possible in a woman her age, I would be forced to alert the front desk. Bogor abounded with many good to excellent private hospitals. For those who had the brains for biology and the balls for business, ownership of a private hospital, particularly in upwardly mobile, growing communities, like Bogor, was a permanent passport to professional and personal success. But only in Asia.

Christ, I thought, maybe Lilith was pregnant. Maybe the man with his feet in the clouds, landed infrequently and left something more than skid marks on the tarmac!

With a supreme effort to control my heavy breathing, I casually strode into the lobby of the main building, which I reasoned had to be Lilith's destination. I sat down and picked up a brochure which touted the reasons why the purchase of a time share package in Bogor would be a prudent, almost providential, investment.

I had run as fast as I could to get as far ahead of the woman as possible. No sense attracting attention as a couple who appeared to be in the midst of a domestic spat. And no sense following a strategy involving speed again, I thought, until I had done some laps around a gym to reacquaint myself with a childhood friend named, Stamina!

After what seemed like an inordinate amount of time just to follow the same path I had taken, Lilith appeared at the front door. Hesitating, she lingered for a moment and then lurched into the lobby. Instead of heading straight ahead toward the check-in desk, or to the bank of elevators on her left, she abruptly veered to the right and, bent over in pain, staggered down the corridor like some urban, gut-shot victim of a 'pass-by' shooting. She must have known that the short, dead-end hallway ended with the oases needed by those caught short during their prolonged games of social mating.

Another interminable, 'stop sign' interlude I thought. A woman could vacation in a wash room stall and attend to whatever part of the body needed attention, almost forever. This time though, this bloody time with Lilith, this was not going to happen!

On the dance floor of life, if one were to partner with Lilith, one had always to remember to maintain the lead. If not, the woman would not only step, step hard on all ten toes but would also put knee to partner groin in true gleeful, girlish, ghoulish fashion, just for good measure.

The public, as well as guest room toilet facilities at the Bogor resort were Western in design and decor. No holes in the floor mounted on raised, ceramic platforms for squatters to do their business on this property. No! American Standard was the brand name of choice when it came to the evacuation of potty produce anywhere on the property. After all, any visual or olfactory evidence left behind of the elimination of bodily waste by other guests would definitely dissuade anyone from visiting the retreat a second time.

The washroom for women was empty. No guests occupied any of the first, five toilet stalls, no patrons were cleaning up at the sinks on the opposite side of the room, and no maid was present with both hands extended; one with the offer of a terrycloth towel and the other ready to accept a tip for the service which was redundant.

Only the sixth cubicle at the far end of the room, the one designated for handicapped patrons, the one which was two times the size of the normal stalls, had someone seemingly penned up inside. The moaning, the grunts and the thumping of torso against the walls of the enclosure suggested entrapment more than it did safe refuge for the private and personal business of bowel evacuation.

I scaled the side wall of her enclosure from the adjacent stall and landed noiselessly beside Lilith. Ignoring the potential of disturbing migrating gall stones or rupturing an already inflamed appendix, or even witnessing the crimson tide of monthly fertility renewal, I wrenched her from the floor back up to her perch, slapped her hard across the face, and then pushed her back down into a squat so that her buttocks were just inches above the floor.

Misdemeanor or felony charge, it didn't matter. Cops almost everywhere followed the same routine with all who would be spending the night behind bars. Stripped from the waist down, told to squat, and commanded to cough, was the step by step means of acquiring the litmus test to prove that the anal cavity of the prisoner was void of foreign, incriminating or possibly dangerous, objects.

"It doesn't matter how I got here. It doesn't matter how I knew that you would here and it doesn't matter how I know that you are probably suffering from some sort of bowel obstruction. What matters, you stupid little bitch, is that I have your number. Got it! Your bloody number…, and right now…, you belong to me!"

I looked hard into Lilith's eyes. There was personal recognition of the person barking and taunting her but there was no sign of fear. And there was no hatred either. All I could see was pain. Excruciating pain! Good, I thought. Compliance was what I needed and if it had to be born of unbearable discomfort, then so be it!

"Let's make our little interlude as short as possible, shall we. Pretend that you are my prisoner. No! Pretend that you are my patient. Can you do that! Just pretend and just do what I tell you to do. Do exactly as I say. Doctors always know best! Now cough! Cough hard, like you're a terminal lung cancer patient. C'mon, you're dying of cancer. Look, you've coughing up blood already. See! You sloppy little bitch! It's all over the floor around you."

Lilith peered down at the thin trail of viscous, slightly bubbly diarrhea that had pooled on the floor below her and, seemingly oblivious to the smell, looked away.

Nothing happened. Nothing, it seemed, was lurking or lodged there. Groaning, the woman fell over on her side and, rocking back and forth, rolled up as tightly as she could in a sort of compressed fetal position.

Christ, I thought, maybe her problem involved some abdominal organ failure.

Gray's Anatomy, the authoritative British text on the subject, described the perineum as the superficial transverse strip of muscle that passed between the exterior anal sphincter muscle and the scrotum in males, and with females, the vulva. Normally an erogenous zone to be sure. It was anything but that when it was my middle finger that was pressed into service along that particular isthmus of Lilith. I pressed hard, almost stabbing at Lilith's 'P' spot much as one would at the round, dimpled button beside an unresponsive elevator door.

American draft dodgers from the Viet Nam conflict in the 1960's, those who sought refuge on abandoned farms in Quebec just north of the Vermont border, those who made fashion statements by parading around topless, those who gave and got head with impunity, in true Woodstock style, they were, for me at least, characters from the land of the arcane, from the land that had the Iconoclastic River flowing through it.

They were my source of information about how to assist someone when a digestive tract 'bottleneck' brought everything on their Interstate highway of excretion to a standstill.

The procedure seemed to be practiced quite often among them. They ascribed the frequency of its occurrence, in part, to the hard, mineral laden well water, the water that stubbornly refused to provide lather on wash days and the water which they relied upon for drinking purposes.

The other culprit was the lentil. The little seed, the little seed that was cheap, formed the foundation for their nutritional support. Dollars, even Canadian dollars, could be stretched a long way when the main ingredient in soup, stew or just protein on the plate, partnered with white rice of course, was the brownish, little kernel that resembled bird seed.

But that particular bird seed was a rich, dietary source of iron. And that made the lowly lentil a binding agent that was rivaled only by cement.

Forcing the two middle fingers far down one's throat or that of the victim, sufficient to induce the gag reflex was the first step. Bathed in viscous fluid, multiple attempts, all painful, to slide the two, lubricated fingers between the sphincter muscle and the bulbous obstruction were then made. That was step two. Step three was an unrelenting repeat of poking, pressing and pushing until successive penetrations were achieved. Deep throat lube could, for obvious, bacterial reasons, only be harvested once. Subsequent slipperiness came from expectorated spit or water, preferably warm, which was positioned in a bowl close by.

Step three with Lilith was accomplished thanks to the thin, metal tube that fountained water upward from below the inside rim of the toilet bowl. Rarely available in North America, the stream of water directed at one's undercarriage, post waste elimination, and its volume regulation by a tap beside the toilet bowl, was considered, other than where the pulp and paper industry maintained an army of political lobbyists, the only sane and sanitary solution to the removal of external bacterial presence 'where the Sun never shines'!

Vast tracts of soft wood trees were thought to be of far more economic than ecological importance. They were harvested, reduced to mash, bleached white, rolled up, and then flushed back into the fresh water system. Rendered potable, it was thought, only after being treated in a never ending cycle of chemical baths. Among educated, responsible people, except for those in the land of the free, free to be obstinate, it seemed, this was a 'no-brainer'!

Lilith was beside herself in pain. Her arms were wrapped tightly around my shoulders almost, it seemed, in an attempt to achieve a sort of relief based on transference. Transference of a debilitating condition, to rid herself of the vicious creature that had bitten her, a nightmarish beast that refused to release her from its grip, in favor of another, any other, who was close by.

Hers could have been a game of playground tag. Tag, in which the person who became 'it' would become the Biblical, 'Job' of affliction. But without the presence of a caring or a conciliatory God.

Thank you, I whispered almost audibly. Thank you, thank you, thank you both for being there.

My gratitude was two-fold.

One. There was a chocolate bar in my pocket! It allowed for a successful probe of Liulith's lower bowel. The exploration should have concluded with a bow to 'Mr. Cadbury'! The confection had readily melted on and between my fingers as well as around the perianal area of my patient. Lubrication made easy via confection!

This permitted my fingers to find and fumble with the hard shelled, tubular object that nudged up against the interior wall of her lower bowel. It was not composed of compacted fecal matter. The sides of the object were too rigid and too smooth. And it was perfectly rounded at the one end I could touch.

And two. Lilith's problem was mechanical obstruction, not some metabolic disorder. No self-flagellation would be needed by me as a part of the post-game, possibly post-mortem, analysis of events.

The woman had obviously been in a hurry to conceal whatever it was, or whatever it contained, otherwise, why not just deftly insert it in her vagina. Incriminating evidence, evidence contained in rolls of Kodachrome film, taken by Greenpeace women exposing the work of the whalers of the world, or by female spies capturing, with stills, the malfeasance of bellicose powers, evidence that was hard to defend against detection, had a history of remaining safe and easy to retrieve when that particular orifice was called to active duty!

I was done. Like an obstetrician assisting in the delivery of a breach birth infant, I had reached in and repositioned the capsule so that it was aligned with the descending colon and then had just let nature, assisted by the Cadbury Company, follow its evolutionary mandate!

The capsule noiselessly fell to the tiled floor like a freshly hatched chicken egg. Before Lilith had a chance to notice, let alone respond, it was quickly kicked across the floor toward the sinks.

Stay ahead of the woman. Do not let her take the lead, I reminded myself.

"You have a job ahead of you, missy. So, if you want to show your gratitude for everything I have done for you tonight, then clean this place up and clean yourself up too. Make the place look like nothing ever happened. It's your mess and you are responsible. So clean up 'well' or explain yourself 'good' to the first, curious member of staff who shows up.

This is what you need to tell your associates, before the visit to Bali High Art occurs. The meeting at the Bali property will occur two days from now. All of you must follow the written instructions contained in this envelope. The date of our little get-together is not negotiable. Be there or bugger off and don't bother Dr. Rajawane or me again! Got that!

And…, oh yes, one last thing. In case you are still living in a serene state of ignorance as to my identity…, Michael Campbell, I am Michael Campbell.. Got it!

The Michael Campbell! I am the guy…, the guy that you and the motley crew you work with forced to return prematurely, from the Caribbean. I am the guy with the close business associate, one Colonel Satu, the gentleman you have repeatedly threatened over the past two weeks. I am the guy you have to get past to even get a glimpse of the property that is home to Bali High Art!

But despite of all of your collective obfuscation, we, Dr. Rajawane and I, have decided to meet with you and your group, as I have just said, at Bali High, the day after tomorrow. But, be warned, we are not impressed by anything contained in your written correspondence to date. So start working on a new proposal which you, collectively, think will convince us that getting into bed with you, so to speak, will be in the best interest of Bali High Art.

The best of British luck with the challenge and the invitation my dear!"

I winked at the woman as I slid the envelope, without protest, between the second and third buttons of her blouse. I opened the stall door, skipped across the room, scooped up a bundle of loose paper towels folded between the sinks, and threw them, like a bundle of newspapers from a moving truck, toward the dry area of the floor in her stall.

Feigning the brisk washing of my hands in the sink, I removed the greasy ruminants that were both biological and British in origin from my prize and slipped it into my pocket. Lilith would be left thinking that the plastic chamber of little secrets that had produced all of her horror had simply been sucked away, along with the dam burst of built up waste in the toilet bowl, with the first flush.

It was not clear whether Lilith had heard any of my parting remarks. She apparently was having none for me. She was alone in a world of her own and she was 'tickled pink', as my mother would have said, to be in the middle of a new found world of 'painless', normalcy.

She was completely free from pain and she seemed, like a little child with a new, miniature dish set, delighted just to be able to ponder the 'do-able' details demanded by the mundane task before her. Rudimentary tasks requiring simple eye-hand co-ordination. Tasks unimpeded by the electric fence of illness. Personal clean-up or make believe table set- up, it didn't matter. All that mattered was that she was capable once again.

John Clark, a former, 'head-hunter', friend of mine, a man whose job it was to steal executives away from 'donor' companies and feed them, for a fee, to 'client' companies, had been diagnosed with cancer.

He had responded so well to chemo therapy, he was told that not only had the disease gone into remission, but that it had disappeared completely from his body.

Cancer-free! I am cancer-free. Michael, can you believe it! I am cancer free. This became his mantra for the next six months. He was energized. He was exonerated. His death sentence had been commuted. He had become, once again, a trekker on the high road of life.

That exuberance, that 'player plus' mentality, lasted right up to the resurgence of the leukocytes, his white blood cells, in their futile attempt to mount a defense against a second, stronger rush of rapacious 'c' cells. A sort of cellular cannibalism played out in his body. A Civil War, almost! The cells that came to dominate from within were the harbinger of a new and lethal order. They had been, from his very conception, programmed to proliferate and ultimately, prevail.

I knew the Bali High Art meeting would not bode well for any of the players in attendance. There was, in particular, a sense of dread about the vulnerability of Lilith. She, like her name sake, would be most prone to perdition at the hands of the Devil who, from the outset, would be dwelling within the details. A black force which would, without compunction, dispense diminution to any who attempted to court his disfavor.

Lilith did not belong to the company. She was not even an associate member in good standing and more, she represented a foreign, an untrustworthy element trespassing in the Elysian Fields of American espionage. She would have been viewed as a threat to any on-going stability, to the comfortable status quo, to the turn of events in America's favor which, from the perspective of those in Virginia, only covert, hard work and expertise had made possible. Meddling would not be tolerated by those zealots whose job it was to mold and maintain the company culture, a culture which was founded upon a virulent strain of xenophobia.

Worse, she was a woman who was scared of dying. She was a woman who was even more scared that she was not scared enough to satisfy the God who had scared her since childhood. And her face wore that fear like a badge. The woman was a magnet for misfortune.

Chapter 17

Strange, I thought, airports were never named after women. Airplanes and ships however, were always considered to be feminine but that might have been, as opined by Chester Nimitz, a Fleet Admiral in the US navy, because they, the sea going vessels of war at least, were so expensive to keep in paint and powder!

I. Gusti Ngurah Rai had been a fighter for Indonesian independence, post-World War Two. The Dutch had attempted to, ironically enough, take back what they felt was theirs, just like, less than a decade earlier, what the Japanese had set out to accomplish in South Asia and the Nazis all over Europe. A long history of occupation, they reasoned, sanctioned their repossession of the archipelago which straddled the Equator.

The man died a hero, while battling that 'Dutch treat' notion. The country of Indonesia was born and his name was given to the airport in Bali which was, next to the Sukarno Hatta, in Jakarta, the busiest one in the country. It was simply referred to as "Gusti Ngurah" airport by all who passed through its 'portal to paradise', plate glass doors.

I had made a habit of always being early for business appointments. It had afforded me the luxury of time. Time to smoke, think, to smoke, strategize, to smoke, create opening gambits, to smoke and play the imminent game of chess in my mind until I lost track of the board positions of the opposition pieces and my own as well. And still smoke.

George Carlin, an American social commentator and funny man, was no stranger to the ingestion of compounds designed to alter one's perception of reality. One of the more innocuous of his addictions, or at least one of the few which was legal, involved Lady Nicotine.

In his signature, staccato, stream of consciousness delivery, he explained, to a reporter, how he was able to quit that particular addiction, cold turkey. Stated simply, tobacco ceased to pass his balance test. According to Carlin, there were three elements involved in the pursuit of personal gratification through physical intimacy with natural and synthetic mind altering compounds.

Procurement, Preparation, Pleasure.

When the third 'P' in the process reigned supreme, the preceding 'P's' were but necessary steps to be ascended to achieve Nirvana. But when the first two factors began to out-weigh the third, even when the third was increased in volume to sustain the power of some long ago, initial rush, it was time to stop.

Buying bloody smokes had, for me, become a nuisance. Stores, corner shops, even ubiquitous street hawkers were everywhere when you didn't need them. Books of matches, and lighters were rarely kept around the house in sufficient quantity to have one at arms-length, at the ready, and the potted plants scattered around the house always seemed to be too far away when butt burying was in order.

The toasted taste of tobacco, the pleasure that had punctuated my youth, ebbed as that chapter in my life drew to a close. I had switched from the red pack of Marlboros to the 'lights' in the gold box, but that didn't help. 'P' plus 'P', in sum, came to out-weigh the final 'P' in the addiction equation.

My habit of arriving well in advance of the agreed to time persisted, despite the Indonesian proclivity for 'rubber time', their being late, almost always. The gray clouds of exhaled smoke that usually attended my early arrival were replaced by the 'lung-loving' large, fluffy variety found only high up in the sky.

I was nervous. I was nervous about the meeting which was about to commence. I was nervous because I was too well prepared. Facts, too many facts, were going to be made to fit into a funneled format that would, only maybe, foil my uninvited guests.

First and foremost, I was responsible to protect Dr. Rajawane and the fledgling crew of Bali High Art. That, I knew, would be no small undertaking, in large part because of what Lilith's bowel obstruction had revealed. The note inside the small, plastic case cracked the code of intent and revealed that my supposed suitors were, in fact, my adversaries.

My attempt at the washroom sink, post Lilith delivery from pain, to rid the plastic capsule of its unsavory, greasy skin had inadvertently, allowed warm water to seep inside. Unfolding the soggy mass of paper, back in my room, was like wrestling with a wet, tightly folded napkin from a Chinese restaurant. And my meaty fingers, which less than deftly sandwiched the piece of dripping flimsy between two, dry, face clothes, did not help.

The writer of the hastily scrawled note had used a cheap, ball point pen. 'Hilton Jakarta', was all that remained undamaged at the top of the page. Most of the hasty scribbling had been drowned in the sink and no museum quality restorative work would have breathed new life into my bathroom blunder.

The words, those which were left, like little blue, islands on the page, were mostly blurred but the intent of the missive was abundantly clear: know and maintain a focus on the objective, know the weaknesses of the adversaries, do what had to be done to ensure success at any cost. It was a page right out of a tome written by Vince Lombardy, the patron saint of American football. 'Winning isn't everything…, it's the only thing'.

In fewer than twenty, hand written lines, words and phrases like, tasked with assignment, of urgent concern and immediate resolution, Achilles heel, kid card, deliberate, and dispatch, screamed that 'NO' was not to be viewed as anything more than an adversarial point of view requiring stronger, more coercive, negotiation tactics.

Coming home empty handed was not an option. It was a page taken from the manual of life lessons followed by the mothers of Sparta whose sons served empire. Their parting comments to their progeny, as they prepared to march to war was, 'come home with your shield, or come home on it!'

The CIA, as proud, protective mother of America, was resolute in its preparedness for perpetual war with the rest of the world.

I knew that my invited guests would come to the meeting armed. I certainly was. My concealed weapon was thanks to a safe house in Denpasar. Firearms, forged travel documents and a sort of Halloween haven for moustaches, wigs, foundation make up, horned rimmed glasses, clothes for both color and style changes, to make me look like another, any other, of either gender, lay scattered about, but at the ready.

All alter egos waited patiently behind a false wall that served as support for bookshelves which were student certified sloppy.

My tea party guests would have had their side arms waiting for them in a restroom in the Arrivals area of Gusti Ngurah airport. CIA, s.o.p.

I tapped the envelope that was nestled at the bottom of a deep inside pocket of the jungle jacket which I was wearing. I called it that even though people remarked, whenever I wore it, that I looked more like a foreign correspondent than an explorer. Beige in color, it was all pockets and stitched loops. It was too over the top not to be real. It was my ticket to look like a sleuth on assignment for some prestigious publication. The intrigue which it created was sometimes amusing and almost always annoying.

A great source of vexation at times, would have been a nineteenth century way of expressing the problem. 'Pain in the ass', would have been both upbeat and better. The buttons, and zippers and Velcro which conspired to cover every pouch made for maddening misplacement when something was needed in a hurry. Passports, plane tickets, room reservations, credit cards, all fell into that category.

The saving grace of the jacket was that a heavy object, like a hand gun, could easily be tucked away and held secure on either side of it. This allowed for perfect 'concealed-carry' and the weapon could, in an instant, be retrieved and leveled at anyone who posed any real and/or present danger.

The brown manila envelope, which lay flat inside the oversized pocket of my Walter Cronkite jacket, had been handed to me by the young man on duty at the front desk of the Lembah Bukit Raya in

Bogor as Dr. Rajawane and I were checking out. It was one of my major weapons of preparedness.

"A young lady, a guest with us last night, just like you, Mr. Campbell, a guest who checked out before you this morning, instructed me to give this envelope to you. And, and, only to you, Mr. Campbell. She said 'Please', she was very strong with her words, 'Please', she said, please tell Mr. Michael Campbell to give the envelope to Mr. Brian Law when you are together in Bali… and she said you would know when is the right time…, she said only when you are together in Bali."

Taking my cue from the demeanor of the front desk fellow, a young man turned ecstatic acolyte, a convert who was completely enamored of the ravishing beauty who had chosen him above all others, to deliver an important diplomatic pouch to a fellow guest, I fished around in my wallet and found an American ten spot. Surreptitiously I handed it, along with a wide, grateful smile to the man whose mission had tragically, from his perspective at least, come to an end.

My meager contribution would serve as a compliment to the folded bank note which would have been concealed in the outstretched hand of the women with whom he was now hopelessly in love. A woman against whom all future females in his life would be judged. A woman against whom all would be found wanting, because all would fall short of the high water mark served up by imperfect memory!

The envelope contained two sheets of paper and four, black and white, glossy photographs. One sheet listed two individuals as well as, what I assumed were, their addresses in the state of Virginia. A Mr. James Rutherford who resided on South Stewart Street in the town of Hampton and a Mrs. Adele Law of Grange Drive in Aberdeen Gardens were, according to the hand written note at the bottom of the sheet, recent recipients of copies of all four photographs.

Each candid shot, taken quite clearly without his knowledge, featured the man, Brian, photographer pleasing, frozen on his back. With his feet raised high in the air, he seemed ready and willing to foot print paint the ceiling if given the chance.

All four images, studies in adolescent self-absorption, were interrupted only slightly by the naked back and buttocks of a female who, as she hovered above the crib-creature, appeared to have something cinched very tightly by black straps around her mid-section and upper thighs.

It did not require the logic of an Agatha Christie to conclude that the gentleman named on the piece of paper was one of Brian Law's handlers at Langley and that Adele was the wife of the man in the pictures who seemed to be very content without her.

The meaning was below the deductive reasoning power of her alter ego, Hercule Poirot as well. Only a fool would miss the implicit meaning in the visual message which was as large as a theatre marquee. Mrs. Law would be struck numb-dumb by what she saw. Was her husband a liar and a cheat…yes…, was her husband homosexual or, or, at least bi-sexual…, yes…, was immediate action required to distance herself from this stranger she did not know, this stranger whom she had never known…, most assuredly…, YES!

Rutherford, on the other hand, would have seen nothing more in the photos than an operative who had been exposed, an agent who had gone rogue. Brian Law would be viewed as a minor player who had just become a major security risk. And immediate action would be required to permanently distance the man who had morphed malignant from the ongoing business of the Company.

The real power behind the promised poison of the pictures required the analytical capabilities of both Christie and Poirot combined. To be fully understood and appreciated the observer had to be able to applaud the perverse.

No one, other than Brian Law, would ever receive the incriminating evidence. The idea of certain disaster was all that would be required.

The seed of 'secret revealed' would be planted in Brian Law's gut by a gardener who possessed twice his intellect. And as unwilling host to the bad seed, he would nevertheless, become its growth medium. He would fixate on inevitable, catastrophic end points and…, he would self-destruct as a consequence of that process.

"This does not appear to be written by someone who was nurtured in the tradition of the Western ethos. It speaks to brotherhood, to the community of the spirit of all mankind. It is of the earth. If it is, in fact, North American in origin, then the author is a native, a member of a tribe whose thought processes are of some antediluvian time. Measured and somewhat mystical, it could be European. There is an overwhelming tranquility in the adversity, maybe even perversity, of it. It is hauntingly beautiful."

Those were the words which Dr. Rajawane delivered to the air in front of him as he finished reading and re-reading the one line statement on the second page which had been placed in the envelope.

'The kindness in your cruelty makes me like me best when I am with you.'

I had folded the piece of paper neatly and had found a ready and remote pocket for my prize.

People in airports swarmed the 'arrivals' floor like primitive vertebrates. As with most vulnerable denizens of shoreline shallows, the survival of these creatures was predicated on a fraud they were able to practice, perfect and hence, perpetuate. By swimming together in a tight ball, individuality was lost. They resembled little more than a mass of floating tidal trash. Only when one of the wiggling creatures decided to change direction did the rest, 'en masse', follow suit.

My guests emerged from just such a 'mal de mer' of mindless movement on the concourse floor and brought my musings to an abrupt end. On with the mundane business of my own, not so special, survival, I thought sardonically.

My mother used to swear, politely, under her breath, when unwanted visitors showed up at the front door.

True to current, generational subtext, the word 'fuck' formed on my lips as I peered at the four horsemen from whose mischief I had chosen to protect Dr. Rajawane and the whole Bali High Art ensemble as well.

I willed myself into creating a reality that differed from the one in front of me. Crotches. I thought of crotches. I had engaged at least one of my physical senses in prolonged intimacy with every crotch that walked on two legs toward me.

DJ had played lady Lord Chancellor with her pants down. My eyes had feasted on her promise. Renee, the girl next door, had air brushed herself all over my body as we furtively allowed every sense to over flow our disparate worlds.

Lilith and I had painted and pained ourselves through every consensual position of copulation explained in text books devoted to the subject. Every position, that is, except vaginal penetration.

And Brian, ah yes Brian, the man whose bum had become as familiar and mundane as a scenic photo on a bank calendar. It had been witnessed enough, through sight and wall thumping sound, to force a familiarity which almost fostered the belief that it had a separate and distinct existence all its own.

Primitive thought made for a raunchy readiness.

The arrival of my suitors was met by the exercising of the seventeen muscles in my face needed to create a large grin. Put vanilla extract under the nose of mama rabbit and she will accept her young even when they reek of misguided human coddling.

Amused by my own musings, I stood and waited for my guests to initiate the dialogue. I needed their utterances to better understand what it was that they hoped to accomplish with or through me. And I hoped for at least a hint as to their level of optimism regarding their ability to secure the sought after prize.

I wanted their silences too. Without the tone or timbre of their words, I wanted the something in their body language that would hint at the true trajectory they were prepared to trace in pursuit of the endpoint of our strange interlude.

Were they of the opinion that success was completely within their grasp or was there a subtext of trepidation!

I was expecting Brian Law to play Pestilence and speak for the remainder of the assembled quartet; Death, Disease, and Hunger, but I was wrong.

"Well, good morning Mr. Campbell…, Mr. Michael…, Michael. How nice it is to see you here in Bali. Paradise for all of us, to be sure and…, the perfect place to begin the process of future partnership…, perhaps! Oh…, sorry…, maybe I'm getting just a little bit ahead of myself. Sorry. And, and, I seem to have lost my manners as well.

Michael Campbell, allow me to introduce or reintroduce, in some cases, my associates, ah…, the rest of the team members who wish to meet with you and…, and…, Dr. Rajawane today."

Lilith's flat, somewhat self-conscious delivery had sounded more like that of a secretary reading the minutes of a senior executive meeting to a televised audience. Missing was the voice of optimism, of excitement, which usually attended the commencement of something big and bright for everyone concerned.

Totally absent was the kind of ebullience, of bravado exhibited by self-styled architects of innovation, those who were charged with the trumpeting of the good tidings that triumph and fulfillment were at hand.

Perfunctory handshakes ensued with each, save Lilith, who deliberately looked away as our fingers and flesh met. She subsequently returned my gaze but hers was a pointed, penetrating look undoubtedly reserved for the few who were blind to the bigger than billboard reality which her physical presence presented. Both beauty and the beast were in attendance.

"So you're the guy who keeps that cardboard cut-out of a Colonel on a leash. Not exactly a prize specimen of a military man, I must say. A friend of yours I am told. Anyway, irregardless of that fact, where is the other impordant member of the prize Bali team. Is there a doctor in the house? Ha, ha. Where is the doctor, what's his name, Rogerwally…, nah, that's not it…, Dr., Dr. Ragerwainy, yeah, something like that."

It was merely a time-tempered, matter of fact, I thought, that this man with the inadvertent ability to murder language would be mine.

The Mercedes chosen to take the mavens of mischief to the shores of Lake Batur resembled a small school bus. A disproportionately high roofed cube on wheels, it had a door, on the right side, for the driver and one on the opposite side for the front seat passenger. A sliding door on the passenger side provided access to the cabin. Two bench seats comfortably seated four adults and in the rear of the cabin, baggage space was sufficient to hold the stacked remains of combatants in a failed, third world country, coup attempt.

My gut told me that initially I had been viewed by the apocalyptic four as the man to be courted or crucified. But their most recent intel update had precipitated my immediate demotion in favor of Dr. Rajawane. I was now seen by them as merely an office boy. The women looked at me as though they didn't know me. Brian looked at me as though he didn't want to know me. My responsibility would end with their safe, prompt delivery to the man who mattered, the real boss of Bali High Art.

A stroke of luck, I thought. The three women, if so inclined, could have spilled their tales of intimacy with me, exclusive intimacy they believed, to one another, and that would have proved to be very problematic indeed! But their enlightened self- interest had dictated otherwise.

So the three monkeys; see no evil, hear no evil and speak no evil, coupled with an inarticulate Mr. Numb-Nuts, filled the passenger roster of those seeking to buy or bully their way into paradise!

I loved the demotion. I did not have to ingratiate myself to any of them through small talk. In fact, I could ignore them completely. And I could count on their reciprocity. I would have the two hour plus trip due north all to myself. I would be able to revel in the kaleidoscope of costumes and culture, the real Bali, which lay just beyond the garish beaches of Denpasar.

Of course, I would rise to the occasion, Phoenix like, once we arrived at the site. But, in the meantime, the other school bus students could be ignored. The only preparation needed was to review the plot line of the Norwegian child's story, 'The Three Billy Goats Gruff'.

It would have to be reverse engineered to fit a certain, new reality of course, but when delivered to my crotch mates as part of my opening remarks, it would provide the punch which I needed!

"Welcome aboard Bali-Air. Today, we will be flying at a scheduled altitude of two and one half feet. A smooth flight is expected. However, we are anticipating a little turbulence due to the condition of the upcountry roads in Bali. We shall do our best to avoid the air pockets caused by the potholes encountered. No detour is expected at this time and we anticipate arrival at the gate on schedule. Thank you for flying Bali Air.

For your comfort and convenience please note that the settings for climate control, seat adjustment, music selection and earphone location are to be found in and around the console located to the right of your seat. Bottled water is stored to your right, beside the seat, as well. Two pit stops are planned during our trip.

More, if deemed necessary. Any questions you might have about the people and places that pass you by on the reality side of the tinted glass, will be cheerfully answered by either myself or our driver, Sarwono. So, sit back and enjoy being taken for a ride."

I didn't care whether they heard or followed what I had just said. I didn't care if they were even remotely amused by the attempt at parody. I didn't care if a distinct discomfort started to gnaw at their guts as they began to realize, one by one, that their self-imposed, increasingly isolated position made them irretrievably vulnerable.

This time around, 'clerk with a car', notwithstanding, my job was to send a clear and compelling message to the masters of these marionettes. Hands off Bali High Art! Any quality control or compliance assessment of my mission would be rudimentary at best. The outcome, I thought ruefully, would, in all likelihood, more resemble a post-op, mop-up, than anything else.

"Daddy look, the fishy tuna are all wearing their slippery clothes that are too small for them. They are ready for kinder…, kindergarten but they look like babies in little baby clothes that are too tight. See, the other fishes on the table. Look! See! They all have shiny shirts on that fit. But not the tuna! Maybe the tuna in Bali are poor and maybe they have no money to buy new clothes. Do you think all the tuna in Bali are so poor like that Daddy?"

Christina always commented, with a wide grin, on the sleek, young, blue-fin tuna, the morning catch, which were laid out on rickety, weather beaten tables beside the road between Denpasar and Lake Batur. Ranging between two and three pounds each, they were ready for purchase and the pan.

The frequency of our road trips to Bali High, voyages which followed the winding sandy margin of terra firma along the rugged coast line of the Indian Ocean, made for easy recall of past, pleasant banter we had shared. Ruminations I thought, as I stared down at my lap, ruminations as rich and rewarding as the verdant, fecund landscape itself.

"Welcome to our first pit stop. Everybody out whether nature is calling or not. After you rid yourself of the salty sediment in your black water tank…, 'pee', for the benefit of you landlubbers, come and witness how real salt from the sea is harvested. Learn the secret, the magic ingredient which turns mediocre stove top diner disappointment into pure, gastronomic delight!"

All four pilgrims raced for the toilets only to find that the one and only facility, an outhouse, and a dry bog at that, was occupied by a member of the salt selling staff. Dutifully, they got in line and feigned interest in some far off distraction which only they could perceive on their private, but predictable horizons.

Narko was the man I had stopped to see. Narko was the man who Christina and I had always stopped to see. Short of stature and decidedly rotund, a diet of too much rice and noodles turned to sugar in the gut of a diabetic no doubt, he was the old Sorcerer right out of the Disney animated movie, 'Fantasia'. He was the man who seemed to make sea salt spring from the sand, and glisten like late season, north face, mountain snow.

Up until recently, he had effortlessly hoisted the giggling Christina up above the wooden yoke which straddled his shoulders and placed her almost on top of his head. Without ever looking down into the shallow water or at the rutted pathway created by his daily treks, he had made child's play of the play with the child above him.

Practice something long enough and perfection invites sustained performance.

With the suspended, stitched leather pans at either end of the yoke-like, balanced shoulder brace, he would artfully dip to port and then to starboard catching just the right amount of ocean water in each swoop to complete his rendition of blind justice and the scales she held in sacred trust.

Up until recently. Increased age, a condition from which, it seemed, he had been spared for a generous period of time, coupled with the additional bulk that a growing child cannot control, forced cessation of their cross generational connectedness. But their banter with less demanding, dare-devil antics continued without abatement.

Narko's routine, followed daily, was to make the water laden trip from sea to sand in order to plant what would be harvested once evaporation took place. Balinese tide levels, being less than two feet, posed little problem for the man with the practiced feet.

Once the slight grade from the water's edge to dry, level land had been achieved, he would slowly walk up and down well, worn paths which separated parallel rows of raised mounds of sand. The leather ladles were tipped to a tune which only Narko knew and the salt laden water was sprinkled with never a miscalculation on the tops of the rows of sand.

Narko's several plots of land resembled neatly cared for potato patches. My Western way of thinking had it that a farm promised a reward for hard work once a year. The Asian 'salt from the soil' counterpart made the same sort of deal but it paid off without fail, each and every day.

Wire sieves were used to separate the sodium chloride from the sand. Six inch wide bamboo poles which were split and placed face up on benches cradled the crystalline prize to facilitate the final drying process. A five hundred gram plastic bag of the white treasure would cost the consumer, if Indonesian, two thousand rupiah. And if the client were foreign, ten thousand rupiah would change hands. And both were made to feel that they were getting a good deal from the shy, rather retiring, ruddy faced man.

Ironic I thought. The Turks and Caicos Islands had been a major sea salt producer until the 1950's but competition from other parts of the world, notably India and Africa, coupled with the lack of a deep water port spelled their eventual business demise.

Narko was the deep water port for his enterprise but father time would prove, ultimately, that the proud Indonesian man lacked sufficient depth as well. The man's muscle would be bested eventually by the force which yielded only grudgingly to human toil.

"I don't think the man has a tooth left in his head," said the Ambassador from Snideland.

That was all anyone said about their short stay in Narkoland.

"Look at the face on your dollar bill. That man was also toothless. That man had false teeth made of wood. Any junior student of American history knows that," I added with the same contempt captured by the emissary who had graced us with his presence.

That was all anyone wished to say about their short stay in Narkoland.

As always, a carton of Marlboros acquired at a duty free shop in Changi Airport would be found by my friend subsequent to our departure.

Nothing further was voiced by the man with the practiced eye for detail until we had passed by Pura Goa Lawah, the second Hindu shrine along the chosen route to Bali High. The route was of my deliberate choosing, in large part because it allowed those with sight beyond the mere sentient to experience, as we journeyed north, the transformation wrought by nature to regain its own. The clipped, calculated, convenient growth of all things green in Denpasar was inexorably replaced by nature's own symmetrical order for all living things sourced from the soil.

People lived in greater harmony with nature, the further north one voyaged. Away from civilization, and man-made claptrap, nature's superiority, her graceful dominion over all things, her silent stage direction was never questioned or assailed.

The holy ground upon which the temple had been built was too good for the fools in transit with me. The serenity, the symmetry of the masonry forming the exterior walls of the buildings, the terraces and their balustrades, the sheer spiritual splendor of the island of tranquility made the notion of inviting my unwashed, 'bats-in-the-belfry' cargo to linger longer seem a sacrilege to the real bats who made their home among the hollowed out rocks of the hallowed shrine.

I knew the game I was playing with myself. Reduce the enemy to the two dimensional and detestable through over generalization and vilification and subsequent banishment would not only be made easy, it would, in fact, become assured.

"Why does the Indonesian government not do something about the swastikas that are plastered all over the fronts..., the front bricks of the old, stone forts that we passed by just a couple of minutes ago, just back there. I know the Japs were here in World War ll, the little bastards were everywhere in Asian after Pearl Harbor. But I didn't know that some Krauts..., some Germans were here with them.

Such a bloody simple job it would be to clean up. Just wash the signs off the stones with ammonia or pound the living shit out of the Nazi walls with a hammer and chisel. Why don't they just do something to clean up? What will all of their precious, money bag, tourists think! Those signs are an insult to our American boys who fought and died for freedom in World War 11.

A Goddamned insult! That's what I say. Just an ignorant insult!"

Fascinating, I thought, to observe how the misinformation of a few could morph into the misperception of the many just through the persistence of the telling of the fabrication.

Was the CIA rewrite of history, the foundation upon which it seemed, too, too much of their adventure and misadventure in the world was based, a function of jaundiced, jingoistic group think at the highest level?

And did their poisoned perceptions then seep down to infect the troops thereby dooming so many of their end-game initiatives to failure!

Or was the current clutch of spooks, those who had more recently developed the flight feathers of field agents been able to soar like Eagle Scouts less and less, because others, the more seasoned, mercenary misfits within their ranks, come to dominate the field of battle more and more!

Did the current wave of uncouth Philistines come to the table ready to play already armed with personal, asinine assumptions about the role of the good guy in a hostile, un-American world? Did their 'minute man' mentality manage to creep upward through the ranks, like capillarity, and ultimately mold major elements of Agency policy! Who knew?

There was a crooked man and he walked a crooked mile. He found a crooked sixpence upon a crooked stile. He bought a crooked cat which caught a crooked mouse, and they all lived together in a little crooked house!

Either way it seemed, the bigger the lie the more credible it became with each, embellished telling.

The crooked cross story I had concocted to assuage the indignant Brian Law was met with greater interest than the truth about Washington's dentures. Swastika facing right was for fascists and their final solutions. Swastika facing left was a Buddhist symbol for good luck. Forget the direction for Hindus, the dominant religion found in Bali. Their truth would not be understood, nor matter!

As he struggled to force the two facts into his small, mental foot locker, swastika left and swastika right, it was clear that his concentration was focused upon the two directional facts which gave the symbols meaning. Remembering what he had heard and retaining the information by lip-reading rote was sufficient. Other spiritual connotations, like gossamer from different galaxies, would have been foreign to the man and therefore beyond any need for an attempt at retention.

Chapter 18

"Allen Dulles was the first civilian Head of the CIA. His reign lasted about ten years, throughout the 1950's, the Eisenhower years. You all knew that, of course. Add to that fact though, the name of the man who was Secretary of State for that same period of time. For all of you non-history buffs, his name was John Foster Dulles.

Ah yes, the Dulles boys. Brothers who strolled the business boardwalk between New York City and Washington, DC. Prophets of power to be sure, and Presbyterian to the core. Anti-Roman Catholic, anti-negro, as they would have termed people of color back then, anti-Semitic, and most assuredly, rabidly anti-communist."

"Michael, speaking for myself and I think, for the rest of the group, I don't believe that this is the time or the place for one of your pet past-times namely ranting, or at least rhyming off, a revisionist view of American history…, particularly in view of the fact that you cannot even claim citizenship…,"

That was the first full thought to be worked into words which was allowed to escape from the lips of DJ since her arrival in Bali. Her first utterance, that is, directed at me. She had elected, it seemed, to play dumb when within earshot of her associates, as a defense perhaps, against possible allegations of unabashed camaraderie or, more likely, collusion. I was, after all, seen as the enemy, the two dimensional paper tiger who stood between them and the strategically sound initiative, whatever it was, that would make the world safer for democracy!

"Sibling rivalry. Remember the term, 'sibling rivalry'. And, while you are at it, remember, by rote, for recall later, a second expression, 'genetic hegemony'. America has been governed by alternating versions of these two concepts, sibling rivalry and genetic hegemony, from its very inception.

Your forbearers took flight from the servitude imposed by European royalty almost three hundred years ago only to bestow total political power upon a select few, rich, white, male, slave owners, whose descendants have decided America's role and direction in the world ever since.

Anyway DJ, further to your concern about my non-sequiturs at such a high altitude, let's start by establishing where the true allegiance of each one of us lies, shall we.

So, the Battleford Group, Rubicon Inc., the Ramparts Group, and Playfair Enterprises…, four companies and four individuals at the table. Who is the spokesperson for each? Or can we agree that the incestuous relationships among all four companies make each the bastard child of some unknown, yet to be named, 'other'.

I, on the other hand, represent only the 'true-to-testament' wish of the late Mr. Tan. The sole mandate of Bali High Art is to celebrate Asian art in its multiplicity of forms.

Whoever orchestrated your collective love letter fest should have been more attentive to the choice of expensive stationery used, especially for letters of introduction, one chance to make a first impression, and all of that.

All four missives were written on paper containing the same, water mark. All four were stamped as well with signs of collusion. Vocabulary choice, sentence structure, deductive logic, and win/win outcomes, all are tell-tale signs of the Central Intelligence Agency mind set at work. Nothing more than a cursory glance at any of the recently declassified CIA correspondence is needed to prove the point.

Just one more thing about the similar water marks on all four letters of introduction. All of the bookies in Vegas and Macau combined would be hard pressed to arrive at favorable odds on that resulting from mere serendipity. So fraud cannot be ruled out as a part of what you view as a fair and equitable negotiation process. You want to win. You need to win. That is obvious.

The Company, as some who watch too many movies call it, seems to have a strangle hold not only on the common sense element in all of you, but on your collective capacity for honesty and integrity as well. The CIA motto for covert operations, how does it go again…, ah yes, 'money no object, no holds barred, and no questions asked'.

Remember, rash rationalizations make rogues of us all.

So you attempted to create a first impression that you were independent entities but in fact you are merely clones of one another. An ill-advised strategy I would say because you have done little more than discredit an agency of the US government whose efforts are fundamental to foreign policy. Credibility lost!

Informed guesses are almost as good as irrefutable facts, wouldn't you say? Now it is my turn to play with persona. This is, after all, my house…, you are my guests, and I feel obliged to provide you with a modicum of entertainment which will, it is hoped, both amuse and inform. Pretend you are watching a documentary on PBS. You know their MO…, a never ending fetish for facts that only an army of book worms could marshal and make memorable…, that only studiousness and due diligence could render irrefutable.

My ramblings should shed some light on why it is that we are all huddled together in a cramped, rather uncomfortable cabin atop a cliff at the south western end of the Bali High Art property. We should be sipping something pleasant in the presence of compliant company beside pristine Lake Batur which is about eight hundred feet, straight down, below us. I am aware of that. But cake comes before meat and potatoes only in the dictionary. Let's wrestle first with the large issue before we engage in any 'Unbearable lightness of being', discussion."

I spoke to the air in front of me just as a drill sergeant might to a platoon of new recruits. No attempt was made to accommodate the lowest level of intellect in the group. Forbearance would be the first fluffy sentiment to be forfeited.

"You have all heard the story of the Old Troll and the Billy Goats Gruff. A Norwegian tale that is frequently told to children, I think that it is particularly apt for all of us assembled here, right now, in this rustic, little cabin, in the middle of nowhere.

My role in our little piece of theatre will be that of the Troll, and therefore, you are all Billy Goats. You can decide among yourselves who is strongest, who has the best butt…, based on rank…, or past performance of course, but trust me, the number of chevrons on your sleeves will prove to be somewhat of a moot point.

Let's just say that all of you 'would be grazers' in this field of desire are beholden to me. I am the shepherd, the gate keeper, the one with the real positional authority and I will decide whether or not any of you will receive a "get-out-of-jail-free" card.

The merits of your proposal, as they relate to Bali High Art, will be the only criteria used to determine if a satisfactory outcome, from your perspective and mine, is possible. This strange interlude of ours, will either be precursor to something of consequence in the future or it will spell curtains for you and this…, this…, amateurish, off, off broad-way production. It all depends on you.

I will not be butted off my bridge by brash, bull shitters with big horns!

Everyone looked down at their laps like aging ladies distracted because they had lost count of the stitches in their Christmas knitting project. I continued with my half-rehearsed treatise in spite of their visceral lack of approbation.

"Think about the government agency you represent. And know, by the way, that I know the agenda…, the one that has been set for you to follow. So visualize the big picture…, see your role in it, and imagine whatever wiggle room you might be able to manufacture as trusted operatives of the Central Intelligence Agency.

Use the benefit of hindsight. Create a win/loss ledger in your mind. Think about the state of the world right now. Has your organization, your Company, been a bulwark against past and present political, economic and social excesses in the world or has it always been more a laboratory with the express purpose of manufacturing malicious, military intent? A rhetorical question to be sure.

Let's take a short stroll down some of the broader boulevards of history. Think, for example, about how the State Department and the CIA have worked, most times in tandem, but sometimes not, to ensure the sustained growth of NATO as an anti-communist military force in Europe…, and the world for that matter!

Put the Lockheed Martin SR 71, black bird, spy plane into that equation of military dominance. Starting in 1966 and continuing for the next ten years, those manned missiles made of titanium proved themselves to be able to fly higher and faster than any machine the USSR had ever been able to launch as a defense."

"Michael, Michael. Please, stop right there. You are right about the titanium. But do you know where that metal is mined? Do you know what country has the richest deposits of titanium? Without it the Black Bird could not have earned its reputation for invincibility. It would not have been able to fly at over 3000, no, 3500 miles per hour for extended periods of time. Over twenty years of service…, twenty-two years by your count, in a league of its own, almost besting the Greek God, Icarus, by flying close to the Sun in the process …, a remarkable, American engineering feat. And, and, mainly because of titanium…, I, I don't think you have any idea as to the pivotal role the CIA played in acquiring that scarce, expensive, silver colored, commodity!"

Now apparently, it was Lee's turn to play clucking hen in the roost. My long shot gamble using the Lockheed Blackbird as bargaining chip, as bait, had paid off. I was counting on at least one of the players knowing the back story which had ceased to be a secret, among those in the know, years earlier. In the absence of a leader in the group, she had decided to volunteer. Using her spy plane knowledge as a fulcrum, she was, I knew, attempting to reset both the climate and the course of the faltering meeting.

I stared down at the table top in front of me and remained quiet. I wanted her to appear to have just acquired control of the conversation. That might motivate the others to step up to the plate. To actively participate. I needed someone, anyone, to best me…, as a means of refocusing all of them on their goal. It had become something of a mirage, it seemed, a mist shrouded target that was rapidly disappearing below a distant horizon.

They all reminded me of kids from the sixties, kids in adult guise, college students, who had just successfully staged a 'sit-in'. Once in the Dean's office though, despite their feet up on his desk and large, lit cigars everywhere, they became lost, little children who secretly craved attention and guidance because they had no clue as to what to do next!

With a choir of accomplished mutes as backup, Lee decided to continue her story of the big, black bird that flew fast, a cappella.

"Titanium is mined primarily in the USSR, up until now at least, and the CIA managed to get it in sufficient quantities to satisfy the Lockheed SR-71 project. Through the successful rouse of establishing a series of dummy purchasing companies, companies which operated mainly in Europe but with world-wide connections, the CIA succeeded in beating the Russians at their own game.

Anywhere outside the confines of this room, and that intel..., that intelligence will emphatically be denied."

"Yes, naturally..., and of course you realize that your disclosure about titanium acquisition is rather ironic. It seems that fraud factors frequently into the CIA formula for success..., fake companies for titanium and fake, almost photocopied letters of introduction to pave the way for the acquisition of a Balinese base to snoop on neighbors across the Indian Ocean and around the South China Sea.

Just an educated guess, you understand!

So, thank you for your candor. Just know that your words, with the potential to be used as weapons against you and your associates, will not leave this room. The walls of this hunting shack do not have electronic ears and all of us know that slipped secrets lead to the silence of slit throats..., so..., back to our favorite aircraft which is, appropriately, cloaked in black.

It is worth noting, I think, that the Indianapolis 500 road race in the sky has cost America about three hundred million per plane, per year. That's three hundred million dollars per SR-71 Black Bird in active service. How do I know that, it doesn't matter how I know that..., it's too, just too, too damn late to matter!

Some would say that the number becomes a little easier to swallow if it is looked at it in terms of dollars collected each year from US citizens who file income tax returns. Let's say the number of tax payers, working stiffs over the age of eighteen, is less…, considerably less than the three hundred million mark.

Each plane, therefore, costs every tax payer about two bucks a year to stay in the air. Still, a lot of money just for the bragging rights that go with being able to capture aerial 'Kodak Moments' of countries without their consent.

The Central Intelligence Agency as a deft defense mechanism against the Russian bear is not a definition which is universally held. You are viewed by many as a Department of Dilettantes, who strut a catwalk of your own creation. You first espouse and then attempt to eradicate people, regimes, and political philosophies by turn. Sometimes on a whim or frequently in response to the paranoia of a one term Administration…, or merely as a fashion statement which reflects transient, populist, perspective, wouldn't you say?

You are classic xenophobes. Non-Americans are seen as enemies from the past, with a past, and the 'now' is populated by allies, always, it seems, with Achilles heels, and the future is frequented by usurpers of American hegemony bent on fracturing your notion of 'manifest destiny'. Will the circle forever be unbroken!

Or, perhaps, you are little more than ponderous pretenders on the parapets of make believe castles manning the walls above the moats to keep the minions down below from ever rising up and biting you. And you condescend, occasionally, to lower the draw bridge, almost disdainfully, to allow some of the current 'in people', to enter your rigged reality."

"What absolute nonsense! America has always fought for what is right. From the earliest colonial times, independence and self-determination have been fundamental to our way of life… And…, and…, unlike others, who were part of the British Empire; India, Australia, and yes, even Canada, who groveled and, well, like all who see virtue in being meek, gratefully and graciously accepted all the tidbits of responsible, self-rule, bestowed by British Kings and Queens living on the other side of the Atlantic Ocean. Not just for years…, but for generations, we…, yes, a capital WE, prevailed. 'Colonial' as a mind-set and 'compliance' as a virtue represent a guaranteed recipe for servitude."

"I'll grant you that Lee, but remember, from the earliest colonial times Americans and Canadians and Aussies have been on the same side of the moral fence as mother England. They have perpetuated the worst British brutality of all. Man's inhumanity to man, is what I think most people call it. All four countries have a history of heavy handed colonialism. Why? Because colonialism is the catapult to capitalism.

Territorial governments in Australian and Canada, the fledgling government in America, all emulated the use of colonial claws or perhaps 'maws' would be a better word, of Mother England. All four, all white to the core, chose to trample their indigenous peoples through,

One: the possibility of an omniscient, vindictive, three headed, Christian, God,

Two: the probability of contracting a fatal disease; tuberculosis or syphilis, and

Three: the certainty of early departure from family and field due to gun powder."

"That's the past seen through the lens of the present, Michael. Spilt milk, at best! Anyway, don't be like the rest of the world. Don't be foolishly sentimental and don't be jealous of our success. America was pre-destined to be great…, a World power, no, the world power, no, the world power that has had no equal and…, and, for that, she shall never be embarrassed or ashamed!"

I had to admit that Lee did sound and look good when she wrapped herself in the Stars and Stripes. The nods from her two associates and their mumbled agreements with her closing statement signaled the passage of her private members bill of entitlement as birthright by a majority vote of one. Lilith and I, for very different reasons, chose to abstain.

"Touche, Lee. Your content might be suspect but I do like your style. And in that same vein, here is what one of your fellow Americans had to say about his beloved country of birth. He termed America, 'this monster of a land', and he was no less a person, no less a literary light than John Steinbeck. You would know him for his famous novel, 'The Grapes of Wrath'. In it, America is presented, among other things, as a limitless land of opportunity for those who have, and use, what some would term, 'true grit'.

He meant to say, with the quote, that the immensity and diversity of the natural resources found in America dwarf those of any other land mass that has ever come to acquire political status as a country..., at any other time in all of recorded history. And the cornucopia of natural resources did, in no small way, make possible the emergence and the sustained presence of the American empire. Nothing succeeds, it seems, like excess!

But apart from the raw materials needed for might, the theft of the land from the indigenous Indians, some see that as genocide, and the institution of slavery as a mainstay of commerce in the agricultural South, when cotton was king, provided the two main social pillars upon which your Republic was founded.

And quirky sibling rivalry, plutocracy, and family hegemony in the political arena have consistently produced the preferred players of governance."

"All of this is tangential, Michael. Do you really need that much humoring?"

DJ did not look at me as she spoke. Instead, her gaze remained fixed on her small tote bag which had been placed within easy reach on the table in front of her.

"This won't take long DJ. I'll give you the short, 'crib-note' explanation of the 'whys' which block your way to lake front property in Bali. Trust me, this is all leading to a place where we all need..., where we are all destined, to be. Bear with me. It's important. Just bear with me, please.

So, take the friction, among brothers and sisters, resulting from their jockeying for favored positions within their families. It is commonly referred to as sibling rivalry. Heat and light, and maybe sometimes, might, result. I've already mentioned the Dulles boys, Allen and John, add to them JFK and his older brother, Joe junior, both recipients of the Purple Heart medal for bravery during World War Two.

The same holds true for JFK and his younger brother Robert as well. Both Presidential, one in reality and the other in hope, both following the advice of their father, Joseph senior, 'fuck as much as you can, as many as you can, for as long as you can', both bedding generations of movie stars from Marlene to Marilyn, as a means of assuaging the Freudian angst of their dear old Dad and, in the process, both creating their own versions of 'Profiles in Courage'. Ha!

And very quickly, there is genetic hegemony or, in the vernacular, fucking your way to family fame and fortune…, through nepotism and political dynasty. The Union Army General, Arthur MacArthur, and his son, General Douglas MacArthur, both recipients of the Congressional Medal of Honor for heroism in two very different wars, the Adams boys, John, President number two, and his oldest son John Quincy, President number six, and the Roosevelt clan, let's not forget them, Teddy, number twenty-six and FDR, number thirty two in the Oval Office.

All men of destiny, all dedicated to American style democracy, all decidedly at the helm of American imperialism and all contributing sculptors to the frieze of fact and fiction which crowns the world and gives foundation and form to it.

And…, and, finally, and in conclusion, we have the plutocrats, the Medici families of the great American Renaissance. Included in that august group would be the Adams family of course, the Rockefellers, the McCormick's, International Harvester farm tractors for every field and furrow, the cornucopia of Kennedys, and the Bushes, you know, George, the invisible one, the VP under President Reagan. His Texas money will ensure that at least one of his progeny, probably Jeb, will be stage managed into the national spot light in the not too distant future.

And that's mentioning only a few of the notable players who, hiding in the wings away from public scrutiny, pull and pluck at the strings of political power on the national stage and ultimately on the world stage as well.

American royalty and the never ending Horatio Alger, 'rags to riches' story to be sure! And all framed by a Norman Rockwell tableau of favored, white America.

And that's before any comment is made about the lower echelon political elites, those who perch and preen themselves in the Governor's mansions of every state in the Union. Their brands of nepotism, their 'Tammany Hall' politics of 'special interest group' pandering, of influence peddling, and their financial malfeasance on a truly monumental scale, have always fueled federal aspirations and have been, as an aside, fertile fodder for the tabloid press."

I paused, half expecting my audience to get up and vacate the room. They didn't. Their eyes, their eyes which were completely glazed over, told the story. Not one of them was actually listening to my ramblings, my rehearsed rational, for the dismissal of their Bali High Art proposal. An observer might have suggested, indelicately, that in the face of their 'constipated' business construct I had responded with a 'loose stool' rebuttal. Neither side had demonstrated the 'regularity' needed to reach even a tentative consensus.

"OK, so let's move on then…, Maybe just a quick word about the history of the CIA involvement in South East Asia, particularly in French Indo China. You are all familiar with the relationship between the Company, Air America, and the shipments of 'hard rice'…, you know, rice measured in the millions of units…, each unit containing 130 grains of encased lead, which were…,"

I stopped mid-sentence. Why go on. Why go on just to amuse myself with a recitation of high school history. Too much of the same old song, I thought. The ballad had a plot line which was transparent. The discordant players had become caricature cut outs spouting worn out lines and the only moral to be learned from the drawn out morality play was that virtue, for my audience at least, lay in playing dead. Easier to stifle my motivation, they must have reasoned, than to try to seal up the gushing geyser of words which showed no signs of abatement.

Time for something different. Time for something current. Time for something probably not yet on their radar. Time for dirty laundry, Texas style!

"Forget French Indo China and its reincarnation as Viet Nam. Defeat of Western powers, from both Europe and the Americas, in South East Asia, needs more Pulitzer Prize caliber scholarship based on yet to be released documents from the national governments involved. You know, Statutes of Limitations, national secrets acts, and all of that!

So let's talk for just a minute about the ongoing, CIA proxy war with Russia. You know, the covert conflict which started in the late seventies with an annual budget of five million dollars and, within two or three years ballooned to more than five hundred million bucks per year. Bullets and bombs are, after all, expensive!

The largest funding for secret, undeclared war in American history. An economy within an economy according to some observers! The battle ground is Afghanistan, through the Mujahideen, and two American players of note, civilians actually, include the God-fearing, politically powerful, hater of godless communists, Charlie Wilson, the long term Congressman from Texas, and a wealthy, influential Houstonian named Joanne Herring. Together, they share both bed and right wing bidding. Operation Cyclone was the name given to the secret operation which has now spanned close to ten years."

"No! I want you to stop all of this nonsense, Mister Michael Sir! You have got to stop right now! We have all had enough of your anti-American point of view."

"Well, if cyclones are not to your taste, Mr. Brian Law sir, then how about complicity…, CIA complicity in the assassination of John Fitzgerald Kennedy. You must have heard of Jim Garrison, the DA in New Orleans. You must have followed some of the news coverage of the investigation he and his legal team have mounted against individuals and government agencies thought to be responsible for the crime of the century. Think about it. The CIA and President Kennedy on a collision course regarding the continuance of the Cold War. We all know who represented what in that tug of war, don't we!"

"This is preposterous. I will have no more of it. I will have none of what you are saying about my country. None of it! Do you hear! None of it. Where did you get all of this nonsense that you are parading out in front of us as if…, as if, it was all true…, as if it was all fact!"

"The investigation got quashed but at least Garrison got the Zapruder tape of the fatal shots released to the public. So much for the Warren Report and its purported accuracy…, all 888 pages of it!"

I was beginning to feel like Muhammad Ali as he stood over the beaten Sonny Liston in Lewiston, Maine. First round vengeful venting at its best!

"Correct me if I am wrong, but I believe that it was Christine Keeler, a great American educator, a founding member of the American Civil Liberties Union, a woman who could not hear because she was deaf and a woman who could not see because she was blind, a woman who wrote and talked about the survival of the fittest way back…, maybe sixty, no, maybe eighty years ago or more…, even though she was a cripple, what with no sight and no hearing, almost none anyway, she was…, yes, she was a great woman who believed in the science of u-genetics.

She was way ahead of her time. Way ahead of her time. She believed in helping God to do His work to make His people better. Yes, to make the population better, physically and mentally, through proper breeding…, each tribe of people should look to their own kind to increase their own numbers and…, and medical surgery, irregardless of how young is the age, that should only be for people who are whole. Mixing rotten ones with ripe ones is bad for the whole crop. She reminded us that people were made by God and that they were made by God to be in His own, perfect image.

You just have to spell the word J-E-R-U-S-A-L-E-M out loud, and then see the word you just spelled in your head. You will see that the three letters in the middle of the word spell USA. Our work is against the godless Communists, the heathens, the lesser races of mankind, all the Godless people of the world. That is our manifest destiny. And we cannot fail in the face of the God given command to rid the world of its wrongs. We have to make things right, that's all. Yes, make things right!"

The roar that was to have been Brian Law's response to the front row center ticket he had been given to our rendezvous, proved to be little more than the squeak which a child creates by allowing air to escape slowly from the stretched neck of an inflated balloon.

Now it was my turn to look to my knitting. I had no idea what to say or do in the face of the 'faith and fractured fact' flatulence which had just escaped from the man who sat across the table from me. Almost like insult added to injury, he sat self-consciously emboldened by his misinterpretation of the attention he had just garnered. Pride seemed to be winning the war against pusillanimity in the meager mind of the unfortunate man.

Maybe I could start with the personage he had mentioned who was, according to him at least, a beacon for the brave new world which was wistfully wished for by some and, willed ruthlessly on the world by others.

Only Langley, operating in a third world country like Indonesia, would have the temerity to task 'C' players with a 'B' objective and expect an 'A' outcome.

Christine Keeler! My God, Christine Keeler! It was unlikely that any of the other assembled guests had ever heard of the 'femme fatale' woman/child from the expired empire which had, on its deathbed, aided and abetted the creation of Commonwealth.

Christine Keeler had gained notoriety as a nineteen year old fashion model who, in 1961, got caught up in a love triangle involving the Secretary of State for War in Great Britain, John Profumo, and a Soviet attaché in London, one Captain Ivanov. He worked in the Russian Embassy. The resulting fear of a security breach and the lurid accounts of 'menage-a-trois' sex trysts reported in the tabloids, forced Profumo to resign, the then Prime Minister, Harold Macmillan, to retire, and the ruling Conservative Party, to relinquish power following their defeat in the subsequent general election.

"Christine Keeler was a silly little slut who, in the early sixties, proved the old adage, which most men never seem to learn, that the fucking you get, when you rob the cradle, is not worth the fucking you get. She, like an adolescent Mata Hari, caused the down fall of a high ranking British Cabinet Minister, his boss, the Prime Minister, as well as the fall of their ruling party, the Conservatives, in Parliament."

I gambled that the somewhat raunchy response provided by the former Lord Chancellor of the Turks and Caicos Islands, DJ, to the mention of the 'femme fatale' of a generation earlier could be built upon to awaken libidos and loosen lips, albeit at Brian's expense.

"Even before the Biblical story of Sampson and Delilah, pussy power could and did precipitate outcomes which were past the purviews of many Prime Ministers and Presidents, of kings and Pharaohs as well. David survived Bathsheba only because his God was a misogynist. But even he paid the price through his progeny.

Pussy power, it seems, has always posed a more potent, a more powerful threat to political stability than all the photos taken from all the Black Bird spy planes, combined."

I grinned at my audience and…, I lost the gamble. The room fell eerily silent.

"I think Brian meant Helen Keller. She supported the ACLU from its very inception and she prevailed in a world where the word feminism had not even been coined as a political or social term…, before women even had the right to vote in America. She stood out as a voice of reason despite the absence of two of her five physical senses. I remember the woman's writings and her accomplishments so well…, she was a hero of mine during my undergraduate days. She died only recently…, maybe ten or fifteen years ago, in the late sixties, I think it was."

Lee's words were measured. Her voice, like incoming tide water, swirled around and lingered long on each syllable which was uttered. It was as though she was speaking of a more than mortal being. She had steeled herself to speak of a noteworthy woman but it was clear that she was doing more, much more than that. She was praising America for having spawned such a sterling specimen of womanhood. She was the deliverer of eulogy, the recognition of recently departed greatness, to be sure! But her remarks were more homage to the fertile muck from which Americans of note materialized, those paragons of virtue who provided the 'Lincoln log' foundation for the American monolith, for the American myth, than anything else!

Maybe the off, off Broadway production which had been decided upon, subconsciously, by Brian Law was based on Helen Keller's biography, 'The Miracle Worker'! Maybe it was fiction fucking with facts that had produced his flatulence!

"Yes, Helen Keller. That's what I say, Helen Keller."

Brian's voice was almost accusatory. We should all have had enough common sense, as only Lee apparently had, to have known whom he meant just by the manner in which the woman and her achievements had been described.

The man had become something of an inner tube which had been pumped to a point of over inflation. The seal between the rim and the rubber tire on the front wheel of his Schwinn, American Flyer had burst. Oblivious to any potential performance shortfall, Brian seemed to be steeling himself for a rough uphill ride even though his rear axle of a brain provided only one forward gear and his wounded front wheel offered little mental stability and even less maneuverability.

Slow, deliberate, straight line logic was his only means of ascent. And that was an option for which he had the least aptitude. He was, at best, what my college friends often termed, when referring to a bombastic professor, an old fuck with an intellectual hard-on!

Emboldened though by the further impact his words had achieved now that the minor detail of identity had been established, he seemed to have girded his loins for combat. He was ready to conquer the mountain of mischief which had risen up in front of him.

Not to lose the momentum created by the Keeler/ Keller moment, Brian gathered himself up and pointed his thumb and fore finger at me much as a child might when firing a make believe six shooter at imaginary Indians who were attacking on horseback. They, of course, were circling the settlers in a clock-wise direction, while the covered wagons, moving counter clock-wise, lurched and lumbered together, waiting for the cavalry, which was just over the hill, to arrive.

The man had the demeanor of Chaplin's, 'Little Tramp'. His mental gears, most of which lacked sufficient cogs to sustain measured movement, positioned him as the squeezed, hapless victim in the portentous film classic, 'Modern Times'!

"Are we supposed to be impressed by your ridiculous, high school take on the state of the world? What total nonsense! Preposterous! Anyway, I thought we were here to discuss our contribution to the success, the real success, the financial success of Bali Art on High or whatever you call it…, High Bali Art…, ahh…,"

"Is anyone else in favor of a short break? The air is getting a little stale in here and I think we would, all of us, benefit from a few minutes outside just to stretch our legs…, and…, and…, think through, as Brian just said, what our next steps, concerning Bali High Art, should be."

"Good for you, Danyea. Spoken just like me…, a true outsider. One who knows the music but doesn't play it all that often. I agree with you. We all need some fresh air. It could be that some people in here talk too much. Anyway, it's potty time and I'm going to be among the many today Michael, who will literally and figuratively piss on your parade, ha, ha!"

To them, the young Miss from the Middle East seated in our midst was Danyea. To me, she was Lilith. She had insisted on the name of the half-forgotten, fallen angel. To her masters, I wondered, was she someone else. To herself, was there another name that mattered, a name that had meaning in her life, or was it just the day of the week or something as primordial as progesterone which determined who she would be on any given day!

The Beatles' ballad, 'Rocky Raccoon', a musical parody of cowboy confrontation in the old west, came to mind. Dan, a man from Dakota and Rocky Raccoon got in a gun fight over a lady. That femme fatale had personal moniker issues as well. 'Her name was Magill and she called herself Lil, but everyone knew her as Nancy…,'

Rocky Raccoon had been seriously wounded in the saloon shoot-out and Gideon, now a man, not the evangelical Christian organization, in his efforts to ensure Rocky's revival, had checked out of Rocky's room just prior to the gun-play in the not-so-O.K. Corral. This left nothing more than the religious tome, which bore, not his name, but that of the religious group, to console the stricken loser-in-love. A metaphor perhaps, for the convoluted nature of Christianity!

DJ did not wait for agreement. She dashed outside and ran in the direction of the only other man made structure within sight. A small wooden shed with a rudely fitted door, it resembled many built in colder climates, where the road to the farm house and the road to the rest of the world met.

Enterprising fathers were the architects and their offspring were the grateful recipients of the plank and paint protection. The shelters from the cold of winter, for those forced to wait every morning for the metal boxes on wheels which were painted chrome yellow, were not an attempt to imitate some 'Fallingwater' esthetic of Frank Lloyd Wright. They were more prophylaxes against frost bite.

As I stood at the window and gazed out at my guests, I was struck by two of the common place pairing rituals, usually seen on play grounds and in school yards, which were being played out.

Fleeting vignettes of camaraderie and conflict were being show cased at either end of the long bamboo bench which acted as a barrier between the eastern edge of the cliff and the void of vertical descent just beyond. The masks depicting comedy and tragedy, part of traditional theatre motif, were not needed. The pivotal importance of center stage had been usurped by the smiles of the schemers to stage right, and the frowns of the forlorn to stage left. Center stage had been 'upstaged', and it seemed that it would remain conspicuously abandoned and void of drama throughout the intermission that punctuated our Balinese tragicomedy.

DJ and Lee sat almost nose to nose at one end of the bench whispering about the turn of events which was forcing them to confront not only my obfuscation but the obtuse, ineptitude of the other member of their team.

Lilith and Brian, on the other hand, gave a very entertaining, albeit shortened version of fractured matrimony. She too was nose to nose with her partner but only between violent kicks at the legs which protruded from below the bench seat. Whether the targeted legs were those belonging to Brian or those of the bamboo bench, was not clear!

Which was worse, I wondered. The combined malevolence of compatible conspirators or the ferocity of individual wrath forged in the furnace of unfulfilled promise.

In preparation for the return of my uninvited and unwanted guests, I checked the positioning of the weapon in my pocket. I verified as well, where the imaginary 'X' on the floor would be to satisfy the crude triangulation needed to align my back with DJ and Lee were I to require an uninterrupted line of fire. The vantage point would be engineered based on a supposed need to face Lilith in mock or meant confrontation.

"Michael, you are so full of yourself and boastful of the rewrite of American history that you have learned from paperback books sold in drug stores, that it is pathetic. So, let's put the shoe on the other foot, equal time you could say, just to be balanced and fair. I am going to tell you some of the stories, some of the true facts, we have learned about you.

You talk a lot about the so called mistakes of the CIA so let me tell you what we have found out about some of your mistakes. And, unlike the case with all of your stories, we have the proof that what I am about to say about you is all true. Yes, I am going to paint a picture of you Michael, warts and all, that is not very flattering. Your failures outnumber your accomplishments by a long shot.

And that is why I do not think, no, why we do not think that it is right for us to be working out a plan, or at least trying to work out a plan about the future of this property with someone like you. You are not at all qualified to represent the best interests of this property now or in the future either, for that matter. There, I have said it. And I know that what I am saying represents the opinion of everybody else in this room.

In a word, Mr. Michael Campbell, you are dishonest. You are a liar and a cheat. And…, and, you cannot be trusted!

Feel free ladies, to jump in anytime if you want to add more to what you remember our sources have been able to piece together about Mr. High and Mighty here. Mr. Bali High and Mighty who thinks that he is better than we are…, Mr. High and Mighty who thinks that he can stop us from successfully completing our mission that will guarantee success for high art at Bali for all the truly deserving people who will come here."

The second round of trench warfare had begun and the opening salvo had been fired before I had finished placing the cans of Coca Cola, Sprite and Fanta, in clusters, on the table. The company from Atlanta which had, more than a century earlier, captured cocaine in a bottle, had seduced and secured Indonesia without a fight and 'the real thing' had never relinquished its decades old strangle hold on the soda pop market which straddled the Equator. It was a very lucrative market, to say the least. Two hundred million thirsty throats, and counting.

Stackable tables and chairs made of utility grade plywood and metal tubing had been sent to our, 'room-at-the-top' perch within the first week of our occupancy of the Tan property. Mr. Tan, the man who had literally and figuratively 'willed' Bali High Art into being, had viewed that part of the property as a personal refuge, whereas, for some who succeeded him, it became an extension of the bustling business center down below at ground level.

Those managers and minions who were charged with the transformation of flight of fancy into design of fact and function inhabited a self-made world of daily cacophony, a discordant 'wall of sound'. That was the price that had to be paid. That was always precursor to the symphony of successful creation.

The cliff top retreat did however keep most of its aura of splendid isolation. It remained a place away from the concentrated clangor of people with purpose, of people in pursuit of a prize. It was a Godsend.

The 'U' shaped configuration of the tables in the cabin allowed for easy dialogue among practiced and plodding players alike. It granted the chairperson of any assembly complete visual and vocal access to all members of the group. Graphics could easily be projected on the wall, which faced the open end of the 'U', by covering it with a stretched bed sheet. A Kodak Carousel slide machine added the finishing touch. The scene could almost have been mistaken for a 'pump-up-the-troops' meeting venue anywhere in urban or suburban America.

I carried my chair toward the back of the room and placed it a few feet away from the inner edge of the table which formed the base of the letter 'U'. That positioned me directly in front of Lee and DJ. Like bookends, Brian Law and Lilith sat at the tables which were on either side of and at right angles to the one where the dynamic duo sat. He was to my right and she sat facing him, on my left.

We must have looked like a touch football team, with me as quarterback, ready to rethink our offensive options in a choir like huddle. The form looked right for synergic results but dysfunction was the definite foregone conclusion. No bridge could span the yawning chasm between the noble and the nefarious, between art and mere artifice.

I sat down. I bowed my head in an attempt to project contrite silence. And I waited for the next round of enemy fire to commence.

"So, where did I leave off? Oh yes. We know all about your background and we know that you have a long history of lies and just…, just doing whatever you want to…, just to please yourself, just to make you happy at the expense of others around you. We know, for example, what you have done that has caused pain and sorrow and disappointment in people who trusted you, who believed in you, completely.

You let them down. In fact, your whole history in South East Asia has been a steady stream, a steady, long story of ego centered actions…, of decisions, that have caused great suffering for the people who loved or respected or…, or, relied upon you, over, over the last ten years…, over the last decade."

"Good background introduction Brian, but to save time, let's move on to some specific details that we think disqualify Michael as a bonefide representative of Bali High Art.

If it's OK with the rest of the group, I'll start. And I will begin with Michael's separation and the subsequent divorce that left his wife and two children high and dry, without support in Manila. The city was foreign to them…, they had no friends and his wife's family, I believe her name was Lydia, was on the other side of the world, in Toronto, Canada. Talk about unconscionable abandonment. Talk about antisocial, criminal behavior!"

"And not only was there the hanky-panky that went on before the separation, the major cause of the break-up, according to our sources, but it continued long after the family moved back to Toronto as well. Michael continued his mischief, his conceit, his deceit long after his separation from his wife and family with junior members of his staff, suppliers to his company, as well as a steady stream of 'street meat' from local bars and night clubs. Michael looks out only for number one. He has no interest in the welfare of others."

'Criminal behavior', 'welfare of others', I must have been the topic of discussion between Lee and DJ on the bamboo bench during the break. How else could their thumb nail sketches of my peccadillos have been delivered so smoothly. They sounded convincing even to my ears. Practice as precursor to perfection, I thought sardonically to myself.

"And when the company offered him a promotion in head office, in Europe, not only did he turn down their generous offer but he also, just before he quit, sabotaged the operation in the Philippines so that his successor could not help but fail. Michael wants to win all the time and Michael not only wants to win but also Michael wants others around him to fail. Not the kind of man I want to do business with…, especially when this Bali project is based so much on integrity and honesty and fair play!"

Brian Law was enjoying his unexpected moment in the limelight. Whatever I could do to maintain his chosen role which seemed deserving of center stage, I would. Silence was, it seemed, more than sufficient.

"And let's not ignore what Michael did after quitting his job as the Country Manager of a prestigious drug manufacturing company. To add insult to injury he opened a whore house in Manila and lived off the avails of prostitution. I think it was called Casablanca or Casanova or…, Casa something or other! Some name that sounded Spanish anyway.

And then he abruptly left Manila and the Philippines after less than two years and joined this Col. Satu character in Jakarta as a partner…, a partner in crime, that is.

Satu is and was a well-known, small time racketeer who operated, no, he still does, in the tenderloin districts of every major city in South East Asia. By joining forces with a man like that, Michael went from being a prominent, successful business man, worthy of respect and deserving of praise, to a small time hoodlum deserving of nothing more than thorough police investigation and pity."

I was getting a sense of what the hapless women of Salem must have felt like when they faced their young accusers who were suffering from the hallucinogenic effects from having ingested too much bread which was riddled with mold. Witches, warlocks and dunking ponds were definitely 'Dead-Pool' spaces on the board game of life. And they were avoided best by those who knew and threw only dice which were loaded! Clint Eastwood and Dirty Harry, notwithstanding!

I was relieved. Words had been rhymed off but nothing was said! I could afford the luxury, the flippancy of likening my character assassination at the hands of the Kellogg cast of characters, Snap, Crackle and Pop, to the lunacy which occurred in seventeenth century America. My accusers, although filled with poisonous vitriol, lacked the vital information about my past which might have made a difference. They knew some of the superficial 'what' of Michael Campbell but the 'why' of life changing situations and the 'how' of event resolutions completely escaped them.

I was in attendance for my own obituary, one which focused on chronological facts, but one which was bereft of backfill.

For the price of a cup of coffee, any junior product manager with my former pharma outfit in Manila could have served as their 'secret' source of superficial information.

Not knowing whether to lead with my strong suit or my long one, I decided to continue to gamble with factual flippancy.

"So, it appears that your intel has caught me, figuratively speaking, with my pants down. Touché! A great segue though, I must say, into why the Company, the OPC specifically, you know, the Office of Policy Coordination, so prosaic don't you think, the covert crowd who specialize in global coup d'état, will never succeed with any future clandestine initiatives in Indonesia.

Why, you might ask! A quick history lesson. It's 1958. Indonesia is in the throes of replacing one national leader with another. Sukarno is being ousted by another military man, one generation his junior, General Suharto. Complicate the turmoil in the country by adding a virulent strain of communist witch hunting to the mix. Confuse matters even further by having CIA pilots instruct and fly with local Indonesian airmen on bombing and strafing runs over military targets commanded by senior Indonesian officers who were trained in the USA.

A civil war, with America on both sides, a civil war which would have been humorous were it not for the fact that more Indonesians died in the two year blood bath than did the number of residents of

Dresden who were fire bombed into extinction by Allied planes in World War 11. One hundred thirty thousand German civilians died in that devil's inferno. No strategic advantage was to be gained. The target was a civilian population center. The stated goal was psychological disequilibrium. Dresden…, Denpasar, dots on a map, no difference!

That fiasco made the CIA the laughing stock of the world intelligence community and a perpetual, pernicious 'iblis', devil, in the Indonesian psyche.

So why all of my blather about sibling rivalry? Because your government institutions are fashioned along the same lines as your favored families. That's why. So instead of you trying to win points on the international stage, your handlers in Langley should have deferred to the State Department on this one. Everyone knows that 'State' is your rival when it comes to international affairs. But if results matter, then…, so what!

George Shultz, you know, George Shultz, the current Secretary of State, he would have been greeted with open arms by President Suharto. George Shultz, or even his emissary, would have been seen as a real diplomatic catch. George Shultz could probably have acquired government approval to set up wire taps on every citizen in the country, if that was what he wanted. But only if the concessions, say in East Timor or Irian Jaya or Kalimantan were generous enough!

Successful negotiations need to be done with clout not with clowns whose pay scale is one level above that of an analyst. Just possibly your efforts would meet with greater decision maker approval if you targeted some of the more remote areas of Indonesia, the ones which I have just mentioned.

'Every man can stand adversity, the true test of character however, is to give him power.'

Do you, any of you, have any idea what American politician of note said that? Of course you don't! Not one of you has even the remotest clue as to who the author was. It is a quote from Abraham Lincoln. Now ask yourself, how can anyone possibly know what path to follow to ensure a productive future, either personally or for the benefit of the country, when next to no knowledge of the past exists.

I mentioned the term, 'genetic hegemony' earlier to describe the favored few among American families who have dominated American politics since early colonial times.

Some lived up to Lincoln's comment on character and power. Most, however, did not. The question is, did that matter? Did incompetence or did indifference in the White House spell lasting disaster for the country. No! Never! And why not?

Because, as John Steinbeck put it, America, with too much of everything, was born a monster.

So dilettante or a disgrace while in the Oval Office never mattered. The padded walls of perpetual plenty have always protected the Republic from remorse and ruin.

Some would suggest that going through the expensive and time consuming motions of having the general public vote for a President every four years is a waste of resources. Why not just let the members of the Electoral College choose someone, anyone, with a heart-beat and be done with it. Constitutionally, that is already within their purview. The Founding Fathers had no trust whatsoever in the analytical quotient of the common folk!

In summary then, Ladies and gentleman, I am of the opinion that your country is broken and not even Hubert Humphrey and all of LBJ's horses and men can ever put it back together again. JFK conspiracy theories notwithstanding!

And on a personal note, I already have a distinct sense of what all of you think of me and I want you to know that my opinion of you, all of you, is just as flattering. I am Godfather to Bali High Art in ways that your intel could never reveal. I am by blood, by disposition and by promise more a parent to this enterprise than any actual sire could ever be.

Your task appears to be to wrest this property away from its rightful owners in order to enhance some ill-conceived strategic advantage somewhere in this part of the world. But no plan of action has been presented, nor will one ever be, because none exists. There are no artist's sketches of any 'castle in Spain" to present. There is not even a mock-up of a project blue print which could be rolled out as a crutch, as a cue card strategy to create the illusion of commitment and competence on the part of the Company which you represent.

Nevertheless, I'm going to guess that Alice Springs in the Northern Territory of Australia is the most likely object of your ardor. Specifically we could focus on a top secret installation, ha, ha, in Pine Gap. You know, start with a small communications outpost and allow it to morph into a major defense complex. The Bali equivalent of Diego Garcia in the Indian Ocean, perhaps. Spy on those who spy for you. That seems to be how that cynical piece of defense logic works.

How far the world has wandered from the attitudes expressed in the writings of Robert Baden-Powell. A military man, he was, among other things, the founder of the Boy Scouts movement. On the subject of gleaning the secrets of those whose behavior is hostile, spying in other words, he favored clandestine observation to gain intelligence. Stealth and cunning always trumped deceit. To be better informed and hence gain the upper hand, it was his contention that one had to out think the enemy.

Today that notion of out-thinking the enemy, as opposed to out cheating him, is so far out of favor, that it seems to have sunk below the mere atavistic, what grand-dad's grand-dad thought, and come to rest in the antediluvian depths, before there was Noah's ark and before there was the great flood.

So, just know…, my mission today is to rid this property of you and the Machiavellian mischief that seems to be your stock and trade.

So, I'm ready. Give me your best shot! Make it a good one because this might very well be the last chance you will ever get!"

"Irregardless of all of that, it is impordant for all of us to remember that his renumeration package is above the level of a clerk, as he puts it, because his paycheck comes from crime."

It was less than reassuring to note that Brian Law did have a memory for some facts. That they bordered on the absurdly irrelevant appeared to be of no consequence to anyone.

"Michael, you just talked at length about the future of the United States of America. You have issued what amounts to a dire warning concerning my country's very future. But what about your future,

Michael? What about the future for you and your daughter, Christina. How safe are you, how safe are you and Christina right now, right here, right now, so far away from your country of birth, from where rule of law prevails and is taken for granted."

DJ did her best to replicate the reassuring voice of the major female spokesperson for UNICEF, the United Nations International Children's Emergency Fund. Even her punctuation purred almost as perfectly as did that of the svelte Audrey Hepburn. She was the designer doyen, the poster Mom of means beseeching the world to approach starvation, especially among the very young, with compassion and of course, cash.

Thank God that the corpulent and bearded Peter Ustinov had not been the only voice for the agency, I thought to myself. Even for a chameleon like Donna Jean, matching his voice would have been a stretch!

"Michael, your history of exhibiting care and compassion toward others has been abysmal. This is your big chance to make things right. We are offering you the opportunity to correct that character short fall, to correct it with your own daughter..., Christina.

You should leave this place Michael. You should leave it with your daughter. You should leave it soon. It is time for you to go home. Leave the little details of the day-to-day operation of the place to others..., others who are more adept at...., at, seizing opportunities for growth when..., when they are up for grabs on the negotiation table."

"So that's it! Are you finished Lee? Either I succumb to the thinly veiled threat implied in your comment about the safety of my daughter and leave Bali forever or..., or, I take the road less travelled. I follow, ironically enough, I choose to follow in the footsteps of each one of you!

Instead of cowering under some rigid roof which shelters rule of law somewhere, I would prefer, as is the case with you, Lee, to throw caution to the wind, dismiss the potential for personal embarrassment because of ability shortfall, and become, metaphorically speaking, the best backyard builder of patios on a street, any street, of my choosing, in the world.

And DJ, like you, I would prefer to continue to prevail over every snow storm, which unpredictably batters every safe place, including Bangor, Maine, on my own terms.

I, Lil…, Danyea, I would stop tolerating those who try to tell me when to strike the iron just because they think it is hot. Instead I would vote, as I believe you have, to seek more intimate association with those who, by disposition, make the iron hot by continuously striking.

And Brian, I too would choose to do what I think you are seriously considering as the next chapter in your life. I, like you, feel compelled to increase the frequency of the absences from the far away, stateside, gamesmanship which has to be played. Lingering there for too long, in that mental space, only serves, as you know only too well, to syphon off physical and mental vigor and…, and, at the same time, diminish the sweet smell which comes only with the fresh air of personal fulfillment. And when your considerable vigor is more strategically deployed, something you know from personal experience, you are better able to serve the Company's unofficial motto, which, as you know, is…,

'And ye shall know the truth and the truth shall make you free.' John 8:32

The truth, in all of our lives, is that bravery is a function of controlling fear, not just being fearless. I vote therefore, to follow a path, torpedoes be damned, which parallels those which each of you has chosen to embrace and hold dear.

It is hard to best the Bible when an expression pertaining to the human condition is needed. 'Such shall yea sow, so shall yea reap'. Galatians 6:7.

But today, in this place, and with this thorny, contentious issue before us, the best, the only outcome we can hope for, I fear, is that we can agree…, to disagree.

My Israeli friends never tire of telling me the story of their perpetual run-ins with representatives of neighboring, hostile Palestinian settlements. The Jewish take on the futility of attempting to negotiate with their Arab neighbors is that, 'They never miss an opportunity to miss an opportunity!'

Sisyphus and up-hill, rock rolling redux, perhaps!

Sometimes there are great divides separating people which prove to be insurmountable. Sometimes that is due, in large part, to self-definition being a non-negotiable bargaining chip."

While delivering my moment of Greek mythology, I turned, faced DJ, and silently released from my clenched fist the chromed cork screw which I had taken from her hotel room in the Turks and Caicos Islands. It was the same cork screw which had drawn blood from Jonathon's neck, an event which had happened, what now seemed like, decades earlier. He was the fisherman with no hooks, he was DJ's protégé and he had been, maybe, DJ's potential marriage material.

The hand held kitchen appliance fell to the table top in front of her. It tumbled and came to rest with the business end facing in her direction. A high stakes game of 'spin-the-bottle' was being played in earnest and her turn to perform had been called.

The look of incredulity on the woman's face as she stared at the inert object and then up at me would have merited an honorable mention for emoting on cue at any actor's workshop.

The lethality of the little object and the lack of compunction to use it exhibited by the man who had thrown it, the man who was hovering over her, was not lost on DJ. Neither was the dawning realization that the head long rush into what was thought to be the easy acquisition of a prestigious prize had left her and her cohorts completely exposed and vulnerable.

"Daddy!

You are very bad you know! You are very bad because, because…, you know why…, because always you tell stories that are too long. Look! Already the people who listen to you, the people who have too much Coca Cola, already, you make them ready for nap time!"

Chapter 19

The Hotel Kompas was an aging hostelry situated in the heart of the business district of Jakarta. Subsequent to its cornerstone having been laid, the ensuing structure had enjoyed a certain prominence, albeit brief, on the city skyline. That was based on its splendid isolation. But the inexorable gear shift of urban expansion to 'fast-forward' had spawned business entities whose glass and steel stables created towering canopies of overarching splendor which made the cozy, comfortable guest house seem dated, and doubtlessly doomed to a premature 'wrecker's ball' demise.

True to its name, this little gem of a hotel was the only one I had ever visited which possessed an eight point Compass Rose; the four cardinal directions, North, East, South and West, as well as the four, less prominent, inter-cardinal ones, just for good measure.

Stretching maybe thirty feet in diameter, the carefully crafted circular inlay of polished marble dominated the lobby floor. More public art than pedagogical device, I sometimes wondered though, whether the rendering of the nautical insignia faced true north or magnetic north or, during darker, less romantic, moments, I wondered whether it faced in a northerly direction at all!

Only foreigners with too much time on their hands would choose to perch on the horns of that particular directional dilemma, I thought, almost smugly.

With the North Star never serving as a point of reference below the equator, I had to settle for second best. As a guest in the hotel and when business demanded early morning occupancy of a lobby chair, the capital 'E' on the floor always appeared over the steaming rim of my coffee cup. Mutely, it pointed past the revolving glass doors in the lobby, and beyond the stately palms which lined the boulevard to the main road, to the newly lit lantern of life which could only be viewed through a squint, on the distant horizon.

Rising up like a strung, hunting tipped arrow, between sunrise and sunset, the Compass Rose needle for North was as true as any floor rendering needed to be!

"Michael, you have surpassed the mandate implicit in the task which you burdened yourself to complete. Look at what you have done! Look at the faces of your guests.

Now please, please my dear boy, now it is time to allow me to assume the reins so that our noble steed, Bali High Art, can be brought back safely to the paddock. Please, Michael. Go now, take the two girls. Go now to Jakarta with them. Phone me two days from now when this invasion has been completely repulsed and vanquished.

I shall do my very best, my son, my very best, to meet the challenge that remains in a manner which will, I pray, mimic your own!"

I had left without speaking another word to anyone in the room. I had left, not because of those whispered words delivered to me as we had ostensibly greeted each other with a sustained hand shake. I had left because the good Doctor had spoken to me with his eyes. And the tone he had used was from another place, another time, another mammal. His guttural utterance was that of a lowing, post-partum female, alone with her new-born foal in a protected corner of a field. At once maternal…, paternal…, collegial, and conspiratorial, it left no room for debate. It whispered words which were final.

For the first time ever, I was annoyed by the two girls whom I had in tow. Both were needy. Both occupied worlds, separate worlds, whose gravitational pulls promised to disrupt the sought after season which my singular orbit had made certain.

Both girls were, of course, happy to see me. It showed. They giggled and danced around the way students do the last day of school before summer break. All smiling faces and elastic bodies, they were caught up completely in the ecstatic embrace of unfettered exuberance. They were in love with life and life had given them a free pass…, promising only to catch up with them later on down the road.

But they sapped the energy I had become comfortable using just to fuel the machine which was me. I felt like I was, in their lives, what the Hotel Kompas had become in mine. Safe, sheltering and void of surprises, both of us were taken for granted by those who frequently hovered close. We were softly abused through innocuous indifference when apart and by impatient annoyance by expectation shortfall when we were not. Age had reduced both of us to a utilitarian status. Kompas and I occupied corners of world which had become cluttered by all of the 'other' of the moment. We both enjoyed the casual disregard reserved for a favorite pair of well-worn shoes.

I had bought a Rubik's Cube for Christina and another for Rebecca in the Domestic Terminal of Gusti Ngurah Airport prior to our departure for Jakarta. Sharing, I knew, was not a personality trait of either girl. I thought the, 'oldie but a goody' popularity of the toys would keep both of them amused during the flight. I was wrong. One was too young to sustain interest in a multi-colored, plastic box which twirled, while the other would never be old enough to delve into the challenge, the personal annoyance and frustration, merely to reap a visual reward of so little consequence.

I made a mental note to myself. The following day, as they shopped their little hearts out, I would surprise both of them, 'new' and 'ownership' being as close to adolescent logic as the two words were to each other in the alphabet, with their very own Sony Walk-Man cassette players and, of course, as many tapes as MTV deemed necessary.

What the two 'fading fad' items had in common was personal distraction masquerading as entertainment; a cube which relied on rapid eye hand co-ordination, and a sound system, in miniature, which, when deployed, made the listener vulnerable to collision with any moving object, anywhere out there in the real world.

What the two, 'fickleness of fad' items also had in common, which endeared them to me, was the rendering of the user to absolute, albeit self-imposed, silent isolation.

When Christina had been younger, we had spent so much time together at the Kompas Hotel, that my daughter had fostered the believe that the room across the lobby and up ten floors by magic elevator ride was our private home and that the pool, shrouded in well pruned shrubbery, was our exclusive swimming retreat. Pleasant, home cooked moments had always paved the way for comfortable conversation between us. The Sun had lingered long in the languorous, Asian sky. So, so many times it had toe toasted us but, in retrospect, the magic moments had been all too, too infrequent.

Early mornings and late afternoons were non-negotiable pool times. Mad dogs and Englishmen might go out in the noon day, tropical sun, but we chose to retreat to the air-conditioned comfort of the malls to attend to the shopping which had been promised and re-promised and re-promised again.

Litany as lacquer on the spoken word that had been loosed!

With what seemed like bales of stone-washed denim stacked on both beds in the girl's room, it was hard to tell whether the chlorine and pumice tumbled fashion statements were ready for relocation to Bali or for a clothing bin operated by the Salvation Army.

Both Christina and Rebecca seemed genuinely happy with what the hunting expedition had 'bagged'. And, like the 'Ted Truebloods', who wrote adventure stories for outdoor magazines, they wanted to tell and retell the tales of their latest trophy hunts in the wilds of boutique clothing stores. And they wanted to do it with a table top filled with food.

We sat on cushioned chairs around a circular, glass toped, wicker table. It had a large, striped umbrella growing from a slender bamboo stick which poked through a small hole in the middle of the glass. We had all made choices from the laminated menus, based on color photos of the selections. No thought was given to the nutritional quotient or caloric count of any of the items chosen.

Both girls were wearing bathing suits. One wore an outfit which was too big and the other was decked out in one which was too small, far too small. Both attained forgiveness, however, one for innocence and the other for exposure, by being fully wrapped in large, beige hotel towels. A rendition of the lobby compass rose was emblazoned on the towels with navy blue embroidery. The blue and beige pieces of terry cloth looked more elegant than the hotel and its surrounding property deserved.

I chuckled at the rectifying reality, the usual antidote to pretense, displayed by the compass quarrels being waged in front of me. The 'true-north' arrow on one towel pointed disapprovingly at the other which, in turn, pointed back at its accuser with equal distain. Denigration meant more than did direction to some. The girls had the innate capacity, when together, to create discord even, it seemed, when in the roles of 'would be' cartographers.

"OK guys. While we are waiting for our food to arrive, I wonder if the two of you can help me out with a little problem, no, a little puzzle I have which needs to be solved. It's not exactly the same as a Rubik's Cube…, you know, getting all the colors in the right place…, I know, maybe I can explain what my problem is by using a little story…, a little, make believe fairy tale.

I know, I know. Before both of you complain about my, 'not too long ago' and 'not too far away' story beginnings, just be patient. I promise that this one will be very different. Naturally there has to be a magic kingdom in the story though. No good story would ever be complete without one. Right!

Right! Well, at least that ho-hum fact is out of the way. So, this magic kingdom is different…, very different from every other one I have ever described to you before. The kingdom in today's story is not really make-believe. There are no kings, there are no queens and there are no dragons to fight either. It is a real place and we all…, you, both of you, and me, and most of our friends live there…, in that magic kingdom, all the time.

So listen up, Rebecca and Christina, this story is for you because it is all about you!

Anyway, both of you should listen carefully because it's time to pay the piper. That expression means that since I did something nice for you, clothes and cubes and cassettes, right, it is only fair that you do something special for me in return. And that something nice from you will be to listen to my story, think about it, talk about it together, and then give me some suggestions about what I should do. No, what we should do, so that there will be a happy ending. Then everyone in the story, including any kings or queens or fire-breathing dragons for that matter, will be able to live there happily ever after. Ha, ha, that's a joke, ha, ha, ha."

Christina and Rebecca eyed each other, smiled conspiratorially, and nodded their acquiescence. I knew that the consent form they had just endorsed was roughly composed of ten percent politeness, tinged with curiosity, and ninety percent placation.

This was not the time to tell, to tell anything. This was, I reasoned, the time to 'trip the light fantastic', with or without the consent of the poet, John Milton or any musical accompaniment for that matter! Keep the conversation light and weave a story line which remained 'Allegro-brisk' but decidedly nimble and nonchalant as well.

Keep both kids conspiratorial through engagement and above all, keep both of them committed to sustained contribution to a rational conclusion. 'From the mouths of babes', might flow a straightforward solution to the dilemma caused by the infantile behavior of all of the adults in the service of all things secret.

"So picture where you both live right now in Bali. And if you had a friend with you, a buddy sitting at the table with us right now, someone who had never been to Bali High Art, how would you describe the place so that your friend would have a clear idea of what your home is like?"

The girls looked at each other, grinned and stared down at their laps. Both flexed their fingers and stretched out their arms as if preparing for the fast and furious kid's card game called, 'snap'.

Then Christina and Rebecca bobbed their heads in unison much as two students would during recess immediately after accepting an invitation to jump into the horizontal whirligig of a double-dutch skipping rope. Satisfied with their degree of physical and mental preparedness, a version of what sounded like a Polynesian welcome chant, began.

"Bali High is big, Bali High is best,
Our Bali house is very big, more bigger than the rest

Our Bali house is two floors high, our Bali house is white,
Our pool is very big and blue, and it is, 'out of sight'
Bali trees are mostly tall, and Bali bugs are mostly small
Bali days are super bright, Bali sunshine is just right
And when the bats come out to play, they only fly around at night
Bali High has people too, who love to sing and dance
They laugh a lot and play a lot, so sadness has no chance
Bali High is our home, home sweet home for us
Bali High is where, we always wish to be
It is the very best because, it makes us safe and free
Bali High is big, Bali High is best
Bali High is where, we really love to be
It is the very bestest place, a place could ever be."

I was so enthralled by the paean the girls had created, seemingly on the spur of the moment, about a place which was, granted, only a mind-set away, that I was totally oblivious to the arrival of our waiter. He stood ram-rod straight beside the table with an oversized serving tray poised to the side of his head above his shoulder.

The young man, almost regal in his burgundy and gold vest and matching pill box hat, could have been an extra hired for a back-up role. His foot tapped in perfect unison with the 'paddy-cake' flurry of the four, female palms which slapped against one another and, to accentuate the rhythmic beat, on the table top as well. The grin on his face was in direct proportion to the size of the tray which was lowered to the table top once the recital ended.

The jingle had Christina written all over it. Rhyming couplets were her forte when the spirit of the Bard moved her. Rebecca added the booming, almost baritone voice which did command attention, if nothing else.

Every food group which deliciously poisons a person over a lifetime was present on the platter perched on the side of the table. Granted, nutritional facts were printed on most packaged foods, but an 's.o.s.' warning concerning the addictive levels of 'sugar or salt', present in our restaurant food was absent. Most munchers of fast food were more than willing to ignore the potential for some distant disease or disability in favor of the immediate gratification of great tasting fried everything. We were, it seemed, members in good standing, of that tribe.

Burgers, French fries, onion rings and calamari, all with individual dipping sauces, would be washed down by the Coca Cola which stood at the ready in beaded, beckoning bottles.

And all of those empty calories would serve as mere prelude to the, 'please, just one more', Silver Queen chocolate bars which were stacked like kindling wood underneath a generous supply of paper napkins. The peanut yellow and red letter wrappers seemed to whisper, 'Warm fire in your tummy if you eat me first. No tummy room for Silver Queen is the very worst.'

Wording thoughts in imitation of my daughter's stab at iambic pentameter did have its limits!

"What a great way to show your true feelings about Bali High. I agree with both of you. I agree with you completely. Bali High is the very best place for all of us to be. But those people, the three ladies and the one gentleman who were in our look-out cottage on top of the cliff, they are not nice people and they want to make Bali High a bad place. They want to use it for an Army station. That would be bad for everybody. That would be very bad for everybody, for all of us who live there."

I stopped to see whether my words were having the same alienating effect on my young audience as had been the case with my armed guests. Instead of cold, sullen stares, I was confronted by two faces which were studies in rapt attention.

"I told all the people who were on the mountain top with me the story about the billy goats gruff and the old troll who lived under the bridge which they wanted to cross. I told them that they were just like the billy goats and I was the same as the old troll. I was the guard of the bridge and I told them that they should go far away and find another different place with a bridge to cross over…, to use for their sneaky spy hideout."

"Den of Thieves. Den of Thieves. My Dad always said every day that in Singapore he was surrounded by a Den of Thieves. You should tell them to go there, to Singapore because already there are many bad people there. That's what my dad always said. I heard him…, every day…, he said that…, Den of Thieves."

"Thank you for telling us what your Dad said Rebecca. Remember, he was the man who came up with the idea of Bali High Art in the first place. And it is his money that is paying everybody who works there right now. And his dream was to make Bali High a beautiful place for everybody and we will make sure that bad people do not ruin his dream. All of the people who will come there deserve to be happy.

I told all the bad people to go to Jakarta or to Kalimantan or to Irian Jaya to see if the people there wanted them and their bad army ideas.

But you two arrived at our secret hide-out at exactly the right time. I was going to get angry with those people and start to yell at them. But you two saved the day. You arrived at just the right moment so that Dr. Rajawane could talk to them some more and more politely than me. I know that he would make them understand that we did not want them to stay with us anymore. Yes, you two and Dr. Rajawane were great!

But tell me, how did the two of you make up such a wonderful poem…, I'm going to call it a poem…, because it had many words that rhymed, just like in a song. How did you find all the right words so fast after I asked you to describe why Bali High is the 'bestest' place in the world?"

"Because Dr. Roger-Wally asked us the question same like you did Daddy about the home we have at Bali High. Before we take the truck to come to visit you and the ladies and the man. He told us baby story too about the bad people who were with you high on the mountain."

"Only the baby story of Dr. Rajawane was the one about the fly and the bumble bee. You know the one…? Only in this one we are like the fly and the bad people are same as the bumble bee. And, and Dr. Rajawane asked us if a fly could marry a bumble bee and we said NO! No because the bumble bee would sting the fly and then he would be died."

Rebecca, pleased with her contribution to the discussion, took a huge bite out of her hamburger, sat back in her chair and allowed Christina and myself to supply the remaining annoying little details to the story. But the broad, defining strokes of the tale had been supplied, exclusively by her.

"Fiddle dee dee, fiddle dee dee, the fly has married the bumble bee,

Said the bee said she I'll live under you wing and you'll never know I carry a sting…, fiddle dee, dee…,

See that part! That's where the bad bee would sting the poor, little fly under his wing where she was staying."

Christina grinned widely. She had remembered the critical lyrics to the verse and, in so doing, had contributed as well to our adult, very serious, conversation.

Both girls needed to be players on the playing fields chosen for them by fate. Both girls were vain and highly competitive. Both girls would come to occupy worlds which were light years apart.

I coughed, I hoped convincingly, into one of the napkins as a means of masking my laughter. Dr. Rajawane and I had chosen the same strategy as a means of acquiring a kid's take on the situation. We had played the role of Aesop, the story teller of myth from the sixth century BC, the personage whose name defined story line as secondary to the allegory, the fable, the moral to be learned from it.

The child's tale which I had chosen involved the potential for murder most foul due to unlawful trespass whereas the Doctor's nursery rhyme bordered on being a cautionary tale about the pitfalls of miscegenation.

I couldn't wait to get back to Bali to face the man and demand an explanation…, over the second or third glass rimmed field of ice which floated in the best liquid concoction any nation had dreamed, distilled and distributed to a waiting, grateful world of course!

I would congratulate him on his imaginative approach to problem solving and, at the same time, I would enjoy mounting a feigned but credibly wrathful diatribe concerning his thinly veiled racist allegory involving the coupling, sanctioned by religion in the form of Parson Beetle, of two, consenting insects. I would suggest that his point of view was both anachronistic and misguided and that his decision to disseminate it to impressionable young minds was short sighted, anti-social and criminal!

My return was going to be one of triumph, regardless of what transpired in my absence. If conquering hero was not in the cards then I was more than prepared to assume the role of Joker and trump whatever game remained to be played.

I had confidence though that either the good doctor had found a way to banish the four horsemen and their self-imposed apocalyptic views or to dialogue with them, without my prejudicial views coloring the outcome, with sufficient savvy to formulate a salvage strategy which would not endanger the body politic of Bali High Art.

I couldn't wait to get back to Bali for another reason. I needed to catch up on two nights of lost sleep.

I had felt obliged, during our two night stay at the Kompas, to sleep fully clothed in the large arm chair in my room. It was adjacent to the one occupied by Christina and Rebecca. The door between the two rooms remained open all night, at the insistence of both girls, because, I was told, their knowledge of my proximity should something go 'boom' in the night, would allow them to escape to somewhere safe and secure.

The light in my bathroom had remained on and the door between the two rooms was kept only slightly ajar. The floor surrounding my chair had been littered each night with any and every portable thing I could find which, if accidentally disturbed, would produce a noise loud enough to interrupt my fitful sleep.

My crustacean like retreat behind a moat of the miscellaneous was prompted by the unsolicited groping of my person by the woman-child in my care.

Not so much an aggressive sexual gesture with supple fingers promising a passionate pastiche aimed at arousal, Rebecca's fleeting flutter of finger tips was more like the cold but approving sweep of the hand over a smooth, recently polished, surface of wooden furniture.

Two or three times during each of our two days together, as she innocuously passed by me in the hotel, in the mall, or beside the pool, and always while looking the other way, she would quickly swipe her hand across the zipper of my pants and continue whatever she was doing as though nothing out of the ordinary had happened. Never was a word uttered by the girl who let her fingers do the walking!

Taken aback by the intrusion into my private space, but giving the girl the benefit of the doubt, I assumed that she was merely experimenting with her budding sexuality. She was just directing her attention toward someone she knew, someone she knew would be safe. Someone she knew who would not get angry. Someone she knew who would not 'tell' on her.

Darker meanings did however quickly follow my initial Pollyanna perception. What if the girl was, in fact, trying to seduce me. Maybe it was her adolescent way of demonstrating her superiority over her rival. A perceived competitor who was less than a quarter her age.

What if she had inadvertently witnessed couples 'doing the dirty' behind the bushes on the Bali High property. And what if her voyeuristic experience was titillating enough to prompt her to want to play the same 'grope and grunt' game.

What if her behavior was a reaction to the sinister actions of a Bali High member of staff or member of the work crew. What if the girl was being molested!

Both Dr. Rajawane and his wife, Edith, had to be informed before further complications, like an unwanted pregnancy, arose.

The wellbeing of Rebecca was at stake to be sure but so too was the impeccable reputation of the fledging, Bali High Art.

Chapter 20

"Frank Netter! I don't believe I know a Frank Netter. And you say that, like you, he is a medical practitioner? Where does he practice medicine? Here, in Indonesia, or, with an Anglo name like that, in the UK..., or maybe the US?

Frank Netter..., Doctor Frank Netter..., The only Frank Netter I have ever heard of is the medical illustrator whose work is sponsored by Ciba Geigy. You know, of course you know, those handsome, conservative green, hard covered books which are devoted to human physiology and concomitant pathologies. The ones which have the heft and hard cover, fabric feel of inspired authority. The ones which grace every medical library in the world. And that same Dr. Frank Netter is the man who is solely responsible for the contents of all thirteen volumes in the current set. Quite an amazing, creative accomplishment!

And all from humble beginnings, too! Think, the 1930's, the launch of digitalis by Ciba as a therapeutic response to congestive heart failure or atrial arrhythmias and the introduction of the Netter illustrations of the heart to support promotional efforts with physicians.

Dr. Netter's accumulated, prolific collection of organ system illustrations have, almost single handedly, brought clarity to the art and science of medical diagnoses for lay and licensed readers alike.

And, in the process I might add, they have, in their current book form, contributed greatly to the prestige of the Swiss pharma house which sponsored their creation. Those tomes helped position drugs such as Ritalin, Maalox, Otrivin and more recently, Voltarin, just to name a few, which Ciba Geigy has in its pharmaceutical armamentarium, as the most widely written script items, in their respective therapeutic classes, in the world, over the last fifty years.

His work, underwritten by Ciba Geigy, which has brought so much clarity to the practice of medicine is right up there with another pharmaceutical power house, Merck, and their Manuals of Diagnosis and Therapy.

Prestige through professionalism spells profits. Right! But that is a story for another time perhaps."

"Perhaps and yes, that's the man I mean. And those are the Britannica like books, which you so eloquently described, which Edith and I believe are the main culprits in the drama which has our young Rebecca plunging into a flirtation, no fixation, with the male reproductive apparatus.

As I mentioned earlier, in response to your report of having been molested while in Jakarta, that very same female felon has a recent history of surreptitiously pawing me in much the same manner. And her condition seems to be progressive in nature as well. There seems to be an increasing frequency to her 'hands-on' approach to sexual exploration and gratification, one that I am loath to acknowledge."

"Well, at least she has chosen visuals which are anatomically correct and 'to scale', I might add. At least our lady in waiting will have fewer illusions, based on Netter's illustrations, as to what her connubial future might hold in terms of size! I believe that the only part of the human body which can increase in size four fold is the pupil of the eye! Ha, ha, ha.

But seriously, Frank Netter as a source of post-adolescent pornography! That would be enough to prompt the man to quit his lucrative creative impulse and return to his original professional calling which was more Hippocratic than it was high illustrative art."

"Naturally, both Edith and I will continue to monitor the situation. For the time being, the best we can do is to keep her sufficiently occupied with her 'on sight' duties so that, by the end of the day, she is too tired to think, let alone act on some imbedded Freudian impulse.

Dr. Maria Widjaja, a child psychologist of my acquaintance has agreed to visit Bali High within the next week or so. She will be introduced as a colleague of mine who is on a working vacation with us. But the raison d'etre for her presence among us will be to befriend our Rebecca and get inside the mystery surrounded by the enigma that is the young lady. And hopefully, give both Edith and myself some insight into how to help our Bali High blood line, cope with the challenge which nature has fashioned like a fence in front of her."

"Whatever happened to the time when scratching an itch was the best medicine for it!"

"The only thing missing in that 'Old School' remark is the class tie. The one which would be used by the politically correct chorus to throttle those words before they cleared your throat!

So, back to our discussion of those who wished to do harm. Now I know how you were able to run right over our 'spooky' friends at the Bali High mountain retreat. You flattened them with facts. You 'Frank Nettered' them to death!. And you left them as mangled and ultimately motionless as road kill. All that remained for me to do, after you and the girls left, was to clean up the mess which was left in your wake.

Disposal of the detritus was child's play. A splendid meal, civil discourse, which included a passing comment as to the highly structured executive decision making process adopted by Bali High Art and…, and, over night, five star accommodation in the white house didn't hurt.

Nor, I might add, did the news, which I shared with them, that the Commandant of the officer training facility in Surabaya had accepted our invitation to send his students, on a quarterly basis, to Bali High Art.

Something about advanced physical exercise with a focus on the martial arts as well as taxing mental gymnastics which will delve into, 'The Art of War', by Sun Tzu, seemed, in tandem, to capture his attention.

Along with the fact, of course, that Bali High Art would pay the freight for the budding defenders of the Republic. Protection, albeit symbolic, comes at a cost.

So, with plastic smiles on their faces and bobbing gestures of simulated gratitude, they almost fell over each other in their haste to get into the van which was waiting for them the following morning.

Their body language screamed away, get me away, anywhere away from Bali High Art. Get me far, far away from the ignominious defeat suffered at the hands of amateurs. Get me away too from the near Donnybrook which was averted only by the arrival of the old man, and two, squawking kids.

Just get all of us to a place, a mental space, where we can pretend and then persuade ourselves that the backwater retreat on Lake Batur never ever existed.

Denpasar would serve as portal to certain Hades. They knew that. But the frantic faxing of their failure to their handlers somewhere oceans away, would be less onerous than one minute more spent in the shadow of the great white house, the great, impregnable, white house in primitive, upcountry Indonesia."

"Interesting that you should choose "The Art of War' as a tantalizing tidbit for the military men in Surabaya to mull over. The theme of the text, one which predates Christ by half a millennium, can be summarized by one, simple, declarative sentence.

In any conflict, complete victory is achieved when the enemy is subdued without ever fighting.

Based on what appears to be our complete victory over perverse and pervasive evil and flush with the fact that not a gun shot was fired, even though every player in 'the room at the top' was armed to the teeth, maybe we, you and I, are best qualified, to deliver the course material that speaks to the legacy of the old and venerated Chinese master, Sun Tzu. Ha, ha, ha!"

"Don't go too far down that road of self-congratulation and rationalization young man. Remember George Bernard Shaw and his observation concerning the status of the player and the pedagogue.

'Those who can..., do. Those who cannot..., teach!'

"And based on my pedestrian experience with public education, I would add, ...'and those who cannot teach..., teach teachers!'

Oh, just out of curiosity Dr. Rajawane, did Brian Law volunteer any information as to his planned itinerary over the next week or so? Back to the US or..., maybe lingering in South East Asia a little while longer..."

"Brian Law..., Mr. Brian Law..., Let me see..., let me see now..., You know, I cannot remember ever having met an individual in the employ of a national government, one empowered to do mischief, one sanctioned to influence the stability of other nations, and by extension, the world ..., who proved to be so bereft of intellect.

I suppose he could be excused for uttering words like, 'impordant' and 'v-hickel'. Accent is, after all, a function of geography. But his bastardization of the language of the Bard, the language the Brits perfected, the language of nuance, the one which has fueled the politics of science and the science of politics as well, the same one that has driven much of artistic expression throughout the world for the last a thousand years, assails a polite listener's ears much as offal does the nostrils of a pedestrian in an urban slum.

Non-words like, irregardless, mediocracy and renumeration pepper his prose and totally distract the unprepared listener. Whatever meaning he may have wished to impart was lost. And he seemed to be at his pompous, bleating, attention getting best when using polysyllabic words. They managed to further mangle the only bastardized language he knew..., American!

Ah, the language of America, that wayward, undisciplined, linguistically abandoned child of English! The isolated 'ivory tower' few notwithstanding, its undisciplined presence has put a ceiling of what the culture, no, what that empire has been capable of achieving. Ideas which rock the foundations of conventional wisdom are rarely conceived and when they do manage to see light of day they are still born. The lexicon that gives license to thought is lamentably lacking.

You see, the issue with people like Brian Law, and others in positions of power just like him, is no small matter. Rudimentary verbal skills and an under developed reasoning ability usually go hand in hand. The former can be symptomatic of the latter. And of course the reverse of that maxim is true too!

A vicious circle of verisimilitude perhaps!

And therein lies the problem. His number is legion and it is on the march. Sound bites on every screen in every living room and political catch phrases replacing substantive content on the part of elected officials exacerbate the intellectual emaciation of the American body politic.

Stop me Michael. Stop me before I drown in my own diatribe!

I don't know why you would have any further interest in the man and I don't understand why you would care about his whereabouts. But yes, since you ask, Brian Law did mention, during our one white house evening meal together, that he would remain in Jakarta for a few days prior to his return to America. He mumbled something about the Philippines and brewing political turmoil in Mindanao.

The Christian majority at odds with small, vocal enclaves of Muslims. The mirror image of Indonesia, as you know. The Roman Catholic Church whose liturgy, especially the celebration of High Mass, is recited by priests in Latin and Islam, with its focus on the Koran being taught only in Arabic, champion two languages which are relegated to isolated minorities. One by history, the Roman Empire, and the other by hubris, the Saudis of Arabia. Students of antiquity or families fueled by fossils. Minutia or Myopia. Choose your disease!

No wonder misunderstanding and mistrust abound. People don't even understand their own religious tenets, let alone those of their neighbors, those that differentiate and divide, those that define discord in communities and by extension, entire countries as well!

One ironic result of insistence on religion by rote is that Faith becomes the only bulwark against the bent views of the favored, frocked, powerful few. And, fighting others who have been spoon fed from a different cup, becomes the only means of salvation.

Heaven is assured only when the heathen have been vanquished and immortality is made certain only if the mortal sins of vanity and venality are assuaged."

"Faith that the God chosen for you by circumstance is the right one and faith that those who provide worldly guidance to achieve that particular God's grace in His Heaven are either divinely directed or devilishly deceived sufficient to sustain the ruse ad infinitum."

A codicil to 'Pascal's wager' if ever there was one! You and I have talked about the man before. The seventeenth century theologian, mathematician and philosopher, he was a trail 'Blaiser', the pun is intended, in the formulation of 'probability theory'. And ask me nothing specific please, concerning that theory and, as a reward, and I will make my point concerning Pascal succinctly! Ha, ha.

To paraphrase the man; humans bet their lives on the existence or non-existence of a God. The rational response, he believes, would be to believe. Why…, because if proven wrong, then losses, worldly pleasures and luxuries, will only be finite in nature. If proven right, the believer will receive infinite gain – eternal Heaven and, and, let's not forget, avoidance of the infinite loss…, eternity in Hell.

Definitely a probabilities game of 'Snakes and Ladders'. But Pascal would say, one well worth the toss of the dice!"

"But, my dear friend, I fear we do digress.

Back to Brian Law. I am asking about him because he wormed the details of the disposition of the Tan estate which pertained to the Bali property, from the lawyer in Singapore, one Mr. Whitehead. And Whitehead, for a fee, always for a fee, told him everything. Everything as he knew it, at least!

The result was that we were faced with a conspiracy which was cancerous in nature. Bali High would have been rendered nothing more than an empty shell fronting for foreign intrigue. Without an aggressive treatment regimen, our plans for an Asian cultural presence would have succumbed to malignant, end game politics. And posterity would have been among the victims. In fact, it would have topped the mortality list!

Our initial approach involved chemotherapy. We managed to sufficiently poison the patient by presenting it, the property, as being too open to public access by all the wrong people to ever be seriously viewed as a secure station. And we even suggested other, better situated locations for 'spy in the sky' antics both inside the country and further afield throughout South East Asia.

That particular cancer which we just faced might be in remission but its causation is still alive and no less virulent. It must be removed. Surgery is needed on Mr. Whitehead such that his carcinogenic presence will be alleviated…, permanently!

And our friend, Brian law, can be an unwitting asset, a consulting physician, if you will, with a second, informed opinion relative to the pending, surgical removal procedure."

Sometimes a half-truth was better than no truth at all. I felt that I owed the good doctor at least that much. The whole story, and my role in it, the whole saga of my relationship with Mr. Tan and Mrs. Tan in particular, would have revealed a certain treachery on my part. What I had chosen to become would have been seen as tantamount to treason. It would have been a game changer for both of us.

In jeopardy, truth be told, would have been the trusting relationship which existed between the doctor and me.

In jeopardy, truth be told, would have been my continued participation on the Board of Directors of Bali High Art. Disqualification would be immediate. Disqualification would have been merited based on conflict of interest.

In jeopardy, truth be told, because of my savaging of Dr. Rajawane's belief system, his concept of good and evil, right and wrong, friend and foe, would have been the man's very equilibrium.

In jeopardy, truth be told, would have been the man's capacity to cope. The exposition of the real, royal-rascal, me, would have done to him what I hoped to inflict upon Mr. Whitehead through similar deceit and devilry. It would have undermined both the mantle and the bedrock upon which the soul of the man rested.

And the resulting fault lines would forever cripple the topography, his 'lay of the land' which, hitherto, had been buttressed by girders of trust and truth-tempered behavior. Truth-tempered behavior which demanded reciprocity.

"So Brian Law is merely a resource to be exploited to get at the potential for a mother lode of information…, the personal, perhaps damaging details which pock mark the life of Mr. Whitehead, renowned lawyer, an oxymoron if ever there was one, and hopefully late resident of the Republic of Singapore.

Let's not forget, at my meeting with him, the meeting concerning the bequeathal of Mr. Tan for the Bali High Art project, that he attempted to swindle millions of dollars from the project by amateurishly altering the amount stated in the bona fide will.

And he was the squawking Myna bird who put the 'B-Team' working for the CIA and the equally inept agent from Egyptian intelligence, the Mukhabarat, on our trail. The song he sang for them, or maybe just for Brian Law's ears, about real or imagined "Achilles' heels we might have possessed, weaknesses which begged to be exploited, undoubtedly came at a steep price.

The man is a whore!

Mr. Whitehead is the man who believes, who prays, that he is the biological father of Geoffrey Tan, the only son and heir to the bulk of the Tan fortune. Why? To gain access to fabulous wealth through a bona fide, albeit secret son, perhaps..., but more, I think, he wants to make the statement about himself that parenthood, his, merits respect based on that simple, biological accomplishment. He wishes to wrap himself in the falsehood that he has made a meaningful contribution to society. Ironically, that fraud will, he believes, endow him with a certain, indelible legitimacy. He wants progeny as an insurance policy to ensure his place in posterity!

That is why I requested that you falsify a statement of paternity listing Mr. Tan as the Ivory Snow man. You know, just like the soap flakes which are nine-nine and forty-four, one hundred percent pure.

Irrefutable proof that Mrs. Tan's husband was the donor, the dispenser of the seed, the deflowerer of the maiden..., maybe..., the one who put the bitch-mother's reproductive wheels in motion!

Mr. Whitehead is the man who was slavishly in love with Mrs. Tan. He wanted to be her suckling son, her harboring husband, and, believe it or not, her submissive sex-slave lover..., forever.

That last fact is the gob of icing on the cup-cake that is Mr. Whitehead. He is the corpulent man, one of many in positions of trust and authority in Singapore by the way, who showed up regularly, like an errant school boy, ready to receive his humiliating punishment from the perverse, dungeon disciplined Mrs. Tan. She met his needs by donning a black, latex, cat suit. It was outfitted with an appendage in front which was not standard issue at the moment of her birth.

I will kill every concept of legitimacy in any sphere of human activity which the man perceives to be his by virtue of birth, circumstance or good works. Like an annoying insect with a sting, I will annihilate him between my proverbial thumb and forefinger!"

"Michael, I think it would be wise for you to do nothing regarding Mr. Whitehead for at least two, maybe three weeks. You have become too emotional to be effective as the gardener who can rid this world of the weed which is Mr. Whitehouse. Remember it was Sun Tzu who suggested that a warrior choose his battles well. Know when to fight and when not to fight."

"I appreciate your call for calm, cool, collectedness Doctor, but the man in Singapore will not be permitted to continue the comfortable float down the river of life which remains…, which nature has allocated to him.

Not only do I wish for his immediate encounter with that roaring waterfall of Divine retribution but his appointment as well, with the unforgiving boulders at the bottom of the precipice.

That is his concept of purgatory, not mine. I want him to become the active agent in the process of his own demise. The silent plunge of a man into an abyss of his own creation…, That, to my mind, would be true poetic justice!

And don't forget, Sun Tzu also said, 'Know yourself and know your enemy. Create a plan which is unique and disguise it well.' I believe that I know both players on this field of battle well enough to wage war successfully and only a little fine tuning is required to my campaign strategy to ensure a quick and decisive victory.

I know I can play Trojan horse to the smug Mr. Whitehead's walled city of Troy."

"Somehow I knew that the military man from antiquity would factor into your retort. And somehow I knew that you would not be dissuaded by my call for caution. You have already donned your armor. And you have mounted your warrior steed. All that remains is to make certain that the sword you are carrying has been sharpened enough for the task at hand.

The letter pertaining to the parentage of young Geoffrey which you requested is ready. And, I must say, I am impressed by the 'doctored' document which my imaginative staff created. It should serve to compliment the quiver of arrows which you have already assembled to fight the good fight.

One word of caution though. If you are going to play 'matador' in this particular bull fight, don't leave your banderillas, particularly the barbed stick of parenthood, in the tormented bull for too long. Anything more than a cursory examination of it will reveal its sorry lack of authenticity."

"Yes, I thought of that possibility. I had planned on presenting Mr. Whitehead with your 'evidence'. Let him hold it, let him read it, let him read it over and over if he wishes, and then, minutes later, make it disappear. The memory of the missive is all that will matter.

Back to the arrows in my quiver, as you so picaresquely put it. Let's talk about people and their frailties. You're a man of medicine. You've seen more than your fair share of human suffering and tragedy. What makes people crack under pressure?"

"Well, let's look at your question from the opposite perspective. What makes some people strong in the face of hardship, abuse, and undeserved, from their point of view, setback. What character traits do some prisoners possess which leave them relatively unscathed by the experience of incarceration and subsequent societal rejection.

Why do some patients, faced with the assault, the insult, of progressive, debilitating, and ultimately fatal diseases, remain optimistic, or at least reconciled to the end game which is their prognoses?

To my mind, it's not the severity of the pain which any of them suffer; the plebeian, the prisoner, or the patient. It is the perception of their place in that predicament of pain which is the predictor of response.

A simple example of that would be the removal of a tooth. A tooth yanked out, while the victim is strapped to a chair, done simply to induce pain, as in torture for political ends, will, in most cases, serve to either stiffen the resolve of the victim or prompt him to abjectly surrender. He will either fight the foe fiercely in determined silence or fold, like a jib-sail, in a flurry of loud, flapping shreds before the angry, all powerful wind which has bettered him.

Pull the same tooth for medical or aesthetic reasons, and the patient is both accommodating and grateful. The same pain is seen as a minor, transient discomfort, a precursor to the pleasure of anticipated, positive change.

The plebeian draws strength from the perception that his house is in order. The teachings of his God have been followed 'religiously', as it were, good works have abounded and, and…, 'God's in his Heaven and all's right with the world'. With a bow of appreciation to the Victorian poet, Robert Browning, of course.

The prisoner's source of strength is his concept of 'future'. He holds to the belief that he will ultimately be vindicated or that he will eventually exact vengeance.

And to accomplish either of those outcomes, a sustained future focus is required. Strict attention must be paid to nutrition, prison food being a challenge at the best of times, and a military modeled, daily exercise regimen must be followed. Preparation through personal discipline, as price to pay for payback!

The addition of messaged tattoos to the skin for all to see, aid and abet the metamorphosis from man to machine with a mission.

The patient is strengthened by becoming a parishioner of John Donne. The seventeenth century English poet and cleric, who penned the thought that, 'every affliction is a treasure'.

From his pulpit the Reverend Donne would have preached that hardship was a constant in the lives of everyone. Hardship was not visited on anyone by an uncaring, malevolent God. Hardship was a trial by fire to determine individual mettle and unswerving faith in the way of the Lord. John Donne, most assuredly, John Donne, at his Divine best!

So it is important to remember that your man in Singapore is full of himself. Alone and completely full of himself. And filled with the notion that what he has done during his life time has been, for the most part, right and beneficial for the majority of those affected by the results.

You, for example, might have been seen by the man of manners and decorum, well, most of the time at least, as a young, arrogant, upstart who stole the attention and the affection of the old man, Mr. Tan. You seduced a defenseless aging man, an ailing man who was at death's door. He was not in command of all of his faculties. And you intentionally pulled the wool over his eyes for your own, selfish gain.

Know the far side, Michael, the Alice through the looking glass side, before you sally forth onto this or any field of battle. He feels as virtuous as do you. He feels as wronged by capricious circumstances as do you. You two will simply be combatants using separate optical devices to determine where you are.

Virtue and vice will not be squaring off against one another. Good, will not be pitted against evil, nor will the former necessarily prevail. Yours is not a morality play. The winner of the contest will be the one with the speed and dexterity and drive to deliver the first, debilitating blow. This is not Hollywood. No dénouement has been written into the script. There is no script. There will simply be an outcome…, one in which there will be only one man left standing!

Remember, whether as plebian, prisoner or patient, both you and the legal-eagle in Singapore possess the predilection, the perversity and the capacity to don any or all of those personas. Both of you can, when necessity knocks, morph and chameleon yourselves into the emotional color needed to blend personality type and requisite thought trappings perfectly.

Both of you are equally adept at play-acting roles. And donning the disguises, the self-vindicating rags of rationalization which are needed to make the chosen role of victimization fit most comfortably and most convincingly are, for both of you, mere child's play.

Just don't allow yourself to be victimized by an opponent who is as capable of the noble art of deception, an art form dominated by those who can make themselves believe in their own capacity for transcendence, as you are!"

"Hmm…, the analysis of the relationship between thoughts, feelings and actions…, and the social masks one might don as emotional prostheses to create order and safety in the midst of malevolence..., I see, I think I see.

For the plebian it is performance of persistent faith in order to see God. For the patient it is to see God through sickness. And for the prisoner, it is to play God through premeditation.

Why Dr. Rajawane, are you talking about the early signs of schizophrenia? No! Never mind that. I already know what your answer will be.

Apophenia, a word that eludes most dictionaries, is a term coined by the German psychiatrist, Klaus Conrad, about twenty years ago. It is the condition wherein people mistakenly see connections and meanings between unrelated things; gamblers and their pet number systems, people, their egos and something about central positioning in the universe...,"

"And let's not forget another word that same, good doctor created namely, PAREIDOLIA!

You seem to forget Michael that I loaned you a hospital copy of Dr. Conrad's work on the presentation of the initial stages of schizophrenia quite some ago. And I am still waiting for you to return it to its rightful owner!

A literary type with light fingers. That's what you are!

Pareidolia, a subset of apophenia, refers to, as you undoubtedly remember, the condition wherein a patient sees, that is the pivotal word, sees, an object, pattern or meaning where, in fact, there is none. The face of the man in the moon, rock formations which resemble animals, clouds...,"

"And don't forget, closer to home, along the road between Ujung Pandang and Toraja in Sulawesi, there is the Gunung Nona, the Mountain Miss. The narrow trough created where two adjacent hills meet is thought to resemble a vagina. And that natural formation is more than a soccer pitch long!"

Remember Michael, it was Ralph Waldo Emerson who said, 'A man is what he thinks about all day long!'

Chapter 21

There was something warm and comforting about returning to a city which I knew so intimately. There was something empowering about the revisiting of former haunts so rich in memories of people past and the patina-like pleasures which had attended them.

The familiar colors and contours of the urban set design, the silhouette of the Indonesian capital, had served as mute backdrop for my dalliances so delicious…, as well as the bouts of despair which had, all too frequently, dropped the curtain prematurely on desire leaving me destitute and far beyond mere despondency. And those, 'at the edge' outer limit experiences which defined my flat earth existence, had managed to manifest themselves in both generous and equal measure.

I felt in synch with the rhythm, the giddy rhyme and reason, the vital signs of the sea port which was sinking into the sea, in synch with the sinking city of Jakarta which everyone knew was being reclaimed by the Java Sea.

It had, from the outset, served as surrogate for the long lost, sheltered bedroom of my childhood. Sins committed in that confined space were neither misdemeanor nor felony in nature. They were merely infractions, seen only by my fellow conspirators, my four friends, the walls. And they steadfastly maintained the covenant which afforded me unwavering and impenetrable cloister.

The 'rule of law' I had fashioned for myself, reduced any wandering from my paved road of reason to mere, manageable miss-steps. Strict self-governance and absolute adherence to tree house regulations reigned supreme.

A rigid code of behavior, one which had ordeal by consequences attached to every action conceived and consummated in that nine foot by twelve foot space, prevailed. Crimes of thought which traversed the twilight zone to the temporal were permissible in the room where I ruled only because I possessed the currency of contrition needed to always make payment, to make restitution, on time and in full.

Jakarta was my private Petri dish, my growth medium as well. Its fecundity brought closure to my adolescent flights of fancy. Bathed in the blessing of personal inconspicuousness, almost invisibility, just another stupid tourist gawking indiscriminately at everything both monumental and mundane, I possessed the license which gave full reign to the pursuit of personal liberty. And that gave form to what had hitherto been little more than forlorn, freckled, fanciful, fulminations. Rages against, what Shakespeare would have termed, 'my outcast state'!

In Jakarta, be it conspirator, agent provocateur, criminal or conqueror ..., I was the enlightened despot. I was the unquestioned king!

I knew that Brian Law was hard wired to blindly follow the herd instinct and return to his favorite, his only, grazing padang in Jakarta. Not only would the Hilton be his hostelry of choice, but room 837 would have been more than merely what he wanted, it would have been what he absolutely needed.

Using my frequent guest status as leverage, along with a smile and a neatly rolled twenty dollar bill, I managed to reserve room 835 for a two night stay. By balancing on top of the high-backed upholstered chair in the room and leaning on the wall against which it had been snugly pushed, I was able to position myself in front of the grate located about a foot below where the wall and ceiling met. It covered the return air duct for the air-con unit in the room.

From that vantage point, any noise which emanated from the adjacent room tumbled down the hidden, air circulation conduits and resounded with the clarity of a ringing bell, declaring that Sunday worship was about to commence.

I took a chance and waited for just the right musical notes to escape from my next-door maestro, Brian. I did not have to wait long and I was not disappointed by the noises caught by the rectangular tunnels of air. Groans from one end of his GI tract and escaping gas from the other, created two, harmonious, cresting waves.

That moment, just after the explosion of methane gas and just before proof of manure manufacture snaked into the waiting bowl, would be my cue to act!

Most guests, when alone in their rooms, eschew closing the bathroom door. Something about trees falling in the woods and noises not made if no one is there to hear! And the sounds of my man at work were unmistakable!

I leaped from my perch, grabbed my prop, tip-toed out into the corridor and politely but repeatedly knocked on the door to the room where pooh production was in progress.

"A letter for Mr. Brian Law. A letter for Mr. Brian Law."

I tried to sound like a town crier announcing the arrival of an important dignitary to an assembly of curious townsfolk. But with a heavy, Asian accent.

"Just leave it on the floor in front of the door and I will pick it up later."

Brian's voice was distant but clear. He was annoyed by the interruption to the satisfying, parent-pleasing business of elimination which, were my assessment of the man correct, represented the major achievement of most of his monotonous days.

"A letter for Mr. Brian Law from Dr. Rajawane. A letter for Mr. Brian Law from Dr. Rajawane."

Even I was annoyed by my flat, repetitive voice. And so too was my target. He had managed to stop mid-movement and his bowels were not happy.

"I told you to just leave it at the door!"

Brian must have hopped up from his throne, with pants only at half-mast, to confront his antagonist on the other side of the door. I could hear the muffled thuds of his feet on the carpet as he stomped toward his enemy. I bleated out my massage one more time.

"Letter from Dr. Rajawane to Mr. Brian Law very special. Must have Mr. Brian Law to sign paper. Must have Mr. Brian Law to sign paper, please."

I was proud of my broken English. Not only did the man forget to 'peep-hole' the person outside in the corridor but, in his rush to swing the door open to verbally assault the intruder, he neglected to connect the security chain to the door.

I put my back into the best football block I could manage. It worked. Brian went sprawling to the floor, all arms and legs that flailed about in the air. His flabby stomach was laid bare and his under wear received more daylight than did the unzipped, rumpled Levis which were tangled in knots around the calves of his legs.

I shut the door quickly behind me. I locked it, and strode over to a corner chair which was beside a circular table close to the window. I sat down and looked up, apologetically, almost meekly, at my host.

"You, it's only you! What the hell do you want? You should be embarrassed to even show your face. You…, you…, the tough talking guy who needs a couple of kids and an old geezer to rescue him from complete failure. What the blazes do you want?"

It was easy. This was all too easy. The man placed all of his emotional cards face up on the table before the bidding began, before the trump suit was determined.

"I thought that it would be appropriate Brian, you don't mind if I call you Brian, to have a few moments together to…, to review what happened in Bali and to…, to look to the future to see what opportunities might await both of us."

Brian looked down angrily at his shirt tail which stubbornly refused to hide behind the belt loops of his jeans.

"You want me to comment on your behavior in Bali, to comment on where we stand regarding High Bali development and…, and…, best of all, you think that after you insult all of us at Lake Batber that…, that…, I would want to talk, to talk to you about some future plans we could work on together. Why, you must be mad. You must be insane!

Get out! Get out of here right now. Get out of here right now before I call security to have you kicked out on your irresponsible…, your uppity ass!"

"Aren't you at least going to offer me something from you mini bar? It was a long trip by taxi to get here to see you. We had to fight our way through a lot of traffic to get here just to see you. Couldn't you be just a little bit more accommodating, a little bit more sociable?"

"You wish! I want you out of my room. I want you out of my room, right now. Do you understand? Right now!"

Brian rose to escort me to the door. He stopped dead in his tracks when he saw that I was not acceding to his wish.

"OK, so what do you want to do? Fight! C'mon then. I was second runner up in the boxing club of my high school."

I didn't know whether to laugh or cry at the response of the former pugilist of limited renown, standing in the middle of the rope-less ring in front of me. His clenched fists were raised to a height which rendered them incapable of warding off attack and flat-footed, he almost fell over the coffee table as he advanced to the rear! A sand crab mounting a feeble defense against a hungry seagull, came to mind.

"Stop being so dramatic. Save your energy. You are going to need it. Here, look carefully at the contents of this envelop. Try to guess who gave it to me. How long have I had it, and what…, what options do you think you have to minimize the damage which this evidence, in the wrong hands, will cause to you.

What are you going to say to your wife, Adele and how will you deal with your boss, James Rutherford. Both of them, for different reasons of course, probably can't wait to get their hands on you back in Langley, Virginia. Strangulation might be an idea they have in common.

Remember World War two and the strategic error committed by Adolph Hitler. Remember the strategic blunder which cost him the war. He opened two fronts, the original one, in the west, Europe, and a second, in the east, against Russia. But he was capable of mounting offensive action in only one theatre of conflict at a time.

How are you going to fight the good fight with Adele in one corner and James, your boss, in the other. There is no time limit on how long you can take to mull over your options, Mr. Brian, sir!"

I sat back in my chair and watched the shell shocked man first go through the perfunctory motions of flipping through the four photos and the mailing information like a disinterested customs official might with a proffered passport.

Without taking his eyes off the papers which he knew spelled poison to everything near and dear to him, he spread all five pieces of paper on the desk top as though in readiness for a clandestine aerial photo shoot with a miniature camera. It was as though their separation and exposure to day light might somehow mitigate their lethality.

He became a junior sleuth in a Hardy Boys story. He became a neophyte government agent, ready to reveal a truth in the clandestine world of spies. But all he uncovered was evidence, incriminating evidence, irrefutable evidence, which implicated, convicted and condemned himself!

I got up, went to the mini bar and filled the fold in my arm with two bottles of spring water, two shot size bottles of Chivas Regal, and two glasses. I dropped the assorted collection of glass noisily on the opposite side of the table from the life draining documents.

Brian was oblivious to my machinations. He was bent over the papers on the table in fierce concentration like some grand chess master vainly seeking a way to wrest brilliant victory from defeat at the hands of an unranked upstart.

I settled for a bottle of spring water. Neither the moment nor the man merited a quality scotch. And besides, it would have been wasted on my taste buds. They, like the man seated on the far side of the table, had been collapsed like a beach umbrella in anticipation of stormy weather.

"I…, I'm going to be sick."

Brian's prognostication, directed at the wall which separated him from his desired destination, was all too accurate and only a little bit too late. The ice bucket I held in front of him, like a make-shift feed bag for a mule, caught most of his initial offering but not all of it.

I jumped ahead of the stricken man and quickly lifted both the toilet seat cover and the toilet seat just as he sank to his knees and embraced the oval, porcelain water trough which endeared American

Standard to washroom builders and washroom users throughout the world.

'Sight' and 'smell' being the two 's' words which follow immediately on the heels of the first one, 'sound', when personal business in a water closet is in progress, lend, by extension, compelling credibility to a fourth 's' word, namely 'skunk'. Aversion to…, and avoidance of that reality, spelled out in black and white, is always prudent…, and a well advised precaution when confronted by the ever 'present danger' of fouling a crime scene with foot prints! CIA jargon, notwithstanding.

I smothered the half-digested spill on the floor between the sink and the bath tub with a large towel.

Retching, regaining his feet and releasing unfinished lower bowel business before his bottom reached the rim of the toilet bowl, became Brian's alternative to the parlor game of musical chairs. The plastic seat, like a halo, remained upright on its hinges above his head but well below his mental radar. The piece of molded plastic was unnecessary. It was not required by a body which had become an automatic expulsion machine.

It was as though the man was defined by elimination. It was as though the man's derriere could not get positioned over the bowl fast enough. It was as though his face could not get close enough to the sullen swirl of swamp water, the bubbly mass of suspended mash which he had created. It was as though his mouth, now void of discharge, had volunteered his face to act as surface skimmer of the brown, putrid porridge which had replaced the toilet water in the bowl.

A face cloth soaked in lukewarm water seemed to provide the maternal moment needed to remind the man who was entrusted with a nation's secrets that a world beyond the bathroom floor existed and that it beckoned.

"Do you really have to be here with me! Do you really have to see me like this! Do you think that maybe I could have just a little bit of privacy."

"No sir. I don't think that you should be left alone right now. Maybe you have a condition which is more serious than your symptoms, diarrhea and vomiting, suggest."

Left alone, never on my watch you slithering snake, I mumbled under my breath.

"But somehow, I doubt that. Get over yourself. For God's sake, smarten up! I am the wrong person for you to play 'baby' with. You have no control of your bowels, like a baby. You have no control of your sour spit-up, like a baby. And now, you think that you can whine, just like a baby, as well! Think again mister man!

Here, have a drink of mineral water. You are dehydrated and you need to do something right now about your breath."

Brian Law would never have been left alone in the bathroom. Not on my watch. Too unstable. Too many places to conceal weapons. And in the case of the compromised CIA agent, too many options to mull over. Too many aggressive scenarios, some of which might include me as victim. And possibly, given the apparent depth of his despondency, a very viable way to counteract a cruel and uncaring world by inviting Mr. Death to sit beside him at a table in the Hilton Hotel, in Jakarta, in Indonesia. From obscurity to honorable mention on the Memorial Wall in Langley, Virginia.

Suicide as solution. Suicide as salvation.

Better Dead than living in Dread as replacement for Better Dead than Red, the mantra of the Dulles descendants from the 1960's.

"I know who gave you this envelop you know."

"Do you really. OK then, give me your considered opinion as to what the contents of the envelop and my surprise visit to your room are all about. Think big picture when you consider the story that will accompany the pictures of you and someone playing make believe man on top of you. Try hard to think beyond the confines of the play pen which seems to be your chosen reality.

There will be a test at the end of this strange interlude involving you and me. And if you receive a failing grade, your reward will be the total obscurity which attends all those who vanish without a trace. You will go unacknowledged on the Wall of Shame, Pain and Ineptitude that hangs on some lobby wall in Langley, Virginia."

"I know who gave you this envelope. She, I mean Danyea, did. She was mad at me. We had a fight and she said that she would make me pay..., that she had more power and authority than I did..., and that I would be sorry that we ever met."

Words of wisdom heard at least once before from the same source, I thought.

"Think for a minute. How could she get even with you by using photos that incriminated her at the same time? Get over yourself. You are of little or no consequence to anyone. Anyone who matters, at least. Your face dominates the four photos on the table. But so what! The number of shots taken of the incriminating encounter or others with similar compromise is probably measured in the hundreds. You are nothing but collateral damage. The target of the campaign to clean house, to get rid of dead wood, is the woman whose back and back side figure prominently in the shots I just gave to you. Of course, the woman with you in the photos is Danyea.

But it is not your Company that is doing the house cleaning. The agency responsible for the photos is from the Middle East..., from her part of the world..., from either Israel or Egypt. She is their property. She is their puppet.

I received the envelope with the photos anonymously via the hotel concierge in a hotel where I am known in Bali just hours before we met in the airport. My guess is that it is either the work of Mossad or Mukhabarat. That detail does not matter to either of us though. One works in much the same way as the other. Both derive their legitimacy from their lethality.

Both countries maintain espionage networks that are interchangeable in that they never forget transgression, they never forgive performance short fall and they never fail to act decisively to rectify a situation.

Remember the '72 Olympics..., Munich..., Palestinian Black September..., eleven Israelis dead..., Mossad, with tacit Israeli government endorsement, is still, to this day, in the process of eliminating every person responsible for the planning and execution of that operation.

That decision was not based on any support for rule of law. No judge, no jury, and no jurisprudence. It was revenge. It was and is the precise surgical procedure..., the intervention..., that kills a cancer when it threatens the existence of an organism…, a society…, of a state. 'Never again', is a better motto, for country and individual citizen, than most. It is definitive!

"That sounds more like the law of the jungle than anything else to me. Eat or be eaten. That's what animals do! People have souls. People are beyond mere animal, stimulus-response, behavior."

"That sounds like, 'the pot calling the kettle black'! We could, perhaps, talk about Guantanamo Bay, Kennedy's Bay of Pigs fiasco or Reagan's Iran Contra affair some other time. Suffice it to say that there is a veritable horn of plenty in the world concerning man's inhumanity to man. Perhaps in the next life there will be time, time to prepare a face to meet the faces that we meet, time for you and time for me, time yet for a hundred visions and revisions before the taking of toast and tea.

There are many such love songs and that of J. Alfred Prufrock, as told by T. S. Eliot, is only one of them.

So let's bring all of this, from amateur sport, to professional hits, to Bali adventurism, home to roost, shall we! Danyea will pay the price for the Bali fiasco even though you were a co-conspirator and equally complicit in the cock-up that occurred between Danyea's man, Saladin and my man, Col. Satu.

You were the man on the ground in Singapore and in Jakarta. It was your job to be on top of things. Your squealing pig in Singapore, Mr. Whitehead, was less than candid with you concerning the details of Mr. Tan's will which pertained to Bali High Art. As I just said, the man is a pig who straddles any feed trough put in front of him. He gorges himself at one end and simultaneously disgorges what he swallows but cannot digest, at the other…, much as you just did.

What you got from Whitehead was a self-portrait rather than a sober, actionable profile of me. As a result, you, and your associates, mistook me for some two-dimensional, cardboard cut-out character whose love of money trumped every other concern in life. Why did you not consult DJ and Lee. Both of them knew me better than did that larcenous lawyer in Singapore.

A composite character sketch of me could have been created, warts and all, which would have at least suggested viable strategies to wrest the place away from its transitional owners. Instead, you, Lee and DJ rode recklessly over the hill, like the US cavalry. Spurred on by your sense of invincibility and the arrogant notion that somehow, spontaneously, you would, collectively, arrive at a mutually satisfying solution to the obvious stale mate, you succeeded in doing little more than shooting yourselves in the foot!

You and Danyea should have fucked less and fashioned viable plans of action more. In the future, assuming that you have one as an operative with the Company, strive to do a better job of vetting the people who stage your events. Remember, any event is mere prologue to the actionable outcomes which it spawns.

You are wrong on another count as well, Mr. Brian, sir. Adele and James Rutherford have not and will not receive copies of the damning documents that are now in your possession. And no other copies exist!

I was sent the photos and the addresses of the two people who apparently matter most in your life, to use as bargaining chips, as blackmail, if you pushed too hard for a Bali deal. It could be argued that my daughter, Christina and her friend, Rebecca, arrived just in time to save you from a fate which, from your perspective at least, would have been worse than death.

Anyway, what makes you think that Mr. Rutherford's closets are skeleton free and what makes you think that Adele sleeps with her legs crossed every night during your prolonged periods of absence?"

"How dare you talk like that about my wife! You are absolutely disgusting!"

Puritan pronouncements seemed to trump prurient possibilities in the minds of some.

"Know that there are people and powerful interests out there who are diametrically opposed to what the CIA would like as a construct on Indonesian soil. And know as well that I would have fired the torpedo that would have sunk your ship without giving it a second thought. At the time you were nothing more to me than a minor annoyance.

But the photos from someone's candid camera now belong to you. You can frame them for display over your mantelpiece, if you have one. You can store them in a bank for safe keeping, to share and enjoy with your future grandchildren. Or you can ceremoniously destroy them by throwing them into the campfire that celebrates your oneness with nature somewhere in Appalachia. That's entirely up to you.

The wheel of fortune is in perpetual spin for all of us. Maybe that's a sentiment with which we can both agree.

At any rate, now I'm going to talk about potential partnership between us.

But my gift of partnership comes with a price tag…, a sort of long term installment plan to ensure mutual security."

"You expect me to believe that these are the only copies of the photographs. I was not born yesterday, you know!"

"Like I just said. Get over yourself. You are not a player. You never were!

The photos in front of you are the only ones I am aware of. Other mug shots of you would have been shredded because you are not a person of interest to those who spied on the dramas that took place in your bedroom…, bedrooms. You do not matter. Get it! You do not matter. The net was cast to catch Danyea. The operation was successful. Nothing more needs to be said.

So let's move on shall we. Listen to my proposal. You can come out of this mess, if you play your cards right, smelling of roses.

First, let me tell you what will not be in this partnership for you. No money will ever change hands and no physical evidence will ever be amassed which could prove to be compromising to either of us.

We are both in the business of information gathering. We are both prudent and deserving of the trust, based on past performance, which the two separate but parallel intelligence communities we serve, have bestowed upon us.

Here is what I propose. I will be your eyes and ears inside Indonesia. I will supply you with the information back-fill needed to more fully understand the dynamics of the situation on the ground in the archipelago. State secrets are not part of the portfolio being offered. They are outside of my purview. But what I will share with you will most assuredly enhance the intelligence quotient, as it relates to South East Asian politics, of the US of A.

Case Number One:

The Indonesian air force deploys Soviet, Sukhoi, fighter aircraft for coastal surveillance in Kalimantan. They fly out of a place called Taracan. And so do fixed wing, single engine aircraft with over-sized landing gear, piloted by American, Viet Nam war vets. They tired of carpet bombing Cambodia and decided that flights of mercy were more in line with redeeming behavior. Maybe they are part of the group you mentioned earlier. Maybe they found their souls flying over some pot-holed runway somewhere.

The point in all of this? The point is that some of those military aircraft crash in the jungle. They crash because of faulty parts and even greater faulty repair procedures. The graduates of the Mekong Delta know where the crash sites are located. Put two and two together. If you wanted downed aircraft parts, say for reverse engineering to acquire a metallurgical profile for comparison purposes, this child adventure story might be of some help.

A second scenario. Think of East Timor. Think of US interest in deep sea trenches between Indonesia and Australia. Ditches which easily hide submarine movement between the Pacific Ocean and the South China Sea.

Next, think of Indonesian spies in East Timor. Think of their point of origin. The Armor Division of the Indonesian army in Jember, East Java. Inconspicuous place. Think about their rank. Corporal. Knowledgeable of army discipline but of sufficiently low rank to ensure a natural, subservient posture while working in the field. Pre-military background. Farmer. Easy fit in Dilly, the capital, or anywhere at the low end of East Timor society. Religion. Christian. East Timor is a territory dominated by the Roman Catholic Church – a vestige of Portuguese colonialism.

What the Company would or could do with 'Genesis' information like that is best left to the moles that scurry about their business in the catacombs beneath Langley, Virginia."

I deliberately stopped talking. The better I felt about myself and my managed outcome, the more I realized that I had commandeered the microphone for too long.

"So you are talking about soft information. Soft information that could be acquired anywhere, by anyone and at any time. There is no such thing as a free lunch so, what do I have to do for you in return?"

"Soft information, as you call it, is like gold. Pure gold is brittle and, other than in ingot form, quite useless. It is only when it is combined with silver, copper, or zinc to form an alloy, does the precious metal become malleable and hence durable as well. No intel is of use in isolation from everything else. Context and creativity have to be added to establish structure within which to work. You know that!

Let me give you an example of how, what you call soft information, could work. Let's use your informant, your fat, font of information in Singapore as an example.

You talked to the man. You probably talked to the man many times…, and at length. You are a practiced interrogator. Give me a snap shot of our lawyer friend based on your encounters with him."

"That's classified information. I cannot divulge what was said to me in confidence. That would not only be unethical but foolish as well. If my informants lost confidence in my honesty…, in my integrity, in my silence concerning matters that involved them, I would lose my credibility, my reputation…, all of my effectiveness in the field."

Under the table I clenched my fists in rage. I grinned at the man and counted to five. Ten was a destination too far down the road from my residence in the town of Tolerance. Rage was however, immediately replaced by regret. Brian was not being facetious. Brian was not playing at being 'dumb' with me either. Brian Law was only capable of being Brian Law.

"Of course, Brian. That only makes sense. A man is only as good as his word. Of course. You are right.

Just simple, harmless things though. Like what does Mr. Whitehead do during his spare time. Does he enjoy any hobbies. What makes him happy and content. What makes a God fearing man such as Mr. Whitehead happy and fulfilled."

"He collects stamps. And so do I. His major focus is on the stamps issued by South East Asia countries during their colonial periods between 1850 and 1950. He showed some of his collection. Most of it is stored for safe keeping in a bank safe deposit box in Singapore though. We talked a lot about stamp collecting because I am a philatelist too. I focus my collection on the stamps of the Thirteen Colonies but his collection is much larger than mine. He has more money to spend and more time to devote to his collection than I do. Anyway, it was a pleasure for me to have met a man like Mr. Whitehead.

Oh, and since you asked about what makes him happy, he told me that he is a Member of the Board of the Sisters of Mercy Orphanage in Singapore. He is very proud of his contribution, both in time and in money, to the good Sisters over the years. I sort of got the idea that the Orphanage will receive a generous sum of money from his estate when he passes on to his just reward in Heaven."

No more snide remarks about Mr. Whitehead's corpulence or corruptness would pass my lips when the Eagle Scout from the CIA was within earshot of my sometimes cavalier comments, I promised myself.

Cast your net on the other side of the boat and you will be justly rewarded. We should all strive to be fishers of men, I thought. The Sisters of Mercy Orphanage in Singapore! What a splendid piece of serendipity! My map for mischief with Mr. Whitehead had just been printed and posted. And Brian Law had been the cartographer!

"Thank you Brian for the interesting bit of information that you provided. That's the kind of intel I meant. So you see, armed with that kind of knowledge, I would do my homework, I would study up on the stamps of that era in South East Asia before I met with Mr. Whitehead again.

If I could recognize the stamps that were rare, the stamps that were from a very limited print run, the stamps that might have contained errors as a result of a faulty printing process, I would feel so much more at ease with Mr. Whitehead. I would be much more confident in negotiating business deals with him as a result of something that is as simple…, as straight forward, as a stamp.

Don't get me wrong. I don't mean that stamps are simple. I mean that a little bit of knowledge about the likes and dislikes of the person across the table from you, can make a world of difference to the outcome of any discussion. Do you know what I mean?"

Even I didn't quite know what I meant.

"So, earlier you asked, what you can do for me in return for my soft information feed on all things Indonesian.

Simple. I want you to act as my radar. I want intel on three different parts of the world. I am asking you to share what your Company gathers, information wise, about Saudi Arabia, Malaysia and Pakistan. Specifically, information about terrorist groups or their sources of funding…, those individuals, in other words, who wish to wreak havoc on Indonesian society. The Islamic factor in all aspects of Indonesian society; military, political and economic, is unstable enough. It does not need outside influence to stir up an already simmering pot.

"And how do you propose that we stay in touch with one another?"

"You go to a university library and you read the lost and found items in The Times-Picayune, one of the better tabloids from New Orleans, the Sunday edition. Search under lost animals for an Irish setter named 'Fire'. Just phone the number and follow the instructions that will be given. My contact is via The New Straits Times, Kuala Lumpur. Sunday edition as well. I will be looking for notice of a lost Basset hound who answers to the name of 'Butch'.

Any questions, concerns, comments? Now is the time. Tomorrow will be too late."

"You said, two parallel but separate intelligence gathering communities, before. What does that mean? Who do you work for exactly?"

"Most people would say that success comes to those who play the game of chess through the perfect positioning of and intuitive interplay among the pawns and pieces at the player's disposal on the board at any given time in the game. Most people who play the game know that pawns, though important from a positional standpoint, carry less individual value than do the clergy and nobility who are lined up at the start of the game, behind them.

If you were to say that the Company you represent in the intelligence community is comparable to a pawn because it follows, is reactive and responsible to government policies and directives, you would be wrong.

If, on the other hand, you were to state that it is more like a chess piece possessing a greater independence, a sort of sound reasoning and clearer sense of priorities because it must be out there, on its own, making decisions, initiating actions, all of which are fathered by gut feel, with taught tendrils of plausible deniability of course, you would also be wrong.

The CIA is just one of many national governmental creatures with international bite. And it, like all of its counterparts in the world, trading in the currency of the secret and the sinister, those of friend and foe alike, has distinct limitations. It is merely one of many 'boogeymen' outfits which flexes its narcissistic bent on a finite field of play, with finite player capability performing for handlers who possess equally finite, self-serving goals. Your Company, like most, is all too predictable but, at the same time, irrepressible. The beast cannot be killed.

It could be said that I work for an enterprise which transcends the national, which marshals the parochial and more often than not, plays parent to the squabbles and sibling rivalries which define all myopic, territorial driven, imperatives.

That's it Mr. Brian Law. That is all I can say about my employer. Is there anything else we should discuss before I take my leave?"

"No, I think it is all good. The Times-Picayune in New Orleans for me and The New Straits Times in Kuala Lumpur for you. Sundays. No, I think that's it. It is all good."

Brian Law shook my extended hand much as a politician would after kissing too many babies while out on the pre-election hustings.

"Very good then partner. Have a safe trip home and know that I will respond to any missive you might send within a week of its receipt."

I was out the door and gone before the man had a chance to move a muscle.

Most of what I told Brian Law was truthful but it eclipsed his shallow notion of gravitas.

Some of what I told Brian Law was untruthful but that was beyond his intellectual grasp.

Little of what I told Brian Law was important because facts eluded his feeble grip.

None of what I told Brian Law mattered because all had evaded his glazed gaze.

Brian Law was the kind of creature who was conditioned to wrap himself in the warm blanket of the familiar, the affirmative, and the fundamentally false.

* * *

You can fool some of the people, all of the time, and

You can fool all of the people, some of the time, and

You can fool all of the people all of the time when you control the form, focus and frequency of the messages dispatched to them by friend and foe alike.

With apologies to Abe Lincoln!

Chapter 22

It was a truism, when travelling by road anywhere in South East Asia, that, as a foreigner, you never took the wheel of the motor vehicle in which you rode. All expats knew that. The concept of 'All' did, however, entertain the notion of exceptions, from time to time.

Nobody walked anywhere in Jakarta. Too primitive for the locals. Too dangerous for the foreigners. Black head hamma, as they were called, human insects that collected and consumed the cash crops of others, busied the air everywhere. Those who flaunted bling on their person while in public to those who sported swaying swags of cash in accessible billfolds were easy targets.

All mobility, whether by rattle-trap or Rolls Royce, depended on the marriage of a metal frame to two or more wheels and, of course, a motor made functional by fossil fuel. And that specific black gold, supplied by Pertamina, the state run oil company, was dirt cheap because most of the generous government subsidy which the firm enjoyed was passed on, by law, to the consumer.

The result, at any time of the day and throughout most of the night, on all major arteries throughout the capital city, was traffic congestion on a scale which was found to be acceptable only in the third world. The horn blowing, oxygen depleting, time wasting nightmare was not only a statement of conspicuous chaos, but it was, as well, the source of a dull, debilitating headache which diminished both physical and mental acuity.

Never a source of embarrassment or shame for municipal administrations, predecessors made for great 'fall-guys', it was proof positive that when one factor, motor vehicle ownership, increased exponentially while the concomitant element, road reach and readiness, remained constant, crippling civic atrophy and truncated commerce, would follow.

The latter consequence was, in actual fact, only partially true.

Commerce, of a sort, rose, like new, green shoots, from the scorched forest floor of human presence via the pernicious celebration of the 'now'.

One such commercial enterprise involved school aged children, mostly boys, who aided and abetted commuting motorists in their attempt to circumvent the law. To ease morning and afternoon traffic congestion, the government had instituted a '3 in 1' program, for every vehicle on the road that followed the daily arc of the sun.

One car, one occupant, was an American standard which the rest of the world lacked sufficiently deep pockets to emulate. To achieve the magic number of three people per car, Indonesian commuters had attempted to enlist the help of discarded fashion manikins as passengers. But no amount of make-up or discarded clothing allowed them to pass police check point scrutiny as bona fide, day-time, office dwellers.

Fast kids, those who could make the run from suburb to down town street corner, hitch-hike back to the same or similar pick-up point and repeat the sequence, might complete four or five runs in the a.m. and one or two less than that in the late afternoon.

A good day would net them $4 or $5 US. And that princely sum poked a large hole in the argument made by their teachers that lingering long in school to learn would ultimately be rewarded by fat pay packets. The kids behaved as though they were the spawn of the adults who swam upstream every day of their lives. Attention was paid to the potential for payment in the present and the future, with its promise of rich reward beyond the horizon, could go and 'fish' itself.

A second creative approach, to turn traffic adversity into financial advantage, was created by boys who were somewhat older than their 'pick-up parade' cousins. Their strategy for success was to impersonate police officers who were trained to direct traffic.

Positioned at busy intersections which had no traffic lights, side roads which emptied on to major arteries and at breaks in the six foot long cement road dividers strung haphazardly along stretches of wider than usual sections of road to create boulevards, they were the directive force, the only force, to be reckoned with in the Marlboro country where men, machines, and motor oil mixed.

Equipped only with whistles and arms that flexed like those of fullbacks who were ready to straight arm anyone who dared get in their way as they ate up opposition yardage during their broken field runs, fearlessly, they faced the constant glare of oncoming head lights. They were the maestros, the matadors who confronted the madness that ruled the roads of Jakarta. They made mere pennies per manoeuver but volume trumped price points, always. These stars of the street were handsomely rewarded for their daring-do exploits.

The game they played was reserved only for the young and the nimble. And the success of that subset of entrepreneurs was based on a universal acceptance, among those bogus officers of the law, of individual territory integrity.

Women were not absent from this cadre of creative capitalists. Their specialty was more of the heart and not of the 'how-to', mechanics of running the daily gauntlet between cops and choke points along the routes to the city center. Theirs was the art of the soft sell!

With borrowed, some would say rented, infant or toddler in tow, they would position themselves along the curbs or astride the narrow islands which separated two way traffic flow, or close to intersections regulated by traffic lights. 'Red' would signal the commencement of their slow walk, with child in tow, beside the idling, tin and tinted glass islands of opportunity.

Eye contact with each and every commuter was critical to their success. Human pain and suffering and desperation, desolation, and depression were best transmitted by facial expression. And that was a learned behavior. That was a form of method acting, make believe which made good money for the practitioners of poverty who were plausible. And good money was usually complimented by mounds of items no longer of value to the driver of the vehicle. Dr. Scholl shoes, any sizes and all colors, 'T' shirts in need of washing, toys with one part missing, half-filled coloring books and gaudy, costume jewelry completed the Santa's workshop 'take' on most days.

Unlike their male counterparts who had to tread water in the same 'swimming hole' of traffic every day, these mothers of milk and kindness had to be mobile. They had to change the location of their Mother Theresa machinations frequently. Nothing dulls the dulcet tones of pulled heart strings more than over exposure.

Still others, among the inhabitants of the islands in the stream, the players in the daily street pageant, could usually be counted on to be present and accounted for, though in much smaller numbers, when mischief was the means by which mercantile ends were to be met. Most were men but women merited an honorable mention.

Operating mostly at night and on secondary, feeder roads to major thoroughfares, ones with ditches on either side, ones hemmed in by heavy foliage, ones which were poorly lit, pot holed and sparsely populated by pedestrians and vehicle traffic, these opportunists preyed on those who drove large, unwieldy vans, like the Toyota Kijang or Panther.

Those who appeared to be feeble, lacking in dexterity behind the wheel, those who seemed to be frightened by everything in front of them on the road, inexperienced, and, most importantly, those who looked like they were female, based on traditional garb like the hijab, were the targets of choice.

Female victims were preferred because violence was not one their primary reactions to shock and, critical to the success of the ruse was the selection of a driver who would possess an immediate willingness to display and act upon sympathy and compassion…, and generosity!

The MO, as news stand detective novels would have it, the modus operandi of the thief, was simple. He would choose the right type of vehicle with a single occupant, a female driver, and follow it a short distance on his Kawasaki or Honda motor bike. Remaining to the right of the targeted van, between it and the ditch, he would attain and maintain the same speed and remain in the driver's 'blind spot'. That was just behind the driver's door.

When a straight section of road, one that was almost pot hole free was encountered, the motor cycle driver would deftly lean the handle bar of his bike into the side panel of the van. In one fluid motion, the bike jockey would then jump free of the sacrificed bike and allow the staged collision, now a certainty, to occur. No thought was given to staging the appearance of a bloodied, collision victim. The gravel at the side of the road would take care of that!

The fraudster would assume the position of a semi-conscious person by sprawling on the road beside the front wheel of the idling van until he was joined by the distraught driver. With drama queen theatrics he would feign a broken appendage. Arm, leg, finger, rib, it didn't matter. Groans and grimaces, to give the scene an appropriate sound track, were a must.

The next step in the process leading to financial reward was wreckage removal from the scene of the accident. The driver of the van had to be convinced of the need to drive the motor cycle victim and his damaged machine to the nearest hospital or clinic. Neither the police nor an ambulance would show up if the perpetrator worked quickly.

The strategy was to get hurt, slightly, but look as though the injury was severe. The victim had to remain sufficiently coherent to provide road directions to the distraught driver. Once at the medical facility, the fraud artist would be met by accomplices, usually family members, and his faked incoherence could resume. The driver of the van, still suffering from a certain disequilibrium, if not shock, would rarely connect the dots of hospital location and victim family presence.

Hospital forms would be completed correctly and in detail by the visibly distraught next of kin.

The paper work was critical to the financial success of the exercise because that would ensure the vital information about the person responsible for the mishap, the hapless driver of the van, would be recorded. Name, residence address, telephone number, place of employment, perhaps, and credit card details, maybe, would provide 'bank vault assurance' that all financial matters which would result from the mishap, would be promptly and fully addressed.

All medical bills, doctor consultations, prescribed meds, x-rays, potential hospitalization and possible rehabilitation would, by default, become the responsibility of the actual victim of the accident because the cyclist would have no money and no means of livelihood. Prolonged financial support for the now disabled victim would be a 'bonus' possibility as well.

'Knowledge is power', or so the aphorism suggested.

Knowing the game, which reversed the roles of victim and perpetrator, and knowing that victory would go to the player with the better sense of immediacy, of timing, of rational thought, was critical to averting personal and financial dislocation and, given third world proclivity for social spin, long term tragedy!

The day following my 'Treaty of Versailles' encounter with Mr. Brian Law, I found myself stuck in traffic just as the Sun was disappearing into the grey smog which substituted for the horizon in Jakarta. I had been successful in purchasing both Remy Martin and Chivas Regal, cognac and scotch being necessities of life for some, but I had been less fortunate replenishing my cache of cigarettes.

Marlboro was the brand and Marlboro Lights, in white and gold packs, were the smokes I preferred. I had had to settle for the regular cigarettes in the red box but I rationalized the less than ideal purchase with the faulty logic that I would smoke less because I did not particularly enjoy the pungent aroma or taste which the regular, red, Philip Morris moments, provided. Anyway, I reminded myself, I had quit months ago!

Little was planned that evening in the house that was beside the house that had been the residence of the recently departed, amorous, American Miss who had called Houston home.

Strange, I thought, how some women who linger long enough in your life to make an impression, take up residence in your room upstairs, spread their bric-a-brac everywhere in it and stubbornly refuse to leave. Thoughts of Renee seemed to visit themselves more frequently with each passing day. I missed the matriarch, the Southern belle, the

Andrew Wyeth, egg tempera, fresh faced woman more than I cared to admit.

Spiders and the webs they had spun across most windows and doors, mutely attested to the only form of trespass experienced next door. The elegance of arachnid handiwork, more compelling and credible than any cop, crime scene, tape, provided the proof positive I needed that the former Lee residence was bereft of any recent human visitation or occupation.

Minutes passed before I realized that my taxi had come to a complete stop just inches away from the car in front of it. A glance out the rear window of the motionless Blue Bird, revealed a long string of imperfectly aligned head lights which seemed to stab, almost accusingly, at the immobile obstructions in front of them.

The trapped machines, at least twenty in total, snaked their way down the street in single file, like flies stuck to an extended strip of sticky brown, fly paper. A ghostly white hue, which at first, seemed almost religious in intent, battled for supremacy, in the heavy, humid air above the road, against the billowing, blue clouds of engine exhaust. Their mischievous mingling merely added an eerie element to the growing misery which now included a cacophony of discordant car horns.

Major mishap more than minor road obstruction was, I thought, the likely cause of the road infarction. And, to paraphrase Winston Churchill and his dismissal of prepositions at the ends of sentences…, the situation I now faced was something up with which, I would not put!

'Power sailing' was always my immediate response to being becalmed while at the helm of a vessel which relied on sheets and sails for motive power. The auxiliary, the stink pot, the part of a sail boat which received more than its fair share of distain, that is to say, the motor, was always called upon to assist the hapless, flapping sails. And that was despite the distain of purists who, like true masochists, expected, no embraced the notion that the journey toward destination, by sloop, ketch, or yawl, should, by design, be punctuated by discomfort.

I paid the taxi driver double what the fare would have been had we been able to reach my abode, grabbed my two bags full of sin, and strode off toward the front of the line of traffic. Idol curiosity, more than concern for casualties, pushed me forward. The reason for the wrinkle in road reliability was of less importance to me than rehiring the services a new and unfettered taxi cab somewhere beyond the traffic bottleneck.

My intent was to escape the moment and retire to my island of tranquility which was not in the main stream of anything. My idea was, for the remainder of the evening, to just enjoy my own company and perhaps, the companionship offered by a reasonably, well written book.

'Watch what you ponder, it may precipitate a certain prescience', could have served as suitable sub-title beneath a photo taken of the elements which created the head of the 'road kill' traffic snake.

Set design perfect and 'lights-camera-action' positioned, were an idling, white colored van with its headlights on, a distraught Muslim woman wearing a full, black, burka, a motor bike resting on the ground beside the van with the back wheel still turning slowly and a young man whimpering softly as he rocked back and forth in an attempt to nurse the bleeding lacerations which began below the knee of his right leg and extended down to just above the ankle.

During the short walk to the scene of the crime, I had put on my aviator style sun-glasses and had pulled down tightly on my baseball cap so that the sun visor rested snugly along the top of their metal frame. The mask did not hide the fact that I was a foreigner. My walk, talk, skin pigment and posture made that impossible. Large, reflective lenses and a logo free head cover did offer some degree of anonymity. That was the hope. The potential for facial recognition by the limited audience of curious bystanders and other drivers in close proximity to the 'carnage', was next to nil.

Due diligence done with deliberate speed to defuse the situation would, I knew, destroy any individual capacity for accurate memory or account of the supper time, silly theatre played out in the gathering gloom of the residential road.

The supine victim suffering loudly from superficial lacerations, his location almost on top of the downed bike, the burka lady whose capacity to view her surroundings was akin to that of someone looking through the mail slot of a suburban front door, the perfect alignment of the van on the road to ensure an effortless, rapid escape, everything seemed staged by an amateur. It was too perfect! It was the work of a director who was still awaiting peer approval. It was work which made text, and even sub-text seem superfluous. Symbolic imagery seemed to want to go it alone.

The only layer of meaning which mattered to me was that I had been robbed of a smooth, uneventful, return trip home by some street failure fishing for easy funds.

He now owed me and I was going to collect. Placing the two brown bags just under the front bumper of the van, I went to the door on the driver's side and extended my hand to the crouching woman whose demeanor was one of debilitating remorse…, almost akin to that of a captured war criminal.

"Salamat malam, Ibu. Apa kabar?"

The 'Hi and how are you' salutation was met by a quiet, reserved, almost apologetic, 'Kabar baik', by the woman who appeared to be in the process of going through the mental list of males in her life, those who would not be supportive of her latest traffic misadventure.

It was clear from the immediacy of her response and her effortless, coordinated gate, as she allowed me to guide her to the opposite side of the vehicle, that she was uninjured and in complete control of her faculties.

Waiting until she was comfortably seated inside, on the passenger side of the truck, I patted her on the forearm, and, as I closed the door, I gestured to her to push down on the door lock.

For a couple of seconds, my mind went blank. I could not remember what I was doing in the middle of a congested street in the center of Jakarta and I could not focus on what I had planned to do next. The lady in the van, the lady whose vanity went beyond the secular, whose inflated sense of self resided in the religious, was someone I knew. I knew her smell which was more than mere manufactured musk. I knew her body reaction to my touch. In spite of her flowing garments, I recognized her posture, her stance. I was familiar and comfortable with, and quite enamored by her distinctive perambulation.

Christ, I thought. How many women did I know! Their number was far from legion. Don't allow transference to distract and derail, I almost said out loud. Too late to change tactics. Too late to ponder some 'perhaps' person who is of no consequence. Get on with the deed. Play with the 'maybe' and the 'perhaps' when the dance of dislocation is done..., when the urge to play avenging angel is assuaged and the villain vanquished.

I returned to the cyclist and, without a word, lifted him off the frame of his machine and half-carried him toward the front bumper of the van. I reasoned that the glare of the front head lights would blind those gaping few who stood in front of us and block the view completely of the victims of schedule disruption who were founding members of the 'big-wait' club, who brought up the rear.

I quickly retrieved the motor bike. I stood it up and walked it toward the front of the van and its former rider. I leaned it against the front grill between the two headlights. Both wheels rolled easily and appeared to be undamaged.

I pulled the two paper bags from beneath the front bumper and placed them in front of the flummoxed man on the ground. Like a practiced chiropractor I pulled and pivoted the man's four appendages in rapid succession and, just for good measure, poked and pinched at the meager musculature which defined his chest and abdomen. His head and neck were tested in much the same way as Christina's Barbie doll had been, post turkey baster cauterization.

No words passed between me and the man on the ground. All communication with the downed cyclist was through impromptu sign language.

I grabbed his chin and roughly pointed his face toward me. I pointed at him with my forefinger, then at the motorcycle and then at the alleyway which was to the left of the van. I followed the same 'connect-the-dots' pantomime two more times before I turned my attention to the bag in front of him which contained the carton of Marlboros.

I kicked the cardboard carton to his side, took out my wallet and, just inches away from his face, peeled fifty thousand rupiahs from the inside compartment reserved for paper money. He was going to be offered $25 US and not a penny more!

Another piece of finger pointing theatre ensued. This time the magic wand of the substitute Tinkerbell touched the forehead of the not-so-lucky contestant, then the bike, then the direction of the escape route down the alley, and after a slight pause, the Philip Morris moments in a box and the crisp Rupiah notes stacked neatly at his side.

It was clear that the fellow understood what was happening and what it was that he was being offered as reward for his efforts. Something in the young man convinced him that negotiation would be a logical next step.

He pointed tentatively at the remaining bag and the two glass necks which, like tubers, seemed to be sprouting up from deep within the dark brownness. I looked at him quizzically and just as he was about to begin his finger point at the inclusion of the booze in the final settlement, I hit him hard on the side of his head just above his cheek bone. I coughed loudly as the slap landed. Open handed and with the wrist relaxed, the blow delivered a sting which was guaranteed to increase in severity for minutes after the initial blow was delivered.

The manoeuver was borrowed from spin-cast fishermen. If one wished full utilization of fishing rod capacity to deliver a lure a great distance over the water, wrist action snap was essential.

The manoeuver was a favorite among Indonesian mothers who wished to convey their disapproval of a child's behavior and their demand for cessation of it. Most often the blow would be delivered mid-sentence by them, no facial expression would betray intent, and the speed with which the punishment was delivered left the recipient wandering whether the source of the painful assault was 'Mom' or some deranged beast who lived next door or under the mattress.

I finger pointed one last time at all of the elements which were critical to his escape equation and I took his downcast demeanor, his staring at the bag of booze, as acceptance of the compromise, of the less than successful negotiation process.

He slowly stood up, stuffed the money in the non-bloodied front pocket of his shorts, and stowed the cigarette carton in a compartment located under the passenger seat of the bike. He mounted the motorcycle, started it up and pointed the front wheel at the agreed to side road.

Just as he was about to put the machine in gear, he grabbed at the bagged bottles which had been left beside the bike. I lunged at the little ingrate and managed to dislodge the prize from his grasp. The bottles fell in one of the muddy puddles which pock marked the road.

Appearing to guide the young man to the alley way he had chosen, I grabbed him under his left arm and with my thumb and forefinger pinched him as hard as I could. This was standard operating procedure in Indonesia. This disciplinary action, taken from the unpublished Indonesian woman's manual on effective child rearing techniques was what every Indonesian child remembered most vividly about his or her mother.

Wailing like a banshee, the little gangster drowned out his own voice by revving up the motor of his bike and, like a shot from a catapult, disappeared in a cloud of blue-white smoke. I had one more manoeuver to execute before I could comfortably, 'blow the popsicle stand'.

Like some sort of benevolent overseer of the event, I returned to the van with my head bent downward as though on a quest for anything which might have been left behind by either of the two players featured in the recent drama. I stared at the ground along the side of the van, bent down, pawed at it, ostensibly to pick up something of interest, visited the rear of the vehicle, paused to ponder the ground again and then continued my complete circle check of the big white monster.

I wiped the trace of mud left on my right hand down the side of my pants, collected the fermentation in a bag, opened the driver's door, mounted, what in an earlier age would have been called the running board, got in, shut the door with a deliberate deftness, noting that the pilgrim who was Mecca motivated was still there, put the tin heap painted white in 'drive' and slowly drove away.

Any local Dick Tracey types who might have formed parenthesis around the Kijang would have been hard pressed to remember anything more than the color of the license plate. Both front and rear rectangles of tin had had their number and letter configurations obliterated by the road muck of monsoon Indonesia.

"You did not have to go to such great lengths just to see me, you know. Your presence is my pleasure…, particularly when I see that you are in peril. Peril which is sometimes self-inflicted, as you know, or peril provided by those who are pernicious…, peril is peril nonetheless.

You know, in truth, I believe that you are a seer!

You are the one who can reconcile cruelty and kindness, the one who can descend Dante's ladder to the depths of conceit, of deceit, of self-love, and know all the while that redemption derived from energized eroticism, electric ecstasy, and eloquent eulogy, is at hand through unwavering and sometimes, unrequited love of another."

I expected a denouement…, a flourish of triumphant shedding of…, the renting of garments…, the abandonment of societal…, of religious constraint, the tumbling down…, the cascade of beautiful, black tresses, but that was not to be!

The eyes behind the mail box slot stared at me coldly. There was no hint of recognition in their dull luster. Only the annoyance of having to be grateful to a stranger for a matter that could have been settled by an amount of money, a trivial amount, a sum which would have been considerably less than the price of a mediocre meal at an equally mediocre restaurant.

"You speak like a man who is educated.., well educated. You speak very fast and you speak with very much affectation…, no, very much alliteration. The music you make with your words does not make much sense. This is what I think. I don't know if I can say it this way but you speak with too many flowers in your prose. They get in the way of your purpose."

The voice I was listening to behind the layers of linen-like material was somewhat muffled and distinctly deeper than the one I knew and had expected. It was like that of a young man, feigning a baritone voice to buy booze while underage. It bordered on being contrived, like a less than mastered, foreign accent. The intent, to add credence to a cardboard character, failed miserably.

Flowery speech! That's what the woman was accusing me of practicing. The accusation was not new to me. In fact, it had been a frequent 'no-go' sign along my road to relationship building in the past and, when left unheeded, always spelled disaster. My love of words, my loquaciousness, was viewed by some shell-shocked veterans of the protracted trench wars of the sexes as proof positive that I was all form and no content. The package was the prize. No promise was inside!

'Prose getting in the way of purpose', that's what she had said. What a fascinating way to express a personal criticism of a recent benefactor, I thought. I was amused more than I was annoyed by her sober, almost stern, demeanor. It was a new approach to reproach for me and, as such, I found it somewhat intriguing.

"My name is Michael, Michael Campbell. May I ask what your name is…, after all we have something in common. We are both victims of the same road accident. So we share a commonality and we sort of already know each other…, at least a little bit, don't you think?"

I found my self-confidence ebbing and my interest in trying to engage someone whose only desire was to escape, had begun to disappear like trapped water in a cupped hand.

"Leorah…, my name is Leorah. L, e, o, r, a, h, Leorah! It means, I have light. I am a person of light!"

"And if I may ask, Leorah of the light, do you have any siblings…, I mean, do you have a sister perhaps who is about the same age as yourself? The reason I ask is because you remind me very much of a lady I met recently who is visiting friends in Indonesia.

We have met quite a few times, in Jakarta and, and in Bali as well…, there is a strong family resemblance…, you look very much like her, from what I can see…, that's all."

Silence, my question was met with complete silence. It was as though I had never uttered a word to her. It was as though she had misconstrued what I had said as an amateurish 'come-on'. Finally, under her breath, almost like a faint whisper I thought I heard her mumble, "No, there is just me. I am my only family."

An even longer, uncomfortable silence ensued. I could feel the rising tension in the woman. She fingered both sides of her shawl almost in an attempt to shrink into its folds and disappear. Her discomfort was caused by me. I knew that. But I was powerless to mollify her misgivings. I was the strange man beside her who had commandeered the lion's share of an already confined space. I had robbed her of any 'own space', in the already uncomfortable box made of metal which was the front passenger section of all utility vans. This was a, 'déjà vu', Yogi Barra moment all over again!

Lilith had been forced to endure the pain, the embarrassment, occasioned by the multiple baptisms of fire wrought by my hands, before anything approximating civil discourse between us had blossomed. The little Miss Look-a-Like beside me would not be spared the same 'breach-birth' discomfort. The payment be exacted from her for the process of 'becoming' was going to be just as steep.

"My house is close by. I need to stop there for a couple of minutes. Just long enough to clean up the outside of your big white machine where the guy on the motor bike ran into you. No sign of a collision means that there was no collision, right, ha, ha…, and just long enough for me to get my car out of the garage. That way, you can follow me in the Kijang until you get your bearings…, until you know exactly where you are. Then I can return home and you can drive the rest of the way back home…, back to where you live. How does that sound?"

"No, thank you. That will be fine. I can make my way home from here. Maybe you can get a taxi. That would be better for …, if you got a taxi to take you home from here."

I hit the brakes hard. Leorah braced herself just in time to avoid a collision with the dash board. I rolled down the door window, got out of the van with my sopping wet booze bag in hand and slammed the door shut.

"My advice to you, Leorah, is to get rid of this rented machine first thing tomorrow morning. Ask the guy you leased it from to supply you with another one of a different color. And avoid travelling anywhere in this area. Avoid the scene of the accident completely. Do that for a least a month. Do it so the little highwayman you met today will have enough time for his wounds to heal and maybe, with a little luck, to try his luck elsewhere. Do it so that he will have enough time to forget about you and me and everything that went wrong on the road which, hopefully, will be less travelled by him in the future."

I felt like adding that the bill for my carton of smokes, the ransom paid in cash, and my steep consultancy fee for benevolent road assistance would, unceremoniously, be shoved down her throat via the rectangular hole in her head scarf. But her 'insensitivity' and my reciprocal 'insult' would not segue very well!

At the very least, my displeasure helped me decide that she would get no Ketok Magik'. Neither as advice nor as restorative action. That was the least I could do out of spite..., out of the 'more' that I would have done had there been a kindred spirit!

Ketok Magik was a business which specialized in repairing the minor bumps and dents, the superficial scratches and scrapes, which befell most vehicles at one time or another, on the congested roadways of Indonesia. Located throughout the country but situated most often in large urban centers, they were the clinics were plastic surgery was performed quickly, cheaply, and in strict secrecy, on the nation's wounded rolling stock.

Behind locked gates surrounded by six or seven foot high wooden fences, hot water, drain plungers, WD-40, acetone, grease and various lengths of lumber would be used to 'magically' restore the vehicle to its mold memory, pre-collision condition. All motorists were required to wait patiently outside the 'O.R.' compounds while the doctors of deception did their work.

Insurance companies were deliberately kept out of the news loop with the result that, individual insurance rates never increased. Typical of the third world, I thought..., elaborate construct to partially forestall and hence completely disregard, systemic malaise!

Without looking at the woman, I quickly walked to the rear of her vehicle, crossed the road, and disappeared down a narrow side street. I knew that it connected with a thoroughfare where the light blue rattle-traps for hire, the busy little army ants of metropolis, would be parading along, in single file, their prescribed patch of pavement.

Chapter 23

'Home is where the heart is', or to quote the German author, von Goethe, 'He is happiest, be he king or peasant, who finds peace in his home'.

The refrigerator rewarded my rummaging around by supplying a tray of vintage ice cubes sufficient to last the evening and a frozen pack of Marlboro Lights as well. The latter a compensatory gift, I chose to believe, from the Gods of the Carolinas for my generosity with their most favored commodity. A commodity whose mythic worth was on a par with the gold, frankincense and myrrh of another larger than life story. The cellophane wrapped box of smokes had become wedged behind a Styrofoam tray of out-of-date hamburger meat, at the back of the horn-of-plenty, freezer unit.

Like an escapee from any politically motivated purge, the rolled tobacco had avoided being caught up in the first sweep of likely haunts which harbored 'enemies of the state', and had become dependent upon the silence of the shadows to act as a shield against authority which would have banished the platoon of twenty soldiers to the garbage gulag.

The disappearing trick, the subsequent waiting game…, the dependency upon the passage of time to purge and the gifting shift in the direction of fickle political winds, only rarely coalesced to produce conciliatory, almost common weal, closure.

A plastic bag of chocolate covered raisins completed my quest for a well- balanced evening meal. And my ring side seat in the mosquito proof porch which over looked the less than pristine water in the unattended swimming pool, consummated the marriage between gastric and visual compromise.

The first scotch had been served up, savored and swallowed. Its sibling was awaiting the same fate. Philip Morris and his favored son, the Marlboro Man, did not fare as well. One inhalation of the Madison Avenue promise of pleasure resulted in the lit thing between my fingers being violently stabbed to death in the glass dish which had been pressed into service as an ash tray. Funny, I thought, how a fast friend from the past could morph into a repulsive monster so easily and so fast…, and so permanently!

Stick with what works, I said under my breath. Stick with fermentation and simple sugar confection.

Select a candidate and then stick with the choice. That defined my relationship with Mr. Brian Law. Decidedly a character of confection, if ever there was one. Yes, Mr. Brian Law and his pin prick of a presence on my mental map of eminent, not so notable and decidedly unremarkable, personages.

A silly magpie of a man, he was in imminent danger of falling off the low level, Langley perch to which he had been assigned. An innocuous man, whose perceptions, whose beliefs based on those perceptions and whose resulting actions…, squawking and wing flapping like some caged bird, would lead not only to his demise, but also entrap those who could be paper traced back to him as well.

Which was worse, I wondered? The man who was under employed and bored to death or the man who was overwhelmed at work and ready to welcome death in response to any number of work place triggers.

A cynical truism concerning modern corporate life was that all people eventually got promoted to their own level of ineptitude. Under employment and over employment, it was thought, were time triggered in every individual and no one was immune. Widgets, weapons for war, government engineered social programs or cleric-to-laity blueprints for salvation, the nature of the product or service being offered up for consumption, did not matter. People charged with the pursuit of the perfect production method always represented the weakest link in the business practice chain.

Books had actually been written by individuals who managed to climb up a sufficient number of rungs on the corporate ladder to reach a position of authority such that they could, through delegation, deception, obfuscation, absenteeism, plagiarism, and deferral, get away with doing absolutely nothing during their first full year in a new position. Senior management indifference and ineptitude seemed to dove-tail well with the Machiavellian, detection avoidance maneuvers they employed.

The 'nothing' the neophytes did was never exposed while it, the 'nothing', was a work in progress. Their 'nothing' only reached the light of day when they trumpeted their accomplishment in print..., and collected royalties from book sales in recognition and celebration of their moral bankruptcy.

Neither a moral code nor a compass to ascertain direction was ever included in the work belt selection of tools which hung from their waists. But that was of no consequence, because the work they were charged with completing was of no real consequence to the financial complexion of the corporate. Minions minding the minutia of the shop.

Adults perpetuating adolescent play. Perhaps!

Innocuous ineptitude as half-brother to the diagnosis of benign, corporate tumor.

A well-defined, rigid moral code, combined with insufficient business acumen and weak interpersonal skills more often than not, spelled irreversible disaster. Suicide, business set back, and the collateral damage of truncated careers for associates, usually defined the scene of the crime.

Everything which had transpired between Brian Law and me had been verbal. No written document, no incriminating photos, no hard evidence of any sort, no taped conversations, would ever, could ever, be produced. No prints..., therefore, no accessory after the fact, no proof of malfeasance, or collusion, no 'nothing' to prove that anything untoward had ever transpired between us.

Any investigative trail would turn cold before it got to my door. Foot prints in the soft soil of the rose garden outside the ground floor window of a purported crime scene would not be mine.

Should Mr. Brian Law, my favorite member, in good standing, of the Dan Quayle Fan Club, succumb to recrimination, and resort to finger-pointing or mud-slinging, no jury could be convened, let alone be convinced to convict based on the hearsay and uncorroborated evidence he could provide. Anonymity and innocence were assured. Disavowal of any knowledge of Mr. Brian Law and his antics would be the only defense I would ever need. The man and his life of dreadful desperation would remain forever below my dignity as a topic of discussion!

A face full of chocolate seemed appropriate after putting the issue of Mr. Law to bed. I wanted a sugar 'buzz' and I needed some sort of stomach lining if I were to continue to imbibe from my hard fought for, 'Regal', prize.

I was wrong. The raisins covered in chocolate which was not chocolate, only succeeded in ruining the heather-honeyed moor which my mouth, after three stiff shots, had become. No matter, I thought, the evening was still young. There would be time, time to think, time to ponder the wonder of the world, time to ruminate on one's place in it, time to dispel through drink, the dreariness that shortfall in expectation precipitated.

Yes young..., the evening was young..., yes, young, young like little Miss Kijang..., Little Miss lady of light..., little Miss Leorah. The woman with the Jewish name. The woman who walked and talked the role of the Moor, the devout woman who dressed the demand of the Muslim creed. The woman I thought I knew. The woman who said she did not know me. The woman who claimed to have no siblings..., no duplicate, no 'Alice through the Looking Glass', double.

Either my physical senses had betrayed me or the serene, no, the shell-shocked woman I had met on the darkened street in Jakarta, was lying. I had been wired, for as long as I could remember, to trust what my blood hound, pronounced proboscis in the middle of my face, told me. Olfactory sensation trumped both sight and sound. I could smell the presence of Lilith on that street in Jakarta and I could almost taste her presence as she sat, obediently, beside me in the white, rented van.

And those sensations of her had excited me! Truly excited me. I felt that I was in the presence of the author of the arresting treatise, the pain and pleasure portrait of the oneness we had wrestled away from adversity. I was with the one person in the world who, by dint of intellect and emotion, had captivated my imagination in a way which was unique, was unsettling, was so very, very decidedly delicious.

So what to make of the two solitudes, the two worlds, mine and that of the femme fatale who was all fatwa. The Kijang lady had to be lying about the non- existence of a sibling, either a look alike sister of the same approximate age or an identical twin. Maybe. She must be lying about the absence of a Lilith or a Danyea, as a distant blood relative. Maybe.

Or…, or…, the Kijang lady was, in fact, Lilith, in disguise, in character as a ruse to conceal both her real identity and the nefarious nature of the clandestine operation tasked to her. Maybe. Or the Kijang lady was Lilith, in character which was outside of and removed from her conscious state of being. Maybe.

Some choices, I thought. Either there were identical twins on the loose in Jakarta or there was a woman of my acquaintance, a woman who had at least one other woman, alive and well, residing inside her head. Both 'people', competed for a public presence and the ensuing rivalry between them ensured that the sentence of schizophrenia or multiple personality disorder would remain immutable.

So, the creature whom I had met on the road was a nobody, or a somebody related to Lilith, or a somebody known as Lilith, to Lilith, or a somebody not known by Lilith, but still Lilith. Or maybe every player in the 'rag-tag' ensemble of real and imagined characters was just damaged goods. Maybe all of them had recently fallen off the back of a truck in Manhattan somewhere in the vicinity of 7th Avenue and 42nd Street!

Discount designer duds for designing damsels in varying degrees of deterioration and distress! Maybe that too!

Trust the merchants of misrepresentation in the Middle East to come up with the wrinkle of look-a-like spies. That was assuming, of course, that neither of the two women, if there were two women, had facial features which were marred by dermal imperfections, dental abnormalities or other discrepancies related to trunk and limb formation which could be used to differentiate one from the other.

Espionage operations sponsored by any number of countries with cause for the clandestine, with a need for strategic versatility in their spy network, would be clamoring for their or similar services. Twins who were almost joined at the hip would be in greater demand, on a long term lend-lease basis, than any Hollywood stunt men…, or stunt women would ever be.

The phlegmatic woman who had stood beside the waylaid Kijang had been real. That was the only fact which passed a reality check. Everything else was the proverbial riddle wrapped in a mystery inside an enigma.

I had no idea as to the destinations listed on the travel itinerary of the woman I had known as Lilith. Once she left the Bali High Art property, she might as well have sprouted wings, and, like some venerated archangel, flown away to where ever she was needed most, maybe to write in riddles for others more deserving than myself in some distant galaxy.

Maybe my fixation on the young woman and our unfulfilled moments of prophetic prose had unduly affected my perspective. Maybe I had started to see things which were not really there. Maybe I was experiencing a bout of apophenia. Maybe I was mistakenly seeing a Delphic Oracle in women's weeds whom I wish fulfilled as Lilith. Maybe I was being introduced to my own early stages of schizophrenia. Maybe I was being introduced to a new partner in life!

Quickly I fixed myself another drink. The tawny spirit that smiled as it left the neck of the bottle was strong, the ice from the tipped tray was watery weak, and some of both trickled down the wrong side of the rim of the glass in a conspiracy of non-compliance.

No matter. The vexation from Virginia, Mr. Law, had been dispatched and, 'The Three Faces of Eve', the movie experience for which I seemed to have been afforded a front row seat, for the stage adaptation at least, had been easy to follow. It had featured only one character. And the actress in my private screening was much better looking than her silver screen counterpart, Joanne Woodward, had ever been.

Ms. Woodward won the Academy Award for her sympathetic portrayal of a woman suffering from multiple personality disorder. But that was in 1955. In that year, the president of the US was Dwight D. Eisenhower! That post-war, ebullient time of America 'rightness' in the world helped to explain what Paul Newman said about the woman who was his wife.

According to him, Joanne was the stuff from which steak was made and all other woman who expressed a romantic interest in him were nothing more than hamburger meat. An interesting culinary analogy, I had thought, at the time. Women as chattel, moveable pieces of meat, as most Muslim men might have it, or women as feedlot managed sources of protein destined for the digestive tract and the inevitable expulsion as effluent.

Time for a male rethink of their mothers, their sisters, their wives and their daughters. Time for the minority to re-evaluate the majority of the global human population. Time to fully fathom and find favor in their splendid reality and, in the process, find greater favor with self!

Alcohol was better than corrective lenses. Clarity of vision and capacity to knowingly express facts and feelings, commonplace for citizens of the planet, Erudite, were always in evidence when alcohol was speaking and when no one was present to corroborate what was said. When the room was empty, and the gut was fermentation full, even the speaker was denied memory of eloquence.

Eloquent memories. Eloquent memories in miniature. Memories which had defined the last six years of my life! Memories which made their continued manufacture, a personal mandate…, a personal mandate which was sacrosanct.

What was the matter with me! I was forgetting about the other young woman, the slip of a girl, the other weaver of magic with words, the miniature Madonna of the hard hats, the party crasher who, inadvertently, had saved the day for me…, for everyone, with her pronouncements from the pinnacle which rose above the Bali High Art enclave.

Yes, what about her! What future had been fashioned for my little Christina! What future had been secured for her! I had spent less and less time with my darling girl, the only person in the world for whom I had an unqualified love, and even less time positioning options to enhance the pedals of the rose poised to bloom in full profusion.

Options had been bandied about in my head but all of them, upon subsequent reflection, were limited and most seemed fatally flawed.

I had started with blood. The family of her deceased mother in Monado, or the remnants of mine somewhere in Toronto, or maybe in Vancouver. I had lost track.

Viven had told me, before the birth of our daughter, Christina, that she had had a son with an Australian intimate and that the child had been given to her mother to raise. The mother relied on the financial support of her daughter to survive. That required Viven to travel extensively to keep the money flowing.

Companionship and support, doing the chores which required lifting or pulling or pushing, for the ailing mother on the family farm were provided by the young grandson in exchange for a loving place to call home. Grandparent, parent, child, role rotation was commonplace in the bartered business of family life in rural, upcountry Indonesia. Add nieces and nephews and relatives once removed to the list of the reassigned and it was easy to understand why most Indonesians in any given town or barrio felt that they were related to almost all of their neighbors.

Had Mr. Death called on me and not Christina's mother, then a life spent padding about, bare foot, on dirt floors and pursuing dreams and aspirations which were rooted in a life of subsistence would probably have been sufficient. What a person did not know, did not, apparently, hurt them.

But the roles of the quick and the dead were reversed. Christina had always been with me. She experienced a life predicated on the Western notion of personal independence, freedom from drudgery and conspicuous consumption. And that would, not only, never change but it would, in fact, expand, based on heightened expectation and subsequent broadening of scope.

Yes, a half-brother resided in Monado. But if bridges were to be built to include access to him, their construction would begin with her full agreement and only when she had legally come of age. And that was a generation away from fruition.

That left my family. Lydia, my former wife and our two sons, Philip and Stephen, who were twenty some-things by now. Both, assuming that I was the sire of both boys, were half-brothers to Christina. Both would have been indifferent to the arrival of a little girl whose skin was two Crayola colors darker than theirs.

But all three would have quickly developed a resentment of the child because of her interruption to their precious little myopic worlds. And that alienation would have spilled over into overt animosity shortly thereafter. Proof positive of my ability to move on and embrace a new life would have cracked their egg-shell assumption that I would be forever wounded by the self-induced loss of their presence in my life. No trip to High Park in Toronto or to Stanley Park in Vancouver would be in the cards for either of us in the foreseeable future.

I shifted from blood to social bonding as the next parameter, as the next port of call on my ethereal journey in search of safe haven for my supposed 'child in need'. Dr. Rajawane and his wife Edith, came to mind. They were next to merit consideration and they were alone in that regard. There was no one else in my life with whom I would place any degree of trust, trust to selflessly parent my most precious cargo.

But Dr. Rajawane simply did not have the time to devote to a child. He had never had an offspring and Bali High Art would be worse than a teething baby for the foreseeable future. Edith was simply too old for motherhood. She had no experience with the condition and she was just too, too, old. Her stamina was now measured by the cups full, and common sense, which had always been the hallmark of the woman, was in ever diminishing supply. Both would be more than willing to accommodate me. Both loved Christina dearly. I knew that. But both would be overestimating their capacity to effectively cope long term with a girl growing up!

And any school located close to the Bali High compound would have been so parochial as to make Christina's experience with formal education in the Turks and Caicos Islands seem almost 'Ivy League' in comparison.

Anyway, what was I thinking! Enough of this nonsense! I was the father of the delightful slip of a girl and I had the responsibility, the duty, no, the overwhelming desire to be with her, to be by her side, always. I would sacrifice whatever was necessary to see that the corner stone was laid…, the corner stone upon which her values, attitudes, and sense of self-worth would be built.

So, both 'blood' and 'bonding' were out of the question as sources of supposed child support. That brought me to the last alternative I could think of and that was 'boarding school'. Anywhere in the world would have been viable had money been a determining factor. But that was definitely not the case. Boarding school might have been a sound choice had no parent been present.

However, institutionalizing a child, regardless of the academic reputation of the bricks and mortar location chosen, would have amounted to dereliction of duty bordering on criminal neglect and abandonment. Widget replication was not ever going to be in the cards for Christina. Psychic death at the hands of devout Jesuits would never be played out, like some parlor game, either. Not with my little Miss Someone, my little Miss Someone who possessed the better part of me more than I could ever lay claim to that same better part of me!

Only one option would ever make sense. It was the only choice with which I could ever feel comfortable. And that was to become Christina's brood hen. In our little nest in Jakarta, I would provide enough warmth, security, and nurturing to satisfy my chosen brood of one. From a house our new home would be hewn.

Jakarta would be our city of residence. The house I was holed up in would change, too many bad experiences for both Christina and myself, Siti and Jessica, one a maid and the other a miserable next door neighbor. I would find an au pair, a nanny, a governess, a live in maid, a somebody, a competent somebody, a compatible somebody who had the age, the experience, the disposition and maybe even the dried up libido to meet, unencumbered, the daily needs of Christina and the developmental wants I had in mind for her.

And Jakarta catered to expats who had kids in tow by offering a wide variety of private schools with names which harkened back to British colonial times…, times which were never part of the Indonesian experience! The Trafalgar School for Girls, Summerville Academy of Arts and Sciences, and The Townsend Preparatory School, came to mind.

I knew that too much of my affection directed at Christina had been based on performance…, hers…, and too much of the reward system I had concocted and delivered was based purely on the pecuniary. I kicked at a cushion close by, missed it, and almost fell in a clumsy heap on the floor.

Time was of the essence. I knew that. I had to start…,

Something went 'boom' outside, in the night. Something went 'boom' next door, in the back yard of the former Lee family residence. Someone had bumped into something in the dark. Maybe in response to my spontaneous eruption of frustration and exasperation with myself. Maybe not. Regardless of the cause, I knew that I was no longer alone with my thoughts and, in the same instant, I also realized that being ensconced in the most flimsy of structures attached to the back of the house, made me vulnerable, very vulnerable to attack!

Ignoring the dead cigarette, which fell into my lap, I grabbed the glass ashtray beside me and held it poised above my shoulder ready to heave at the head of the intruder. Failing that, I would use it as a dead weight in my clenched fist to either hit the person in the upper body or cause a diversion by lobbing it into the swimming pool. I shrank into the far corner of the couch hoping that I would be befriended by the shadows which engulfed the over-stuffed piece of furniture.

Well organized thugs, spontaneous opportunists, or bored teenagers whose families lived in the compound, it didn't matter. It didn't matter because they all would pose a high potential for doing damage to anything or anyone who got in their way.

The intruder or intruders would almost certainly be male. They would be young and they would probably spook easily. Little provocation would be needed to spark a violent reaction in them. Fear or vengeful retribution would fuel the same result. They would have 'cased the joint' or joints, just minutes before their decision to strike or maybe they had driven by the houses days earlier.

Regardless of when they were first made aware of the abandoned properties, the would-be thieves would have come to the same conclusion. The two houses represented a 'grab and run' opportunity which was guaranteed to be risk free. The two adjacent properties, despite transparent attempts at creating the illusion of occupancy by using light timers in one or two bedrooms in each of the houses, screamed of vacancy and opportunity. One empty house would act as buffer for the other. Passers-by would be totally oblivious to anything which might have been construed as untoward.

The only effective defense I would be able to mount against the menace would be a fast and forceful offense. And words would not be the weapons of choice. I was at least twice as old as the intruders and I was at least twice as drunk! There was no George Foreman left in me. No stamina. No capacity to 'take it', the physical abuse, nor any energy reserve to dish it out.

Any 'Rumble in the Jungle', Congo style, would have spelled curtains for me. And more than a memory of Mohammad Ali would have been needed to do the devil's deed! Stepping into any boxing ring of life, going the distance, all ten or twelve rounds, would have been out of the question.

And so I was hiding like an errant schoolboy on a piece of aluminum lawn furniture, in a screened sunroom, at night. Think you silly bugger. Anyone could drink like a fish so try acting like one…, an apex predator from the depths…, a shark! So, what were my assets, I thought. Mobilize what you have. Think scenarios. Plan for the best but be skeptical and be prepared for the worst.

My occupancy of the place, or at least my specific location in the house or on the property grounds, could not have been known by the interloper and his accomplices. And I alone knew the locations of every moveable and immoveable object on the lot. Memory provided me with the night vision which my adversaries did not possess.

Become a night feeder. That's it. Become a marauder who knows no fear. Become an object of stark terror. Savage the prize and then swim away to wreak havoc elsewhere.

I quickly tiptoed across the sunroom floor, opened the screen door and ran on the balls of my bare feet toward the gate which separated the two properties. For the first time since taking up residence, nothing had squeaked when it was trod upon or when it was opened slowly and deliberately!

My focus was diverted for a few, precious seconds as I recalled that the same gate had served as portal through which, my farm fed foe from Texas had made her triumphant but truncated appearance on the empty stage which had been the backdrop of an earlier life, a much, it seemed, a much earlier life.

I disappeared behind the overgrown shrubs which, like silent sentries, guarded both sides of the entrance to my former Bower of Bliss. I nestled in between the hedge and the fence and managed to approximate a credible gargoyle squat just as the unseen and uninvited intruder tentatively tested the gate latch.

It seemed that I was being confronted by a gang of one.

I exploded from my hide out and ran headlong at the crouched form and, visualizing through my mottled memory, my best shoulder block on a high school tackling dummy, I drove the marauder away from the side of the fence and, indifferent to a referee call for unnecessary roughness and a subsequent fifteen yard penalty, I pushed the hapless creature into the deep end of the swimming pool.

I did not know what to do next. Was I to save the culprit I had just tried to drown or was I to deny the thrashing scoundrel in the cesspool in front of me any means of escape. Was I to show compassion for a fellow human being who was in trouble or was I to vengefully punish his ill-conceived, antisocial behavior.

The choice was not an easy one to make. The difficulty arose because I could relate all too well to the unfortunate man's circumstance as he thrashed about in front of me. Discomfort trumped danger and immediate embarrassment outweighed any concern for future run-ins with the authorities. I knew all of that from personal experience.

As a kid, I had spent one week each summer with my cousin, Alton, on his family's farm. Hide and go seek had been a favored game for youngsters with too much time and too little money. Places to hide on a working farm were limited only by a kid's imagination. Silos topped the list of great hiding places. The sixty foot high, circular, cement block storage units which were securely anchored to adjacent barns offered hiding places to accommodate every level of concealment ability.

Like medieval castles, or look-out towers, as we called them, the over-sized exclamation marks which rose high in the sky, stood empty, or almost empty, during the month of June. But between the end of June and November, crops like corn and soya beans were harvested, as was the hay, which was baled. The latter was stacked in the lofts of the barns, while the former, the grains, were augured up to the tops of the silos where gravity took over and filled the winter larders from the bottom up.

I was with Alton during the second week of June. We were playing hide and go seek with some of his friends. I thought the empty silo had a cement floor. I jumped down to the base which was about three feet below the barn floor upon which I was standing. I sank up to my neck in the smelly, liquid sludge which had pooled inside the base of the storage unit during the rain drenched, post winter, months.

I am told that I went berserk and that Alton and his friend had, with no small degree of danger to themselves, managed to pull me out.

Being stripped naked in the middle of the barn yard and being hosed down with ice cold water like a dog that had lost an encounter with a skunk, was the stuff from which indelible childhood, traumatic, memory was made.

Being reduced to uncontrollable tears and being forced to succumb to new-born nakedness in front of Alton's family and friends, including the girls from neighboring farms, ranging in age from four to fourteen, was also the stuff of dysphoria. And that state of mental discomfort remained with me like an unattended, simmering pot on the stove..., for more years than I care to recount.

Only one false move, one false move anywhere, at any time in one's life, and, automatically, one was transported from recognized, respected player with social status to hapless loser…, and all in a heart-beat. 'April is the cruelest month', according to the poet, T.S. Eliot. The month, in northern climes, noted for regeneration and the resurgence of all things new and alive, is also the month when suicide is most prevalent. April and June share the same season.

Break and enter, trespass, theft, property damage…, nothing merited a conviction…, a sentence which included a yoke across one's shoulders weighted down by an unattended, simmering pot of anger, embarrassment and remorse.

I crouched down to get a better look at the aquatic animal I had trapped in the swimming pool. Immediately, I scrambled to prostrate myself in front of the thrashing individual and shouted as loudly as I could to break through the wall of shrieking sounds and splashing water which the trapped creature had created. I splayed my legs and dug my stiffened toes into the soft earth. I grabbed fast to the raised edge of the pool with my left hand to further anchor myself against what I knew would quickly follow.

"Grab my hand. Just grab my hand. And pull yourself along my arm to my shoulder. Use me as a ladder to get out of the water. A ladder…, you know…, rung by rung. Climb along my body until you can roll unto the ground. Stop yelling and just do it. Just pull yourself, arm over arm, up the side of my body and then roll to safety. Roll to the ground beside the pool. Just roll to the ground beside me."

Like most people who cannot swim, like most people who cannot see or touch the bottom of the body of water which surrounds, no, engulfs them, like most people in that traumatic situation who sense the close proximity of another person, the drowning victim will always fight mightily to pull the person on shore into the water to act as a buffer, a shield, between them and the sure death which is already kissing at their face. Personal survival becomes paramount and all else mere pastiche.

The panting, bedraggled monster from the black lagoon no sooner made landfall than the commencement of a 'drum roll' assault of small, flailing fists on my upper torso, began.

I rolled over once to escape the onslaught and, staring into the face of my assailant, I started to laugh uncontrollably. Life was just too bloody bizarre, I thought. Just too cracker crazy to be taken seriously.

"What is the matter with you, Michael Campbell? I come all the way across the city of Jakarta, just to see you, and..., and..., this is the reception I get. What is the matter with you anyway! Why do you feel that you always have to hurt me? Why do you have to be so physical..., so violent..., so rough..., are you..., are you not, at least, a little bit happy to see me?"

There was playfulness, a coquettishness, behind the rebuke in the voice. There was an expectation of reciprocity as well. Genuine happiness made the voice sing. The message was as clear as any in a written contract. There was a finality to it as well. The tone of the voice demanded immediate recognition and reward.

The voice belonged to Lilith. I knew that I was talking to Lilith. Not to Danyea. She had been left behind at the Bali High Art compound. Not to Leorah either. She had been left behind as well, in some other century. No, this was Lilith, in the flesh, Lilith. This was the lady I knew. This was the real Lilith ready to pick up where we had left off at the Bali High compound and, just before that, in the public washroom of the Lembah Bukit Raya resort in Bogor.

"Am I happy to see you, you ask? Well, let me answer your question this way. I want you to take off your cloths, all of your clothes, immediately. Any trace of the brackish, the rancid water in the pool has got to go and go now, right now. Your clothes are history, you can borrow some of mine and your bod, your complete body, from head to toe, needs a thorough scrubbing..., skin, hair, nails, the works. And I am here, fair but frustrated maiden, to volunteer to do the dirty job that needs doing.

Look, just to prove that your health and welfare matter..., matter a lot actually..., after your unfortunate tumble into the black water in my back yard, ha, ha, ha, I will scrub you clean myself. That's only fair..., fragrant water in exchange for filthy water..., and all in the space of a few, short minutes! And..., and just to prove the seriousness of my intent, I will prepare to begin the alchemy, the miraculous transformation, right now!"

Without waiting for a response, I took two steps back from Lilith and, in less time that it took for her facial expression to change, I disrobed, leaving only Calvin Kline between me and the flummoxed woman. Only the smile on my face was offered up as an apology for my social impropriety.

My clothes, having proved their worth as part of a makeshift ladder, were in as much need of incineration as were those of the salvaged lady. Flaming clothes be damned, I thought. There was a bigger fish to be fried right before my eyes!

Without hesitation, Lilith had followed my lead and, like someone who had been raised on a kibbutz somewhere in rural Israel, disrobed more quickly and more completely than had I. Soiled, white sneakers, with socks stuffed inside, sat on top of a neatly folded, albeit soggy, mound representing the sum total of her arrival wear.

All she wore, apart from a sort of dangling G-string created by her hands which were clasped in front of her, was the nonplussed look of someone looking at another someone who had just witnessed a nativity scene of nakedness…, the removal of every stitch of clothing, and the resultant cultural quicksand, for the observer at least, of not knowing where to focus one's gaze.

Her face mockingly mirrored my conundrum. The piece of prose below a photo of it could have read, 'HELLO! You have seen and felt most of the moving parts already Mister Man. So why the problem when the fully assembled production model is ready to be taken out on the road for a ride?'

Sarung sepatu, O.R. disposable slip-ons were stacked like kindling wood at the back door. Patio dirt was best left outside as patio dirt. It was too labor intensive to clean up. The resilient, paper like galoshes with elastic tops were compliments of Dr. Rajawane. They allowed us to noiselessly skip from back door through kitchen and corridor to the bathroom while maintaining a muck free floor.

Most men view one room in their abode as being special. One room that trumpets their unique identity or ability to create. One room which positions them perfectly for seduction…, of themselves or of others! Opportunity and proclivity being willing and equal partners in any case!

For some, it would be a recreation room replete with stuffed animal heads, taken with great skill and even greater expense from some remote location in either Alaska or Africa. Others might have a room with a laterally rolling step ladder to allow access to a whole wall of unread books. For others still, it might be a living room dwarfed by an oversized audio-visual system which reduced the reality of normal sight and sound to second tier status.

For me, it was the bathroom.

My buttons got pushed by the water works needed to make that particular room an extension of the grandiose me. Journeyman experimentation with installation was a part of the process. Toilets, bidets, sinks, all required seeming veritable mountains of PVC pipes of various lengths and diameters. Fittings like elbows, u-tubes and plugs, had to be seated and sealed together by great gobs of ABS solvent and cement.

Sketches had to be created to show proposed water flow routes, much as pirate treasure maps, supplied to eager kiddy campers, were needed to trace the route through sand and secret tunnel to the 'X' spot where the treasure lay buried. Simplicity was the key to success whether digging for stuff which was stolen or devising drainage routes which were subterranean.

The form and resulting function of the 'root ball' of pipes beneath the floor had to satisfy three parameters. The pipes had to be angled downward in the direction of the main stack to take advantage of gravity to ensure water flow. Dripless water movement meant that pipe fittings had to be snug, and an over-abundance of glue had to be at hand and kept ready for application at all times through constant stirring before and during application.

And last but far from least, a sufficient number of u-tubes to create water traps, had to be installed to alleviate any possibility that uninvited odor would succeed in taking up residence in the room known lovingly by some as the water closet or by others, who were somewhat less sophisticated, as the pee-pee parlor.

Of course, the out of sight, out of mind, mechanics of the installation had to be pleasantly pedestrian. Pleasing house guests and their penchant for the practical was paramount. Elimination, the irritating interlude between rounds of drinks, hands of cards, or practiced peccadillos among those married to others, needed to be innocuous, and uninterrupted by mechanical malfunction. The water works had to be almost automatic in order to successfully pass the tolerability test.

Complexity reared its ugly head however, when a shower configuration of some sophistication was added to the mix. My statement of individuality saw the creation of a plumbing 'ménage a trois'. An oversized, flat, circular, chromed shower head protruded through the center of the shower stall ceiling.

It was joined by two others, both of similar size and appearance, which were nestled into the far corners of the glass cage. They faced kitty-corner into the shower area. They were positioned at chest level and could not only be switched on and off but also manually adjusted up and down and, to a limited degree, side-ways as well. All together, the fire ready, special sprinkler system became the holy trinity which cleansed and purified all who pilgrimed their way to my suburban 'crystal cathedral'.

When in operation, and viewed through the front of the Plexiglas enclosure, the nod to Niagara surpassed even the wildest imaginings of Frank Lloyd Wright and his iconic property, Fallingwater. With all fixtures in full flow, a suburban car wash, missing only the oversized revolving brushes, also came to mind.

The simple, original tune of tumbling water morphed into a symphony of sight and sound when plumbing crosses, tee fittings, clamps and straps were added to the subterranean matrix. A simple, straight forward treasure map was replaced by a visually challenging aerial view of a Santa Monica Freeway ramp interchange configuration.

The crowning achievement in an otherwise ordinary bathroom, this splendid shower configuration did bestow one more blessing. It obviated the need for a bath tub. The human goblet of cast iron, made only marginally acceptable by machine application of some spray paint color of the month, occupied too much space.

And, when given the option, no thinking person would actually choose to sit in a suspension of tepid water and dissolved dirt! That would be tantamount to reversing the swimming pool to shower sequence which had just concluded.

My shower mate had a raisin sized mole close the crown of her head as well as a darkened blood clot under the thumb nail of her right hand. Both would pass as distinguishing features. Both would have to be sufficient because even after a prolonged, head to toe, vigorous rub down, nothing more, mark-wise, was revealed.

I had stopped my U2 flights over the land which was Lilith, only when my eyes ceased to detect the slippery splotches of swimming pool sludge which had insinuated themselves into every cuticle, crack, crevice, and hirsute hiding place that the woman possessed. Only when my hands were met by taut, unblemished skin did I relent. Only then did I return the body I had borrowed to the woman who owned it!

Thanks to the rain makers that had assaulted her from all sides, the bedraggled burglar had been reborn. The mantle of muck was gone and in its stead there stood the unadorned promontory of youth, a Lady Liberty whose radiance went beyond that of mere torch in outstretched hand. Lilith had become both squeaky clean and cat walk ready for reveal in harbors both safe or sinister.

The young lady had remained mute and compliant throughout the decontamination process. She had stood ramrod straight when required. She had lifted her arms out and away from her torso when nudged, she had bent her legs at the knees to affect a semi-squat, and, she had leaned over from the waist to touch her toes in rote response to my beckoning. She behaved like a keen, compliant, neophyte recruit in residence at the 'farm', or whatever name had been given to the facility which had housed her during basic spy training in the Middle East. She wanted to please and she was pleased to be able to please the person who needed pleasing!

"Three things will make me happy, Michael. One, I want you to leave me alone for a few moments. Two, I want to wear the black kimono hanging on the back of the door. Three, tell me please where I can get a glass of water. You cleaned everything, I mean you really cleaned everything…, except the inside of my mouth. I can still taste the sewer that you think is a back yard swimming pool."

"Privacy is yours, a new tooth brush in the drawer beside the sink is yours and a glass of soda water will soon be yours. Just give me a second. I'll be right back.'

Not for the first time, I was relieved that the woman I had body blocked into a dead pool in the middle of the night had nothing more to show for her ordeal than soiled clothing.

"So, simple things first! How did I know your address? Renee Lee! She instructed me to meet her here..., next door, at her house, before we flew to Bali. She wanted it understood that my role, during our meeting at the Bali High Art property with you, was to be that of a silent observer. She called what we were about to do a 'game' and that in the 'game' there would be only one winner. I was to think of myself as someone who was seated in the cheering section, as someone who would provide support, verbal support, only when called upon to do so by the person in charge..., her, the cowboy..., the cowgirl, no, just the cow, from Texas!.

Lilith had wasted little time completing her rudimentary toilette. Wrapped from head to toe in the black terry cloth robe, and with a half empty glass of soda water in hand, she had silently padded into the living room just moments after my arrival with my own glass, one which contained distilled tranquility, along with a touch of fresh water, as well.

She glanced around the room, and decided to take up residence at the far end of the same, well-worn, piece of carved mahogany that I occupied. If, as the saying went, nine tenths of the law was predicated on possession, then, squatting rights should have been mine. Eschewing the invitation inherent in the other seven or eight bum perches made of lacquered teak or ebony or sandalwood which were spread about the over-sized living room, she chose to slither onto the seat located at the far end of the stick of furniture that belonged to me.

And out of hubris, like a sort of elephant equipped Hannibal, she gaveled her glass down in the middle of the end table almost as though it were the scepter that proclaimed the legitimacy of her authority over the four legged creature which she had just captured.

Her rational for literally 'dropping in', to my house, to my living room, to my lap, was fuelled by her history of hurt and of subsequent quirky intimacy with me. I knew that! And it followed that choosing a field position with strategic advantage, a perch from which to launch a campaign of seduction, would be paramount in the mind of any scheming female Lothario. Sexual stereotyping notwithstanding! Her machinations aimed at molding something memorable out of our long awaited tryst, were at once, touching and titillating.

I was as giddy with glee as a teenage boy when first he was struck by the realization that his female friend, the toothy, grinning girl by his side, was 'hot-to-trot'. I just knew that by the end of the evening, we would both be slippery, satiated and spent. Conspirators without conscience, we would both know that, before the new day dawned, we would have danced the dance of the damned.., deliberate and delicious and all so ever devilishly slow!

"Now, for some of the things which are not so simple to answer. Like, why I am here to see you? Well…, maybe the best beginning of an answer to that complicated question would be, my Uncle Afzel!

Do you have any idea how good you were against those three CIA buffoons sent to bury you at Bali High? Facts just came out of you like…, like…, like pounding rain water from the shower in your bathroom. How can so many facts, so many details of details, just come tumbling out of you so easily…, and for so long. And you were talking about a subject that they live and breathe every day. They should have known everything there was to know about the Company they work for. Half of what you said to them came as a complete surprise.

All Dr. Rajawane had to do after you left was to behave like the true gentleman that he is. We were fed well, treated with respect and then patted on the head and sent on our way. You two play in a different league. That's all, a different league entirely.

And I got to watch all of it. I had a front row seat for your whole performance. I knew that I would never be asked my opinion about anything, so I was free to do what I wanted. So I just stared at your crotch the whole time and tried to imagine what you would look like with your pants down!

I pretended that I was fourteen again living with my parents in Cairo. I was alone in our living room with my favorite uncle, the brother of my mother, my Uncle Afzel. He was younger than my mother and he stayed in our guest room while he finished his graduate work at university.

He was just like you. He was very smart and he could talk about many things. He used to read out loud to me from,' The Prophet' by Kahlil Gibran, all the time…, when we were alone.

My memory, for some things, is pretty good too! Not as good as yours…, but when something worthwhile…, something really worth remembering is said or when something happens to me, I never, ever forget.

'Out of suffering has emerged the strongest souls, the…, the most meaningful characters are always seared with scars.' I like that. People become strong through suffering. Trite but true. I liked the thought.

And…, and…, 'If you love somebody, let them go, for if they return they were always yours.' Are you ready for this? 'If they don't, they never were.' I really like that one! If you let the people you love be free, then you will be free too!

And…, and…, one more, the one my uncle Afzel read to me all the time…, all the time…, 'One day you will ask me which is more important? My life or yours?' He always stared into my eyes when he said the next part. Always…, 'I will say mine and you will walk away not knowing that you are my life.' I remember, my Uncle Afzel cried the day he left my parent's house. He cried really hard at the train station too when he hugged me and said goodbye."

"I used to have a book of Kahlil Gibran quotations as well. It was my bedtime read every night when I was an undergraduate student in Montreal. His words, his thoughts, made me feel that all was well…, all was right, with the world.

Let me add one or two more quotations, les beaux mots, to your list…, maybe we were both suckled, ha, ha, nourished by the same food for thought. 'Trust in dreams, for in them is the hidden gate to eternity', and 'Generosity is giving more than you can, and pride is taking less than you need.'

The sentence structure of that last one and the concept being expressed always reminded me of the famous slogan of Karl Marx, the one that gave a rational, humanist face to the frightful, dark horror that was the reality of Stalin's communist state.

'From each according to ability and to each according to need.'

Great stuff when you are young..., when you are among those of a certain age who believe that being in love with love is noble. But remember Mr. Gibran was, what I would call, a recidivist romantic. He fell into the emotional trap of thinking that altruistic generosity was consistent with engineering the best out of every personal experience."

I chose not to pursue the man and his work any further with Lilith. Dead at age forty-eight because he turned himself into walking liverwurst, would not have been in keeping with the mood manufactured by my fellow lover of limpid literature.

I chose not to pursue the subject of Kahlil Gibran any further because of what the man had done to himself. The rogue's gallery of Johnny Walker, Jim Beam and Jack Daniels notwithstanding.

My decision to cease and desist from further focus on the man of Lebanese birth was bolstered by the piece of specious theatre that began to unfold in front of me. The one act, one player performance stared Lilith, playing herself.

During my animated, somewhat amateurish, anti-communist rant, the woman had, with eyes fixed on me as thought my words dripped with portent, slowly slithered down into the corner of the sofa and positioned her body so that her left elbow supported her upper torso on the wide arm rest.

With deliberate slowness and a successfully managed grace, she hoisted her kimono exposing the lower part of her reclining body, from the waist down. The tawny, tautness of her bottom and the shadowed treasure it harbored were demurely covered by her right hand. Bemused, she peered out at the world like some Renaissance, Raphaelite cherub, at once the complete embodiment of self-consciousness and coquetry.

"Maybe you remember my little love note, Michael. The one I gave to you in the envelope with the pictures of the male member of the 'three blind mice' team. That line of love is very special to me. My uncle Afzel gave it to me in the train station just before he left...., just before he left and never came back. He told me that it was another quotation from Kahlil Gibran. He said that he wished he had written it himself because he said it was how he felt, deep in his heart, about me.

So, I gave it to you, Michael. Maybe he had fallen in love with me the same way that I have fallen in love with you!"

'The kindness in your cruelty makes me like me best when I am with you.'

Kahlil Gibran remained her bait of choice in a tackle box of limited lures and I was powerless to protest.

The juxtaposition of concepts and alliterative use of words usually found in the work of Kahlil Gibran yes, maybe…, but that part of the line was banal pastiche…, there was more…, the Jungian theory of the collective consciousness maybe…, people connected to each other and their past through their ancestors…, a shared set of experiences…, personal meaning given to the world acquired through connectedness with others,…or, or…, Nietzsche's, 'Man Alone with Himself', That, or because something is irrational is no argument against its existence, but rather a condition of it'…, but a little known, unpublished piece from the hand of Mr. Gibran, definitely not!

"You said before that you thought Dr. Rajawane and I play in a different league. I take that as a great compliment, Lilith. You should know that I shared your love-line with my friend, the good Doctor, and both of us agreed that it represents an expression of deep emotion that belongs in a different league, a league of its own, all by itself, as well!"

As the comforting lines of congratulation continued to flow, Lilith expertly separated her vaginal lips with her thumb and second finger and deftly inserted the tip of her forefinger at the base of the crevice she had created. She gently started to caress the no-go zone between her legs that hitherto had been deemed in need of defense. Each caress finished with a flourish of thrusts in and out of the wet, willing orifice.

"Michael, I want you to do two things for me please. Come over close to me and…, and lick my fingertips so that they are all wet and slippery. Then move back to your own seat and take your penis out of your pants so I can see it."

I started to comply with the first request immediately but attended to the devil's business of the details she had requested like a man cradling his first glass of newly fermented fruit from his own vineyard. Time stood still. The tense was present perfect.

All five senses stood at attention and were accounted for. All five senses would be deployed more than once because satiation had developed a close affinity for saintliness.

The look, the feel, the odor, the taste of a woman's body, any portion of it, even the appendages, represented the treasure of every age. The first etchings on stone walls by cavemen, the age of enlightenment and its depiction of the female form with paint and pallet, the age of disillusionment and the advent of three minute ditties on vinyl about Mary Lou and Peggy Sue, all paid homage to the female form. When flying in formation with function, the symmetry of fit was golden, Fibonacci numbers, $2+3= 5$, $3+5= 8$, $5+8= 13$..., notwithstanding. Women were not defined by any mathematical formula, they were the formula itself!

When face met female form midsection, the configuration of viewer eyes, nose and mouth, fit the female house of fecundity; clitoris, labia and vaginal opening, perfectly. It was a glorious manifestation of the natural world! It was true even at the cellular level. Drugs, pharmaceutical or otherwise, derived their efficacy either as cell receptor agonists or cell receptor antagonists. Their effectiveness stemmed from fit..., they worked because of, or in spite of, fit.

I was a man teasing time by savoring every second of my serendipitous bliss. Each fingertip smelled. Each smelled of the ripeness of a healthy woman. Each glistened as it became bathed in the viscous saliva from the deep throating of my troughed tongue. I had ignored Lilith's request for finger-tip attention only and the deep guttural sounds emanating from her throat, suggested that she had forgotten the directive, as well.

She moved her hand quickly from my body to hers. She smeared the viscous cargo over her mound much as a dry-wall worker would when 'mucking over' an exposed seam. She made the voyage from sea to salt mound, she made the same voyage as did Narko, the salt man from Bali, three or four times, before she decided that she was sufficient with salt to satisfy the brightest rays of the Sun.

The 'kid canoe' that was hemmed in on all sides by mesmerizing, Michelangelo molded flesh was knowingly stroked much as any vessel would be by a knowing, practiced paddler. The gunnels, the labial lips, both majora and minora, as well as points forward and aft, the clitoris and vaginal opening, all received lingering, flexed finger fondling.

The rude analogy, female genitalia to a tipsy water craft prompted a burp-like laugh which I quickly covered up by feigning a cough. I could not believe what was transpiring. I could not fathom the depths of emotional despair to which the young lady had been allowed to descend…, despair which demanded a drama of the demeaned to assuage.

My timid, almost apologetic penis made an appearance which resembled that of a child who had been rudely awakened from a blissful sleep only to have to stand stupidly, rubbing his eyes, in front of a semi-solicitous uncle and aunt, the names of whom were not known, the names of whom would never be known.

"It was fun to imagine what you would be like behind the zipper in your pants…, just like it was fun with my Uncle Afzel too! Ooh kaay! Now I know what both of you are like when you are sleeping…, and soon I will know what both of you are like when you are not…, sleeping that is. Ha, ha!

Lean over toward me Michael. I need more of what's in your mouth for my fingers. So tell me what Mister Moron, what Mr. Brian Law did when you showed him the photos and you told him that copies of them had been sent to his wife and his boss in America.

Lilith, freshly furnished with slurry, increased the speed of the digital manipulation of her genitals in anticipation of my reply.

"You are making a big mistake Lilith. You are making the mistake of thinking that I, just like everyone else who was in attendance at Bali High Art, believe that you are simple…, that you are stupid!"

The girl immediately stopped playing with the upturned maritime vessel at anchor below her rumpled kimono.

"Of course you gave me the dossier to give to Brian Law and you instructed me to tell him that copies had been sent to Langley, Virginia. Of course you did.

And of course, I did not. I did not comply.

I know you better than that Lilith. You are like me. Why actually hurt someone when the mere idea of hurting that someone is even more devastating to them. Why go to all the trouble and work of sending pictures when the enemy believes that they have already been sent and received."

"See, that's what I really like…, no, what I really love, about you. You think around corners. You shoot straight but your bullets curve. The conclusion you delivered to those seated around the table in the little cabin at Bali High Art, was absolutely brilliant. Pissed off and yet through a mask of humility, you anointed each with a paean for future perfect performance. It was absolutely brilliant! You gave a synopsis which was more like a sonnet. It enjoined all to aspire to greatness."

Before she finished her thought, I joined her busy hands and stabbed two or three times into the mouth of the river from which all life flowed with my tongue. I loved pussy. It was at once forbidden, it was religiously kept from public view by fashion, its bouquet was more varied than all the wines of all producing countries combined, and it tasted of triumph, of tenderness, of travels to be taken as often and for as long as possible. I was beginning to sound like old man Kennedy giving 'birds and bees' advice to his wide eyed, impressionable sons.

"No, no, don't do that Michael. That is not what uncle Afzel would have done. It is not in the rules. We must follow the rules. This time, for sure, we must follow his rules…, we must follow them together."

It felt like I was talking to someone who claimed to be able to see ghosts. A silly notion from most but when Lilith implied it, she seemed to almost levitate!

"Sorry, Lilith, I hope I did not upset you. But listen, I covered your ass, figuratively, not literally, by telling Brian Law that you were the person who was being blackmailed. He was not the target of anyone. You were. Period! Mossad or Mukhabarat, some people in some group wanted to get rid of you. Some people in some group wanted you dead.

He bought my piece of fiction, not because of its plausibility but because it was the only story that provided him with a place to hide from the shit storm which he knew would occur, which he knew he could not survive. End of story that will never end for him!

In fact, I convinced Brian Law to become a partner of mine. We have agreed to share intel which relates to Indonesia and other strategic locations in South Asia and South East Asia. Only from time to time, of course, and, because my partner is Mr. Brian law, time to time means never."

Lilith resumed taking care of personal business, but with less vigor. Less was more. Less was more than enough. Her head was tilted back so that, had her eyes been open, she would have been staring at the ceiling. Shivers, like those that ripple up and down the back and hind quarters of a horse during a rub down after a strenuous trot around the paddock, captured the central core of Lilith's body. Her extremities twitched and quivered in synch with the growing musical strains that seemed to be rising and reaching a crescendo from somewhere within.

To hell with the man in the myth, I thought, the one whom Lilith had locked away in some revered, memory vault. I had to be on the platform, close to the track, smiling and waving, when the fast freight train thundered on through.

My thumb banished her forefinger which poked distractedly, like a nosy guest, around her castle keep. As I thrust my appendage deep into her warm, wetness, the other end of her skiff received a liberal painting, with broad brush strokes, of the anti-fowling preparation which only my lascivious, forty percent proof, tongue could provide. We were joined together in a rhythm that was at once universal, ageless, a presence made, 'present perfect' in the extreme.

A bed sheet being twisted and squeezed by hand after a machine washing to prepare it for the back yard clothes line was Lilith's uncontrollable wringer-washer response to her orgasm and, as collateral damage, to my head which was trapped between her rigid, vice-like thighs.

Youth sometimes is not wasted on the young!

As regular breathing was restored, the world we shared slowly came back into focus. We arranged ourselves so that clothing covered most of our bodies. We remained side by side but allowed for space between us to occur.

The silence between us was not uncomfortable.

"Tell me Lilith, do you have a sister…, a close sister…, maybe even a twin?" I continued to stare at the wall on the far side of the room.

Lilith jumped as though she had come in contact with a bare, live wire. She struggled to disengage herself from our entanglement and, only partially succeeding. She rocked herself into a cross legged pose in front of me.

"No one has ever asked me that question, Michael. No one but you has had the interest…, the imagination…, no, more than that…, more than that…, the concern…, the compassion to ask such a question.

No one has ever asked me that question and, and, I am not sure that I know how answer it. The truth. I will answer your question with the truth. Yes, the truth.

Identical twins. I am an identical twin. I am Danyea and my twin sister, who was born only minutes before me, was Leorah. Her name means, 'light', 'I have the light'. Identical but different. We were never the same at all. Just like our finger prints, we were never exactly the same.

Leorah was the favorite child of my parents. But Leorah is dead. She died when she was young, very young.

We had never even visited the area south of the Sahara Desert where the disease that killed her was worst. And even though only two percent of the people who did get it, died, she was one of those unlucky ones.

She accomplished more, especially playing the piano, than me. My parents loved her more than me. I loved her more than me! But she is the one who got meningococcal meningitis and died from it at age thirteen. That is why there was room for my Uncle Afzel in our house. The room of Leorah was vacant because she died."

"You are a brave young woman to talk so candidly about the traumas in your life, the setbacks that would have crushed most other people."

I did not know what else to say. 'Poor little you' remarks would be insulting and attempting to prompt greater disclosure, immediately after our variation on sexual intercourse, would have simply been in bad taste.

"Michael I have to go now. Can I borrow your robe? And maybe a pair of swimming pool flip-flops. Clean ones. I will return them the next time I see you. Don't worry, my purse is in the van. I have to go. I just have to go. Don't worry, I know my out of here. Thank you for everything. I just knew that you would be the way that you are. Thank you."

I did not follow Lilith out to her car that was parked in the driveway next door. Her visit had not been the annual drop-in of someone for whom there was emotional connection or of someone of considerable consequence. So the insult of mouthing road safety slogans and weather trivia was eschewed.

Instead, I peeked out the living room window and watched a white Kijang disappear behind the hedge at the front of the place. I could not make out the license plate number because road grit and grime had completely obliterated it.

The silence which followed her departure was deafening. Kahlil Gibran paid me one last visit. 'We are all like the bright moon, we still have our darker side.'

Everyone, it seemed, had their own silo of suffering, and in its shadow, a sorrow sulked…, one that could not be assuaged.

Chapter 24

As a child I had developed an exercise of sorts which had provided the mechanism by which I had been able to gratify my every adolescent need and desire. It worked best on Saturday mornings because that was the one day of the week when hot porridge, brown sugar and cold milk did not define the beginning of my day. My mother's stick to your ribs, love food, was not the issue. Her strict adherence to a fixed serving schedule was!

Still half asleep and lying flat on my back, I would remove the pillow from beneath my head. Next, I would pull the bed sheet up tightly over my head, hold it in place with my clenched fists and close my eyes. Slowly I would start to roll my upper torso from one side to the other and then increase the speed of the roll to get in sync with the rhythm of an invisible metronome which ticked away inside my brain.

After a minute or so, the uninterrupted rhythm of my rolling allowed my mind to take flight and soar to any destination I desired. One frequent whistle stop was at the Texaco gas station that I wanted my mother to buy for me. It was made of thick, durable plastic, that's what the advertisement in the window said, and painted the same white color with green trim as the real thing. Two gas pumps were standing at attention in front of the station. One contained 'Fire Chief' gasoline and the other, for more powerful cars, contained 'Sky Chief', the best gasoline of all.

Signage was in the form of a stand-alone plastic post with a large circle on top. It contained a red star and a green, capital letter 'T', in the middle of it. A ramp supporting a narrow road snaked up and around the sides of the gas station and made it possible to drive Dinky toy cars up to the roof. Instead of a hydraulic lift to hoist a pick-up truck or car that needed an oil change, a handy, metal lever was provided. It was the place where I wanted to be on a busy Saturday morning.

The sustained, sightless roll made it possible to not only fly over and around the busiest place of business in town but also I was able to shrink myself down to match the size and scale of those walking around the property on which the station was situated.

I was the boss, the place was mine and what I said was law to all who were within earshot of my words.

Destinations promising fun and excitement, escape from the crushing containment of quotidian suburban certainty were a mere 'rock and roll' away for, in my self-induced trance, I controlled the exclusive Carousel slide projector of life and hence, I determined what appeared on the one and only screen.

Even more frequent than visiting the gas station were my episodes of swimming alone, contentedly, in a warm, sunny, tropical climate. I would be floating on my back or breast stroking my way through a calm sea of Orange Crush soda. Any of the orange drink delight that made it to my mouth as I chugged along doing my best imitation of a frog was swallowed with great satisfaction.

Always, I was swimming in this soda fountain sea toward an island which was close by. Upon reaching the shore, I would roll over and over gleefully in its solid sureness. It was composed entirely of store frozen, ice cream. Not just any ice cream, but my favorite, butter pecan. The frozen confection never melted in response to my body heat. Instead, only a thin layer would thaw, when lightly touched by my finger-tips. Just enough could be scraped up to fill my cupped hand. Every time I went to my island of ice cream, I made a baby-fool of myself by trying to stuff twice as much butter pecan into my mouth as it could possibly hold!

I never told anyone of my rolling exploits alone in my bed on Saturday mornings. And the only proof I ever had that my dreams had actually spun from my magic spinning wheel was the development of a bald spot on the back of my head. It receded when my top spinning days ended but, perhaps as a permanent reminder of those halcyon days alone, I ended up sported a postage stamp patch of hair on the back of my head which was a shade lighter than any of the hair around it.

Had the 'then' doctors possessed the same penchant for labeling childhood behavior, as the 'now' group of practitioners did, armed with a title and a dedicated tribe of 'specialist' health care professionals, my 'condition' might have been termed, Syncopated Fluctuation in Adolescence.

SFA for short.

Had a dietary cause for my 'affliction' been established, an overabundance of saturated fatty acids in my diet for example, the fats found in meat, bagged sugar and salt snacks, any and all ice cream, then treatment would have involved the curtailment or cessation of the presence of saturated fatty acids in my diet.

SFA for short.

Had my mother run screaming to our family doctor with exaggerated stories of my early morning flights of fancy, my obvious autism, and had the good Doctor been unduly predisposed to prescribe a drug in response to an hysterical, anecdotal patient recitation of symptoms, an approach introduced and nurtured by the pharma industry, I might have been forced, at the very least, to ingest truck-loads of Ritalin for presenting with a variation of ADHD, attention deficit hyperactivity disorder.

Insomnia, ironically, would have been one of the side effects, had I been forced to ingest the drug. More seriously, a future of dependence and further addiction might well have followed. The term that could have been used to describe my Saturday morning, transient condition might well have been, SWEET FUCK ALL!

SFA for short.

Crazies are not contagious and crazy is a conundrum of conditioned response.

A few years later, when I developed the stamina to sit through televangelist church services on black and white TV, I saw myself and my circumstance played out in the behavior of the gentle parishioner folk who stood in front of the Preacher and his congregation.

Each, in turn, fell back, in a blissful swoon, when the magic word, 'HEAL' trumpeted the long awaited end to the liturgical ramble which was delivered, without interruption, by the man of God. The forceful thrust of the preacher's palm to the forehead of the saved soul helped, in no small way, to assure the congregation, both in the church and at home in their Lay-z-boy pews, that faith heals and is Heaven sent.

I became convinced that one could, with only a smidgeon of faith and a shit load of ritualized rigmarole, convince oneself of anything!

The only carbonated beverage allowed to enter our house was ginger ale. That was because it was thought to aid in the treatment of sore throats and colds. Ice cream was too expensive to have as a permanent resident in the refrigerator. It made appearances, vanilla only, only on birthdays and at Christmas.

Rolling for me, was not a gamble, it was a sure thing!

Like some sort of pembantu, a domestic, I had spent the morning following my visit from Lilith and her two friends, Kahlil and Afzel, buying food and getting replacement clothes for both of us. Her shoe size had been noted just prior to dropping the dead ones into the inferno which the back yard waste barrel had become.

Strange, I thought, how a person who could be identified so easily at the scene of a car accident or in a darkened, back yard swimming pool, could evade the detection and definition of others. Costume of conscience or convenience, demeanor of the delightful or of the damned, it should not have mattered. The chosen trappings, the choice of social mask, should not have made any difference. When she was up close and personal, the woman was unmistakable.

House burglars stole more than mere goods. They robbed one of personal immunity from intrusion. The sanctuary and safety found in personal abode was dashed. Defensiveness, followed by defenselessness, always flourished in defeat.

People who knew themselves less than did those who surrounded them were carriers of the same stigma. Personal vulnerability was of their creation and it was inexorably exacerbated by the passage of time.

Early in the afternoon, the white van breached and beached, like Moby Dick, in my driveway. Did the unheralded arrival of a monster in my midst make me just another Ishmael, doomed to wander the world alone, without redemption! An innocent victimized by the tyranny of a fickle God. Or was I to be the one-legged Ahab, inexorably drawn to the wrath of the white whale and even in death, serve as a beacon for those who also chose ruin over resurrection.

The devil, it seemed, lived in the deep blue sea, and escape from the clutches of one, sealed the certainty of capture by the other.

The doorbell rang twice, three rapid, loud knocks followed and an attempt was made to open the front door by roughly turning the door knob back and forth. I opened the door with the same aggressive approach used by the visitor while trying to gain uninvited access to my abode.

"Yes, can I help you?"

As the woman in traditional Muslim garb opened her mouth to answer, I rushed at her, roughly spun her around by the shoulders and pinned her face hard against the vestibule wall just inside the door way.

Like a policeman with a captured suspect, one who had been seen fleeing the scene of a violent crime, I forcibly pressed against her shoulder blades with my left forearm so that her upper body was firmly pinned against the wall in front of her. No movement was possible, let alone escape. My right hand was clasped hard around the back of her neck so that light headedness would occur. Her hijab offered her no protection. That's what I wanted. Constriction of the carotid artery. Dizziness and slight nausea but without the risk of my apprehended felon actually fainting. I kicked roughly at the inside area of her ankles, first her left one and then, with equal disregard for possible bruising, her right ankle as well.

"Spread your legs. C'mon, spread them. And stay like that. Let's just see whether you brought any friends along with you, shall we. You know, trusted friends who are small, but friends who have big teeth and know how to go, 'bang, bang', just before they bite."

I often wondered, when a person was being frisked by the cops, or by an indifferent face in uniform, one waving an electronic wand that beeped, at an airport customs booth, whether they believed that the groping and molestation were intentional or was the view that cautious comfort should be taken from the knowledge that one was merely paying the price for vigilance, more accurate!

My thoroughness would leave no doubt in the woman's mind as to which search camp I belonged to. My intent was to find 'concealed carry' weapons but, at the same time, I intended to inflict personal insult by aggressively fondling and assaulting her private parts. I wanted the woman to be defenseless and I wanted the woman to be irrationally angry.

"What the mother-fuck is the matter with you, Michael Campbell. Don't you remember me? Leorah! It's Leorah, you remember, you must remember, it was only a couple of days ago…, you got rid to the little prick on a motor bike who was trying to screw me out of some money."

"Oh now I remember, you're the ingrate of a woman who insists on masquerading as a mail box, with a slot in the front of her face for mail, or is it, 'male', spelled m.a.l.e.! I'm not sure."

"That's an insult to my religion!"

"No it isn't. It is insulting to those in your religion, the Imams, the Mullahs, the Ustadz, who insist that women of the faith sustain a mode of dress best suited for the sixteenth century. It is five hundred years out of date. You could be storing enough weapons under all that fabric to outfit a small army. Your religious men should find another way to keep the females in their flock subservient and obedient. In other words, they should find other means to maintain control and power over the faithful.

Don't feel singled out. You're not alone. Roman Catholic men of the faith, men of influence, Priests, Bishops, Cardinals should find other ways to keep their women down…, in check…, as well. Single, chaste women married to Christ is one thing. But parading them around in black and white habits, older by far than the hijab, is just as antiquated and idiotic.

Reducing over fifty percent of the human population, the female element, in the church or mosque to menial tasks rather than co-managing the future to gain new converts is self-defeating. Both religions are demeaned and devalued by the continuation of the misogynistic practice.

So…, what do you want? What could I possibly do for you that has not been done already, albeit with little or no appreciation.

And how the hell did you find out where I live?"

I released the woman from the cage my body had become and backed away in anticipation of a retributive assault.

The game had to be played. The woman's head was covered, and the finger with the flaw beneath the nail had been wrapped in a Band-aid. No positive ID, no end to the many faces of Eve.

"You are like most men, you know. You think through your dick. When it is out and on the prowl, any hole it can find will do. When it is hidden in its little house made of cotton, it is still in command. When men like you get angry, dick still dictates decisions. Even though it is blind it insists on being allowed to decide what to do.

You, or your behavior is a perfect example. You were angry when you left me alone in the Kijang…, alone and lost on a darkened street in Jakarta. You went to the first busy street you could find and you paid a taxi driver to take you directly home. You were one easy man to follow. And that's because your dick made the driving direction decisions for you.

And what do I want from you? I want Ketok Magik. I have to take the Kijang back to the owner and I do not want to pay him extra because of some little dent that you know how to fix. I know that I am being picky about something small but I have already paid the man too much for a very unreliable, ugly machine."

The game had to be played. Ketok Magik, and the credibility stretch it represented, would have to be accepted at face value. What the woman really wanted was anybody's guess. Retribution aimed at Afzel, aimed at Danyea, aimed at the faceless force that had harbored the meningococcal meningitis, who knew!

But the game could not be one of perpetual defense. It would be too dangerous to afford the woman too much latitude. Any intrigue she might entertain would most certainly position any partner in a precarious, unprotected, probably lethal position.

"OK, so fix the car…, and then what?"

"The 'then what' will depend on how well you fix the car, as you put it. Let me know when you have finished. In the meantime, I will make myself at home by getting a snack and something to drink from the kitchen, if that is alright with you. If there is a kitchen and if there is something in it to eat and drink, that is!"

"Done! Go crazy and make yourself comfortable."

The grin that could have been captured by a fish-eye lens, told me what I needed to know. The woman believed that she had just reassumed control of the situation. The woman was happy with herself. The woman was where I wanted her to be!

A pail of hot water, a small rubber drain plunger, a can of WD-40, a couple of rags and less than ten minutes work and the job was done and ready for inspection.

"Results time, Leorah."

I heard myself chirping like a parakeet in search of a favorite cracker reward. Not too heavy on the 'needy' scale, I warned myself. The Leorah legend would not differentiate between short fall in self-sufficiency and short changing just reward.

"I trust you Michael. I am sure your best is good enough. The man at the rental place will never know the difference. Anyway, come and sit down over here. No, sit at the other end of the sofa. There is something I want to show you."

The 'other end' was where Danyea, aka Lilith, had sat less than a day earlier. And Leorah had occupied my former spot. The carved mahogany couch had a 'casting quality' that I had hitherto known nothing about!

Leorah had helped herself to a pimple-popping, era specific snack which included a coke and a heaping dish of chocolate chip cookies. Apparently she had come to the conclusion that visual exposure to her sugar snack would have been sufficient to satisfy any food cravings I might have had. Nothing sweet was offered.

What else had the woman fixed for herself I wondered, while I had tended to the crate that masqueraded as a car.

"So, I want you to just sit back Michael and relax. Let me entertain you as a reward for all the kindness you have shown to me. Let me make today as memorable for you as our first meeting was for me."

With deliberate slowness and successfully managed grace, Leorah lifted her jilbab and let it fall, in loose folds, on her lap. She smiled winsomely at me and ever so slowly began to open her legs.

"Michael, have you ever had a wish about yourself that you didn't want anyone else to know about? Have you ever had a fantasy that your family and your friends would say was bad, very bad for you. Have you ever, just once, said to yourself that this is your life, it is your body and you should have the right to do whatever you want to do, with it…., with whomever you want to do it with as well…, just to experiment, just to try something new, just a little bit of change with someone else who is close, someone who will not judge, someone who is destiny driven as well… Do you have unfulfilled wishes like that Michael, do you, do you ever…, I bet you do. And just so you know, I do too Michael. I do too!"

Leorah's masturbatory monologue ended just as her fully parted legs revealing a flesh colored, her flesh colored, rubberized piece of plastic reminiscent of an erection that might make a twelve year old, proud.

Despite the synthetic exclamation mark which punctuated nothing in the full paragraph of perfection on display in front of me, I understood how religious zeal had aided and abetted the proliferation of true believers. Completely covered during waking hours to discourage male marauders, both in and outside of the family circle, Muslim women, even when just partially revealed, could, as Mick and the Stones noted in song, 'make a dead man come'!

The scene, the sequence and the soliloquy were, however, all lost on me. Anger born of embarrassment welled up almost to the point of explosion. How had my practiced, searching fingers missed such a large object lodged somewhere on her person? I had finger padded my way around every major and minor topographical feature the woman possessed. Everything on the surface, that is. But the crevices and caves that were the hallmarks of every female from birth, had not been piton punctured or probed.

What a gaff! Suppose the bitch had been harboring a stiletto rather than a dildo! Suppose a lot of things. Suppose you get back to basics more often. Suppose the performance shortfall be a wake-up call. Suppose you consider yourself lucky to be afforded the chance to learn and not repeat the same mistake again…, ever. Suppose you consider that things could have been worse. Suppose you consider death or suppose you consider actually working for the CIA. Death before Dishonor, I say to all those, whose deeds…, and misdeeds, are so deserving!

"I don't know what to say Leorah. You have caught me off guard…, and…,and…, unprepared. First I would like to visit the bathroom. I must clean myself up for you. This is so unexpected. This is really exciting. I feel I must tell you that this will be my first time. I hope…,"

I stopped, feigning lack of words, before my lack of interest or enthusiasm for the role of receiver became evident.

"Yes Michael, everyone is a little apprehensive the first time. But you can trust me. I am knowledgeable in these matters and our sweet little secret will always remain just between us…, between us only. And, just for you, Michael, today we will start small."

"Yes, of course, just between us, us only. Leorah, I want to pay you for your services. I insist on it. I want to pay you well because I can see that you are a person of integrity and honesty. You are like a highly skilled Vestal Virgin, one who is professionally practiced in maintaining the fiery flame to the exclusion of all else."

Among those who were comfortable living with one foot in a world of illusion and the other, planted firmly in a parallel world of delusion, the mixed, metaphorical message concerning the virginal call to the sacred Roman flame made perfect sense. And the wanton mischief of gender-bending, fit in perfectly as well. It was mere sub-text…, and it changed nothing!

"No, no Michael. This will be a moment of intimacy between friends. This will bring us very close together. This will be a bond between us. You will see. Yes, an everlasting, a permanent bond between us."

As Leorah fumbled with her folds of fashion and her fake midget appendage in order to close the distance between us, I interrupted her progress by holding up my hand much as a cop might when stopping traffic.

"No, no Leorah. This is important. I am talking about a business proposition. I want to hire you and your very particular, intimate skills to engage a very dear friend, no, a close associate of mine, a professional man, in Singapore. I want you to help him more fully self-realize. I..., I want you to be my present to him."

"We shall have to talk about your proposal at greater length Michael. It sounds intriguing. But first we should talk about..., we should first talk about the laughter that is in our eyes, we should talk about skin that loves to dance and sing and play with other skin that is just like it. We should talk about our toes that can curl up so cuddly close together, We should talk about many things Michael because we are so very much alike, you and I."

My decision to take the 'long day's journey into night' with Leorah was based on solicitude. Ten percent of it was. The remaining ninety percent was seduction.

Hers..., of me. I wanted the woman. She made me want to want her. I wanted her beguiling smile, I wanted her successful ruse with the rubber replica, I wanted her Karl Wallenda high wire act which traversed separate, disparate worlds, one of irreconcilable religion and the other of ruptured reality, I wanted, I wanted to be utterly and completely subsumed by the facets, the faces of the woman who sat, neatly nestled, beside me..., more, I wanted to harbor the woman whom I knew could never, ever be close to me, I wanted to give succor to the woman who could never, ever be close to anyone!

At that moment, I wanted all that was all of her, everything about her..., I wanted to own her..., I wanted the woman and I wanted her world. The land of Leorah would have a title deed, evidence of ownership, and I wanted to possess it. It had to be mine..., and mine alone!

"I think that you are as happy to see me as I am to see you. A movie star who is older than both of us put together said something like that to a lover many years ago and now..., that invitation to intimacy belongs to us."

I knew that I was trading on a yet to be realized conquest, Leorah over me, and the leniency, the latitude for acceptance of any foolish, adolescent aphorism would be temporarily high.

I slithered over to and across the semi-supine body of my conqueror and concubine. Supporting my weight on my left arm which had been snaked around Leorah's shoulders, I buried my face in the nape of her neck. Purring softly, I licked at her warm softness much as a cat might at its paws in preparation for whisker cleaning. Making certain that nothing obscured Leorah's view of her recently reconstructed crotch, I slowly and deliberately reached over and closed my hand comfortably around her Freudian wish fulfillment.

Uttering a deep, guttural grunt of acceptance, she arched her body closer to mine in perfect male mating ritual compliance. I slowly tongued my way up and down the exposed skin of her neck lingering at both ends of my journey to suck and nibble at the rest stations I had created.

I found myself fighting to remember the right things, the lascivious things, my former lovers had done which had made the mating moments with them memorable. The task was made challenging because not one woman had ever got the ritual completely right. Memories of individual personages did not work, only the panoply of players and their sometimes planned and oft-times spontaneous puddles of delight, did.

Penis play presented one such patch of fake connubial quicksand. Preamble to passion in the male, the fuse to uncontrolled and uncontrollable fucking, the under stimulation of the appendage by the female partner and the resultant 'ho-hum' sex, was often determined by her peer perceptions, her mother's tales, or her own reticence stemming from innate or acquired revulsion to the otherwise innocuous organ.

Noting that Leorah's eyes had remained open and were fixated on the rhythmic 'tug-job' being delivered to the sometime family member who was 'just visiting', I slowly released my firm grip on the shaft, wet my fingers with Leorah's saliva by roughly forcing them into her mouth and commenced a forefinger trace around the glans penis and along the underside where, had nature had her way, the urethra would have been located. Her breathing went from being noticeably strained, to pre-orgasmic.

I knew that I had to accelerate our 'strange interlude', if I were to succeed in my reverse seduction of the woman.

Disengaging myself from my 'looking-glass' partner and collecting as much saliva in my mouth as was available, I kneeled on the floor between her legs and plunged my open mouth down on her semi-erection. Before my gag reflex reaction to the cock from South Korea produced the tears which would blind me, I took note of how the life-like member from a mold was fastened to the wearer.

World War 11 flashed before my eyes. Specifically the calibers of the shoulder weapons used by the Brits and the Americans during the conflict. The soldiers of the former nation fired 303 ammunition while the Yanks used rifles chambered for 30-06 cartridges. The shell casing for the 303 bullet was considered to be 'rimmed' because the base protruded from the bottom of the shell. Whereas the American round was termed 'rim-less' because the lower part of the shell was indented allowing for the base to be the same diameter as the main casing.

Leorah's dick was probably Asian by manufacture but definitely American, rim-less, by design.

Tongue flexibility and positioning along with spit production made bobbing up and down on the sometime shaft of my main squeeze more sustainable than any capacity she had to absorb the onslaught.

My forefinger thrusts in and out of her vagina and the pressing and probing of her clitoral area with my thumb, mechanics hidden from her by her glistening dick and my wet, red face, were the distinct collaborators responsible for her winning the game of involuntary release.

Quick work was made of disengaging the dildo from its harness and reinserting it, head first, into its rightful receptacle. Rimless design, coupled with relentless determination, were able allies against recipient reticence. Role reversal did not occur. Sex for personal gratification, the domain frequented most often by the male, and sex as a means of appeasement, the old and antiquated role dished out to women, remained intact.

The George Carlin Principles concerning human habits, including addiction, were sustained, albeit in reverse. When preparation becomes the addiction, when preparation surpasses pleasure, just keep doing what you are doing. Just do it!

Bacterial banishment from below the belt, even for a few fleeting minutes would always be a messy, smelly, and a time consuming affair. Too much play with the anal sphincter, too much plunging in the wrong sink hole might, I was told by those who were committed to do no harm to others, adversely affect its integrity. Flatulence, adult diapers and colostomy bags might not represent inevitable sequences of anal fixation, but each of those responses to a progressive medical condition, posed sufficient punitive sentence to merit considerable caution.

If one were comfortable cozying up to a five o'clock shadow and a beer breath, both exhibited by a member of the same sex, and if one were content with the warmth offered by an oversized stomach heaving in the dark, emanating from a member of that still same sex, then one's choice would be clear and understood and accepted. That only made sense. That was ironically, the partnership choice of most hetrosexual women!

If, on the other hand, one thought one could dismiss the mantle of homosexuality based on female fakery, then one was deep in the throes of self-denial.

Hetro, bi-, homo, were mere modifiers of the same coupling pageant. Pleasure always precipitated compromise regardless of the choices made. Just pick your poison and position yourself to play along with it!

"You fucking bastard. That is not what I wanted. And you Goddam well know it! I know what you wanted Michael and I was prepared to give it to you. But instead, you insult me with boorish behavior. What the fuck is the matter with you anyway. Are you afraid? Are you afraid to face the truth about exactly what you are, you…, you…, little closet fairy, you…, you…, fucking faggot!"

Not wishing to listen to any more of the foolish ranting of the hysterical woman, I grabbed at her crotch and extracted the plastic prick from her person.

"Leorah, Leorah, where is your sense of perspective. Rome wasn't built in a day. Military campaigns are not won in mere minutes.

Everything that is worth winning, every laudable goal in life, takes time to be brought to fruition.

Look at your toy. It started off the day buried in your secret box of juice. Now, as you can clearly see, it has me dripping down it everywhere. That is progress.

Our juices have met and mingled. So plan for the next time we meet. Plan to move closer to the goal you have set for yourself. Plan to bring a bigger dick. Aim higher, no, aim bigger and thicker!"

"Go fuck your…, your…, No! You are right, of course you are right, Michael. There is always next time. Yes…, to be sure, there will always be a next time. How foolish of me. The next time. Definitely the next time."

With that abrupt change in direction mid-step, the woman was on her feet angrily pulling at and adjusting the dishevelment our romp with a rubber maid had created. Without uttering another word, without glancing in my direction, she turned and strode purposefully toward the door.

"When we meet again, don't forget we have to discuss the business plan concerning a friend of mine in Singapore. Remember money, lots of money, tax free money, in the bank. Think castles in Spain, a villa on the Riviera, a retreat on the isle of Crete…"

The last part of my pitch was drowned out by the door that was slammed shut behind her.

Well, I thought, at least she didn't attack me with a weapon she had concealed in some orifice I had failed to secure. And at least, just maybe, she saw a glimmer of light at the end of her nefarious tunnel. I was not lost to her. She thought that salvage could possibly be within her grasp.

I thought that proper attention could only be paid to the woman, when in her presence, if one armed oneself with a mental bouquet of roses and a strait-jacket.

Two days passed before the other face of Eve appeared at my door. The winsome demeanor and delicacy of step of Lilith, when pirouetting to the strains of the sugar-plum fairy dance that only she could hear, were unmistakable. The reappearance of the woman in possession of a certain magic at my backdoor was cause for relief as much as it was for rejoicing!

I had not been left alone, lost in lingering, lugubrious, thought of the one I wanted, for very long.

"You just stay where you are mister man. Don't move an inch my beautiful man. Tonight is my turn to make music with your body. Just like you did with mine, hmmm, not too, too long ago, as I recall."

Lilith stood framed by the sliding screen door which she had noiselessly opened. Moon glow softly bathed the hair and shoulders of the woman and the lace camisole she was wearing seemed to have been allowed to drip-dry on her after being dipped in an ice bucket of champagne.

Smiling widely, she untied the delicate garment and let it fall to the floor. As she tip-toed toward me, she slowly did a pirouette at the end of the bed. Her generous, cared for body was the stuff of male fantasy from the 1950's. Breasts, belly and buttocks, all were full and perfectly sculptured. All were air-brush perfect under the smiling benediction of the Jakarta…, the Javanese moon.

She tongued her way up both of my legs licking and darting wetly as she went. She stopped only when she reached the intersection of my two splayed limbs.

"I want to go were all the gooey candy is made, Daddy. Can I go to the candy store, please Daddy."

She did not wait for a response.

Lilith knelt down and started to suck on my big toe. Running her wet tongue under the four remaining toes and then back again, she moved to the other foot and repeated what we both knew was prelude to the grand performance.

Gently but deliberately, with her eyes fixed on mine, she engulfed one candy making machine and then the other. As if to coax the manufacture of a few more samples from each, her tongue searched thoroughly in and around every nook and cranny for daddy's promised treat.

"I can smell the candy, Daddy, but I can't taste it. I want to taste it Daddy. What can I do! I know. If I kiss Daddy, maybe then he will let me have some of the candy that I know he is hiding."

Gone was my original notion of prudery in the woman and, in its place, the proud prance of the prurient.

She did not wait for a response.

I loved women who were unself-conscious, who were natural when naked. It spoke to their confidence in what each promontory and mound, every curvature and crevasse, would divulge and deliciously deliver when explored by a knowing, piton practiced mountaineer.

"Lilith, you look absolutely ravishing tonight. Ravishing is the right word, really! But I'll bet you put in a hard day today and that beautiful bod of yours is tired. I have just the right, comfortable seat waiting for you. Just for you. I know you will enjoy the pleasure it will provide. It will relax you completely and, at the same time, dissolve all the knotty problems that this day has brought your way."

"First my kiss Daddy. Then the nice seat for my bum-bum and then…, and then my candy. Ok!"

Kissing a woman who is new to one's lips, new, but not untasted, was to submerge one's face in the nectar that is fresh rain water. The elixir of life that is trapped in a basin of rock far up the mountain where few have ever ventured. It is to lap at it greedily and then with reckless abandon.

"You have been eating cashews. I can tell. Your mouth tastes even better than oral sex. And that's because, yes…, that's because, it's better tasting but, but, just as salty. I like sex in my mouth. When it is salty but not too, too salty."

"OK, lovely lady of the night, your seat is waiting."

"But where? I want to stay here with you Daddy, not over in some corner far away."

"Your wish is my command. Your seat is right here. Not somewhere over there. And it's a front row center seat too!"

As I patted my chest, my woman of the night had to cover her mouth with both hands in an attempt to muffle her laughter. She knew that I knew to push her 'D' button for domesticated dominance.

"So I better be a good girl and not use my very own, private throne the way I usually do!"

Lilith's apt comeback prompted girlish giggles as she mounted the saddle of her merry-go-round horsey.

"There, how is…, uhhh! Where is the go-slow button on your machine, Michael? Uhhh, I should have stayed down below with your candy makers. I was safer down there!"

She grabbed the back of my head with both hands and directed my nose and tongue to where her want seemed in greatest need.

"Oh Michael, I have waited a long time to meet you this way…, someone like you…, someone like you who is…, is so much like me…, but I was afraid…, uhhh, that I was too different, yes, yes, that there would be no other person, oh, oh, yes, someone who just…, just knows what to do…, knows what a partner in trouble…, a partner in intimacy needs, without asking, all the time…, uhhh, and how, uhhh, to do what is wanted, what is needed. Don't stop, don't stop, pleeese don't stop, ever, uhhh."

Kissing, nibbling, tongue probing, licking, nose stretching, inhaling-exhaling as one continuous life-line, the total engagement of every physical sense one possessed was sublime subsumption. The precipice loomed large. The fall willfully into oblivion and the descent into sheer swoon was sweet death tempered by assured resurrection. I was outside myself, inside myself, everywhere and nowhere, without thought of escape.

The experience of a woman offering up her most intimate physical self, her beauty, her vulnerability, her intellect and thoughts, transported me beyond what was, into the realm of what two people in love with like, could be.

No wonder religions, governments, teachers, parents, all authority, conspired to keep the secret safely hidden away from life's neophytes under layer upon layer of moral codes, criminal codes, fear fabrications, and social embarrassment. Societal embarrassment followed by ostracism when discovered.

Unfettered freedom was dangerous!

The knowledge of self, of connectedness with another, of escape with that other to the stars, was intoxicating. Tragically toxic though, to those who had succumbed to the forced feeding of poisonous anecdote,

anecdote that dripped of the antidote to life. Poison fed to them when they had been wide-eyed and wondrous and ready to run. Ready at the starting gate. Societal prison! That bloody misery and its love of company. The complicity of it all!

With my nose buried close to her vagina, I commenced long, flat tongued sweeps of Lilith's sphincter muscle. Her response was immediate. Her thigh muscles tightened around my head. I peered up at the woman who was no longer in Jakarta, no longer in her secure enclave, no longer with me.

Her head lurched back allowing her hair to cascade down to her shoulders. Her clinched hands seemed to be wringing the finish out of the wooden headboard of the bed. Moments passed before any semblance of controlled breathing returned to the spent woman above me.

"Does your seat come in any other color besides flush flesh pink, Michael? I think I want to buy one, no, many, to keep everywhere, anywhere and everywhere, around the house."

Lilith laughed self-consciously as she dismounted and fell in a heap beside me. I gathered her up in my arms and commenced to slowly rock back and forth. Fragrance companies must have experimented with their products to determine the best formulations to compliment a woman's sweat. The bouquet that assailed my nostrils was that of a fresh, young woman. It was as though Lilith was experiencing her first time, again, for the first time. She was mine. Her body oozed that affirmation.

"I still want some candy, Daddy."

"Well, don't forget to be a good girl and share what the machine makes for you. Remember, sharing is caring. Maybe somebody important, maybe somebody in uniform, once said that. It's definitely not original."

My rambling words bounced off the ceiling and got lost in the fading, swimming pool reflected stars. Lilith had already made her way to the candy factory compound. As a courtesy to her host she left an intimate parting gift, a viscous reminder of her visit, behind. She straddled my head with her lower torso and began to nudge, nibble and gently gnaw at everything that her tactile and olfactory senses deemed pleasing. Dominance demanded devotion to detail.

I raked the tips of my fingers over her shoulder blades, pushed deeply into the smooth skin on her back and finished with a vigorous scratch of both bum cheeks. Each time my fingers reached her behind, they lingered longer. They lingered longer as my palms slowly opened and closed the promise that lay, warm and waiting within.

Winning, the bi-product of stamina, was not part of our stolen moments of mumbles and meandering madness together. We were too busy with the aperitif, the drinking in of too much of each other. Ours was not a contest which pit one against the other. Ours was a celebration wherein no victor could be declared. The rhythmic 'warp and woof' of our love-loom and the tapestry which was peculiar just to us, was all that mattered.

We had 'pincered' together, the German army notwithstanding, and we had both emerged victorious. Time, I thought, for both of us to declare an armistice at precisely the same moment. And our mutually agreed to number, the one we shared, the one that fell between sixty-eight and seventy, meant that the moment would be me, Michael dependent.

Burying the end of my nose between her mansion of excrement, no offence to the revered, English poet, William B. Yeats, and her wishing well, I gorged myself on the moveable feast that Lilith had become.

As the lady above me started to quiver and groan more audibly, love-lines from another time and another place washed over me.

I was with my 'Bijou'. That was my love label for her, my 'gem'. She was from Marseille. She was living in Jakarta with her boyfriend and she liked older, fatherly and fastidious men. I must have been double her age at the time. She was just a thin slip of a girl and she always signaled me when she felt discomfort resulting from our prolonged love making.

"Viens Michel, viens pour ton Bijou, viens maintenant."

And on cue, I had learned to oblige and come on command.

My new Little Miss Muffet had squeezed the base of my penis with her thumb and forefinger and was frantically thrusting up and down on my erection that had almost completely disappeared down her throat.

She gagged and retched violently. Her lower torso, commanded completely by her full flight orgasm seemed to be in competition with her body's need to expel what had filled her mouth and throat.

Quickly, she found her way up to my face, planted her mouth on mine and, with a series of guttural, animal grunts, discharged her over-the-limit cargo. I wrestled her torso up and onto my own and effortlessly entered her.

"Michael, I want you to put your candy where it should be, back where it belongs. I want your candy, all of it, to be inside me. That's where it belongs. Please, go down there now and do it. Do it for me Michael, please."

I quickly acceded to her wish and flooded her from clitoris to perineum, the narrow neck of skin that separated one orifice from the other. I returned to the face which was a pastel wash of perfect pleasure and made us as one again.

"Do you think that if we bottled our pleasure together, it would sell?"

I punctuated my question with slow, deep strokes, strokes that were well lubricated, strokes that made suction sounds as the glide in and out increased in speed.

"Nope! Too good for ordinary folks. And too strenuous for the hearts of most, figuratively and otherwise. Uhhh, Michael, where do you get all of your energy?"

"The first letter, in the answer to that question is, 'L', Lilith."

"Michael, I…, I…, just want…, I just want, just want so much to sleep with you. I just so much want to awake before daybreak and know that you are there, right beside me. Can I do that with you, Michael?"

No Lilith…, you cannot, not do that. I insist.

Lilith, let's make a pact with each other. Right here and now. Let's…, let's never let our fields lie fallow. The growing seasons are too few and too short in duration in one lifetime. Our fields are fertile. Ours are ready. Ours are ready for planting. Sundays are thought to be the Lord's Day, the day of rest. But fields, when they are ready, will not…, no, cannot wait for the gods. Attention must be paid to what life demands of us. Every day is precious and the present is the prize. Let's never tire of the giving of self, unabashedly, with all that we possess.

Let's shake on that, shall we!"

But it was too late to garner an agreement.

This woman, this bloody, this beautiful woman who lived in a world so remote from my own, this woman lost in slumber by my side had become, in the space of a few short weeks, someone I chose, during flights of fancy, to view as a soul-mate.

But it was a relationship of rivals..., measured in mere weeks! The romantic in me embraced the poetic notion of, 'injury spawning intimacy'. But cold reality thundered the harsh truth in my ears that soft focus, 'soul-mate' was more subterfuge than substance. Anger prone and hardened with hate, 'cell-mate' was probably closer to our shared realty.

Thoughts that ran to commitment were ill-conceived. I knew that. In my heart, I knew that! A gun would be on the floor, at the foot of our bed, hers..., mine..., it did not matter..., a gun that would speak, in muted tones, to the future we would inevitably share.

Narcissism trumping natural selection perhaps!

Chapter 25

If robots ever took over the world, their Garden of Eden would be Singapore. Plastic faces of placidity and eye averting politeness masking distain and condescension toward everyone foreign, including neighboring Malaysians, reigned supreme. Humans who acted like automatons, and wired machines replete with human gestures, machines that could complete simple, repetitive human tasks were, to outside eyes at least, ubiquitous, interchangeable with their human counterparts and indistinguishable from them as well!

I did not want to be there. It hurt. The prosthetic I wore in my mouth like an ill- fitting denture, repositioned my jaw in such a way that it induced a headache after less than three hours of continuous wear. The restriction even affected how I pronounced the simplest of single syllable words. The horn-rimmed glasses were co-conspirators. They pinched the bridge of my nose blocking any hint of fresh air from penetrating past my nostrils.

And the nostrils of others, others who got close, would not recognize the new smell that followed my every foot step. The deodorant, the bloody cologne, the clothes, even the two-tone, wing toe shoes, were new to me. My stance, my gestures, my demeanor assumed an old world, an Italian 'sprezzatura' splash. My body language changed to project a calculated nonchalance, a look, it was hoped, of natural elegance to accompany my newly acquired sartorial splendor.

The new me was decidedly different. The new me was distinct, very distinct, from the old me. Nothing about the new me was me.

Everything about the new incarnation of me was throw away tricks and trash. Hiding in plain sight was the hope that was fuelled by hubris, nemesis notwithstanding.

This bloody burden had to be endured because some people possessed no sense of honesty, no sense of honor, no sense of social justice, no bloody common sense whatsoever! This bloody burden had to be borne because some deeds needed to be dealt with and delivered decisively in person!

This bloody burden was demanded because deeds, deeds of restitution, deeds that were done by one's own hand were steeped in cultural canon. They were a defining measure of personal merit that allowed for comforting closure. The symmetry needed to redress the imbalance of unnatural, immoral, reprehensible behavior.

'Vengeance is mine, sayeth the Lord', was an edict written in the Old Testament, in the book of Deuteronomy and in the New Testament, in Romans 12, as well.

Being vengeful was, therefore, thought by most Christians to be outside personal purview. Deliberate disobedience was a sin and as such, might merit retribution in excess of the seriousness of the transgression itself! But on the Serengeti Plain of modern day existence, where human jackals and hyenas prowled at will, less death for them meant more, much more, death for others.

God takes care of those who take care of themselves!

The details of the assignment, which had been willingly, in fact enthusiastically, embraced by Leorah, had been delivered, at her insistence, by phone. She claimed that she was too busy to meet me in person and further, she claimed that her window of opportunity to do my bidding was limited to the three weeks subsequent to our one dimensional, truncated, vocal visit.

All of my cards had been played face up and on the table with her. No surprises were hidden in the targeted prize, Mr. Whitehead esquire. The recounting of his failure to fulfill his fiduciary duty regarding the reading of the final Will of Mr. Tan, his willingness to divulge privileged client information, for a fee, to Brian Law, his selection of stamp collecting as a sedentary but satisfying pastime, his bulwark against utter obscurity through association with the Sisters of Mercy Orphanage in Singapore, his parenting impulse with Geoffrey Tan, and his sissy shenanigans with Mrs. Tan, had, I feared, made more for monotonous monologue than meaningful disclosure. Not once did the woman ask for clarification or elaboration on the thumb-nail sketch provided.

I knew the woman was more a spontaneous, reactive wit than a disciplined note taker, but I reasoned that her capacity for recall had been made more than passable through practice in the field. And our agreed to telephone call schedule, at eleven o'clock every evening, would allow for corrections to misinformation or reiteration of information missed.

Ten thousand dollars had been sent to her at her Jakarta residence by private courier to cover her expenses and the promised twenty thousand dollar fee, in cash, was ready for delivery once her fact-finding tour of duty was completed. The logistics locked both of us into a better than legal, business ledger.

Leorah honored her commitment for the first two days. Then, her telephone calls ceased. She had informed me that Mr. Whitehead had been admitted to the Gleneagles Hospital intensive care unit just days before her arrival in Singapore. COPD, chronic obstructive pulmonary disease, a group of progressive lung diseases which, in Whitehead's case, included the 'regular suspects' of emphysema and chronic bronchitis, were the diseases at the top of the man's life limiting list. Obesity and Type 2 diabetes and pulmonary hypertension added insult to already life threatening injury. That was all she was able or willing to report. No info about prescribed meds, prognosis, or analysis of the emotional status of the corpulent patient was forthcoming.

I phoned Dr. Rajawane in Bali and asked him verify the status of Mr. Whitehead in Gleneagles through his colleague connections there. Within thirty minutes of my call he responded. No patient with that name was currently in the facility. Hospital records did reveal however, that six months earlier a man with that surname suffering from the illnesses reported by Leorah, had been admitted to the ICU. But he had been discharged within the second week of his stay once his condition, his conditions, had been stabilized.

Dr. Rajawane was pressed into service, as was the mother of a neighbor who lived across the street from me in Jakarta, to answer any callers who rang up around eleven o'clock in the evening. The caller was to be told that I had gone out to visit friends for the evening but that I would be back by the following morning. Then they were to hang up the phone and ignore any further calls until the following evening. Then, the same message would be delivered to anyone who phoned. No one, I was told, ever did!

A one day lapse in telephone communication was one day too many. I was on a flight to Singapore early the next morning.

In anticipation of this worst case scenario, wheels of reparation had already been set in motion, immediately subsequent to making the deal with Leorah. Project launch was understood. Success based upon sustained thrust of subterfuge had been factored into the equation. And the trajectory to destination of the missiles of malfeasance had been calculated as well! But everything depended on the gyroscope of mutual goal visualization and faith in the promise of co-conspirators.

I did not want to push old man Whitehead from a balcony or down a flight of stairs or even down an elevator shaft. That would have been too easy. For everyone concerned! I wanted despair to persuade, to pull him from the narrow ledge he clung to. I wanted the narrow ribbon of rock that separated him from anonymity and perpetual silence to appear to be his only means of escape.

Col. Satu had been called immediately after I had secured my telephone subterfuge with Dr. Rajawane and Rosa, the neighbor lady from across the street. He was not at home. He was never at home. He was never at home when I needed him. But he always called back, regardless of the hour, if the caller was, to his way of thinking, of consequence.

The phone rang at two thirty in the morning.

"Col. Satu, thank you very much to call me back so soon. Let me say right away what is the subject of my call to you. I need your help Col. Satu, and I need your help very fast. Tomorrow I will fly to Singapore because there is a man there, a very bad man, and I want this man to be dead. This man is the lawyer who cause you and me so much trouble. This is Mr. Whitehead. I know you remember this man. This is not a job for Pearly because I do not wish murder for this man, only I wish suicide for this man. I will explain this next time when we are together and we have many drinks together.

Do you have business partner in Singapore who can help me, who can help me fast with this military manoeuver of capture and contain of the enemy, Mr. Whitehead?"

Mere moments passed before the Colonel returned to the phone with the name and telephone number of Mr. Right in Singapore. I thanked the man profusely and reminded him that we were past due for what I would call a drunken bender and what he would call a night for two men to laugh and be happy together.

The Dukun albatross placed around his neck by Mr. Brian Law and the noose of sorts readied for my own neck by the conspirators, Law and Whitehead, concerning Bali High Art, were more than sufficient motive to prompt the old, quasi-military man to accept the role of, 'accessory after the fact'.

"Thank you Mr. Joseph for interrupting your business agenda to see me today."

"Do not thank me. Thank your good friend, our good friend, Col. Satu. Without Col, Satu, I would not be talking to you, or anyone for that matter, today. Do you know what I mean by that remark, Mr. Campbell.?"

"Then we are brothers of a sort, Mr. Joseph. I owe my life to that man as well. Would you like to stop somewhere and get something appropriate to celebrate our common history and heritage? Something stronger than coffee to toast our benefactor?"

"No, maybe some other time. The bottle of water I have in the car is fine. Tell me what I need to know Michael, may I call you Michael, so that we can set the wheels in motion for the project you are planning in my backyard."

"Here is the relevant data on the man of interest. I scribbled it down while in transit from Jakarta. As you can see, he resides at 360

Admiralty Way. He occupies one of the penthouse suites in the building. I don't know which one. Question! Is there any possibility that your people can determine if an apartment or a condo is available for rent, on a short term basis, which has an uninterrupted view of his residence. I need to observe the man for a few days before I can decide how best to deal with him.

Oh yes, one small point. On this trip to Singapore, my passport has admitted one Cameron Michaels to your island nation. Me! You know who I am but if a name is needed for introduction to an outsider, please humor me by using my sometimes moniker, my sometimes alter ego, Cameron Michaels.

Anyway, concerning any potential place that has an uninterrupted view of my target, please understand that cost will not be an issue. Oh, and one more thing. If a place can be found and secured, then I would need to know the location of a store that specializes in optical equipment. I will need a pair of marine binoculars, powerful ones, and an SLR, 35 mm camera affixed to a tripod..., with a telephoto lens..., and lots of rolls of 36 exposure film."

"Is that all Mr. Michael..., sorry, Mr. Michaels, I mean. Is there anything else you think you will require?"

"No, that's about it. But I need everything on that wish list by yesterday. Do you still think that you can help me?"

For the first time during our discussion, Mr. Joseph allowed a thin smile to faintly flash across his face.

"Well, we shall see what we can do. Rolling back the clock has always been a challenge for me. In the meantime, however, I am very familiar with a tourist trap that specializes in sheltering those on a budget..., money or mischievous intent. It is off the beaten track, I think that is the expression, and even though it might lack certain amenities to which you have become accustomed, it will guarantee your anonymity. I think we both agree, that takes precedence over all else!

The reservation is under the name, Rubicon, The Rubicon Group. Have you got that Mr. Cameron Michaels. The Rubicon Group!"

The man glanced at me just as one would when attempting to gain assurance that the nuanced message which had been sent was received by an individual who possessed sufficient depth perception to appreciate its import.

Through a thin smile that mimicked his own, I gave the man the best response my rapidly summoned wit could manage.

"Of course it is expected that all concerned will PLAY FAIR even if the RAMPARTS are breached. Those who choose to do BATTLE, FORD all streams and rivers that are in their way in order to assure victory."

Mr. Joseph scratched the back of his head, grinned widely and embraced me for longer than was the custom for a man of Asian extraction.

A game within a game was being played. I was being played. I was being watched just as I was about to become the one doing the watching. Mr. Whitehead had been bad. In the eyes of some, Mr. Whitehead had been very bad. The CIA wanted him dead. The CIA wanted him dead by remote control. The CIA viewed me as a convenient agent of death by detached detonation.

It had all been too easy. One phone call from the Changi Airport lounge after the plane landed, prompt pick up by a man in a limousine mere steps away from the arrivals area doors, a truncated conversation with this person of consequence, in some Singaporean circles at least, a discussion which lasted no more than five, maybe six minutes, and a drop off at a non-descript motel/hotel just off Orchard Road.

Col. Satu was indeed the right man to know when rule of law was least likely to ensure success. Col. Satu was the right man to engage when 'smoke and mirrors' was the board game in play. I had the feeling that Mr. Joseph was cut from the same bolt of cloth as was his mentor in Jakarta. Quiet demeanors, reliance on people who played in the corridors of power, deadly when enemies were flushed out in the open, killer instincts that trampled those who got in the way of the triumphs which had, hitherto been, assured.

I felt that I had been ushered into labyrinth of lies and deceit. I felt that I had been conscripted into the serious business of murder by middle management caveat. Langley might not even know the details. Langley might not even care!

"Yes, good morning. My name is Cameron Michaels. We spoke earlier this morning. I believe I have an appointment to see Sister Georgina at two o'clock…,"

"Yes, Mister Michaels, Sister Georgina is expecting you. Will you follow me please."

It was oddly entertaining to remain one step behind someone who seemed to float rather than walk as a means of locomotion. Slippered, Papal steps defined the Bride of Christ who led the way. A utility brand of soap had been used to ready the temporal to meet the spiritual demands of her day.

"Yes, Mr. Michaels. It is a pleasure to meet you. You mentioned, when you called earlier, that a meeting with me was rather urgent. How may I be of help to you, today."

Sister Georgina's gray and white habit left everything about her size and shape to the imagination of the supplicant to whom an audience had been granted. And her face, surrounded as it was by starched white cotton, took on a tempered radiance usually reserved for idealized women whose images hung in art galleries.

Tradition was triumphant. The women of Roman Catholicism and the women of Islam were seen as temptresses by the men of means in their respective faiths and, as a result, walled or veiled cloister was the containment that time consummated and made fast through custom.

Both groups of women were victimized by the family of men who feared and envied them. The gender war had been fought and won long before the writing and codification of the relevant holy texts had been completed. Life on the savannah had been physical in the extreme. And the female role which was centered on domesticity and relentless duplication of kind had, over time, fostered a silent rage, a distinct hatred of self, a view of self as biological trap.

Ironically, that self-loathing had morphed in relatively recent times, partially due to the advent of fertility regulating pharmaceuticals, into a badge of honor which proclaimed that a caterpillar to butterfly metamorphosis had occurred. For the vocal minority at least, the historic capacity to prevail in the face of adversity had blossomed into a combative compunction to control. And corporal presence was the only passport needed to prove citizenship in the new, energizing, body politic.

Being ignorant of the socio-sexual bent of the woman seated across the desk from me, the one who possessed the Bride of Christ credentials, the one who was head mistress of a school for street waifs, I decided to follow my gut instinct. Neither fact about the woman, involving this world or the next, would have necessarily fueled a personal, gender driven, agenda. But neither fact could be ignored either. Positional dominance, no matter how small the universe being affected, was a dance which, once learned, was never forgotten.

I thought it best to assume that Sister Georgina sided with her liberated sisters who resided beyond the walls which defined her existence. The humility needed to show respect for someone who possessed superior knowledge of a subject would not be difficult. The machinations of the Christian trilogy were her domain. Appropriate reaction to her use or abuse of that library of knowledge and to any penchant she might have to play 'bitch-mother-superior' with me, might prove to be somewhat problematic though.

The inequality of the sexes, it seemed, never ended. I needed the woman more than she needed me!

Be polite, be polite and attentive to what is said, be polite and persuasive when called upon to speak, be polite and prepared for setback. And always, always be polite and smile, no matter how uncomfortable the prosthetic mouth piece made the simple act of flexing the seventeen facial muscles needed to achieve a Mr. Happy look, would promise to be.

"Well, perhaps a little bit of personal back ground would be in order. I am the proud father of a five year old daughter, Christina, and together we live in Jakarta…, and sometimes, Bali. I am a single parent. Christina's mother died in childbirth. Nevertheless we both soldier on and make as much music together as we possibly can. That little girl is the light of my life. She is the spitting image of her mother and as such, is living proof, for me at least, that God is omniscient and that God is omnipresent. Praise the Lord and the blessings He chooses to bestow on His unworthy servants.

On a more mundane note, I am a financial advisor by trade. My first, my only job of any consequence was with one of the major investment firms on Wall Street, in New York City. I was an 'IA', an Investment Advisor. My job was to make money with the money of the clients who sought my advice. A select group of investors, they relied on my stock market savvy and the resultant investment portfolios which I offered. And for that service, I was paid handsomely.

In essence all I did was help them navigate safely around the real and imagined shoals of fear relative to the potential for financial loss and, at the same time, protect them from the daily tendency they had toward embracing the false god of greed.

After a decade or so of making money for others, including my firm, I decided to become independent. I took control of my own holdings, meager as they were, as well as those of a very select group of investors who thought more of my expertise than they did the somewhat stodgy reputation of my former firm. That move quickly proved to be successful and that has allowed me to meet and befriend a number of people of consequence in the business community…, people whose operations are centered in capital cities throughout South East Asia.

One such individual is a Mr. Tan who is, or was the CEO of The Good Earth Distribution Company here in Singapore. Mr. Tan, as you undoubtedly know, died only months ago from a tragic fall at his estate in Bali.

The man will be sorely missed…, And…, well…, that brings me to why I am here engaged in conversation with you today, Sister Georgina. Mr. Tan always spoke highly of you and your staff who, in the service of Christ, bring comfort and stability and security to those in greatest need. That is to say the very young, the most vulnerable in any society, the most valuable as well, for they are the future, and therefore the most deserving of shelter from life's tempestuous twists."

"I can see why your investors believe in you, Mr. Michaels. You marshal your thoughts rather well and your mode of expression provides a rather poetic description of a rather prosaic occupation. If I may be so bold as to share that opinion with you."

"Bold is always best, Sister Georgina. Perhaps our disparate worlds are not that different after all. Eschew the faint of heart, to be sure, and embrace the pure in spirit. Celebrate the meek and the merciful for their vision is of God and His ultimate bounty. The Beatitudes, I believe."

"You're novel take on the Holy Scriptures, even though it borders on the profane, is, coming from your world of fear and greed, at least, somewhat refreshing."

"So, the reason for my visit. Yes, the reason for my being here today. I would be very grateful if you would accept this envelop which contains ten thousand dollars, in American funds, to use as you see fit to further your efforts with the young people in your care. I must apologize for being so tardy in its delivery. Initially I had meant it to be a tribute to the man who introduced me to facets of life which hitherto had been outside of my experience."

Sister Georgina took the envelop from my extended hand, slowly opened the flap and tentatively peered at the brick of pressed paper which featured a bemused, Benjamin Franklin peeking up at her.

"Naturally you will require a receipt for such a generous offering...,"

The woman almost appeared to be talking directly to the only signatory to the Declaration of Independence in the room. I realized that it was a stall tactic.

I granted her the time she needed to regroup.

"No, not so! That was the hallmark of the firm, of the world, a form of legal largesse, which I chose to leave behind. This is an offering of the heart in recognition of the gift granted to me by the Lord. The gift of time..., of time spent with a gentleman who was far more imbued with faith than I can ever hope to be."

"I believe an expression common among the laity is, 'God moves in mysterious ways'! That saying would certainly apply to Mr. Tan and the generous endowment he bequeathed to the Sisters of Mercy Orphanage. And it would be equally apt to describe our meeting here today. You are indeed, as was your former associate, Mr. Tan, one of a kind, Mr. Michaels."

"I believe that if a person meets only one person, only one other person in a lifetime, one who is a catalyst for change, one is fortunate indeed! One is blessed! That one person in my life, was Mr. Tan. But not just Mr. Tan…, his daughter, Victoria, the embodiment of accomplishment…, made of the stuff that I would wish for my own daughter Christina…, even some of the associates of Mr. Tan…, his physician, Dr. Leung at Gleneagles hospital, and Mr. Whitehead, the man on the masthead of the Law firm, Wong, Whitehead and Wong, the man entrusted with most of the Tan family legal matters which included the disposition of the Tan estate…, both men of principle, both men of honor, both men of deserved prominent stature within the Singaporean community…,"

Stop, I said to myself. Stop stretching the truth any further. Time for the gamble concerning Sister Georgina's knowledge of the truth about the doctor and the lawyer to stop. Time for the gamble, that she would swallow the bait and be reeled into a net of disclosure that would go beyond Whitehead's philately and philandering, to end. Ride on red for only one spin of the roulette wheel. One spin only! Time for blind faith in the gamble to take over and trump all else!

Ten grand had just been spent. But it had already been spent. Twice over! Only the name of the recipient had changed. Leorah had been supplanted by the Lord Almighty! And the remaining ten grand was to enable me to continue to fly under the radar of nosy officialdom in Singapore. Penny ante stuff. A mere thirty pieces of silver had been placed on the table.

But my Judas Iscariot tale of betrayal was still a big gamble and my ego coughed in my ear that it was one that I could not afford to lose. An almost audible catechism of pleading and supplication rose like a malevolent mist behind the forced grin which masked my desperate hope. Gamble only when the gods are on your side. Through clenched fists, will into being the outcome you want, through gritted teeth will into being the outcome you need. Will what you wish, without reservation!

"Do you plan on remaining in Singapore for the remainder of the week, Mr. Michaels? The reason I ask is, believe it or not, a celebration of Mr. Whitehead's decades long, valued contribution to the Sisters of Mercy Orphanage has been planned for this coming Saturday night.

Four days from now. And..., and..., given your friendship with Mr. Whitehead, albeit through your shared friendship with Mr. Tan and..., and..., your obvious capacity to entertain, I was wondering..., no, hoping that you would consider accepting my invitation to attend our Saturday evening gala for Mr. Whitehead. The celebration will be held at the Raffles Singapore on Beach Road."

'Magnanimous in victory', would have been an appropriate caption under a photo of my face had it given even an inkling of my true feelings at that moment. Winning a bet on the remote possibility of finessing a morsel of information from the woman of God across the table from me, a tidbit that I might have been able to chew on and spit back in Whitehead's face, would have been sufficient. At least it would have been a start down the vindictive road I had chosen. That would have been sufficient, penny ante stuff. But what I got instead was an Irish Sweepstakes, game changing, windfall! I had been invited to speak at a top drawer event on the Singaporean social calendar, in praise of a man for whom nothing but bitter enmity existed!

An impromptu tour was offered of the facility by Sister Georgina as a sort of post coital, intimate embrace. She had given herself to me in the only way permissible under the strict code she had promised before God to uphold.

The Orphanage resembled more a posh, two-story, suburban residence for young adults than it did a dour institution devoted to providing shelter and succor for the prepubescent of Singapore who were destitute. Lush, meticulously maintained gardens dominated the grounds. The building walls were alive with sparrow nesting ivy. The place was a veritable bower of bliss for the blessed whose predicament had been truncated.

A tight weave of red and black bricks snaked among the buildings. In the middle of the property, a large, wooden cross loomed ominously over the South East Asian version of the Garden of Eden. All paths, it seemed, on the orphanage grounds at least, led to the cross.

When casually asked about her charges and the facilities for their education, I was informed that only a few youngsters, infants and toddlers mainly, actually received instruction from the Sisters of the Orphanage. Those who were not whisked away by couples of the Catholic faith within weeks of their arrival, heterosexual couples who resided in the Benelux countries; Belgium, Luxembourg and the Netherlands, were registered with a select few of the private, parochial schools in Singapore.

St. Jude's Academy and St. Ignatius of Loyola Finishing School were, I learned, primary partners in providing elementary and secondary education for the possibly parentless progeny. A modern day version of Moses in the bulrushes, babies in bassinets, infants left at the Orphanage front door by unwed mothers. That was the reward bestowed on an institution which proclaimed artificial birth control to be a sin.

A steady stream of hapless infants, and the cash cow that attended the trafficking of that particular commodity of value. That was the real sin being committed on Holy ground, I thought to myself.

Apparently the waiting list for Singaporean babies was long and I knew that the fees which attended their adoption process were steep. The cozy, 'cash for kids' relationship involving the orphanage, the schools and the national government of Singapore, via grants and humanitarian fund raising campaigns, was too sacrosanct to ever be scrutinized. What the general public did not know, and did not care to know, met with the approbation of all concerned.

Money greased the wheels of the machinery of mercy and any individual trepidation concerning the possible commitment of fraud in the sight of God was trumped by the complicity of the unholy trinity of church, state and private, for profit, enterprise!

Not so ironically, Sister Georgina shifted my attention away from the machine that managed the very young by hinting that maybe my stock market expertise could be brought to bear on the current financial portfolio of the Orphanage. Only a polite over view of things, of course, and only if I had the time, of course.

The tentative request for free investment advice, whether prompted by her fear of missing 'insider' opportunity or from mere school girl flirtation, destroyed the respect that I initially had for the woman. She was no better than the players from the Flavian Dynasty in ancient Rome…, the father, Vespasian and his two sons, Titus and Domitian.

They were the self-seeking frauds, the self-appointed first saints, the Roman-God pretenders, who looked down, in insolent silence on the faithful, from the heights that surrounded St. Peter's Square.

Had I been a bona fide IA, I would probably have recommended that a sizeable portion of her investment portfolio be redirected to the American armaments monolith. Firms like Boeing, Raytheon and Lockheed Martin would have topped my list. And why not! Mother Theresa willingly accepted funding from Papa Doc Duvalier, the deranged leader of Haiti. His was hardly a country capable of humanitarian relief anywhere in the world other than perhaps, inside its own borders.

Everyone knew that the calculating charlatan from Calcutta, Mother Theresa, was in the running for sainthood. Some knew that she paid no heed to basic sterilization practices with the patients who sought treatment under her roof. Few knew that her only motive was to capture the souls of the deathly ill for Roman Catholicism.

The Flavian dynasty playing God or the diminutive Albanian-Indian playing huckster for God, what was the difference? Both traded in notoriety, in criminality. Both traded the infinite for the immediate, psychic gratification of this world. Immensity of impact notwithstanding, Sister Georgina was of their tribe.

To my question concerning the need for, or the desirability of a partner to accompany me to the Saturday night fete for Mr. Whitehouse, I was flatly served up the ambiguous, Oracle of Delphi remark, 'Although I view accompaniment as antediluvian, it is the preferred arrangement of most who will be in attendance.'

I thanked my host for the tour that had been provided, complimented her on the quality of what had been seen and held out a professional card taken from the lobby of the no-tell motel where I was staying. The promise was made to provide a rapid response to any message she might leave with the front desk clerk regarding last minute changes to the guest speaker agenda.

"If I may be so bold once again Mr. Michaels…, You are…, Mr. Michaels…, you are a man who is carrying a heavy burden…, you are a man of much melancholy. Close relationships, close, intimate relationships which will make you whole, will continue to evade you until such time as you unburden yourself …, unburden yourself, through the Holy Spirit, unburden yourself in the presence of the Holy Father. Your worldly riches will multiply but your lack of communion with God will leave you spiritually wanting and alone.

May the God of hope fill you with all the joy and peace of believing, so that by the power of the Holy Spirit you may commence to abound in His everlasting hope.

Romans 15:13"

To that treatise, which I took as a statement emanating from the Jesuit conviction that only the Roman Catholic faith led to salvation, a smugness instilled in every young, impressionable mind, beginning with baptism, I mumbled the only rebuttal that came to mind. I said it to the air in front of my face as I turned and walked toward the front gate where I knew a taxi would provide real world escape.

"Christ commanded us to love one another as He loved us. John 13:34.

One must learn as well, I think, to love the transient, that which is of this world, as precursor to an abiding love of the infinite and the majesty that might…, that mightily dwells in the great beyond.

Love is all you need."

Beatle bullshit at its best, I thought. Beatle bullshit as a saccharine sop!

Chapter 26

"Stay behind the sheer curtain on your side of the sliding glass doors and I will do the same on my side. No sense being found out before we even start. This is the best equipment I could get my hands on…, on such short notice.

You strike me as a man though, who knows more about pointing a shoulder weapon at an unsuspecting target…, a horned mammal say…, or maybe even a man for that matter, than someone who gets voyeuristic pleasure from viewing people at a distance with their pants down!

So forget any detailed explanation of the camera set up on the balcony outside. My idea of a camera is, buy it, take pictures of smiling teeth and then throw it away. So, I will tell you what I was told about how it works but my explanation will be from the perspective of someone inclined and equipped to take down a prized animal at a great distance.

So, instead of seeing a Nikon fitted with a huge telephoto lens sitting on a low tripod, hidden behind a flower box, imagine that you see a scoped Winchester, model 70, rifle equipped with a bipod on the forearm…, or better still, think upgrade. Picture a magnificent Weatherby mark V rifle on display out there. Both are chambered for their respective, 300 magnum rounds. Both are sighted in for the distance between the two buildings and both possess the capability, as you probably know, for decisive, take-down penetration at any range.

Pretend that you are hunting mountain goat or sheep, some animal that is found high up on the side a mountain, one that is always one valley away from where you are…, say in New Zealand, or some other pristine, under-peopled place that is close to where the world comes to an end. The thrill of the hunt is to see and not be seen. Success is always based on stealth. I know, OK, I know. I am speaking to the blessed!

Anyway, you can see that I took it upon myself to provide a spotting scope as well. No need to have to squint through the small view finder on the camera to keep a steady sight line on your target. And no need for unnecessary movement because of a dangling pair of binoculars. Leave them in the living room. From behind the curtain you can scope out the other balconies at 360 Admiralty Way, if you get bored…or horny! Ha, ha, ha.

So, by lying flat on your stomach, you will be able to comfortably look through the scope at your target and squeeze, no push, the remote control shutter button when whomever or whatever you are looking for, comes into view. Automatic exposure advancement means the camera operates the way a semi-automatic weapon does. Taking a picture activates an internal mechanism that readies the next shot…, the exposure, for use.

Remember, the spotting scope is powerful enough, to clearly identify a bullet hole in a paper target at one hundred meters. That should be more than enough magnification for your non-lethal purposes. Right!"

A note had been handed to me by the front desk clerk at the 'no-tell motel' subsequent to my audience with ROI Georgina. Hers had not been the position of king, expressed in the French language, Roi, but more the disposition of a sovereign reigning over a court ruled by the motto, Return On Investment!

The message was as crisp as it was cryptic. 'Be ready for pick-up at front door within fifteen minutes of your phone call. Maintain current residence.' The limo drive from dump to destination of distinction took less than twenty minutes.

"We, or at least you, Mr. Michaels, got lucky. Let's just say that a friend of mine controls the lease for this place. It is, of course, the penthouse which is located directly across from 360 Admiralty Way. Only the driveway connecting the underground parking to the main road, and a few fancy, rock gardens, separate the two towers. The shooting distance, balcony to balcony is a little more than 100 meters.

No need to adjust your sights for windage, elevation, cross wind direction, or trajectory for that matter, ha, ha. Easy shot! Simple, silent shooting!

Take all of your shots during daylight hours. That avoids the need for a flash. Cover the equipment with the rain tarp that is folded in front of the camera lens when you are finished and do not, repeat, do not turn on any of the lights in the apartment at any time, for obvious reasons. When you have finished for the day, take the elevator down to the first level parking area. You will be met there and taken back to your other lodging for the night. The same routine will be repeated the following day and the day after that, if deemed necessary.

We will develop the rolls of film each evening and provide the shots that turn out, the next morning while you are in transit back to the balcony business at hand. Water and snacks will be stored in the refrigerator in the kitchen. I will not see you tomorrow so let me wish you good hunting with prevailing 'down-wind conditions' and sunny, dry weather."

I requested that only one, 4 x 6 photo be developed from each negative. The right size to fit in an envelope which in turn, would fit in a suit jacket, inside breast pocket. The roll of exposed film was then to be destroyed. Bad evidence begging to be found if left behind. It spoke volumes about complicity. It was a road map that any rookie investigator could follow. Both Mr. Joseph and I would almost certainly be cast as the criminals occupying the Coup de Ville that was hiding at the bottom of that Cracker Jack box!

The inane in pursuit of the intimate, Mr. Meat Loaf notwithstanding!

With more than two hours of daylight left in the day, I got permission from Mr. Joseph to stay behind and start the 'tree-stand' hunt immediately. I wanted to linger longer in my borrowed million dollar residence knowing full well that there was only a slim chance of viewing my quarry in its natural habitat in the afternoon.

That didn't matter. I also wanted to be alone. I had grown tired of feigning interest in Mr. Joseph's hunting analogies. I had to indulge myself. I needed to satisfy my curiosity concerning the layout of the 'hunting blind' built for blue-bloods which had fallen into my lap.

Apart from the 'living large' layout of the place, there was its "ivory tower' location. Just like a first base-line, box seat, it afforded the occupant a 'peep-show' glimpse of how others at the apex of the social hierarchy in Singapore chose to languish in luxury. Time to step up to the plate, I thought. Time to test the weapons of choice without alerting 'Admiralty' on the other side of the rock garden. Time too, to put the binoculars to proper, prurient use.

The residence, that had been mere backdrop to the balcony which was to serve as home, was immense. Ten spacious rooms in all, with a maid's quarters discretely distant from the family bedrooms, the regal residence occupied a quarter of the living space on the penthouse floor of the condominium complex.

Wide, floor to ceiling windows punctuated the two adjoining, exterior walls. Both were blessed by gravity defying balconies. Both outside playpens for baby behemoths bordered on being unkempt and in need of repair. Potted plants ran riotously over the sides of their rectangular boxes and down the exterior edges of the balcony floor. The floor itself, like that which was standard on well-appointed yachts, seemed to be of teak and holly design. It needed immediate, restorative attention.

One wall exposure caught the rising sun while the other allowed the residents and guests to bask all day in the exclusive, clothing optional, perpetual summer of a tropical Southern exposure. The home in the sky commanded uninterrupted, spectacular views in both cardinal directions on the compass rose.

Mr. Whitehead's residence, of almost equal size, had western and northern exposures. His abode would be blessed by direct sunlight just when I wanted him to have it most. Early in the afternoon and on into the evening.

Ostentation was the access obstacle to all of the rooms which were threshold thumb-nailed during my leisurely stroll around the elevated estate. Bedrooms were duveted to death. The living room was sound proofed by over-sized, gaudy pillows which seemed to grow out of the floor, and four, cookie cutter bathrooms were all terry clothed in the extreme. The neatly folded, floral patterned, hand and face cloths, some still in their plastic shipping sleeves, whispered 'Do Not Touch'! Every room, with manic intent, was meant to be a cluttered, no-go zone.

The dining room table was set for royalty. Limoges china; dinner, side, soup and dessert plates, with their bold, gold, pinwheel rims were neatly stacked on raised place mats. They were composed of brown and black, flat, stream bed, stones affixed to mesh underlays. The architecture for eating crowded each of the twenty place settings that the ebony slab of wood could accommodate. Each place setting was crowned by enough crystal stem wear to rival that kept at the Palace of Versailles. The centerpiece was an oversized arrangement of plastic flowers set in the belly of a bronzed, mythical Chinese dragon.

This palace was not to be lived in. It was merely a position which the silly rich could occasionally occupy. Like an addition to a fobbed bracelet, it was no more than a trinket to be included in the diverse portfolio of 'easy-divestiture' holdings. I felt strangely pure and somewhat virtuous being able to bypass the entire den of deception and reside, hermit like, in the KBT- the kitchen, the balcony, and the broom-closet toilet.

In preparation for a full day of snooping, starting early the next morning, I decided to 'dry-run' the planned program of the following day.

Slithering along the carpeted living room floor and through the foot wide opening created by nudging the sliding glass balcony door open only slightly, I started the 'dry-run' snoop. Success, I thought would simply be a matter of lying flat on my stomach, hovering over the eye piece on the spotting scope and clicking at anyone and everyone who moved in 'Whitehead Manor'.

The curtain was problematic. It would move if a there were even a slight breeze. Movement meant occupancy. The sliding glass door would have to be drawn almost shut by my foot once I was completely outside and in position.

The plastic pinkness of my face and hands would defeat any attempt at concealment. I needed a mask, light weight, easy to custom shape with scissors, with no interference to normal breathing…, and dark colored, latex gloves…, tight fit…, no compromise to the use of the equipment…, especially the remote camera shutter button or any manual lens adjustment, and gray or camouflage printed pants and T-shirt. Failing that, a camouflage printed rain slick.

I had some shopping to do before my return visit the next day.

I looked down at the machine gun nest of photographic equipment and smirked. My mission was diabolical. Cruel versus cunning, it didn't matter. It had been successfully launched. All that remained was the test firing of the deck armaments. Photos of live action targets would provide that one remaining detail.

The man of limited vision who possessed the magnificent, panoramic view was going to die. His realization of impending death was not going to be measured by the slow motion seconds it took to experience the bottom of an elevator shaft rise up and engulf, nor would it be the rush of air as the ground foliage turned to a greenish-brown, blur, post balcony plunge…, not even the serenity of self-induced sleep in a bath tub warmed by the contained mess from severed wrist or carotid or femoral artery, no, Mr. Whitehead would experience more. Mr. Whitehead would be visited by a living death.

It would be death by destruction of taste buds. Destroy what a man most cherishes…, the gods in his world…, the reputation for goodness in himself…, and you destroy his will, his reason for living. You annihilate him but you leave him still standing. You render him rudderless but with the full sails of involuntary, physiological response still flapping noisily in the wind.

I granted the Whitehead gallery a parting glance as I began the zipper slide and slither back toward the living room.

I froze in total disbelief. I was transfixed by what was standing a mere one hundred twenty-five yards away from me, some twenty four stories above the ground. Like a hunter who spots an eight point buck munching contentedly, at the margin of a field, on the remaining soybeans scattered on the ground, just one day before the hunting season is set to open, I did not know how to react.

Glee at having advance planning pay off…, maybe. Ground teeth in the face of too much, too easy…, too soon…, maybe. Grimace when the difficult dissolves into numb-dumb luck…, definitely!

The Nikon was turned on, the shutter button was grasped in my right hand and I was hunched over the bomb sight of my B-25 bomber before the person across the canyon had a chance to focus on, let alone process the ever so slight movement behind flower boxes made miniature by distance. The busyness of the sister building's façade, rectangles ruled by a crosshatch network of vertical and horizontal support beams, ensured the integrity of my castle keep against any visual breach of its walls. Sister buildings shared similar exterior shells!

It was Leorah. I could tell it was Leorah by the way the woman who was seconds away, as the crow flies, commanded the entire field of vision of the spotting scope in front of me.

Fully clothed in tight jeans and a loose fitting sweat shirt, she appeared to be in conversation with someone in the living room. Her gestures and exaggerated facial expressions suggested the presence of an audience of more than one. As she strutted and cavorted about, like an impromptu aerobics instructor, her attention shifted to the balcony beyond the open, sliding glass doors.

Her mid-section was girdled by what appeared to be a workman's utility belt. Hers was not for hammers, pliers and screw drivers though. As she approached the threshold to the balcony, she grabbed something from the end table to her left and, rather deftly, attached it, mid-stride, by some sort of snap action to the front of her belt.

Seemingly reborn and reaffirmed, and facing toward, she grabbed the door frame with her outstretched left hand and the open sliding glass door with the other.

The woman commenced to swivel her hips from one side to the other, like a hula-hoop hopeful, so that her newly acquired appendage swung back and forth in a measured metronome beat from the upper thigh of one leg to the other.

More than just talking to the air in front of her, she cajoled it. Emboldened by her assured invisibility, her anonymity atop a pinnacle of the world, she mimed her way through every male strut and swagger which defined pre-copulation or at least, sequestered masterbation.

In the middle of swanky Singapore, I was immediately transported back in time to my one and only experience at a nudist colony. Curiosity and time to kill in Paderborn, a small town east of Essen, the place that was home to the occupying forces of NATO, post, World War ll, were the two Devil's devices that prompted my one and only foray into needless nakedness.

Less than thirty minutes, by car, north of the town, was the location of the nudist colony. Less than thirty minutes by car, north of the town and one knew that one had entered the domain of well-to-do German, country squires. Every property would win a prize for perfection. The cookie cutter, perfect fields, the stone and scrub brush hedge rows separating the properties, small, well managed wood lots, and the meticulous, manicured look of machine perfect, planted rows of grasses and grains bordered on besting export quality quilts.

The feast for the eyes screamed of the German penchant for order. Even the elevated deer hunting stands, made of grey, weathered wood, most no more than one hundred yards from the ditches beside the road, seemed married to the concept of utility without ugliness.

Had my knowing driver not slowed down and signaled, well in advance of an unmarked right turn in the midst of this world made permanently perfect, we would have fallen victim, as was probably the case with many, neophyte nudes, to the certainty of collision with the vehicle following our bumper at more, much more, than posted highway speed. And abrupt stopping and backing up after having missed the exit would have been just as disastrous, perhaps more so!

An 'unmarked' right turn was not quite accurate as a description of the location. At the side of the road, where the turn had to be 'memory molded' before it could be consistently made, stood a rather forlorn sign made of twigs. They were nailed to a weather beaten board. It was the only channel marker signaling the turn off to a trail which was little more than a double rutted, foot path. The sign fashioned in skinny sticks, was painted a putrid pink. It was too small to be noticed by most as they whizzed by. People who chose to parade around legally naked outside the town of Paderborn had to be either coached in memory mastery of location or they had to have some fig leafed naturist squat in the foliage and await their arrival.

One of the words fashioned from the small sticks which peeked out from behind some of the leafy ground cover was, 'Himmel', the German word for 'Heaven'. It seemed to be sufficient to direct the pilgrims to the abode of the gods…, the gregarious gods who blessed sagging guts and cellulite with equal forbearance.

The actual nudist colony grounds commenced at the end of the short, pot holed, road which had initially promised, pink paradise just ahead.

The thinly forested grounds were criss-crossed by a series of walking paths, double tracks of mud actually, and they wound around an abandoned gravel quarry which conveniently masqueraded as a lake. That was the outdoor stage which hosted the parade in honor of Narcissus. It was a stage, like those common to the time of Shakespeare, which favored the presence of men over women, ten to one, regardless of the part to be played.

And those men, victims all of the cruel, cold, spring water among the rocks, practiced the same Leorah logic to sustain a hands free statement of their noteworthy manhood! Those, that is, who could still see past their bellies to visually inspect the apparatus and adjust their swagger according to need!

All 36 shots in the Nikon were taken. I did not need a photographic portfolio of the Devil in Miss Malcontent in the next condo complex. Rather, proof for Mr. Joseph of notoriety among the natives, proof of camera capability and proof of personal dexterity and capacity on a field of restrictive play were all in need of check list ticks.

I turned the camera off, covered it with the piece of plastic, slide back into the living room and slowly closed the sliding door. I grabbed the binoculars and watched the woman from behind the curtain intently.

No reaction. No cessation of her antics for the next five minutes. No need to rethink my strategy for the following day. Only I, and a circling flock of birds, pigeons or doves maybe, witnessed the dress rehearsal.

Return to the motel was routine. Routine, if a thirty minute side trip to a store called, 'The Reel Fun House', still qualified the return to the motel as routine. I had told the driver of my wish list for the following day, he had smiled, and delivered me to a place just off

Orchard Road where everything 'Hollywood' was for sale. Nothing new in that, I thought, as I entered the cavernous space devoted to the movies. Tinsel town and the tawdry who plied their trade anywhere pavement and people collided!

What awaited me in the motel lobby was, however, definitely not routine. The desk clerk waved at me frantically as I walked through the front door. He had an envelope in his hand. But his efforts were too late.

"Hello Mr. Michaels. My name is Goodwin. Goodwin Leaf. It is a pleasure to make your acquaintance. Sister Georgina said that I should come over to the hotel to meet you. So here I am!"

I had no choice but to clasp the child-like hand that was thrust out in front of me. It belonged to a young woman whose short cropped, dark brown hair made her look younger than she undoubtedly was. My guess was twenty-six but she looked sixteen.

"I'm sorry Miss…, Miss Leaf is it? But this is not a good time for me. Maybe you could leave a note with the man at the…"

"This is not a good time for me either, Mr. Michaels. Please, can I go to your room…, I have to…, I have to pee. I really have to pee very badly."

As I reached for the note, I looked at the desk clerk and shrugged my shoulders in disbelief and defeat. Appearances. Whatever you do, maintain appearances. I was an innocuous guest who attended quietly to my own business. I had no guests and I made no international calls from my room. A trace on me and my business in Singapore would meet with frustration because, apart from the bogus check-in information left on file, nothing would be known about any Mr. Michaels.

The woman with the weak bladder would have to be disposed of immediately after the water closet fixture was flushed.

Preparedness did not obviate the need for precaution.

Silence reigned as both of us jockeyed for the lead position as we walked-ran down the corridor. The distraught woman barged past me as the door was opened and she was water closeted away before I had the chance to utter even a banality about the sink faucet that continuously dripped or the black spider whose residence was under the front of the Tojo fixture she sought.

Maybe the note in my hand and the woman in my wash room were connected. Of course they were! The 'pee-pee kid' had proffered Sister Georgina as passport to my kingdom called 'Incognito'. Maybe I should read it instead of standing in front of the locked door, like an ill-informed commuter waiting for a cancelled bus.

The three page note, hopefully a manifesto, explained everything…, the three page note, more like a meandering piece of stream of self-consciousness, brought closure to nothing.

Dear Cameron,

> Thank you once again for your very thoughtful gift to the Sisters of Mercy Orphanage. Your generosity will not go unnoticed. Of that, you can be sure. Thank you as well for having accepted my invitation to attend the celebration for Mr. Whitehead this coming Saturday evening at the Raffles Hotel. I know that your presence will liven up an otherwise predictable, pedestrian event.
>
> As an outsider, an individual who is not branded with any local politics nor blemished by local peccadillos or worse, you can champion what is truly being celebrated, namely the faithful and generous character of Mr. Whitehead.
>
> Most of the presenters are life-long associates of Mr. Whitehead. Business partners, lawyers, and more lawyers and more business partners, ad infinitum, or is it ad nauseam! Most, like aging trees in the forest, have moss growing on their north sides, moss which has an unsavory odor. I am sure that the metaphor I have chosen to hint at a certain misalliance among the men with whom you will share the dais on Saturday night, is not lost on you.
>
> Your question concerning a consort for the evening was well taken. And, given your doubtless attention to pressing business concerns, perhaps you have had

insufficient time to contact a possible partner to accompany you on Saturday evening. So, to that end, allow me to take it upon myself to offer a suggestion.

A dear child of my long term acquaintance, a Miss Goodwin Leaf, might be able to provide you with the social symmetry which the event seems to require. She is a young woman who has been a ward of the Sisters of Mercy since birth. She is well educated, employed full time in a position which requires daily interaction with foreigners, self-assured is what I mean to say, and, to be honest, would benefit greatly from the exposure that such an event would provide.

Her friends call her, 'Goodie'. Please do not tell her that I shared that with you. She will be sent to your hotel late this afternoon for your consideration and hopefully, your approval.

I just know that Goodie can rise to the occasion and make a positive contribution to your presence at the celebration. Put it down to premonition!

Call me please, should the need arise.

Sincerely,
Sister Georgina

Over familiarity with a first name salutation, disparaging remarks about Whitehead associates, reference to the woman as a 'dear child', gushing revelation of the nickname of my outhouse hostage, gall to think I knew no eligible women in Singapore, guts to think I would swallow her 'baby-girl' bait as consort, the meandering message reeked of manipulation and Machiavellian mischief.

I had only to read the missive once to know that Goodwin 'Goodie' Leaf was going to be my partner, if not in crime, then certainly in comedic relief come Saturday night. Two could waltz quite convincingly to the tune of, 'Positive Perversity'.

First, I would have to at least appear to have vacated the room of Arborite furniture, Melmac ashtrays and 'good housekeeping' approved plastic cups. A great hole in the wall, hide-out, but a less than satisfactory salon for entertaining a guest. Too much of my business was lying about as well. Too much incongruous stuff which I had no interest in explaining to anyone.

Second, another hotel was needed. A hotel where neither of us would be recognized, a hotel which took cash and asked few questions. A hotel with available rooms on the same floor, a hotel with at least one reasonable restaurant on the premises and a hotel which was in close proximity to a shopping area where formal evening attire could be purchased. I hoped that at least five out of my six, 'wish list' needs could be met under one roof!

Goodwin Leaf was fast. She was fast on her feet. She knew her way around Singapore and she knew where to find the perfect hiding place. The Wayfarer Inn, a nondescript hotel I had never heard of, met all of my needs.

She was fast, as well, to recognize that there was more to 'lock-jaw' me than what initially met the eye. My play acting persona would need perfecting before the Saturday soiree!

And she was irresistibly cute. A cross between Shirley Temple, when she was a kid, and any one of the road waifs in the 'Our Gang' series that played in the theatres of my youth just before the feature presentation. Alfalfa and Buckwheat excepted. It crossed my mind that Goodie's resemblance to the black and white, celluloid youngsters of an earlier era might be more apt than not! That would certainly have created a distinct symmetry, were Sister Georgina to be cast as meddling stage mother. It was a role she seemed desirous of and also almost destined to play!

"So Goodie, let's pretend that this is an audition. You want to be cast as the Queen to my King in a stage production which will run for only one night. And the venue will be no less than the fine old dowager herself, 'The Raffles' Hotel of Singapore located at number one, Beach Road."

"First of all, I don't know why my mother…, my Mother Superior, told you that my nickname was, 'Goodie'. I hate that name. It sounds like I am some sort of candy bar. She, on the other hand, thinks that it is cute. She still sees me as a seven year old child. God works in mysterious ways…, ways that are not always clear to my mother…, I mean to Mother Superior Georgina.

Second, since you now know that 'Goodie' is out, and if you think that 'Goodwin' is too much to handle, then try, 'Lyric'. That's what all my friends call me. Lyric! It's the name I gave to myself. I like that name. I like it a lot!"

Lyric…, Lilith…, maybe the phenomenon of new age women succumbing to the need to self-define was more a movement gathering in momentum than just the myopic machinations of a maladjusted few.

"Let me guess why. Lyric…, Lyric. You think that nickname is apt because, one; the old one really annoys you. It was probably coined by your…, by someone too close to you, so anything else would be better than that and, two; anybody who uses the term, 'Goodie' sounds like the type permanently blessed with a pimply complexion. Actually it sounds like something backup singers would mouth to support a lead vocalist in a rock group.

Of course! Frankie Lyman and the Teenagers. UK rock and roll, of a certain era, at its best! 'So you lie awake just singing the blues all night.., Googy, goody, And you think that love's a barrel of dynamite…, Goody…, goody.'

It is the lyric that defines and differentiates the leader from the other members of the group. Those in supporting roles supply a lot of familiar harmony but the lead singer delivers the message of the song. The back-up boys and girls use time tested, sing-song sounds, like, do-wha, do-wha, da do run-run, and even Goody, Goody, all of which, when repeated often enough, lose meaning…, cannot sustain song identity. Excellence of choral backup does not compensate for lack of uniqueness in a song. Individual identity is lost.

Melodies make a song palatable and lyrics make a song memorable. The lyric is the thing. It is specific, exclusive to one song and to one song only…, the lyric is unmistakable. Its importance is sacrosanct. No phoniness is possible, unless of course, the speaker or singer wants to play with plagiarism.

So, point number three that can be added to your list…, Lyric is a great alternative. I really like that name. I agree with you. The name, 'Lyric' is a perfect fit. You wear it well…,Lyric! From now on, that will be only name which will pass my lips when you and I are together. Deal!"

I grinned at the laughing eyed, young woman seated across from me in the hotel restaurant. She extended her right arm across our small, corner table and shook my hand with a flourish usually reserved for people charged with negotiating international settlements. I smiled back at her despite the pain caused by my jaw jutting insertion.

Something wonderful happens inside a woman when she is the recipient of glowing words which speak to what had hitherto been seen by her as an Achilles heel. She sees herself anew through the fresh eyes of a stranger and is invigorated. Particularly when the flirtatious signal sender is one who does not try to mask obvious affection. The young woman positively glowed.

"So why should I be Queen for a day in Singapore? Let me list the reasons. As the King's trusted Consort, I can supply you with all the dope, and some of the dirt, on everyone, everyone who matters that is, who will be in attendance on Saturday night. When I get all gussied-up, as my Mother Superior would say, I can be quite a head turner. That means either your stock value will go up among the other guests who will whisper, 'who is that old guy with the fetching young woman', or I can be used as a shield to deflect attention away from you and your agenda regarding that old fat fuck, Mr. Whitehead.

Besides, I want to be at the event with the only guy who can still see his feet when he looks down beyond his belt buckle."

I grabbed the napkin from the table and shoved it into my mouth. Nothing else could have contained my laughter and nothing else could have blocked my mouth piece from falling out into the plate of food in front of me.

The self-satisfied grin on Lyric's face made it clear that she knew the job interview was over.

We shifted our attention to the full plates in front of us. Hers was a seafood medley while mine was a toasted chicken sandwich. No attempt had been made to seduce with fine table fare and no alcohol had been ordered. Coke was not just the 'real thing' for both of us the entire evening, it was the only thing.

"Lyric, would I gain any insight into the derivation of your full name, Goodwin Leaf, if I did due diligence relative to the family backgrounds of the Sisters who currently reside at the Orphanage?"

"You must be a lawyer too! You seem to ask a lot of questions to which you already know the answer. You are going to fit in very well on Saturday night. The short answer to your question, Councilor, is, YES!"

"So, I know more about you than I had, at first, thought. And, I am willing to bet that your knowledge of me goes beyond the superficial too. Am I right?"

"Maybe, but not as deep as I would like. For example, are you married, do you have kids and how do you make so much money."

Obviously, sister Georgina had shared little of our conversation with Goodwin, the sometimes 'Goodie' who turned memorable 'Lyric'. Little that mattered, other than the deduced fact that I had money to burn or, as some supplicant of old, money to throw at redemption and salvation, in that order! Smart woman! Let the kid crayon in the new page in her coloring book all by herself.

"The succinct answers would be, No…, Yes, one, and many ways. Full disclosure would be, No - widower, Yes – one girl child, and many ways – most of my money is made while I sleep.

Now, what do you do to keep the wolf away from your door?"

"One girl child…, let's just pause for a moment right there. Unburden yourself and tell me more about the xx chromosomal creature you fathered."

I deserved that.

"It is too early in our relationship Lyric, for you to have to tolerate my tears. I am so sorry. I did not mean to speak so dismissively…, so disparagingly of my daughter, Christina. Sorry…, so sorry. Please forgive my insensitivity, my gaucheness. That is not me. I hope that is not me. That precious little girl means everything to me. Christina is my world all wrapped up in one little person."

I looked down at the table and fought to sand bag the rising tide of tears. But I was unsuccessful. The child, my child had been left in the care of others for far too long. Far too long just so that I could vent my spleen and do damage to some old, fat, fuck, to use the phrase just coined by Lyric.

I was becoming what I loathed most in others. A vile, vane, vindictive old fuck who reveled more in the public pillory of those deemed deserving than in the quiet, corners constructed through personal conviction and accomplishment.

Lyric gently placed her hand over mine.

"It is OK. OK. We all forget ourselves sometimes. In the heat of the moment, we all sometimes forget. It is OK. David was a man after God's own heart. David's crimes were heinous. David, through faith in his redeemer, was saved!

Anyway, following your lead, how do I keep the wolves at bay…, well…, I ride a bus, script talk to strangers and perpetually smile. Full disclosure would be, I tourist guide a 'Hop-on, Hop-off' bus to Marina Bay Sands, Orchard Road, and China Town, in English or Malaysian or Japanese.

And how long have I been doing the streets of Singapore? Far too long! I have given up on finding a debonair Italian gentleman who suffers from a terminal case of spreezatura, you know…, sartorial splendor that looks spontaneous, calculated nonchalance…, or a German Herr in lederhosen who wants to surround me with energy efficient comfort in a boxy, little house in Bonn. I'm sorry. Is my cynicism showing?"

"And no 'ayam kampung', no local chicken, bread and buttered in Singapore, is nonchalant enough or sufficiently renewable energy savvy enough to receive a passing grade?"

"Singaporean men are very intelligent. But they all think like engineers. In fact, most of them are engineers! They like to figure out how things work. If it is not too strenuous, or too dirty, they do like to fix things. But they are worse than useless when it comes to understanding why, for example, a woman will sometimes, cry. Women represent to them, moving mechanisms with too many variables! And they compound that already 'failed' adult response, report card by electing to retreat in silence as a means of managing her anger, her disappointment, her whatever!

Bad example maybe, but you get the idea. Men here have high IQ's but very low EQ's, emotional quotients. If I wanted a functional machine, a robot, I would go back to Japan and buy one. But I want more than that Daddy. I want passion, I want persuasive presence, I want resonance based on mutual respect. Please, can I have just a little of all that in my life Daddy. Please!"

God the young woman was good at creating a diversion, a bridge which allowed even a fulminating fool to save face!

"So, further to the supposedly cynical little you. Nope, your social shirt tail does not need to be tucked in. But you and a struggling doctor have a lot in common. You both are in need of more patients. Which is it though?. Does the word I want end in 'ts' or in 'ce'? Ha, ha!"

The woman who had, moments earlier, dispensed consolation in great, generous gobs, smashed my hand into the chicken sandwich in front of me. This caused the mayo basted pieces of white meat to squirt from between the bread slices and create a white-on-white mess on the table top in front of me.

Shades of Elithia in the Turks and Caicos Islands, I thought. Her, 'White-On-White' pronouncement, the minor masterpiece done in oils, would, even unframed, never be forgotten!

"C'mon, the joke wasn't all that bad! Look what you just did to my 'bird between bread'."

"If your puns don't improve Mr. Mikey, your **pun**ishment might be the forfeiture of flight for any bird, living or dead or between toasted bread, that you believe belongs to your person. And one more thing, your Singapore Santa Clause visit to the orphanage is suspicious at best. When we get out of here and hole up somewhere that is more comfortable, I think that topic deserves further scrutiny."

"I can't eat any more of my road kill so, if you can do without dessert, then we can leave. Choices, always choices. Maybe it is too late to go shopping, so it will have to be the bar, or my room, or your room if we are to allow any more words to come between us."

"The evening is still young and the stores still want your money regardless of their closing hour. We can take the short walk together down the road to your financial ruin right now. Are you going to buy me a nice dress Daddy so that all the nice men at the party on Saturday can have un-nice thoughts about me when they go home?"

The feigned sheepish grin masked the femme fatale lurking just below the surface. The dichotomy was delicious. The desire for her became more, much more than mere want. Lyric was a need. She lived on the breath of others. She left them wanting less for self in exchange for more, much more of her magnificent more.

'Moments' was a retail outlet which specialized in formal evening wear for 'him' and for 'her'. Better than that, rental rates were available on select items in stock.

"The last time I was in here I bought, or was it I just borrowed…, I forget, a dress for my high school graduation. As I recall the Grad was memorable…, good food, good location…, good music…, great gushing 'good- byes' from everyone to everyone…, I was class Valedictorian…, but unfortunately the young man who was to bring symmetry to my presence there was not so good. He did not deliver on expectation.

He and his insecurities have disappeared into the mists of time but thank goodness the store has not. Take the tour and check it out. If you find something worthwhile, let me know. And I will do the same. It's pact time. We have to agree right now that nothing from this store will be worn to our Raffles soiree without partner approval first. OK!"

My goal, in any retail outlet, was always to get what I wanted as quickly as possible and then just as quickly, get out!

I hoped that my Saturday night date felt the same way.

Suit rental was the way to go. No fuss, no muss, and probably no firm fit either. But that did not matter. My choice of mourning weeds to be worn Saturday evening did not matter. They were not important. My evening deeds worn without warning would, however, very much matter!

The victory of one man over another, a victory for vindictiveness over a Versace moment was to be the thing. The only thing! The outfit would never rise above the irrelevant. But the orchestrated plan to eviscerate a man and still leave him standing was the spectacle that would make the evening more than memorable.

"Found you! This is Charles. He is the owner of "Moments' and just look at what he has kept on file since my last visit here as a high school student."

A grinning, white haired man sporting a pencil thin moustache, posted a Polaroid in front of his chest much as a judge might when scoring a figure skating event. Looking more like an ancient Daguerreotype photo, the wrinkled print resembled one in which the iodine, the silver plate and the mercury vapor had long since lost interest in one another. The resulting blur was unkind to both the gangly young girl on display and the 'princess of the prom' dress she was wearing.

No matter. Both players seemed proud as punch! The old man for having the foresight to develop dossiers to ensure future business and Lyric because she alone could clearly see the youthful somebody she had been so many years earlier.

"And you know what? Charles still has that exact same dress, the one in the photo, the turquoise one, the one I wore almost ten years ago. And…, and he told me that with only minor alterations it can be all mine for Saturday night, just like it was before. Isn't that so great! Something old, something new, something borrowed, something blue, and…, and, a silver sixpence in her…, in my shoe."

A traditional rhyme about what a Bride should wear at her wedding to ensure fertility, a fulfilling future with the man of her dreams, with luck and favorable fortune thrown in, for good measure.

A traditional rhyme about the launching of a vessel on the sometimes choppy seas of life, a christened creature of wood and pitch and caulking, the good ship, HMS or USS 'Bride'. But regardless of how ample the beam or how well she had been laid up in dry dock, this maybe new member of the merchant marine fleet would not, could not be granted a permanent berth along my pier anytime soon!

Too much displacement of time and energy needed for a looming Saturday night engagement elsewhere. Too much cargo, precious only in the eyes of the untested captain of the vessel and too much dry dock attention to make even an amateur stab at the creation of a 'Bristol condition' craft that would float without listing to port or starboard.

I was running out of time. My penthouse perch had only two days left under warranty. I needed the shots promised by just one more day of good luck. Telephoto images of some stupid woman sporting a garden hose accessory would fall short of desired lethality.

Lyric would serve well as diversion at the Raffles Hotel but her cost was beginning to exceed her value. I was tiring of the wench. I needed to review my less than logical plan of action. I needed to talk my way through my own inquisition. I wanted to visit more 'what-if' scenarios. I wanted the comfort of me in the company of my thoughts. I needed to be alone.

"So, a done deal then! We pick up our fancy threads any time after three in the afternoon on Saturday. Maybe that's a wrap for today. Any loose ends that cannot wait for tomorrow? No, well, OK, back to the, what's it called, The Wayfarer Inn and…,"

"One last thing at the pharmacy. I need one more thing from the pharmacy. Remember when we met in the lobby of your little 'no tell' motel and I told you that I really had to pee badly…, well that was true but that was not my only problem down under. I sort of need tampons too!"

Lyric looked away from me the way some women would when granting the male listener a period of reflection to mull over the layered ramifications of what had just been said.

The problem was that once I had tired of those in my presence, anything and everything they did or said, regardless of need or nuance, annoyed me. You manipulating bitch, I thought. Monthly visitation of your bloody friend and the Pope and his red army of robed Cardinals would be placated by a rhythm method which always miscalculated the number of days ejaculate bathed sperm remained capable of the zeitgeist of zygote. A worry free fuck replete with a Boston-less cream pie…, my ass!

I was getting old. Talk of plugs as substitutes for pads defined a new generation of women. Only over forties still diapered themselves with a winged response to 'heavy days'.

Toxic shock syndrome, resulting from the loading of one minimouse with a tail immediately after another in the receiver end of a woman's weapon, led invariably to bacterial build up which frequently required rapid, invasive medical intervention.

But the whole topic of female fecundity had become politicized and it was usually relegated to medical journals or to page fifty-seven in popular publications read religiously by women of academic attainment and concomitant attitude such as MS Magazine and Cosmopolitan.

The short walk back to the Wayfarer Inn, with a detour to a pharmacy, was uncomfortable. The normal buzz between us had been replaced by an eerie, palpable silence. Time to marmalade the moment with pointed praise, I thought.

"I must say that I am in awe of anyone who masters a language that is not predicated on the Latin alphabet. Mandarin, Cambodian, Vietnamese, any Asian language that was not influenced by European colonization. That list would, of course, include Japanese.

You have got about five minutes before the doors of the Wayfarer Inn beckon. Give me an abbreviated history of how you mastered the language of the land of lotus blossoms and of the rising sun."

"Not nearly as great an accomplishment as an outsider like you might think. A first cousin of mine was, no, is in the business of shrimp farming in Kalimantan. His only client is his brother-in-law who lives with his family in Japan. He owns a huge cannery operation in Hamamatsu which is about seventy miles south of Tokyo.

And Tokyo alone, never mind the rest of Japan, would be able to devour more seafood than two Kalimantans could ever produce.

Anyway, I was there, living with and working for my extended family for about five years. I needed to get away from Singapore for a while…, and, and Hamamatsu was just what the doctor ordered. Listen, if you want to be fed regularly, you learn the language of survival pretty fast."

"But what about the music of the language. The intonations, the accents, maybe even iambic pentameter, as in English…, maybe the role of the haiku in every day speech. Where does any sense of 'Lyric' fit into the language lines that take their cue from the treble clef?"

"I get your comment about 'Lyric' in the language but your romantic take on talking every day to someone about mundane topics such as, pass the bread, my clothes need to be cleaned, when is the next bus into town, is misplaced. A working vocabulary of about two hundred words, maybe a few more, was all that was ever needed.

Anyway, I don't want to talk any more about something that was a part of my life so many…, too many years ago. I paid my debt. Sackcloth in the desert and all of that. I was chastened for long enough!"

The woman didn't want to talk any further and I didn't want to listen, no matter how grievous the tale.

"OK. Fair enough. This is where we must call it a day then. I have obligations which have to be met, boring stuff really, details which cannot be put off until tomorrow. Tomorrow will be too late. Anyway, the page in my diary called, 'Tomorrow', is already over booked.

So, how about we meet tomorrow evening at about six o'clock, here, in the lobby. If not convenient, then leave a note with the front desk clerk. A telephone number will do. I won't be using the room in the hotel tonight but feel free to stay in the one registered in your name. Use this cash for any room service amenities you might need."

I shoved two hundred dollars, in twenties, at Lyric's solar plexus causing her limp hand to clamp shut on the unexpected assault and then I briskly walked away.

I distinctly heard the words of the surprised woman, which were flung at me like pebbles at a passing car. Anger, disappointment, embarrassment and resignation were in the slurry which cradled the caustic, grape-shot, message.

"Are you sure that you were not born in Singapore!"

* * *

Blending into becoming background to the background, remaining silently at the ready for a quarry that would forever be oblivious to any foreign presence, fit the description most anesthetists had of their role in the OR. They spoke of prolonged periods of boredom interrupted only infrequently by short spurts of madcap mayhem caused by the 'surprise' of uncooperative or under-medicated patients.

Their exclusive responsibility was to secure and sustain complete patient compliance via sedation. My role, albeit with remote, ambulatory patients numbering two, was to shoot and secure visual proof of their lead up to a 'grand mal seizure'. Bad behavior, either as individuals or preferably in tryst-like tandem, would be the bond that we would share. Two as perpetrators in private and one as purveyor to the world. My mission would not be to mollify or mediate but to malevolently manage the role of malignant messenger.

I hated being well prepared. Rested…, ready with ruck-sac filled actual need and whimsy from 'The Reel Fun House'…, rid of an agenda laden interloper with too many names who was just too squeaky clean to be real…, a blank slate defining the day with no detours delineated. I hated the smugness that seeped into the pores of the self-styled superior. Positional power never sufficiently buttressed one against the vagaries of a capricious universe.

Former bar buddies probably had it right. 'Shit happens when your slinky stops on the stairs'…, when sloppiness of thought and action allows the slipshod and slovenly to substitute for detailed, almost demented attention to detail. Then 'Harm's Way' is the name of the road that is taken.

The results of the photo shoot of the previous day had been placed on the floor by the curtain at the sliding balcony doors. Nikon never missed. The stills were 'Sports Illustrated' clear and candid. The contorted face of the 'athletic' woman was a study in effort besting adversity.

Her clothed body however, attached as it was, to a piece of equipment for which there was no apparent purpose, seemed diminished and discordant relative to the pure, Olympian quest captured by her smooth, oval face. Leorah seemed more than game to play her part in a pageant of physical prowess, but less than certain of the exact role she was expected to fulfill.

The mirror in the hallway of my penthouse perch told me that I would have made for a less than stellar leader of the teenage mutant ninja turtles. My rigid, 'Leonardo' mask had been cut off below the nostrils to allow for uninterrupted breathing, but to suggest that a green, 'scaly monster' was staring back at me from the wall would still have been apt.

My, made for dish washing rubber gloves were too small and, as a result, the tips of my fingers and the extremities of my ten, mini prophylaxes never met. Consequently, I appeared to have grown a full complement of loose hanging claws. And my camouflage colored rain cape, when draped over my shoulders, suggested that I had morphed into a shadowy, solitary, misanthropic Hunchback of Notre Dame. Perfect, I thought, for the moments of clandestine, 'Baden Powell' mischief I hoped to catalogue.

My quarry would be able to look but not have the capacity to see. Hunting white-tailed deer came to mind…, hunting the wary animal from a tree stand. The animal rarely looked up. No danger ever descended from the sky, but there was every reason to maintain a constant, 360 degree surveillance of the surroundings at ground level.

The two denizens of the aerial Garden of Eden, the children of nature domiciled one playing field away from me, were very much like their cloven cousins in the forest. They were able to look but all they were capable of seeing was the splendid isolation afforded those of superior means.

Hundreds of thousands, maybe more like millions, spent on a few thousand square feet encased in a bricks and mortar structure which was not aging well. That was Admiralty Way. Nesting birds had aided and abetted the deterioration of the exterior façade. An alarming number of bricks had already succumbed to gravitational persuasion.

Nothing was done about the decay because ground dwellers, those who chanced to look up, never chose to see what was actually there, or not there! The cloud dwellers in the adjacent building, the one I occupied, would have done little more than look smugly, from behind their drawn curtains, at the misfortune of their neighbors. An 'us and them' mentality would have prevailed. And the top drawer folks who occupied superior, senior positions within the Admiralty, rarely ventured beyond the protective glass to the balcony outside without having first fortified themselves with a premium, forty percent proof, libation which altered their 'Dick and Jane' book of 'Look and See' to include only the congratulatory.

Can't fix it if you don't know it's broke!

I looked once again at the battery of photographic equipment positioned in front of me. I checked that the Nikon was 'on', that the camera and telephoto lens were secure, that the spotting scope tripod was stable and, with a slight tap from my foot, that the sliding glass door was only slightly ajar.

I did everything, everything that is, except to notice that one of the main thespians in the hoped for theatre of the absurd production had already taken the stage!

Like a light weight boxer with no knock-outs and fewer wins than losses, the figure caught in the camera lens shadow boxed her way in and out of the frame as though the pugilistic contest had already begun. I already had more shots of Leorah than I needed. Even one of her alone as her imagined self, was one too many.

Her wardrobe of the previous day, gray sweat pants and matching sweat shirt top, had been replaced. My subject was no longer saddled by the black, strap-on dildo and its attendant, dangling cinches. In their stead, my eyes were treated to a svelte, well contoured woman who created a smooth statement which left no participles dangling.

Leorah had chosen a sort of neck to lower leg jump suit as her fashion statement. The form-fit of the garment left not just little, but nothing, to the imagination. Both the front and back of the costume contained a pattern which vaguely resembled a stone wall or the markings on the front and back of a turtle's shell. An oversized, oval crotch opening was punctured and punctuated by a proportionate, seemingly erect appendage which resembled a tri-colored, single-stick, popsicle. It had to have been anchored in place either by a twist in the leotard-like material or perhaps the other end of the hose had been modified and inserted in the vagina or the anus or both. Creative construction, I thought, for connubial bliss with mutual gratification guaranteed!

One photo shot, maybe two, I thought, would suffice of Leorah's current incarnation as a naughty, Mardi-Gras celebrant.

I was hoping, no, I was praying, that my assessment of the Lady from the fertile crescent of the Nile was accurate. She was not the type to practice for days on end for an event best played out spontaneously. Hers was a world of action, not of simulation, not of second guessing. Dressed as she was, this had to be her warm up to the main event.

Almost as a cued response to my misgivings, a figure appeared briefly behind the pirouetting princess and, just as quickly, disappeared. The apparition seemed to be dressed in some sort of brown outfit with white trim. Was my imagination willing the second player onto the stage or was my hoped for reality, truly present and ready to play.

Only a second was needed for a fat man in a bunny suit to reappear. Only a second was needed for me to stiffen in anticipation of the long-shot, the long-hoped for event. Only a second was needed for everything to come to a crashing halt!

I was no longer in Singapore. I was no longer spying on a couple in a penthouse atop the Admiralty Way. I was a kid in Montreal who was about to have his tonsils removed. I was standing in front of the Reddy Memorial Hospital ready to check in to have my tonsils removed. Apart from my Mother, the only other 'person' close by was a gray, pigeon blessed, full sized statue of an angel. I never knew which one of God's emissaries it was, probably one with a penchant for children, but that did not matter.

What mattered was the creature had wings. Partially spread, they extended from behind the knees of the figure to well above the back of its head. They were bigger than I was! They poked out of the creature's back causing what I perceived to be a malformation, a crippling of the spine. What I saw was the greatest fear inducing malevolence of my formative years. An all seeing God who used flying people to spy on and then punish those who sinned. Traumatized by the event, my conditioned response to angels, or more precisely their beating wings, was akin to what I imagined villagers in Viet-Nam experienced when death delivering Huey helicopters insinuated their throbbing, heart-beat presence into the very fabric of family and feudal tradition.

Hatred and anger, born of fear, was transferred to all flying creatures in God's kingdom.

A Huey helicopter had materialized out of nowhere. A Huey helicopter which dispensed death and destruction, a Huey helicopter with deafening deliberateness, blocked my view of the one-time, and one-time only, theatrical event of the season..., the sole reason for there being a Singapore for me!

As the flying thing landed beside the spotting scope, my left hand grabbed at its back and squeezed hard. The whirring noise was quelled but the struggle for supremacy, or maybe it was just survival, continued. Further noise and any visual distraction denoting the unusual were not to be, could not be, tolerated.

With a rapid flick of my hand, the bird's head and neck were thrust into my mouth. The face mask of Leonardo did not move. The upper and middle sections of it had been firmly affixed to my face by large, commercial elastics. With just one, almost motionless, snap of my jaw, the bird's skull was crushed between my upper and lower molars. The hollow bones of birds, when they are reduced to shards, sound very much like finger joints when they are pulled and popped by massage motivated hands. I did not release my grip on the bird until its involuntary muscle spasms ceased.

I do not remember opening my mouth to release the dead bird. My complete attention was focused on the couple caught in the spotter's scope. My thumb pressed the remote shutter button as though in synch with a metronome which was set at a very slow speed.

The bird simply fell from my mouth in a slurry of spit and blood. My mouth had remained open. My yawning mouth allowed for the complete, involuntary discharge of the remnants of the dead creature.

When crows were killed close to the out-buildings that separated the farm house from the fields, one of them was usually pinned to a post and its breast feathers were ripped out exposing a swatch of vulnerable, grayish-pink flesh. The scene was viewed by the survivors of the shooting who sought refuge in a tree about a half mile away. Not one of them ventured anywhere near the scene of the death-trap for the remainder of the harvest season. Crows have excellent eye sight. Crows are smart birds.

No need though for similar, graphic, 'no-go' signs for the relatives of pigeons. Doves are decidedly delicate, somewhat dumb, and incapable of dominant, aggressive behavior by their very nature.

The photo shoot could not have been better choreographed had I created it myself. Shots of 'doggy-style' penetration, missionary maneuvers, stand up comedic stances with Councilor Whitehead on top, on the bottom, on his 'husband's' lap, were easy. They were easy to capture because once the old man clambered into a new position, his body refused to quickly contort into the requested pose. Leorah got bored and both of them showed signs of physical irritation caused by a chronic lack of sufficient lube. Shooting clean stills of a subject suffering from sciatica was a cinch.

Whitehead deserved the special merit award for his credible portrayal of a somewhat obese rabbit. A hair clip holding large, floppy rabbit ears, a vest of simulated white fur that partially covered his chest and a cotton tail attached to the zippered back flap of oversized diapers created an image which was tabloid expose' perfect. Excessive 'salt and pepper' body hair, front and back, rolls of loose fat found more often on a fresh cadaver, and a demeanor which was fumblingly compliant and embarrassingly receptive made for an amateur hour which was, at times, difficult to watch.

I had what I needed. The four or five shots left on the roll of film would be unnecessary.

But waste not, want not, my mother always…,

Something was wrong. The bird was dead. There were no others. Something was wrong. I could smell it. My legs…, something was hovering over my legs. Nothing had alighted on them. There was no pressure being exerted on them. But something uninvited was there.

It took every ounce of self-control that I possessed to stifle my reaction to the stinging bite I received. It seemed to penetrate my clothing and shoot down the length of my leg to my toes like an errant electrical charge from an exposed wire. A muffled grunt masking my promise of reciprocity. I shut my mouth and bit down hard on my lower lip. An errant feather lodged itself between the jaws of the work-table vice my mouth had created. My stomach heaved and I retched audibly. Sufficient drool fell from the corner of my mouth to rid it of the gray plumage and a remaining remnant of bloodied bone.

I was pinned down and defenseless. I could not move, I could not turn to confront my assailant. I flexed my legs tightly around the dog-sized body that had seized me. Slowly and carefully I pushed myself and my 'captive-captor' back and away from the photographic equipment…, it had to be protected at all costs…, to the sliding door which was now ajar.

As I inched myself and my monster back through the doorway, the heavy breathing of the intruder replaced the frenzied biting as causation for my clenched fists.

I turned and faced my attacker. Goodwin…, Goodie…, Lyric…, whoever she thought she was, sat, puzzled, looking straight at me, but straight past me!. She appeared to have been almost wearing the binoculars in the sockets of her eyes like a true race track aficionado. Her lowered jeans and ripped panties had been twisted into a ball just above her knees. The magnified view she had had of The Admiralty penthouse had been sufficient to propel her into a pre-orgasmic flight of self-gratification.

Some innocuous move by me had interrupted her singular focus which had been to keep the two ponies that were about to enter the home stretch in binocular view. That had occupied her right hand. Her left hand, it seemed, had been burdened with the task of bridging the visual and the visceral. Smell suggested that it had been buried deeply in her crotch.

That which was repetitive, almost repulsive, to me, was apparently riveting and raunchy for my uninvited room-mate. The bromide about one man, his meat, and his poison came to mind.

My ass hurt, having been bitten, and bitten hard, just above the balls. It really hurt! The pain was made worse knowing that my cover had probably been blown with the front desk person in the lobby down stairs..., that the mating ritual of the denizens of Admiralty Way had probably been truncated..., and that Whitehead, alerted to the breach in security, had already contacted his unifrmed people and they would ensure the destruction of the undeveloped film.

I was forced to acknowledge that my slinky had got stuck on the stairs. And, as insult was to injury, I knew that, probably more sooner than later, I would also have to eat the details, raw, of Lyric's version of her triumph over my abrupt abandonment of her the previous afternoon.

For the first time in my life I wanted to fuck someone just because I knew how to make it hurt.

Lyric had seemed startled by my 'pop-up' presence beside her at the end of our advance to the rear. She had immediately dropped the binoculars on the carpeted floor and had thrown her arms around my neck. She had lunged at my face and started to kiss at my bottom lip like a hungry bird at a feeder. More, it seemed as though she was attempting to extinguish the remnants of camp fire embers that smoldered at the bottom of Leonardo's chin with a barrage of staccato, woodpecker-like, jabs.

Quickly tiring of her one-sided attempt at animalized acknowledgment, she had resumed wording her way through the teleprompter text which seemingly appeared on the 3-D screen of the binoculars. Peeping through a slight separation in the sheer, floor to ceiling curtains, Lyric sounded like she was trying to keep pace with the sporting event happening in real time across the way at the Admiralty. Her monologue, staccato-like and energetic in delivery, was ironically in synch not only with the choreographed clash of the two connubial cartoon characters but with the curtained audience of two as well.

"What's the matter with you, anyway! Are you stupid! Don't you know anything? Play with me..., fuck me, if you even know how..., don't just stand there like a sore, sad ass..., do something you freaky, old, fuck, do anything Goddam-it, pretend if you have to..., but c'mon..., just do something...,"

Twenty something females did not stay twenty something females nearly long enough. Socially, some might have been a little rough around the edges, but their taste, their warm, wet inner recesses were, for the persistent who ventured past their personal hygiene shortfalls, decidedly delicious. That was Ms. Goodwin Leaf!

Her pungent wall of dried urine quickly gave way to the rutted salt lick so savored by satyrs and barn-yard studs alike.

Tongue, teamed up with two, rubber rigid fingers, trained on clitoris, and the orifice of vagina and of ass, in that order, and the simulated act of sexual intercourse, replete with the orgasm of one, was completed in better than average, Masters and Johnson, stop-watch time.

Our merging was a strange interlude of intimate indifference. A bitter dispeller of the dream, of the desire, that our probing bodies were supposed to fulfill! Too much personal history not willingly shared, I thought laconically.

"Pull yourself together and wait for me at the door."

I could not think of even one word to share with the spent waif beside me that was kind or congratulatory or even conciliatory. In that regard we were in accord.

"Let's save a lot of bullshit talk, shall we. Mr. Joseph, the pimp with the clothes of many colors, the poor excuse for a man who provided your spy perch, is a long-time friend of my family. He is, he was a personal friend of mine too. And so was Mr. Whitehead if you must know. Both are faithful followers…, both were unfaithful lovers…, No! Forget that I said that…, both are generous contributors to the Sisters of Mercy Orphanage…, generous contributors in more ways than one. Money yes, from their own pockets, sometimes…, but also from protecting…, let's call it, the business model of the Orphanage, the commodity, if you like, that keeps that place of God in business.

I have known them for a long time and I thoroughly detest both of them. Bloody hell, I hate both of them. Both of them care nothing for the people in pain, or their progeny, who get fucked over by fate. They rob, rape and pillage like the Philistines in the Old Testament. Both of them are self-centered pigs. Their back feet should be cloven, just like pigs, just like the Devil himself. Unfortunately for some, of which I am one, dealing with those two fallen angels from Hades has been, too often, the only game in town."

Doors opened only to expose more doors that were shut. The water around me was getting too deep and too treacherous. Who was doing what with whom? Who was doing what to whom? Who had history with whom? Was the Orphanage business model Lyric alluded to really predicated on the 'relocation' of infants and children?

Forget the naive notion of babies in bassinettes, and the Moses in the bull-rushes fantasy. This was not good fortune following a few unfortunates. This was child acquisition and distribution on an industrial level. This was societal in scope. This made for multiple, multi-millionaires. This was a slice of perversity worth dying for. This was a slice of perversity deserving of death.

Who else sought to profit from my peevish and protracted game of character assassination! Deceit, it seemed, was the road most travelled by Mr. Whitehead with at least one too many victims, apart from me.

I decided, as I smashed the palm of my hand into the closing elevator door, that my descent from the penthouse to the parking garage would not be allowed to become a metaphor for anything defeatist, Lyric's nasty rumination notwithstanding. The flags of friend and foe had faded into a fog but the battle lines were still clearly drawn. Just soldier on and then get the fuck off this sanctimonious island of fakery as quickly as possible I thought, with a shutter!

I had known from the outset how to present Mr. Whitehead with the pen and paper proof of paternity. Now, like a skilled butcher who could debone a piece of meat with his eyes shut, I knew exactly how to de-present him with that same, deft, twist of the knife. And Lyric would act as the blade.

Chapter 27

Helen Hayes, the doyenne of American theatre, was quoted as saying that the difference between amateur and professional people who spoke in public was that the latter group had learned how to make the butterflies in their stomachs fly in formation.

Made trite by too many self-help books, the idea of occupying space where others feared to tread was, however, singularly satisfying.

Take an emotion which carries a negative connotation, one which is universally held, like fear, and fashion from it the fuel needed to drive what is done in front of others and surprising heights can be reached. The poisoned meat and the meat from poison story all over again, but with a vengeance.

The 'Melmac' motel had been vacated, as had been the Wayfarer Inn. A complimentary room at Raffles had been proffered in advance recognition of the contracted contribution to the Saturday night 'Pig-roast'. Check out was all that stood between me and the Changi Terminal tarmac.

The fit of my suit was fine. Burgundy red, Lucchese cowboy boots said that my place of origin was Butte, Montana and that a close relative was the Marlboro Man. Strutting on an elevated stage, one almost at audience eye level would be perfect. The boots possessed proven comfort for the wearer and their connotation for callous American gunplay on the silver-screen, would prompt contempt among the pseudo sophisticated Singaporean set in the audience. I had factored their hostility into the rhythm and rhyme of my ancient mariner recitation.

The eulogies which preceded my own, were read from notes scribbled on loose-leaf paper by people who did not want to be present at the event, let alone at the lectern. Some were too tipsy to put two, coherent sentences together and others, like one of the Wong partners, was so nervous that he allowed his precious, penned notes to escape from his trembling hands. They fluttered down like ticker tape and covered most of the floor around him.

The result was that, once collected but not collated, the audience was treated to pages three and four being rattled off twice. The speaker was completely oblivious to the public presentation 'murder most foul' which he had committed. Safe refuge at his assigned seat, with a double of something in a glass, something expensive, was all that mattered.

All read their less than practiced pieces in monotone voices that made train schedule delays, announced over the station PA system, sound exciting.

Not much of a comment on the quality of the people chosen by Whitehead to fill the crowd scenes in his life. Better though, than the other element that was present, namely those who wished him to be deader than dead, I thought sardonically.

Death by dead drop of documents had been arranged. A plain, letter sized envelope had made its way to the front desk with instructions to the person in charge to ensure its delivery to Mr. Whitehead.

The Councilor had received the single page note, had read it amidst the din caused by the drivel of the indifferent at his table, had slowly refolded and returned the sheet to the envelope and, with a face devoid of expression, had slid it slowly into the inside breast pocket of his suit jacket.

From my vantage point across the room, I had insisted on the distant location even though it had necessitated a last minute change in the seating arrangement of more than a few invitees, it appeared that the man was no longer in the room with the rest of the revelers. He was lost in the passport jargon of the foreign territory which Geoffrey now occupied. Paternity Index 60741, Alleged Father, 99.998%, Probability of Paternity..., was as authoritative as the Proctor and Gamble claim that their Ivory Snow soap was 99 and 44, 100 percent pure.

The missive, from the mischievous, medical minds of Dr. Rajawane's associates in Bali, was as compelling as the face of Marilyn Chambers, a model turned actress who, along with a rented child, appeared on the front panel of every box of Ivory Snow soap as the symbol of selfless, blessed motherhood.

The box cover that sold the soap carried the same paper thin, misrepresentation of reality as did the Probability of Paternity proof statement. The paper in the pocket of Mr. Whitehead was as fraudulent as was Marilyn Chambers in the role of loving mother.

In reality, she had starred in the infamous porno pic, 'Behind The Green Door'. She resembled the real thing, the bona fide movie star, Cybil Shepherd, but she was merely a look alike. She received top billing in the porno release but she never had to demonstrate any real acting ability. She exposed herself to a leering, rapt audience but she was never required to prove her worth. Her body did all of the talking. She did not have a speaking part in the film.

She, like the bogus document, gained notoriety just by showing up.

A barbed wire fence had just been erected between the isolated man at the party and Geoffrey. He was saying a final good-bye to the Geoffrey who had never ever been his. The boy was walking away from him. He was disappearing into a heavy mist and he was not looking back.

Lyric had promised to retrieve the letter, without the old man being cognizant of, or in compliance with the loss, prior to the conclusion of the event and return it, intact, to me. I did not bother asking any questions that would have hinted at her 'handle' on the 'how'.

Like death on the field of battle, the first letter, the first rifle shot, was to bring the enemy down. A chest shot, one to the heart if possible..., it was meant to immobilize. The second shot was to be the death blow. It was always delivered to the back of the head. The 'coup de grace', as the French would say.

The photos, all four of them, featuring Ralphie Rabbit and Tootsie Turtle on maneuvers, were to be dispatched when the man of the hour ordered his first drink subsequent to my ascension to the speaker's throne.

I became aware of the fact that the room had fallen quiet, deathly quiet. Sister Georgina was staring silently in my direction from her perch at the lectern. So too, was everyone else in the room. Lyric was tugging desperately at my sleeve. Her face was a study in anger, distain and embarrassment. Hardly the face fronting a person that one would ever wish to rely upon when comfort, consideration, and the closing of ranks were needed most. I reached for the bag beside my chair.

The walk from the corner table to center stage was not so much an imitation of the measured march of a soldier in a funeral cortege as it was the deliberateness associated with the trooping of the colors. The placement of an oversized hour glass on top of the lectern, thanks to 'The Reel Fun House', was done in complete, self-absorbed silence.

So too was the fitting and forefinger adjustment of the Buddy Holly, horn rimmed glasses on the bridge of my nose. Every minute on the stage improved the chances that my real identity would assault the senses of the hapless loser Whitehead or, more likely, his consort, the hydra like Ibu-Ms. Lilith-Danyea-Leorah. The wrath of neither player could be contained nor quashed in the fish bowl that Raffles had become. 'Exit stage left', would have been my only option!

The stroll back toward the far end of the stage, gave everyone a chance to size up the next mouth which, they thought, was about to mumble more meaningless memories of the corpulent lawyer in their midst. I had no need for the microphone which was fixed to the side of the lectern, the one most of my predecessors had tried to hide behind.

Beyond the butterflies, Helen Hayes had strung together other pearls of wisdom for those who viewed words, spoken in public, as weapons. 'Speak from the diaphragm, not from the throat', was one such added encyclical sent by the first female Pope of public speaking. Armed with that advice, any venue, save that the size of St. Peter's Square, became the sole domain of the presenter.

"Of course, everyone will recognize what has just been placed on the lectern. Some call it an egg timer. Some call it an hour glass. Regardless of the moniker that is chosen, we can all agree that it is a reliable, albeit somewhat cumbersome, instrument to measure the passage of time.

Ah yes…,time…, time alone, time spent with others, time focused on professional pursuits, time devoted to family or to leisure, time…, time, for all of us, is a finite commodity.

Everyone in this room has been allocated a specific amount of time. It is a precious gift that should never be squandered nor taken for granted. Time well spent must be a priority for all thinking people.

Some do spend their time wisely, but sadly, some do not.

Some devote their time to becoming rich, wealth expressed in worldly goods, yes, but others focus on the wealth that is realized through amassing treasure troves of life-time, magical moments, moments that are then securely locked away in permanent, personal memory vaults.

Sadly, others waste their time and accomplish neither. We all know too many people in that category. No money on deposit and no memories worth recounting. Theirs are lives of quiet desperation. Subsistence is a constant in their lives and surmounting it, an impossible dream.

But enough about those in that predicament. People are the architects of the mansions or of the mole hovels they inhabit.

Back to those who are made of the stuff that matters. Back to the man of the hour.

What some of us have done during our preparatory past to enhance the 'precious-present', the precious present, and what those same few are doing now to ensure the continuance of that 'precious-present', is the stuff of this tribute.

We are gathered here this evening, in this fine hotel, to honor one of those special, 'precious-present' people. He is a man of the law, he is a man of conspicuous compassion, he is a pillar of Singaporean society, he is a man for all seasons, he is our friend and fellow time traveller, he is a truly, gentle, man. He is our very own, Mr. Whitehead!

A toast then, ladies and gentlemen, to Mr. Whitehead."

Audiences were like kids in a kindergarten. When addressing them one had to appeal to the lowest common denominator of intellect if one hoped for understanding and compliance. If one wished to sustain their attention, one had to invent 'busy work' as well.

Eye hand coordination exercises starting with scanning fellow table dwellers, smiling on cue, lifting one's glass to one's mouth, swallowing whatever was tipped into it and returning the glass to a cluttered table without spilling or breaking anything, played perfectly to audience intellectual and physiological shortfall.

"So, back to the hour glass. It denotes the passage of time, as I just said, but tonight it also serves as a governor of my performance. Think of it as a policeman assigned to keep me honest and true to my mandate. To wit, the celebration of the life and the accomplishments of our friend and colleague, Mr. Whitehead.

This contraption made of wood, glass and sand, an Egyptian invention in all likelihood, has provided me with five minutes of measured time.

You, ladies and gentlemen, will decide what my actual time allotment this evening will be. If I become boring, or as some might think, am already boring…, then five minutes will be my full time allotment. If, however, you want more of what I have to say concerning Mr. Whitehead, vote, as did the ancient Romans in their Coliseum, with a 'thumbs-up' affirmation. I will strive to keep the lions of lassitude at bay!

My name is Cameron. Just Cameron for this evening, thank you very much. I am an Investment Advisor by trade and my association with Mr. Whitehead is via mutual friends who tread the narrow path which is bound by fear of financial failure on one side and the contagion of greed on the other.

To the question, where am I from, I would answer, the other side of your tracks.

To the further question, where exactly is that, I would respond, somewhere in another century."

Say something fast enough, with a straight face, and most people will miss it. Say anything fast enough and follow it immediately with a question aimed at them collectively and all people miss it.

"I have a question for all of you. What do you call one hundred lawyers at the bottom of the South China Sea?

The answer is…, a good start!

What do you call one hundred lawyers at the bottom of the South China Sea…, a good start!

Now some find humor in that comment. But think about it for a moment. What would we, as civilized people, do without practicing members of that profession?

People skilled in the law of the land. People like Mr. Whitehead. How would law and order prevail, how would property rights be regulated, how would personal rights and responsibilities be upheld, how would the good citizenship rules and regulations of large corporations be applied and maintained? Rule of Law. Say it out loud. Rule of Law!

Some investigators in the field of sociology have devoted much time and research to what they term, 'The Veneer Theory'. Has anyone ever heard of The Veneer Theory? No! Well, no matter. You are not alone.

The Veneer Theory holds that people are only positive and polite, compassionate and capable of thinking beyond the pettiness of mere self-interest on a very superficial level. They only follow the rules of society out of fear of what will befall them if they do not. According to the Theory, people are by nature predisposed to selfishness and evil.

Please, do not take my word for it. I am actually paraphrasing the words of St. Augustine. Ask Sister Georgina if you doubt me. St. Augustine was of the opinion that each of us…, all of us…, from birth, are vessels of original sin. And, of course, as such, we are all in need of redemption. Again, speak to Sister Georgina!

And redemption, relative to temporal law at least, is best mediated on our behalf by members of the legal profession. I don't wish to suggest that Mr. Whitehead deserves to be addressed as Saint Mr. Whitehead, but he is a man made of the right stuff. And his 'right stuff' is the reason we are here to honor him this evening.

A toast once again…, to Mr. Whitehead.

Future archaeological digs which will uncover the remnants of our empire thousands of years from now, thousands of years after our demise, will spark wonderment in those future sifters of sand who are fortunate enough to unearth the records of our moments in the Sun. The complexity of our society, the recorded checks and balances of family, of community, of nation, of world citizenship will be decoded and the magical matrix of our enterprise will create wonderment and awe in the eyes of those future denizens of the Earth.

And how will this be made possible? Simple. The evidence which will be unearthed, the proof of our proper place among the societies which achieved greatness, will have been compiled and made safe from rot for centuries by generations of dedicated legal professionals of which Mr. Whitehead is one.

Don't toast the man again. I don't want all this adulation to go to his head. Also, I don't want too much of the bubbly to go to his head either. He has to respond to all of this attention later on this evening.

Let's not talk of time and its passage nor of archaeological digs any further. Let's focus instead on something really interesting. Let's talk about the great story teller of ancient Greece, Aesop. Lets talk about his tale of the tortoise and the hare. That story reveals everything we need to know about our multi-faceted man of the hour.

Oh, oh. My time is up! May I beg your indulgence and request another five minutes? I promise more toasts…, and even more refills of your glasses."

I was expecting something, anything from the pockets of people who, I knew, had to be out there in the audience somewhere. From the pockets of people in attendance who would have been entertained by a certain erudition, by jabs of irreverence, even by the jocular irrelevant.

But I was wrong. Silence, silence like that which had preceded my commencement oration, an eerie silence, seemed to have descended over the audience like a pall. With a certain gallows humor, I thought the dead zone I had unwittingly created to be almost poetic. The sounds of silence, Paul Simon notwithstanding, had formed parentheses around my entire performance.

Not even a penny dropped. It would have been a welcome diversion. Anything to break the uncomfortable pause that had people looking around at those seated at other tables to get some sense of what to do next. Our moments in the mortuary were broken by the thin, raspy voice of one person. It was the voice of the one individual in the room I would have counted on least to rise to the occasion.

"Dear friends, I am just as perplexed by this man from the other side of our tracks, from another century, as he puts it, as you are. Maybe he is an ambassador for the territory where the veneer theory prevails. I personally think, based on his conduct in the precious present, that he is more than just an Investment Advisor.

He has all the markings of a man well steeped in criminal law. Maybe that is where we have met. In court. He sounds like most prosecutors, most prosecutors who possess, who project, attitude. The best kind of legal eagle, as my American friends would say, to have in your corner. He reminds me, a little bit, of myself when I was younger, much younger. There is a time in life when a fire in the belly is as common as a waist line that is less than thirty-two inches in girth. There is a time when people and personal position and places of importance are sacrosanct…, a time when God is in his Heaven and all is right with the world. I think that is the expression…, but no matter, the Lord giveth and the Lord taketh away…, blessed be the name of the Lord…,

I vote to give my learned colleague, the honorable counselor, sufficient time to present his case and complete a compelling summary. Subsequent to it, we, as the jury, will be better equipped to render a verdict regarding the man's performance. Was he able to successfully pass the threshold of reasonable doubt? We shall see. Please, carry on my good fellow."

As Mr. Whitehead slowly resumed his seat, the room filled with the muffled noise of chair legs being pushed away from tables followed seconds later by exuberant, resounding applause.

Was the standing ovation a response to his accurate synopsis of my introduction, was it because of the largesse implied in the benediction directed at a fellow barrister, one who possessed the professional traits he valued so highly, or was it that the man simply possessed more power and influence among Singaporean blue-bloods than I had ever given him credit for. Had I underestimated the man? Was I guilty of the same error in judgment again! Had he known my identity from the out-set. Was he merely giving me enough rope to hang myself!

My disguise actually seemed to have worked. At least I had not been shouted off the stage. But the distain in my voice had dampened my delivery. The coach in my head told me to lighten up, pace myself better during round two, no early knockout was likely, and that winning on rounds would, in all likelihood, decide the contest.

"Thank you very much Mr. Whitehead for those very kind words. I shall attempt, Sir, to live up to your expectation and be vindicated by something more than a 'hung jury' decision. I am confident that Justice will prevail!

As promised, there will be more toasts and more sipping to savor select moments. And Aesop's anthropomorphic, a real mouthful of syllables to suggest animals that act like people, story of domination and defeat to wit, the race between the tortoise and the hare, will be skewered, sliced and diced and deciphered. It will serve as a moving, no pun intended, metaphor for the not insignificant achievements of the bold and beloved and sometimes bashful barrister who is seated among us this evening.

Bear with me though as this ugly old guy from antiquity would not have been my first choice as relevant story teller. In fact, I was asked, by a select few who are close to Mr. Whitehead, a close few who are to remain nameless, to build the rabbit and the reptile story into the tribute tonight because the tale was a favorite of the man from Admiralty Way during his early childhood years."

"Whoever told you that? I shall have to get my memoirs published soon, just to set the record straight. Ha Ha!"

The man turned toward the audience in anticipation of an affirmation of his 'beau mots'. He was not disappointed.

Good, I thought. I was being afforded to opportunity to delve into the story and deliver some of the 'puffed pastry' analogies that would please the audience and poison the man who would soon be in possession of the four glossy shots of his impropriety.

"My lips are sealed regarding my information sources. That's the journalist in me talking. Without them, how could I ever hope to be awarded the Pulitzer Prize for investigative journalism sometime in the future? Fear not! Your favorite bed time story is safe with us. Not one of the hundred or so guests assembled here this evening will tell anyone. Trust me on that count my good sir. Our collective lips are sealed.

So, let's look more closely at the story that helped to shape the young Master Whitehead. I believe it is common knowledge that the moralizer of old, used animals to illustrate human strengths and weaknesses so as to not upset the people who were in power at the time. Enlightened self-interest you might say. No sense risking life and limb just to entertain and inform. No one is forever safe from the vagaries of a reigning court.

Some of you might have heard of, or even read the novel, 'Animal Farm' by George Orwell. Another great animal story to be sure. It is a shrewd tale concerning the tragedy of modern day totalitarianism. Think about it. Its lineage can be traced all the way back to the simple stories of Aesop.

Why this abbreviated lecture about animals replacing people in trying or testing circumstances…, because what 'is', more often than not, is predicated on what 'was'.

Our Mr. Whitehead made the bottom ninety-nine percent of his graduating class possible…, Even as a student, he was a paragon of studiousness and seriousness of intent.

When proper attention is placed on the planting of a tree, the eventual, over- arching reach of its boughs is assured. What is planted and then nurtured, bears fruit long after the initial planting is completed.

I am sure that everyone gathered here this evening has a word that they feel best describes Mr. Whitehead. Please, please do not shout any of those epithets out loud. Remember, this is a family oriented gathering!

Just add, if you will, a new word to the lexicon of favorites your currently possess. And that new word would be TREE!

So, the race is on. The race between the tortoise and the hare. There was, of course, a winner and there was a loser. Question! From whose point of view was the story told?

That is not a trick question. The answer is…, from the perspective of the winner. Whose positive personal traits were mentioned most? Whose negative characteristics defined them in the tale?

Whether interpersonal or international, the recorded history of conflict in the world has always been the prerogative of the victor.

Enter Mr. Whitehead. This gentleman is most definitely a man of victory. Graduated summa cum laude from law school, a partner in the prestigious Law Firm of Wong, Whitehead and Wong, a 'go-to' man of action in the larger community, a man whose council is sought often when cool, collectedness is needed, he is a Tom Wolfe character from the novel, 'The Right Stuff'. Why, he just admitted to all of us…, that he is in the throes of setting the record straight, by completing his long over-due memoirs. I rest my case concerning history and the writing of it!

OK! Just two quick thumb-nail sketches of the marathon runners from the distant past before the gentleman-in-waiting, takes to the stage.

But first a word about our egg timer friend at the podium. Shall we keep him in business or not?"

This time the audience, mindful of the regular, grinning nods from the resident legal eagle who turned tricks regularly as a raunchy, 'she-male' rabbit…, tricks for all to see from his penthouse suite, tricks with the Middle Eastern spy who played the role of the, 'she who must be obeyed' character featured in the, 'Rumpole of the Bailey', series on BBC television in the UK, enthusiastically put silver cutlery to stemware, and wed the moment with a clanking wish for more!

"I shall take your rambunctious response as a rather spirited affirmation.

Variety being the spice of life, I shall call upon my partner in crime at this gala event to right the wrong position of the hour glass. Allow me to introduce Ms. Goodwin, my invited guest this evening. I am sure that you will all agree that she is far more restful to the eyes than I ever will be. Some might even go as far as to suggest that her angelic demeanor has been Heaven sent!"

Arm in arm, we made our way to the stage. To the casual observer we would have appeared to have been two people very much attracted to one another. The reality though, was somewhat different.

"I can't get near old man Whitehead. He is protected by the dildo dyke. I said I would get the letter and I will. I just need more time. It will be in your hand sometime tomorrow morning."

"OK. If you say so. Careful of the bull dyke though. She is dangerous when she is cornered. Trust me, I know!"

Lyric chose to ignore the remark.

The clanking of the glasses continued unabated. The impish looks sported by many of the revelers suggested that they were ready for some light hearted fun and less plodding pedantry.

As Lyric finished her task and was about to leave the stage to resume her seat, I reached out and held her by the wrist. Slowly and with exaggerated Sir Galahad, gallantry and purpose, he was the perfect knight after all, who made the Holy Grail his, I covered and clasped the top of Lyric's hand, bent forward in mock chivalrous fashion and kissed the top of my own hand which had covered hers. The audience, those who were close enough to the stage to see what had just transpired broke out in uproarious laughter.

This did not amuse my anointed Queen with the fifteen second reign.

Through the forced smile of a neophyte ventriloquist, she managed to warble her parting remark.

"If we are ever intimate again I promise you that I will find your fucking 'off button' and I shall do to it what you did to the bloody bird on the balcony!"

The envelope containing the pictures of 'paradise lost' was courteously handed to Mr. Whitehead by a bell-boy. It was leaned against a water glass by the man who seemed more intrigued by the antics on stage than any missive that probably promised dismissal of any hope he might have had of 'tripping the light fantastic'.

Perfect timing, I thought. Perfect timing for the resident of Admiralty Way to trip over his own 'feet of clay'.

"The tortoise is a tyrant! Its ancestors go back farther than those of birds. It picked its places of aquatic and terrestrial abode very well. As a species, it has prevailed for more than two hundred million years. Two hundred million years! We, in comparison, have been mucking about for maybe three hundred thousand years. Experientially therefore, that makes us about fifteen percent of one percent as knowledgeable as our reptile neighbor.

Don't mistake me for some mathematical wiz. I worked out the percentage earlier this evening with the help of a Casio pocket calculator.

So this is one of the runners in the Aesop fable. Don't forget, a runner that carries a house around on its back. It has a pedigree in longevity and perseverance. As a child I had a pet turtle. Tortoise, terrapin, the fresh water, edible kind, and turtle.

I like the sound of the word, turtle…, and I called my turtle, 'Tank'. Tank was in love with me less than I was with him or her. Much to the creature's dismay, I had drilled a small hole in the edge of its upper shell so that a tether could be easily attached. This is not an admission of animal cruelty during my adolescent years. The shell, like our finger nails, is made mostly of keratin. There are no nerve endings present. No nerves, no pain! Anyway, as I was saying…, the tether…, because of it I could leave my pet outside all summer, day and night, without fear, or so I thought, of escape.

It took Tank about one week to gnaw through the stout cord and gain that which mattered most to both of us…, to my dismay and…, to his distinct relief and satisfaction…, his freedom.

I never knew Tank's gender. Male maybe…, female maybe, maybe…, male acting as female…, female acting as male…, the possibilities, the mutations and the permutations are endless.

And maybe all of that conjecture did not matter. As long as Tank's family tree produced a new branch…, the continuance of the gene pool for posterity. Offspring! What was done in partnership with others, apart from attending to the business demanded by Mother Nature, was the sole business of Tank the turtle. Ha, ha, ha!

Remaining steadfastly true to his creed, in business, in association with others, and most importantly, in terms of personal comportment is, I would submit, the major characteristic which Mr. Whitehead shares with the oldest creature on Earth.

Statues are rarely erected to exceptional plodders. Speed counts. A man of the law must be smart and fast. He must be thorough and determined. Flamboyant at times, he must know when to bide his time and he must have a sixth sense as to when to pounce.

A toast then, to Mr. Whitehead, a fellow winner of the race, a man who fights the good fight, always…, and a man who can be termed, a veritable 'Tank' of true colors!

Now, on to the other, less trumpeted, road runner. Mr. Hare or, as I prefer, Mr. Rabbit. Rabbits are raunchy little rodents who function best as protein sources for other residents of the animal kingdom. Other residents that possess incisor teeth.

Ask any Australian about non-indigenous species in their midst. Like Aussies, I don't like rabbits. I am allergic to them…, all of them. More than a minute spent in a room with one and I fall into a well of…, if not anaphylaxis, then certainly a sentence completion which would highlight the word, anathema.

They survive and thrive in this world because of their speed when chased and because of their proclivity to procreate. It is the latter of these two traits that deserves greater attention. Stay tuned. We will get there soon.

Rabbits are creatures of habit. Their considerable speed is mitigated by their penchant for running in circles. They will, if the foe persists in the chase, almost always return to the location of initial encounter. Hunters in the know simply position themselves close to where their hounds first started baying and quietly wait for the out-of-breath, Bugs Bunnies to return.

And then, boom, boom, boom, Bugs the Bunny becomes tasty rabbit stew.

Creatures of habit, as I said. The English language abounds with phrases which attest to the reproductive reputation, which the lowly rabbit has acquired. Breeds like a rabbit, multiplies like rabbits, raunchy as rabbits, over- run by rabbits, are cases in point. Perhaps you know of others. Save them for later as they might not be appropriate for the ears of some in attendance here tonight. Ha, ha!

I have watched rabbits through telescopic sights on rifles, not because I am some sort of voyeur but because they are cheaper to bag with a single bullet than by a barrage of lead pellets. A rifle shot versus a shotgun blast, for the uninitiated hunters among you. They perform anytime, anywhere, with any number of willing members of the larger brood…, any number, who happen to hop by and linger in close, too close, proximity.

So, the rabbit might have lost the contest against the slower turtle but the race for rapid reproduction is one which it wins, almost always. I say almost always because, among mammals, the rat wears the crown for winning, placing and showing most often. Rats, bats, and ragamuffins. We are not gathered here tonight to talk of rats! Who needs rats when we have rabbits! So we shall relegate our comments to rabbits. Just rabbits!

So just how does the rabbit response to reproduction shed light on the character of the man seated among us this evening! Simple. Mr. Whitehead is a man who faces in the direction of the future. Future generations of lawyers that is. His lectures, on the subject of family law in particular, are delivered on a regular basis not only to his alma mater, but also to other universities in South East Asia as well, universities with Faculties of Law.

Further, he initiated and has sustained an Articling Program which allows senior law students to work with the legal services team at Wong, Whitehead and Wong. They do everything from research, to drafting letters, to assisting in the review, investigation and resolution of complaints during a nine month, 'gestation' period.

Rabbits require only thirty days for gestation. So budding lawyers are with the master, Mr. Whitehead, for a grand total of nine, rabbit generations. Now that is truly the sign of a forward thinking man!

So whether the tortoise won or whether the hare won becomes a moot point. Mr. White wins because he embodies the best characteristics of both participants in the contest and, I might add, in the contest of life as well.

How many among you are philatelists? Not sure…, Ok then…, How many among you are philanthropists? Ah, a show of hands. Good. Lastly, how many of you are philanderers, just kidding, just kidding! Just so you know, Mr. Whitehead has an impressive collection of post-colonial stamps from this island nation, Singapore.

Therefore, two of the three monikers beginning with, 'phil', the ones I just mentioned, belong to the man who gives new meaning to the term, 'multi-tasking'.

Introspective and/or exhibitionistic, secretive and/or sociable, stingy and/or solicitous, miserly and/or magnanimous, misanthropic and/or magisterial, Mr. Whitehead is..."

The 'rat reproduction' remark or the family of the three 'phils' or the 'and/or' list of culprit and conqueror characteristics must have served, individually or as one, as the straws which, when defining words were blown through them, became the agents which toppled the house of cards so assiduously constructed by the fat man from Admiralty Way. Mr. Whitehead was almost hyperventilating as he lunged at the glass of water in front of him. Some of the attempt at a huge gulp successfully made it to his open mouth. Most did not.

Looking like an aging actor in an ad for Club Med, an actor who had just been doused by a bucket of water to simulate the renewal, the christening of a new, sun drenched, true believer, he stumbled forward. A Director of the scene would have ruefully conceded that the 'action' shot to stage right, would have been one of many, maddening takes required before, 'that's a wrap', would be declared.

I quickly walked toward the tipsy man so that our paths would cross behind the podium, out of sight of most of the audience. My body language and gate projected eager anticipation of collegial embrace.

Just before he could affect a collision, he tripped, sprawled forward with both hands only partially raised and hit his head on the sharp corner of the wooden base of the lectern. I gathered him up in my arms much as one might if one wished to console a wounded friend. I yelled, in mock alarm,

"Get a doctor! Someone, get a doctor! Mr. Whitehead is hurt!"

Blood had started to well up from a nasty gash above his eyebrow. It formed a rivulet which ran to the side of his forehead and into the disheveled gray hair at his temple.

I pressed the first two fingers of my right hand hard against the left side of Whitehead's neck just below the ear and behind the curve of the jaw bone. The carotid controlled consciousness. I held them there, as I smothered the old man's body with my own, for as long as I could. The envelope in his inside jacket pocket was removed and shoved down the front of my trousers.

The handkerchief in Whitehead's suit jacket pocket, which proved to be real, was soothingly placed over the cut so as to create the illusion of concern. I maintained the pose until the harem with the herd mentality arrived. I cradled Whitehead's upper body in my arms as the curious, the callous and the chasers by ambulance drew halitosis close.

Regardless of the man's intent, attack or acknowledgement, the latter had to be embraced if a credible rebuttal were ever to be mounted against any hint or insinuation of the former.

My response to the unplanned event, the accident, was one of silent mirth. The foolish man had unwittingly become the author of a certain gallows humor that had him playing the role of the dupe! The silly man, reacting like a stead at full gallop, to an errant hare that crossed his path, had tripped over his own legs and done himself grievous harm. The man and the little rabbit, the man as the little rabbit, seemed to have a natural affinity, one for the other.

"I'm so sorry. But this accident which just happened to my colleague and friend, Mr. Whitehead, has been very unsettling. Excuse me please for just a moment. I must go to the washroom to get cleaned up. Please excuse me."

I did not wait for a reaction. I handed the supine man over to someone in a suit who was close by. I did not glance at any of the onlookers. I grabbed the hour glass and proceeded past the table which Lyric and I had occupied, where Lyric still remained seated.

"Forget the letter. It no longer matters."

I got no reaction from the young woman as I passed by. She was totally fixated on the center stage production of, 'Life Imitating Art', and its cast of dozens.

I placed the timer down on the table where Mr. Whitehead had been seated. I placed it just above where his place setting had been meticulously reset. I walked out of the Raffles Hotel and never looked back.

* * *

I was in luck. Joseph the Bad had remained for me at least, Saint Joseph the Good. The Good Samaritan, that is.

The four digit code to access the express elevator from the underground parking area direct to the 'peeping-Tom' penthouse had not been changed. Neither had the key card needed to seek refuge in the lap of luxury above the clouds.

The rented monkey suit was stuffed into a plastic garbage bag, the Luccheses since 1883, that's what the inside label proclaimed, were safely stowed in the bottom of my carry-on duffel bag and best of all, the rubberized molded piece of plastic, the jaw breaker that had secured my anonymity, was spit out and squirreled away in an unused sock.

Naked, I sprawled on the floor in front of the sliding glass doors and with my carry-on bag as companion, fell into the blissful sleep reserved only for those who feel that their race has been run. And if total victory remained elusive, then, at least, personal best had been achieved.

Chapter 28

I woke up late. The clock on the kitchen wall silently suggested that it was seven thirty. Late with no excuse. I was not hung over. I had not had one drink containing alcohol the previous evening. I had not burned the candle at both ends. Whatever celebration had occurred, post Whitehead's single car accident, had not included me. Late was a function of time lost in the light of day.

Nothing had changed since my last visit. A left over apple and a banana sat on the counter top close to the refrigerator. Big red sitting, as it did, above even bigger yellow, resembled a semi-colon symbol that a pre-schooler might ponder. A pause in the continuous flow of life, I thought, as I bit into the perfect, aluminum foil ripened fruit from Japan. The banana, from anywhere in Malaysia, would soon follow and then, all three of us would vacate the place for good!

The spy apparatus on the balcony had not been touched. Even the extra box containing a roll of thirty-six exposure film remained, unopened, on the floor close to the curtains.

Buoyed somewhat by the addition of the fruit cocktail to my empty stomach, I decided to shoot the interior of the place so as to have visual support for my tale of temptation for Dr. Rajawane. The name I would give to my grand paean to greed would be, 'Singapore seen from the Top'.

Toilet training, which from earliest remembered times, trumped all else, once completed, allowed for a comfortable return to the curtained, sliding door. At least some final fun would be wrung from the rogue recipe of revenge I had exacted from Mr. Whitehead.

And maybe, just maybe, some fool with a less than licensed libido would be flashing the world from his or her supposed enclave of exclusivity and privacy in a unit located somewhere below that of the summit dweller. Telephoto shots like that would most certainly ensure the rapt attention of the good Doctor. I knew he would cover up his voyeuristic pleasure with 'tut-tut' disparaging comments on the psycho-sexual conduct he was witnessing!

I was about to throw open the curtain and stride out onto the balcony when my whole body froze. In slow motion I dropped my arms to my sides and slowly I knelt to the floor.

I had seen a shadow move in Whitehead's apartment. It was only for a moment. But I knew that the place was occupied. For some reason, I grabbed the film box and separated it from the hard plastic shell which contained the roll of film. I do not know why I did that. Maybe it was because I knew that I would stay to witness whatever post production was about to occupy center stage. I knew that I would assume the same physical position I had always employed as an almost aerial, voyeuristic, photographer. I knew as well, that I would be running the risk of exposing too much skin to remain undetected. It didn't matter anymore. The deed of deliverance was done. Force of habit was more causative than any premonition I might have subconsciously harbored, about what would transpire in front of the camera lens the 'day after'.

The curtain, the sliding door, the slithering, the cloak and dagger stocking of the optical equipment, the loading, the activation, the film advancement via the remote shutter, all were done in less time than it took for the unsuspecting shadow at the Admiralty Way to walk to the bedrooms or the bathroom and then walk back to the living room area that was adjacent to the balcony.

Lilith, in the guise of Leorah, was first on stage. I knew it was Leorah because of the hands-on-hips swagger. I knew that it was Leorah because of the strap-on dick she was sporting. Seven thirty in the morning suited both her and her partner, it seemed. Obviously, old man Whitehead was none the worse for wear. His intimate encounter with the wooden stage prop was not as bad as his bloodied face had suggested.

But the toast-of-the-town lawyer was not the second character to appear beside the arch-villain, Leorah. The rabbit costume of Whitehead fame appeared at the back of the stage but a new player, a younger, a thinner, a much more lithe thespian, was wearing it.

Maybe a recruiting campaign was bearing fruit. Maybe Whitehead was sharing his recent or not so recent find, the lovely, but loveless Leorah, with friends. Who knew! Maybe Leorah had a Singaporean following of her own and a posh play pen atop the Admiralty Way complex was added incentive for them to 'cum-n-pay-n-play'. I chuckled at my adolescent witticism. I chuckled until I realized who the new player was.

Why were some people so accident prone? Why did some have tongues that positioned them to perpetually pirouette on thin ice? Why were some just naturally attracted to poisonous persuasion? Why did some hold in high regard those who were bereft of virtue? Why did some behave like naked newborns on a ward of child molesters?

Leorah aka Danyea aka Lilith was like that and so too was Goodwin aka Goodie aka Lyric! The former was like a daughter-in-law, all legal and moral tendrils clinging, and the latter was like a daughter-in-love, all attraction, all affection and all unrequitedly singing.

Why was the little kid goat there? So close to me and yet so far away. I could have reached out and touched her with my outstretched hand through the spotter scope but I could not raise one finger to help her. Had she not heard my parting comment about the letter in Whitehead's pocket? Had she been caught trying to retrieve it? Had the visual stimulation of others at play been too much for her? Did she think that her playing with fire in the past had left her somehow immune to new flames? Was the whole episode for her merely an exercise in coming of age with the shakers and movers in her more perverted than perfect world? What the fuck was the matter with her!

The routine which lacked a script had the two women play acting boy and girl in love. One finger felt the other while the recipient feigned modesty. One exposed an erection while the other acceded to fellatio.

One achieved penetration while the other fought to gain the rhythm of the one controlling the pump. Multiple positions were achieved with the help of stationary and moveable furniture in the living room. The expansive room, which was the penthouse center piece, underwent an alchemist's chrysopoeia in reverse, gold was turned to lead, and the result was a bastard rendition of a bordello.

Vaginal penetration was abandoned in favor of anal exploration. 'First' with the tongue and proboscis, 'then' with the multi-colored member from a mold. Initial sphincter play was met with spirited response. The attempt however, at penetration with the multi-colored 'then' resulted in an immediate attempt at escape by the wounded goat. The pain of penetration on Lyric's face filled the lens as did the equally dramatic, martial arts hold that was being applied to her upper body from behind by her assailant. The partner who practiced the perverse, the partner with the gun hidden somewhere in the room-at-the-top, won the struggle.

Bright red blood stained the tool and the straps that held it in place. The young woman went limp. The lover from another level of being slapped her unresponsive partner's rump hard much as an inexperienced or uncaring jockey would a mount which was losing momentum as it entered the final stretch.

Leorah's steed did not respond. The rider desisted and disengaged herself from the offending harness and 'crop'. In a fit of anger, she proceeded to beat the downed creature about the head with the very apparatus that had caused the debilitating wound down below.

The American cavalry did not appear over the horizon to save the day, but Mr. Whitehead did. Outfitted with an eye patch over a large piece of surgical gauze, he feebly attempted to push the crazed woman away from her victim.

Leorah, being stronger than both of the other players put together and with skills that were predicated on superior knowledge of human physiological shortfalls, made short work of the new comer to the fray.

And, as a final statement of superiority, she cracked the two heads of her unconscious antagonists together once, twice and thrice. She angrily departed but not before she waved her clenched fist at the inert bodies on the floor, the two who had had the temerity to defy her need to assuage the memories of her Uncle Afzel and the false prophet with the fine words, Kahil Gibran.

Edgar Allen Poe, the tubercular, romantic poet from the nineteenth century, had opined that the death of a beautiful woman was unquestionably the most poetic topic in the world. As an abstraction, perhaps. But on the chessboard of life where the queen was the major player, her demise was tantamount to game forfeiture.

I wiped down the flat surfaces of the camera equipment with my shirt sleeve, slithered out of my nest, slipped the roll of film into my nap sack, sank, unseen in the elevator, past the street level sentry, searched for and found a public telephone and spoke without being put on hold, to Mr. Joseph. The call was short and sweet.

"Get over to the penthouse where the camera equipment is stashed. Get it and get out. Call the cops and tell them to go to Whitehead's place. He is probably dead and so too is Goodwin Leaf. I know who did it. I will take care of it. If you need to know more, call Colonel Satu. He knows how to contact me. Thanks for all your help. Thanks for everything. And…, oh yes, happy hunting with your splendid weapons from Winchester and from Weatherby!

* * *

American preachers, successful ones, very successful ones, had it right when they whined for and got private jets from their congregations. That investment, measured in the tens of millions of dollars, allowed them to whisk among their many flocks and fleece all of them at will.

My call to Perly, my favorite tamer of Komodo dragons in Carita and of recalcitrant Dukuns, like Mr. Saladin, everywhere, and a two minute description, in pigeon English, of my predicament - witness to a double murder, finger pointing and possible charges of accessory after the fact, false entry into Singapore and the need for rapid, undetectable escape, took me, from a public phone booth close to Orchard Road in the commercial district of Singapore to the front door of my abode in

Jakarta, in less than three hours. The Learjet 35 was the favorite for men of faith and felons alike!

'What' you know is always trumped by 'who' you know! A truism in both career advancement and authority avoidance as well. And those two, that led the list of the famous five..., who, what, when, where and why, were not mutually exclusively!

It took as much time for Danyea to show up in my driveway as it had taken me to successfully fly under the radar of two sovereign countries. More, enough time to bury my boots and associated paraphernalia connected with Admiralty Way under differing layers of reality throughout the property in Jakarta and, with enough tics still left on the clock, there had been time to provision shop for the house so that it resembled a 'lived-in', male managed lair.

No words passed between us. Smiling the smiles that are bestowed upon only those who represent the comfortable and the familiar, we helped each other, button-by-button, to disrobe. Our eyes spoke knowingly of the nakedness we shared. Hand in hand, we padded down the corridor to the master bedroom, stopped beside the promised comfort of the well-made bed and kissed.

The possession afforded lips which are fully pressed against other, willing lips, gave way to mutual exploration. Nibbles and nudges, pursing and probing, wandering and remaining behind the warmth of the ear, kiss created wetness beneath the chin, intimacy with intent, made finger fondling, more than meritorious.

We sought to regale what the other wanted. Middle finger nestled in the well of a well buttressed bum. Finger tips lingering on underside of tumescence. Delicate, thumb and forefinger positioning of erection between waiting, warm, abdominal walls. Fingers following trails where tongues and lips had fearlessly trod.

Sitting together, bolt upright, at the end of the mattress. Falling back into its comforting embrace. Rhythmically rolling and rocking from side to side as one, toward the pillowed promise at the head of the bed.

Slowly parting sheets, together, from their proper, patted, position. Watching the snuggle become the supine. Losing self in the smile that served as invitation to occupy space between open, accepting legs. Hearing the whispered sigh and seeing the glance away to avert knowing gaze. Slowly, deliberately achieving penetration. Submission to eyes that searched for signs of pleasure. Acceptance of eyes which delivered the whisper that our coupling was deliciously complete.

"Let's try for a Guinness world record, shall we. Let's see if we can maintain our love-lock longer than any other couple ever has…, ever has in the whole, wide world. I know, I can stay being Danyea and you can pretend to be Leorah. We can be twins who are joined together at the two pee-pee parlors!"

"A joint business venture you say! Naw. Too plebeian, too hackneyed, too not us. We, my beautiful femme fatale from the land of the Pharaohs, are already bigger than the 'one' that is composed of a single 'one' coupled with another single 'one' because together our 'ones' make an even greater, super-sized 'one'. That is our world record. Together, we are the biggest one plus one equals a monster one the world has ever seen!"

"Trust you, my marvelous, magic man, to come up with wordy ways to weasel out of…, to escape from my tender little trap of sinister, sister-hood."

"Yes, yes, we all get to choose our friends, don't we…, but we are all too often victimized by the familial biology which is beyond our bidding.

But beyond our bidding, beyond our beckoning, beyond the warp and woof of best laid plans, lies the bloom. We are in bloom, Lilith. Together, in this place, right now, we are in magnificent bloom and our love making is proof positive of that!

Here, just for you, a few impromptu, impolite, love crumbs to further whet your appetite for the feast in honor of our one and one and always one.

> Suck the little sailor, til he's ready to salute,
> Salivate the sewer, in silent supplication,
> in wordless wonder of creation and…
> Slither, slide and shudder, til the dirty deed is done."

The first three lines of the doggerel each merited hard, double thrusts into the woman below me and the final flurry of words earned three, quick plunges in recognition of the airborne, S's, which were flying in formation.

"Sometimes it is more fun to fantasize while you weave your seductive blanket of words than it is to actually fuck and feel the stabs of your red, wet thing down below my belly button!"

Run from your own mortality through the headlong pursuit of indiscriminate immorality, I thought, as I smiled and adjusted the pillow beneath Lilith's head. Some would see the irony in my musing and, of course, some would not. None however, would miss that particular vagary of the language, relative to 'prick-placement', as a means of assault causing grievous bodily harm, when it was borne on the lips if Lilith.

"Time for us to role reverse by rolling over. Are you with me Lilith? Let's go then!"

The woman held on to me tightly and shrieked much as a child might who was clinging to her dad as they both tested the limits of a new swing in the town park.

Once on top though, Lilith made short work of separating my legs and squirming into position.

She became the groping groom on the first night of the honeymoon who was about to enjoy carte-blanche with the less than discerning or demanding bride.

"Now I call the shots. Now I have control over you. Now it is my turn to determine how deep and how often your disappearing dick gets to dive. You can just lie there and take it like the good, little boy-girl that you really are."

She raked her fingers through my disheveled hair almost with the same degree of fastidiousness that a proud mother would when preparing her prize progeny for the annual school photo. Then, with more force than was necessary, she slapped me briskly across the face. One smack made her feel good, and an immediate second assault was quickly added to reinforce the rightness of her aggression.

No foreplay attended our upturned hour glass performance. It was deemed by the one on top to be not only unnecessary but also irrelevant.

My suggested departure from our initial delinquent, coupling design was a mistake. Whether motivated by my call to creativity or by some internal, glandular mechanism which demanded a player change, like a time-lapse, metastasizing cancer, a tuber, a new shoot appeared to emerge from within the woman. And the condition seemed to insinuate itself into her whole being. At first it was only as an hypothesis but I knew that little could be done to stop it from morphing into a diagnosis..., a diagnosis which would, without fail, be attended by an ultimate dire prognosis.

"You mentioned that you came directly to the house from the airport. Where had you been? Anywhere interesting?"

"Interesting, to say the least. Interesting too, that you should ask that question Michael. The ticket I held in my hand at the Jakarta airport had been issued by Singapore Airlines, but I don't remember actually being there. Oh, I remember certain things but only like they were in a dream. I remember the people too, very clearly in the dream..., but as soon as I wake up, the details of the place and the people just disappear. All I remember is that I was up high, very high, in a very big house. And while I was there, in Singapore, I was at a fancy dress ball. Very noisy and everybody was laughing. Why I was there and who I was with, I don't know. When I wake up, I just don't know."

"Well, did you come away from the experience feeling happy or sad?"

"Another interesting question. I don't know. I just came away from that place feeling empty. That's all. I just came away from that place.., on SQ, away from that place back to Jakarta..., back to Jakarta to see you."

Silence was a great unspoken lie.

Lilith, tiring of her role as tortured prisoner concealing a truth she did not know, or could not remember, and sputtering because of insufficient fuel to sustain her little engine of intimacy that could not, collapsed on my chest. Much, as I had been told by irate but accepting older women, like a spent man who desired nothing more, post ejaculation, than to doze off on his comfortable and convenient human mattress.

Seconds after the commencement of her shallow snoring, she twitched back to life. Startled by something that only she could hear, with her eyes shut, she mechanically stuck the piston back in the engine block. She halfheartedly resumed playing motor to our love making but her miss-firing machine was like one in dire need of a new timing belt. Her thrusting orifice could not get in synch with the less than rigid rod she had to deal with.

"Do you want me to make my version of love to you Michael, or do you want to make your version of love to me?"

"Let's just let our love making follow its own natural path, shall we. Like a stream that seeks the lowest pockets and depressions in the earth, a comfortable bed will be found in which to flow. It will be the one that we, as one river, can call home."

Less to help the struggling 'masquerade man' to perform his duty and more to masturbate myself into the presence of pleasure with the aid of Lilith's body, I dug my heels into the small of her back, and simultaneously finger probed both her anal sphincter and my own.

The unexpected anal penetration prompted Lilith's mid-section to buckle causing her vagina to completely envelop my penis. The awareness of my two middle fingers working in unison in the two 'poop shoots' which were situated, as Lilith would have it, close to our conjoined 'pee-pee parlors', put me in a place…, a warm, wet place, where 'pleasure' was merely preamble to reckless abandonment.

We both knew that the finish line was not too far away. We both commenced the frenzy that would see us trip the shutter on the photo finish. Lilith was game to finish first. I was not ready for either entry in the race to finish at all.

The pleasure of business, in the male mind at least, trumped the business of pleasure…, always. I still had an agenda with the Trojan woman of trilogy; Lilith and Danyea and Leorah. I deliberately lost the rhythm and hence the momentum of our love making. Our crime of passion was temporarily abandoned at the side of the road which lead ultimately, to recidivism.

"Mukhabarat or Mossad, I'm guessing the former. When do you have to leave paradise and report back to the other side of the world about the Bali High Art fiasco?"

Lilith abruptly stopped her perambulation around our stab at practiced procreation. She looked down at me as her face contorted into a snarl.

"That's the most endearing thing you can think of to say to me? That's what you want to talk about right now. What the fuck is the matter with you anyway. I know that you can multi-task better than most, but sometimes you seem to have no bloody sense of priorities. For Christ's sake, focus, focus on me, will you!

We are making love, you idiot. This is not some long term strategic planning exercise for career advancement. Jesus Christ, you make making love a game for losers! Never mind. Just never, God-damned, mind.

That's what you want. OK, that's what you will get. By next week at this time, I will be in Cairo and I will be briefing my misguided, myopic people on the outcome of the Bali High Art initiative.

Nobody likes failure, but, in this case, nobody will care. The initiative was more opportunistic than operational. My job was to track CIA performance relative to their simple objective. Was there some sort of magic associated with CIA negotiation protocols. Was extrapolation possible to better understand and appreciate CIA win column ticks when the stakes would be higher?

I will tell the clowns in Cairo the truth. It was their party, the CIA, and I was relegated to the role of observer. I had nothing to do with the planning or the procedure to be followed or the poor outcome. The combination of you and your doctor friend, Rajawane wasn't it, proved to be too much for Snap, Crackle, and Pop, the CIA breakfast cereal characters, to handle.

Anything else before we get back to the fucking that is quickly becoming the fucking that is not worth the fucking?"

Misandry, man hating, misogyny, woman hating and misanthropic, human hating, no hate gaze was left undelivered by the woman whose self-loathing was Genesis to it all.

'It is far better to be alone than to be in bad company.' So said George Washington. The George Washington. No rebuttal was possible against a founding father of the country!

Before the woman had finished her quality control rant about our early evening 'roll-about', I grabbed her buttocks and like handles on a stationary piece of work-out equipment, I forced her mid-section up and down on my erection with the frenzied focus of a man in lust with a rubber facsimile of a female.

Searching my face for a reason that would explain my sudden, almost berserk, ardor, Lilith became aware of the wave welling up within her that was about to crest. She shuddered and came with a bawling howl which, in combination with her flailing limbs, created the specter of a woman truly possessed.

I, dutifully, played the secondary role of lioness tamer and bowed to her in subsequent, convulsed concurrence.

"Huit sur dix, cher monsieur. Eight out of ten for you my dear sir. Excellent positioning and timing. Sucking or no sucking, your little sailor certainly knows how to salute. I applaud your stamina…, and his as well!"

We slid apart, lay at rest for a few moments and, with more gesticulation than articulation, agreed to an immediate, late afternoon power snooze.

Even though we would probably both sleep through the night, ours would not be the normal 'B&B', bed and breakfast, morning that most neophyte intimates enjoyed. Instead, our stolen moments of reckless abandonment would be blessed by another, less practiced, 'B&B', tradition. This one would be courtesy of the gun manufacturers, Browning and Beretta. One weapon was chambered for the 9mm cartridge and the other for the 22 long rifle round. Both were fitted with suppressors. Both lay on the floor at the foot of our bed half hidden in the folds of the bed cover.

Murder most foul would occur long before the cock crowed thrice.

I knew that between the murderer and the murdered scant space for any light, morning or otherwise, would exist. Only the small detail of who would do what to whom, remained.

Cain, killer of the unborn self, would of course, prevail and prove once again, to be more than able, the angels appointed by God to take Lilith back to the Garden of Eden notwithstanding: Senoy, Sansenoy and Semangelof.